KILO OPTION

KILO OPTION

Sean Flannery

A TOM DOHERTY ASSOCIATES BOOK

NEW YORK

KILO OPTION

Copyright © 1996 by David Hagberg

All rights reserved, including the right to reproduce this book, or portions thereof, in any form.

This book is printed on acid-free paper.

A Forge Book
Published by Tom Doherty Associates, Inc.
175 Fifth Avenue
New York, NY 10010

Forge® is a registered trademark of Tom Doherty Associates, Inc.

Design by Brian Mulligan

Library of Congress Cataloging-in-Publication Data

Flannery, Sean.
Kilo option / by Sean Flannery.
        p. cm.
"A Tom Doherty Associates book."
ISBN 0-312-85256-8
I. Title.
PS3556.L37K55   1996
813'.54—dc20   96-8486
                CIP
First Edition: September 1996

Printed in the United States of America

0   9   8   7   6   5   4   3   2   1

This book is for
my friends and fans at BYC.

KILO OPTION

PART
ONE

1

THE PERSIAN GULF
OFF THE COAST OF IRAN

A dim red light flashed briefly in the pitch darkness as the afterdeck hatch was opened and closed. A man dressed head to toe in black looked up from where he waited at the rail of the patrol boat gently idling in the three-foot seas. A similarly clad figure beckoned, only his silhouette visible against the nearly featureless backdrop. The man at the rail glanced toward the lights along the coast five kilometers to the north, then turned away. He didn't want to lose his night vision too soon.

He examined his feelings, switching between anticipation of the job at hand, fear of failure, and a Muslim's resignation to fate. *"In sha'Allah."* God's will. He whispered the prayer for the future, though he wasn't sure he believed in it any longer.

Jamal el-Kassem made his way forward, his thickly soled combat boots affording him good footing on the wet decks. The boat was a Russian-built Pchela-class fast-attack patrol hydrofoil. At 83 feet on deck the heavily armed boat displaced 80 tons loaded, but with a crew of twelve men she could make 44 to 50 knots raised on her hydrofoils, pushed through the water, or rather over it, by two diesels pumping 6,000 horsepower into two shafts. She was an old boat, nearly twenty years since her keel was laid, and all the more rare because she was the only ship of any consequence left to what remained of Saddam Hussein's beleaguered forces.

This and two F/A-18 Jets was all they could count on, Kassem thought unhappily. Not much with which to win back a country illegally taken from them by the infidels. The memory of the last chaotic, horrible days in Baghdad before the Allied forces had entered the city and driven their Supreme leader into hiding in the desert was a blot on his conscience. If he had fought a little harder, held his post a little longer, used a little more creativity and intelligence in his battlefield orders—if they all had tried harder—Iraq would not have been defeated in the second battle to liberate Kuwait.

The thoughts were almost more than he could bear, as were the memories of his wife and children. He had personally dug their bodies out of the rubble of their apartment building at the edge of the city. They had been murdered in an Allied air strike on the second day of the war, and there hadn't been a thing he could do about it. But that was about to change. Thanks to Saddam. *In sha'Allah.*

He began to chant the Shahada softly. *"Allahu akbar; Allahu akbar; La ilaha illa 'llah."* God is most great; God is most great; I testify that there is no other God but God and Muhammad is His Prophet.

Kassem was not an ignorant bedouin, nor was he a rabid anti-Western fundamentalist, though he felt that he had every right to be one; he'd been educated at Princeton, had lived among the infidels for four long years, learning international law and economics, and he'd hated every minute of his exile. He'd been an outsider. He'd even been called a nigger. His dark-complected face was deeply lined and weathered from spending years in desert combat training missions. He was large, by Iraqi standards, standing over six three, yet at forty-five he still moved like a desert scorpion, ready at long last, he thought with satisfaction, to lash out with his poisonous stinger. This time the strike would be aimed not only at their Western enemies, but also at Iran—a nation of men who should have been brothers, not enemies.

Two crewmen who were making the rubber raft ready looked up expectantly. "We are nearly finished here, Colonel," one of them said.

Kassem checked his watch. It was 1:30 A.M. Iran time. "Five minutes," he said, and was gratified to see their smiles. Good men, too good to continue to waste their lives uselessly. All that would end.

He took the ladder up to the bridge deck where his lieutenant, Karim al-Midafi waited. Where Kassem was large, and solidly built, Midafi was short and sinewy. His muscles stood out from the base of his neck like the deeply bedded roots of a willow that could withstand the most violent storm. Where Kassem looked like a rugby player, Midafi could have been a jockey. He was a night fighter, every bit as competent as his partner. They were friends.

"Are they ready down there?" he asked.

"I told them five minutes," Kassem said.

"The captain wants to see you."

"About what?"

Midafi glanced toward the lights on the distant shore, his dark eyes narrowing. He shrugged. "He wants us to understand the consequences if our mission fully develops this morning. The heathen is afraid for his own skin. He thinks that if we're caught and tortured we'll tell them how we got ashore. Political troubles. He has to be careful now, because too much is at stake. It's money."

Kassem looked into his friend's eyes. "Will he continue to cooperate?"

"If he doesn't I'll kill him with my own two hands."

"We need him to send out the encrypted radio message. We're dead without it."

"He knows it!" Midafi said vehemently. "The bastards are taking advantage of us. When we've regained Baghdad, and our oil finally begins to flow again, I say we treat them the same as they've treated us. We hold them by the balls!"

"In the meantime we need them," Kassem repeated gently.

"More's the shame," Midafi lamented. "They're no different than the Americans."

"Get our equipment and load it aboard the raft. And make sure that we have everything, and that it has not been tampered with. I don't want to be stuck with weapons that are inoperative, or a transmitter that doesn't work."

"I've already checked our gear, but I'll check it again, Jamal." Midafi nodded toward the bridge hatch. "See what he wants. Then make him understand what will happen to him if he crosses us. I swear by Allah, if he does I will somehow come back and put my hands around his neck, even if it means crawling five hundred miles over the mountains and across the desert."

"I'll join you in a minute," Kassem said, and he opened the hatch and stepped over the raised sill into the bridge which was lit only by a very dim red light and the ghostly pale green raster of the radar set.

The captain stood at the windows, studying the shoreline through a pair of image-intensifying binoculars. The helmsman held the boat into the chop while the radio operator listened to something on his earphones. They wore the same uniform as the captain, which was different than Kassem's.

"You wanted to see me, Captain?" Kassem asked. "It's nearly time for us to leave."

Ukrainian Black Sea Fleet Captain Third Rank Vladislav Sidorenkov lowered his binoculars and turned his square-featured Slavic face to Kassem. "We're on station. I wanted to make sure that you were ready before I call for your air strike."

"Karim is checking our equipment. We leave in two minutes."

"Don't be hasty. Your government has very few assets to waste on a futile operation, or because of bad timing, or bad luck."

"Leave that part to us. Just do your job."

Sidorenkov's thick lips curled into a smirk. "Without us you wouldn't have gotten this far."

"It is just you and your bridge crew and chief engineer. We would have drawn the personnel from our own navy."

The Ukrainian laughed harshly. "From where? What navy?"

"Do not underestimate us."

Sidorenkov laid his binoculars down, and motioned to the radio operator, who slid the headphones half off his ears.

"The operation begins in two minutes. Get that off to Base One."

"Da," the operator replied tersely, and he turned back to his equipment.

Kassem studied the Ukrainian. He knew that it was possible that they
would be betrayed. That there would be no boat to return to no matter
how the operation went. This one had already been paid, and he would
leave to save his own skin. Later he could claim that they'd detected an
Iranian warship heading their way and had to run, and he would be believed.
That was the part that hurt the most: The Ukrainian would be believed
by enough of those in the Revolutionary Command Council that Saddam
could be convinced.

"Be here when we're finished," Kassem said uselessly.

"We'll wait until the agreed-upon time. No longer. Afterward we'll get
out of here. We're brave, but not fools, Colonel."

"Is that the message they give you in Kiev? Stand up to Moscow but
not the Iranian navy?"

"There is a very large difference between defending one's homeland and
that of another man," Sidorenkov said with an indulgent smile.

"Yes there is. I suggest you do not forget it."

"I'm here by orders to help a former ally in a last-ditch stand to save
itself. But I will not stick my neck out very far. Nor do I have orders to
do so. Baghdad is no longer yours. None of your cities are. Nor are your
oil fields, or your airstrips, or your eighty kilometers of coast line. Saddam
Hussein only has his deserts, this ship, two jets, and little else. You have
nothing to defend. I will not forget that."

"There is honor and loyalty."

Sidorenkov started to laugh again but then thought better of it. "I'll give
you that much, Colonel. But this is not my fight, it is yours. Get on with
it, and I'll stay as long as I think it is practical for me to do so."

"See that you do."

The hatch opened and Midafi was there in the darkness. "We're ready."

"Wish us luck, Captain," Kassem said gravely.

"Even if you are successful tonight, what will it accomplish?" Sidorenkov
asked not unkindly.

"We're seeking information, nothing more," Kassem replied at the hatch.
"With knowledge there is power."

"With armies and navies and air forces there is power. With money—"

"With oil," Kassem interrupted. "And we have the oil."

Sidorenkov was about to say something when his radio operator pushed
the earphones off his ears. "Base One acknowledges. The mission clock is
go."

Kassem left the bridge without another word, and climbed down to the
gently rolling afterdeck with Midafi. The Iraqi crewmen were lowering the

fourteen-foot black rubber inflatable over the lee side of the boat where the water was calm. The mission equipment was lashed to the floor of the raft in floatable watertight backpacks. Midafi handed Kassem an American-made M-16 assault rifle, and four extra thirty-round magazines of .223-inch body-armor-piercing ammunition.

"If we need all this we'll be in trouble," Kassem said, pocketing the magazines.

Midafi grinned viciously. "In that case we'll take as many of the bastards with us as we can."

His wife and children were safe in the deserts to the far west of the capital city, but he felt the pain of Kassem's loss as if it had been his own family in the rubble. He'd been like an uncle to Kassem's two daughters. But now that their training was finished and it was time to fight, he was more than ready, he was anxious.

As Kassem boarded the inflatable he looked up toward the bridge deck. Sidorenkov came out and stood by the rail. When Midafi had the highly muffled 3-hp outboard motor running and they were heading away from the patrol boat, Kassem looked back again. This time Sidorenkov waved once and went inside, the brief flash of red light all that was visible of the boat which was rapidly swallowed by the blackness of the sea and the jumble of lights on the offshore oil rigs several kilometers to their southeast.

They made it to the stony beach in slightly over fifteen minutes, where in silence they carried the inflatable a dozen meters up into the tall sea grasses and brush above the high-tide line and crouched out of sight of any chance patrol that might be passing. Midafi stood watch while Kassem checked their exact position with a handheld GPS (global positioning system) navigator.

They were within ten meters of their planned landing spot, which placed the Iranian navy base of Bandar-é Emān Khomeini three and a half kilometers up the beach to the east.

Kassem took a pair of binoculars from one of the packs and rose up high enough out of the grass that he could make a complete 360-degree sweep of their position. The lights were confusing at first, making it hard to distinguish between the navy base, the town of Bandar Ma'shur, which had been renamed Bandar-é Emān, and the dozens of oil platforms dotted just offshore. But after several moments he could pick out the lights along the base's perimeter fence as well as those around a low, heavily barricaded installation a few hundred meters from the coastal highway. It was where electricity for the navy base was generated. The feeder lines, like most of the station, were underground to protect them from missile attacks. But the station did have one exploitable weakness. The ventilator intakes that supplied outside air to the diesel generators had to be out in the open, hidden only by camouflage paint and netting. Finding their exact location had taken nearly five months and had cost the lives of three very good men, all of them Kassem's friends. But without that information tonight's mission wouldn't have had one chance in a thousand of success.

Midafi unlashed the equipment and he and Kassem strapped on the heavy packs. Keeping low, and with M-16s at the ready, they raced up from the beach grasses, across the open ground studded with scrub brush and other beach and desert flora, toward the east.

They stopped twice so that Kassem could study the power station through his binoculars. Fifty meters away he could finally pick out the four air shafts clearly enough to make a positive identification. Their locations and configurations were exactly as he had studied from the photographs and diagrams they'd been supplied. He checked the luminous dial of his watch. "We're still on schedule."

"Good." At home Midafi was garrulous, but in the field he was a man of very few words.

Crouching on the hardpan, they unslung their packs. Midafi's contained four lightweight tripods that stood less than a meter tall and were painted flat black for low visibility. Each was equipped with an operator-set firing pack that would spit out an electronic spike after a delay of 0 to 600 seconds. He set the tripods up two meters apart in a straight row.

Kassem's pack contained four specially modified American-made M72 A2 antitank rockets. He took them out, one at a time, extended their cardboard tubes, and handed them to Midafi, who set them on the tripods. Working swiftly, but carefully and methodically, Midafi aimed the rockets at the four ventilator shaft heads which were disguised to look like small fishing shacks, attached the firing harnesses, and set the firing delay for 300 seconds.

"This'll give the bastards something to think about," he said.

"If the jets are on time," Kassem replied softly. *"In sha'Allah."*

He checked his M-16 to make sure it was ready to fire, then headed parallel to a dirt road that connected the power station with the service and supply gate into the base, Midafi falling in beside him in a deceptively slow but distance-eating gait.

They were at their most vulnerable now. A chance patrol might discover them. Motion sensors could have been installed since the last time one of their operatives had been here. Or, and this was the most chilling possibility in Kassem's mind, the Iranians might have planted land mines. It was not uncommon. Iran and Iraq were the most heavily land-mined countries on earth. So many were planted, in fact, that no one had any idea where they all were. One wrong step and there would be a sudden blinding flash, a brief instant of intense pain, and then, for the lucky ones, oblivion.

Within minutes they reached, unharmed, a position twenty meters below and to the west of the service gate, where they crouched in a ditch. Kassem trained his binoculars on the guard shack. He picked out one man inside and two standing together in the middle of the road on the opposite side of the barrier. A fourth guard came from behind the building, joining the two on the road. They were armed with Russian-designed AK-47 assault rifles, and were dressed in night-operations camos.

Midafi touched his arm. "Now," he whispered.

Kassem heard nothing but the sounds of small waves on the beach below, machinery running somewhere on the base, and perhaps a truck rumbling somewhere in the distance. But then the distinctive roar of two F/A-18 Hornets came in very low from the north, shattering the relative quiet of the night so completely and suddenly that any rational thought was out of the question.

The first missile strike took out the guardhouse and gate, and moments later the four LAW rockets across the no-man's land behind them hit the power station's ventilator shafts.

Kassem and Midafi turned their black tunics and trousers inside out, revealing the Iranian Palace Guards' dark camo pattern, then rushed up the hill to the shattered gate and furiously burning guardhouse.

One of the Iranian soldiers was still alive, in shock but on his feet. He turned around in surprise as Kassem appeared out of the darkness. For a moment it was obvious that he thought help had arrived, but then his eyes widened as Kassem raised his rifle and fired three rounds into his chest, blowing him off his feet.

The big diesels in the power-generating station, deprived of air because the ventilator shafts were now blocked, shut down, plunging most of the base into darkness. Only a few emergency lights were on anywhere, and those were overpowered by the blossoms of fire springing up on two of the nearby oil platforms, which the jet fighters were attacking.

The base was coming alive like a suddenly disturbed anthill, but no one noticed two Palace Guard officers racing on foot down the hill toward the heavily fortified administration building at the head of the deeply dredged inner harbor.

They had trained for eleven weeks, every conceivable obstacle placed in their path, and so far their training was paying off. But it was too soon for self-congratulations, Kassem cautioned himself. They still had to find what they'd come for, and then get out with it. Impossible odds. But there were no other choices.

The night before they'd left camp, they'd been brought into the emergency bunker of the RCC where Saddam Hussein waited for them. "Go with the blessings of Allah, and of me," he said. "For our glorious cause!"

Troop transports, jeeps, and armored personnel carriers, along with hundreds of soldiers on foot, some of them only half dressed, were starting to clog the roads. Although some of the activity was moving toward the apparent source of the attack, many of the soldiers were rushing about in all directions. There didn't seem to be any organization yet. The confusion would not last, but in the meantime it was exactly what they'd hoped for.

Kassem pulled up short in the shadows across from the windowless, two-story building that looked as if it were deserted.

Double chain-link fences topped with rolls of razor wire, through which there was only one entrance, encircled the building. Gun emplacements were mounted on the four corners of the roof, which also bristled with communications antennae, radar domes, and satellite dishes. An emergency generator was up and running, supplying power to the poured concrete building, and to powerful spotlights that bathed every square meter of the fence. But there was no movement anywhere.

Midafi studied the entry gate and guardhouse through binoculars. "There's at least one of them hiding in there like a rabbit. Maybe two."

Kassem looked at his watch. "Any second now—"

He was interrupted by a bright flash and explosion at the telephone exchange in the direction from which they'd come. Then one of the F/A-18s roared low overhead, the noise deafening.

"Now," Kassem shouted. He and Midafi raced across the open ground and along the fence to the main entry.

Two Palace Guards, their AK-47s unslung, nervously watched from the door of the gatehouse.

"Open up! We're under attack!" Kassem shouted.

"What's going on?" one of the guards demanded. "The phone lines are down, we can't reach anyone."

"That's why we're here!"

Another rocket landed somewhere along the base perimeter fence, and the second F/A-18 screamed overhead.

"Move it, you godless dogs!"

The thoroughly confused guard motioned for the other one to release the gate lock, and both gates swung inward.

"Who's attacking, for God's sake?" the first guard demanded.

"Get inside, you fool," Kassem ordered, roughly herding the man back into the guard post. Then he shot both men at point-blank range, their bodies crashing to the floor, blood splashing behind them on the walls.

Midafi had the gates closed and relocked and was waving off a jeepload of soldiers when Kassem emerged. They could hear more explosions offshore as the jets directed the attack back to the oil rigs. The night sky was eerily lit by fires.

Inside the administration blockhouse the main corridor was deserted. They reached the broad stairs at the far end and took them two levels down to a pair of steel doors that led even deeper into the bowels of the building.

A lone guard stepped out of the shadows and raised his rifle, but before he could issue a challenge, Kassem shot him in the chest with a short burst, the force of the three rounds driving the man's body up against the wall.

Midafi entered the five-digit lock code their operatives had gotten for them.

Something was wrong. Kassem could feel it in his gut. "The guards," he said, looking back the way they'd just come.

The lock cycled open. "What about them?" Midafi asked.

"There should be more security here."

"The attack drew them away."

"It's not right—"

"We can't turn back, Jamal! Not this close!"

One piece of information is all we need, my brothers. But you must bring us proof. A serial number, a photograph . . . something. It is of vital importance. Worth your lives. Worth a thousand lives.

Kassem nodded.

Midafi pulled open the doors, stepped through, then stopped short, his breath catching in his throat as he stared in open-mouthed awe at what lay thirty meters below.

Four huge submarines, each nearly the length of a soccer field, floated low in the water, their decks nearly awash, the top of their sails, from which the periscopes and electronic masts rose, painted with fleet numbers and the green, white, and red flag of Iran. The warships looked like malevolent sea creatures, dark and ungodly, water glistening off the cluster-guard anechoic tiles that covered their hulls like armor-plated fish scales. Heathen inventions. Satan's tools.

Kassem stepped through the doorway and stood next to Midafi on the catwalk. He too was moved to silence. He had studied the scale drawings and diagrams, had seen the photographs and read the specifications, and he had been briefed by the engineers at the training camp. But he was not completely prepared for the deadly bulk of the four great machines lying in the water below.

Bandar-é Emān Khomeiní Navy Base was Iran's most closely guarded nonsecret. Two years ago Tehran had purchased the last of four Kilo-class diesel-electric submarines from Moscow, and had completed construction of the hardened submarine pens to house them out of harm's way. Massive high-carbon steel doors protected the openings through which the subs would pass out into the Gulf. Electronic surveillance and alarm devices covered every square meter of the pens, and Iran's elite Palace Guards patrolled the base with orders to shoot to kill without hesitation. Because of the extraordinary precautions, every intelligence agency in the world knew what was here, or thought they did.

Kassem felt a sudden, deep sense of despair, and defeat. If these ships were allowed to become fully operational, Iraq would never have a chance of survival. They would be caught between their infidel enemies to the west and a more dangerous enemy here on their doorstep.

The forward loading hatch on the submarine directly below them was open, and a torpedo or missile held in a hoist was poised to be lowered. Whether or not it was a nuclear weapon was impossible to tell at this distance. But it was what they had been sent to find out.

Iran had the submarines. But if Tehran also had managed to buy nuclear weapons from their Russian allies, the threat would be infinitely greater.

It was information that Iraq would leak to the West, if they could come up with the proof.

Three technicians in white coveralls spewed out from an open hatch in the sail and looked up toward the catwalk where Kassem and Midafi stood in the relative darkness. They were armed with automatic weapons.

"It's a trap!" Midafi shouted at the same moment powerful floodlights lit the sub pens as bright as day and a Klaxon began to blare.

Kassem fell back through the doorway as the technicians opened fire, catching Midafi with at least a half-dozen rounds to the gut and head. He was dead before he hit the deck.

It was a missile they'd been loading aboard the submarine. Kassem fixed on that thought. A nuclear missile. He was certain of it. Otherwise why the trap?

But Karim was dead! There was no helping that. And, Kassem realized with a sick feeling, the radio transmitter was in Midafi's pack.

He turned and sprinted back up the stairs to the main corridor as four Palace Guards stormed through the front doors.

"The infidels have reached the submarine pens!" Kassem shouted in formal Farsi. "Thou must block their retreat!"

"How many art there, sir?" the lead soldier asked. He was confused. His orders were to spring a trap on a force of infiltrators, but no one had told him that one of his own officers would be down here issuing orders.

Other alarms were coming to life throughout the compound. More soldiers streamed through the front entrance.

"At least ten, possibly more. No matter what, thou must hold them until I return with help!"

"Yes, sir," the Palace Guard replied, and he led his troops toward the stairs.

Outside, Kassem commandeered a passing jeep and ordered the driver to take him immediately to the Base Security Command Post. A half-block later he shot the man, dumped his body in the shadows, and headed toward the front gate.

Escape by sea was out of the question without the transmitter to call the patrol boat. Nor could he message his own people about what he'd seen. Which meant he had to make it home at all costs.

For Karim's sake. *In sha'Allah.* For Saddam Hussein's return to his rightful place in Baghdad.

2

THE PENTAGON

A tall, moderately well-dressed civilian took his place all but unnoticed in the line of employees, most in uniform, waiting to turn in their security badges. He carried a briefcase in his left hand and his plastic, Level Two badge in his right. He avoided eye contact with anyone, his actions not particularly unusual because he was known by his co-workers to be stand-offish, though efficient and highly regarded as an electronics systems analyst.

When it was his turn he handed over his badge and put his briefcase on the belt that moved through the scanning machine. When it came through he reached for it, but a Pentagon security agent picked it up instead, and a second agent appeared at his elbow.

"If we could have a moment of your time, Mr. Isaacs."

Isaacs had his hand out for his briefcase. He looked over his shoulder, then back at the first agent, a nervous, guilty expression on his face. He pushed his glasses back up onto the bridge of his nose.

He was a square, solidly built man, nearly six two, with thick black hair that he combed straight back without a part. His eyes were wide and brown and serious, and his swarthy complexion, sharply chiseled features, and thick dark eyebrows gave him an aristocratic appearance.

"Is there something wrong?"

"That's what we're trying to find out, sir. It's pilfering."

"What, do you mean like stealing paper clips?"

"It's a little more serious than that," the agent replied evenly.

The man looked to the other agent. "Am I a suspect?"

"We're checking everybody," the agent said. He wore civilian clothes, the bulge of a pistol unmistakable beneath his suit coat at his left side.

"Start paying us more and it might not happen," Isaacs retorted sharply.

The agents gave him an odd, bleak look, then escorted him into a small office devoid of any furnishings except for a table. "May we look inside?" the one agent asked, setting the briefcase on the table.

"What are you looking for?"

"Whatever doesn't belong to you."

Isaacs shrugged. "It's not locked, so go ahead, but you're not going to find anything very interesting."

While the first agent opened the briefcase, the second asked to see Isaacs's identification. He took it out of his wallet and handed it over.

The second agent studied the ID photo, then looked up at Isaacs's face. "What does the *P* stand for?"

"Peter. Gerald Peter Isaacs. After my grandfather."

The first agent took out a thick microchip circuit reference manual, checked to make sure it wasn't government property or classified, then pulled out a pair of complicated calculators.

"Two of them?" the agent asked curiously. "I thought you guys used laptop computers."

"Don't need one when I have access to the Pentagon's mainframe. One of the calculators figures micrologic circuits. The other one is an ordinary scientific calculator."

"Are they yours?"

"The government doesn't feel it's necessary to issue them to us. They know we'll buy our own."

"You have a problem with our government?" one of the agents asked pointedly.

Isaacs looked him in the eye. "I've had better employers."

The agent looked away. There was nothing else in the briefcase. It was closed and the second agent handed Isaacs's ID card back.

"Have a good day, Mr. Isaacs."

"Yeah, you too."

The man identified as Gerald Isaacs left the Pentagon's west exit and took a shuttle bus to where his five-year-old Taurus station wagon was parked. He climbed behind the wheel and, making sure that he wasn't being observed, took out the scientific calculator, switched it on, and pushed the keys for the cube root of 3.71785, then set the device on the passenger seat. Until he switched it off the device would audibly warn him if he was being scanned by any kind of electronic signal, up to and including radar frequencies, as well as the surveillance bands normally used by the FBI's Counter Espionage Division. For the moment he was clean.

He left the Pentagon's vast west parking lot and took the Jefferson Davis Highway to Arlington Memorial Bridge into Washington, rush-hour traffic heavier leaving the city than coming into it. He drove at a moderate speed as he always did, but he constantly checked his mirrors to make certain he was not being followed. And twice he glanced over to make sure his electronic emissions detector was working. He was not a nervous man, simply a competent, well-trained, highly motivated professional who took no chances unless they were necessary to the mission. But the FBI was starting to close in, as he'd known it would sooner or later. The timing, though vexing, would not be a problem, he decided.

He arrived at the Grand Hyatt Washington across H Street from the Convention Center a few minutes after 6:00 P.M. He parked in the underground garage, got a small overnight bag from the trunk, and took the elevator up to the atrium lobby. Passing the cocktail lounge, he glanced inside, spotting the tall, square-shouldered naval officer sitting alone at the bar. Then he took the elevator up to the eighth floor where he used his key to enter a room two doors from the emergency stairs.

An attractive woman in her late twenties, with long light brown hair, high arched cheekbones, and a face that reminded most people who saw her of Kim Basinger, came out of the bathroom. She wore a scoop-necked knit dress.

"It's time," Isaacs said.

The girl smiled nervously, got her tiny handbag, and, checking her makeup in the mirror above the dresser, left the room, not sure what the trick was all about but willing to go along with it to a point because she was getting paid five times her normal fee for a night of escort service.

Lieutenant Commander Tom Stein ordered another Gibson, his fourth since arriving an hour ago, even though he had a two hundred mile drive ahead of him tonight. But this was civilization. Norfolk was the boondocks.

Lighting a cigarette, he sat back and looked around. Already the cocktail crowd was gathering like vultures at a kill. Washington insiders, some of them, he supposed, and he could feel his envy and resentment growing. He belonged here.

He was a career naval officer and he'd always figured that he would have his first star by the time he was forty. His father had. But at thirty-four he'd been passed over twice for full commander because his last two FITREPS had been less than glowing. A friend tactfully suggested he had an attitude problem brought on by too much booze. Left unsaid was a failing marriage. Three strikes and you were out, except in this navy one strike was enough to put a career on permanent hold.

The bartender came with his fresh drink. He finished his old one and traded glasses, slopping a little over the rim and soaking his cocktail napkin. "Damn."

"Waste of a good martini," a woman said over his left shoulder.

He turned around as a young, very attractive woman sat down on the barstool next to him. Her short skirt slid far enough up her thighs to show the dark tops of her panty hose. "Gibson," he corrected.

"Whatever," she said. She ordered a gin tonic from the bartender, and when he was gone she took out a cigarette and lit it.

Stein watched the way she moved. She was hard around the edges, but Washington did that to people, especially young, good-looking women.

He figured she was twenty-seven or twenty-eight. Maybe thirty at the most. She had great tits and a killer ass. Even if he was happily married, which he told himself he wasn't, he could envision screwing her.

She glanced at him. "Are you heading back to Norfolk tonight, or are you sticking around?"

"Do I know you?"

"I work for Admiral Lawrence. Name's Dana Vining. I've seen you around, but I don't think you've ever noticed me."

"I didn't think I was that blind."

She laughed, her voice sweet. "I don't dress like this around the Bulldog, he'd have a heart attack. Besides, I'm upstairs in Analytics. Off the beaten track, if you know what I mean."

Stein knew exactly what she meant. Admiral Lawrence, Bulldog to insiders, was chief of Operations for Naval Intelligence headquartered across the river in Suitland, Maryland. His staff was his and nobody else's. He kept them cloistered like monks and nuns in a religious retreat.

He nodded. "What are you doing here?"

"We're throwing a bachelorette party for one of the girls who's getting married next week. One last fling. Kind of a send-off, you know. Wanna come along?"

Stein grinned. "I thought it was a bachelorette party."

"You only invite guys to a stag party, Commander?" Dana asked, her left eyebrow arching.

"Maybe I'll spend the night after all."

"Better call your wife, you wouldn't want her to worry, now, would you?"

Stein's mouth dropped open, and he felt a sudden hot flush creep up his neck.

"There're phones in the lobby. I'll wait here for you," Dana said evenly.

Stein nodded dumbly and left the bar. It was her eyes, he told himself. They were fucking devastating.

When Stein left, Dana got a house phone from the bartender. She telephoned the room. "We're on the way up."

"Any trouble?"

"No," she answered, and the connection was broken. She hung up, a troubled expression on her face.

Isaacs put down the telephone and went immediately to the door and opened it. The corridor was deserted. He shut the door so that it was closed but the latch did not engage, then turned off all the lights. As soon as he was ready, he took out his Heckler & Koch VP70 9mm autoloader, checked the action, then screwed the long silencer tube on the end of the specially threaded barrel. The gun was an old friend. He waited in the corner next to a floor lamp by the heavily draped windows.

He had no compunctions about killing the lieutenant commander and the girl. Stein was a soldier whose job it was to give his life for his country if the need arose. And Dana Vining was a high-priced call girl whom he'd hired from an escort service, nothing but an ignorant whore whose death would be meaningless. The police would probably not spend much time or effort looking for her killer. And by the time naval intelligence got itself organized to figure out what had happened here, it would be too late for all of them.

He'd been trained by the KGB in the late seventies and early eighties, long before the breakup of the Soviet Union. His first assignments had taken him to the Middle East where he'd participated in dozens of kidnappings, car and bus bombings, airplane and ship highjackings, including the *Achille Lauro,* and even more assassinations and outright acts of terrorism. Any assignment he was given, however bloody or outwardly senseless, was completed. He was above conscience. A half-step to one side of the human herd. Not better, not worse, than his fellow man, just different. He could look upon his work with a clinical detachment. A surgeon cutting out malignant cells was a murderer in a sense of the word, but he did it to save the whole. It was a line of thinking with which the deep-cover agent deeply identified, thus his nickname, "the Surgeon." He was precise.

Born in a small town near Kiev, when the breakup came he had gone to work for the Ukrainian KGB as one of its most important assets. But he'd languished in his job at the Pentagon for the past six months. Until now.

Someone came to the door. Isaacs cocked the hammer and switched the safety off. He would be invisible for the first seconds to anyone coming from the lit corridor into the dark room. But first the door had to be closed, that was the girl's final job.

"Hey, what the hell is going on?" Stein demanded. "What about some light?"

"Beth?" Dana called. "Are you hiding?"

The navy lieutenant commander stepped around the corner into the spill of light from the corridor. He held a drink in his left hand and he seemed confused or drunk or both. He half turned. "Is this some fucking game?"

The door closed, plunging the room into almost complete darkness.

"Christ!" Stein shouted.

Isaacs switched on the floor lamp, and in the sudden glare the navy officer reared back so fast he almost fell over. Isaacs fired one shot, the bullet hitting Stein in the head just behind and above his right ear, knocking him to the floor and killing him almost instantly.

But the girl was gone.

Isaacs rushed across the room, careful not to step in the blood that was pooling around the lieutenant commander's head, and eased the door open. As before, the corridor was deserted. She hadn't had time to make it to the elevators, which meant she'd taken the stairs. He debated going after her, but decided against it. She was a whore and an accessory to murder.

She'd run to save her own skin, not to call the police. He was surprised that she'd had the presence of mind to figure out what was happening. But she'd probably spent a lot of time on the streets, most of the whores Isaacs knew had, and as a result had developed a savviness, a street sense. A cunning.

Locking the door, he turned on the lights and went through Stein's clothes, taking his wallet after making sure it contained his navy ID card as well as his Intelligence Service Restricted Entry Security Lock Card.

He looked at the corpse, and could see the resemblance to himself. With a little makeup he would pass as the lieutenant commander providing he didn't run into any of the man's friends.

Careful not to get blood on his clothes, he hefted Stein's body off the floor and laid it on the bed. He covered it with the bedspread and tossed a towel over the bloodstain and the empty martini glass on the carpet.

When the maid came in she would see someone apparently still asleep in the bed, and leave. It would afford him an extra few hours.

He placed his gun back in his bag, then checked the room to make sure he'd left nothing behind. It took him a full minute to find the spent 9mm cartridge case where it had rolled under the table.

At the door he stopped and looked at the bed. In a way the lieutenant commander was a lucky man. He had a wife and friends who would grieve for him. Isaacs knew that when he died no one would mourn his passing. He had no family, no friends or mentors, no fishing buddies, as Americans called such associations, no one who cared. Only the State of Ukraine was interested in his well-being. But governments, contrary to what their leaders might say, did not spend much time worrying about individuals: they were mainly interested in causes, positions, and strategies.

He placed the DO NOT DISTURB sign on the door, rode the elevator down to the lobby, and took a cab over to a metallic green Chevrolet Corsica waiting for him at the Holiday Inn parking garage on Thomas Circle.

A half-hour later Isaacs was on Interstate 95 heading south toward Norfolk, Virginia.

3

THE UNITED NATIONS

The twenty-plus acres along New York City's East River with its modernistic buildings, statues and sculptures, and flower garden is a place of hope, seen by millions of tourists who are given guided tours in twenty languages. Fifty years ago the General Assembly accepted $8.5 million from John D. Rockefeller Jr. to purchase the first parcel of land, and the rest was donated by the city. In 1948, the US Congress gave the UN a $65 million interest-free loan to build the now famous structures.

But the real purpose of the organization isn't pretty buildings, magnificent statues, or restful gardens, it is peace and human dignity, agreed to by more than 150 nations. To these ends, among others, nearly everyone who is assigned to one of the delegations works very hard. Dozens, even hundreds of agencies, commissions, committees, councils, and organizations have been created by the United Nations during its half-century of existence. Among them is the Security Council's Peacekeepers, whose broad charter is to act as policemen for the globe.

A small suite of offices on the seventeenth floor of the Secretariat Building housed the Peacekeepers' First Response Inspection Forces Intelligence Unit. Operated by diplomats, most of whom were intelligence officers from a half-dozen member nations including the United States, Great Britain, and France, FRIFINTEL was a data-link customer of the National Security Agency. The product sent up from Fort Meade was carefully screened before it was released. Nevertheless it sometimes contained startling information that had more than once sent an intelligence officer scrambling for independent confirmation from his own government as well as instructions on what to do next.

Frances Shipley, a commander in Her Majesty's Royal Navy, was mindless of the fact she was alone in the unit's secured communications center.

She stood at the ultrafine-detail full-color laser printer that was slowly cranking out satellite images from a US National Reconnaissance Office KH-14 bird in geosynchronous orbit over the eastern Mediterranean. It was after 6:00 P.M., and she was late for a date for cocktails with an American marine captain also assigned to FRIFINTEL. But that was forgotten now.

The region including Iran, Iraq, and Kuwait was at peace, coerced to it by the Allied Forces which had participated in both wars to liberate Kuwait from Iraqi control, and held to it by the Middle East General Accord on Peace—MEGAP. Allied forces were stationed on the ground in Saudi Arabia and Turkey. Advanced Radar Tracking and Surveillance units were set up in Kuwait. And the United States maintained a constellation of three satellites over the region, with overlaps as far north as Kazakhstan and as far south as the Arabian Sea.

Ten minutes ago NSA had sent a flash message to all MEGAP observers. At approximately 2200 hours GMT, two fighter/interceptor aircraft had appeared out of nowhere and had briefly attacked a number of Persian Gulf oil platforms belonging to Iran. Weapons used were probably Mk82, 83, or 84 low-drag (Slick) conventional bombs. A total of eight strikes had been counted on the preliminary pass. The timing and the weather had been just right so that much of the attack had been photographed by the KH-14, the high-definition images downloaded to a NSA installation in northern England, and retransmitted across the Atlantic to Fort Meade. Still unknown, however, was the country of origin of the jets which had disappeared from MEGAP radar into the mountains to the north as quickly as they had appeared.

Pictures three through seven, and eight, which was just emerging from the printer, showed the heat blossoms typical of weapons strikes. A NSA-supplied overlay showing the coastline and the position of the town of Bandar-é Emān, as well as the near-shore oil platforms, made it perfectly clear that it had been the platforms under attack. Iran's major enemies in the region were Israel and Iraq. If the attack had been made by the Israeli air force more planes would have been involved, and there would have been a lot more damage than Frances was seeing. Only two platforms had been hit. On the other hand, Hussein didn't have the jets, so far as anyone knew, and attacking a couple of oil platforms wasn't worth the risk of losing such valuable assets if the Iraqis did have the jets squirreled away somewhere.

She took photographs one and two, which were establishing shots before the attack began, and photographs seven and eight, which showed the attack in full progress, across the room to a worktable. Adjusting the overhead lights, she carefully examined the shots with a powerful magnifying glass, her medium-length blond hair falling around her pleasant oval face.

One of her specialties was photographic interpretation. What she was seeing did not quite match what NSA said she should be seeing.

On photograph one, she picked out what she was certain was the bloom of a rocket strike, possibly an AGM 65 Maverick air-to-surface missile, which the Israelis had and the Iraqis used to have. Right behind it, on photo two, was another series of three, possibly four, very small blooms. The problem was they were inland. The first part of the attack had been directed against a shore target, not the oil rigs.

NSA hadn't picked up on it or they considered the inland shots extraneous. But she was certain of what she was seeing. The heat blooms were not stray reflections in the camera's lens, nor were they brush fires. They definitely were weapons hits, the three or four smaller strikes probably caused by hand-launched weapons.

Frances looked up from the images, her gray-blue eyes sparkling in the harsh lighting, her full lips compressed as she worked it out in her head.

The Iranians had plenty of oil platforms in the Gulf, but so did the Kuwaitis to the southwest. It would have been more understandable if Saddam Hussein's rebel forces hiding out in the desert had gone after Kuwait's assets, not Iran's.

But there was something else there. Something on shore, just south of the town of Bandar-é Emān. A much more interesting target. One of more significance.

With a growing sense of excitement, Frances activated a computer terminal and brought up the unit's archival files on that section of the Iranian coast, including the latest information on Iran's military installations. The satellite photos were standard 100 centimeters square. Matching the number of square kilometers of terrain covered by photos one and two, she printed out a map of Bandar-é Emān Khomeiní Navy Base on a sheet of clear plastic 100 centimeters on a side. This she brought back to the worktable and carefully laid it over photograph one, bringing the main features into alignment.

Using the magnifying glass, she studied the position of the single rocket strike against the clear chart overlay. With shaking hands, she moved the overlay to the second photograph and studied the positions of what she could now make out were four smaller strikes.

"Bingo," she said in triumph. She knew damned well what was going on, even if she didn't know who was behind the attack, or why.

Someone came in from the outer office. "I thought I'd find you here, darlin'."

Frances turned as her date, Captain Terrence Reilly, strode across the room, a bemused grin on his rawboned Texas features. He was an American Marine intelligence officer assigned to FRIFINTEL, and Frances, who'd been brought up in an advantaged London neighborhood, found him primitive and devastatingly handsome. Though it was bad politics to mix work and pleasure, especially in an Interpol-type intelligence unit, they'd been lovers for a couple of months. The relationship would not last, Frances knew that, but while it did he was like forbidden candy, which was the best explanation she could give herself because even she didn't understand why she was doing what she was doing. One thing in his favor was that he was one of the finest intelligence field officers she'd ever worked with.

"Sorry, Terry, but something's come up," she said. "Take a look at this."

"What have you got?" Reilly took the magnifying glass from her and leaned in close to study the photograph and overlay, going over it in minute detail. Next he placed the overlay atop photograph one and studied it as carefully. After a few moments he looked up. "Where is this?"

"The Iranian naval base at Bandar-é Emān." Frances handed him the NSA flash message.

When he was finished reading it, he studied photos three through eight, then went back and studied one and two again, this time taking a full five minutes.

"There's no question they hit the oil rigs, but unless I'm dead off the mark, they also mounted an attack on the base," Frances said.

"You bet your sweet ass they did, darlin'," Reilly said. "The first strike on the back gate looks like an AGM, maybe a Maverick air-to-surface missile. Everybody out there has them."

"Could have been a mistake," Frances played devil's advocate. "The lights on the ground would be confusing to a pilot."

"Bullshit, and you know it," Reilly said mildly. "The three shots on the second photograph are definitely M-72's."

"I counted four. It's the power plant for the base."

Reilly shrugged. "The attack on the oil rigs was diversionary. Whoever did it wanted someone inside. Could be the Israelis."

"They would have hit harder. No screwing around. And the attack would have been better organized."

"Were they going after the subs?"

"Presumably, but there's no evidence to suggest they were successful, except that the base loses power by the fourth photograph."

"They used the M-72 rockets to hit the air shafts for the diesels," Reilly said distantly. He was thinking.

"They made two other rocket strikes to the base's perimeter, but there's no other real damage that I can see."

Reilly focused on her. "Maybe they weren't there to sabotage anything. Maybe they were after information."

"Like what?" Frances asked. "Everybody knows that the Iranians own four Russian subs. Even the Iraqis know that."

"Yeah, but what kinds of weapons are they totin' these days? Ever wonder about that? Maybe somebody has."

"Nuclear?" Frances suggested, hardly daring to say the word.

Reilly stared at the satellite images for a long moment. "No way of knowing, unless we could get in there for a look-see." He turned back to Frances. "But the missiles are for sale. Just because it hasn't happened yet doesn't mean it won't."

"That's a cheery thought."

"Yeah, isn't it. We'd better call Charlie. He'll have to take a look at this." Colonel Charles Renaud was the current chief of the mission. He was an intelligence officer with the SDECE, the French secret intelligence service.

"We're going to have to send an inspection team over there posthaste," Frances said. "Have Charles set it up. And count me in." She got her purse and coat and began stuffing the photos and the overlay into her briefcase. "You can make copies of these. They're in memory."

"In the meantime?" Reilly asked.

"I'm going down to Washington to see a friend. I'll call as soon as I get there."

"Should I be jealous?"

Frances grinned wickedly. "Extremely, *darlin'*. But if I'm right he's going to save us a lot of work."

4

WASHINGTON, D.C.

The man Dana Vining had known as Stewart Mann was gone. She'd watched him cross the lobby, and from a position near the front entry she had watched him drive off in a Yellow cab. She'd even memorized the taxi's shield number. Insurance, just in case. But it had taken nearly half an hour to rouse herself out of the booth in the coffee shop one level below the atrium lobby. She was very badly frightened.

In the three years she'd worked for Uptown Escorts she'd grown used to the quirky, sometimes bizarre actions of her customers. The service supposedly prescreened the really dangerous types, but her boss, Heidi Kahn, figured a little controlled kink once in a while wasn't necessarily a bad thing. Heidi, who'd founded the service and ran it with a velvet glove, liked to think of herself as a big sister to her seventeen girls. Nothing was taboo, nor was any problem too big or too small to bring to her, day or night. "We're in the kind of business in which we have to rely on each other," she told them.

This time, however, Dana figured the jam she was in was too big even for Heidi, because she thought there was a good chance that Stewart Mann had killed the navy lieutenant commander. It made her an accessory before the fact. It was she who had lured Stein up to the room to his death.

It was a very long way back to her student days at NYU, she thought.

She took the broad stairs up to the lobby and crossed to the bank of elevators. Her dress was tight and revealing, but Heidi insisted that none of her girls dress like whores, and none of them did. Although she got a few stares, hotel security paid no attention to her.

The lobby was busy. The cocktail hour was in full swing, the piano bar was packed, and the early pretheater dinner crowd was beginning to show up.

Waiting for an elevator, she looked over her shoulder toward the main entrance and studied the people coming and going. Stewart Mann was not among them, and although she didn't think he was coming back, she didn't want to encounter him now. It was his eyes, she told herself. They were dead. Like a vampire's.

When the elevator came, she hesitated a second, almost turning away, but then she stepped aboard and rode it up to the eighth floor. This was one situation she couldn't run away from. If Stein was dead, she would have to do something about it, although at the moment she was finding it difficult to think exactly what it was she could or should do.

The corridor was empty, as it had been earlier. Again she hesitated by the elevators, wanting to get the hell out of there. She glanced at her image in the mirror above a table. She looked pale and out of breath.

Steeling herself, she went down the corridor to the room where she'd brought Stein. A DO NOT DISTURB sign had been put out, but there were no indications that anything was amiss.

Making sure she wasn't being observed, Dana placed her ear to the door and listened for a few moments, but there were no sounds from within.

Christ, what was she doing here? The money was good, but God in heaven, how could it happen like this? How could she have gotten in so deeply?

Using the magnetically encoded key card, she unlocked the door and pushed it open a few inches. The lights were off inside, but in the light from the corridor she could see what appeared to be a towel on the floor. She couldn't imagine what it was doing there.

Stay or go.

She stepped inside and, holding the door open behind her with one hand, flipped the light switch. The floor lamp by the windows and a lamp on the table in the opposite corner came on.

"Lieutenant Commander," she called, her voice wanting to catch in her throat. There was no answer.

Stewart Mann was gone, and it was possible that Stein had left as well after whatever business they had together was finished. But for some reason she didn't believe that.

Allowing the door to close, she stepped the rest of the way into the room, then stopped short. Someone was lying in the bed, covered head to toe with the bedspread.

She stared at the figure for several seconds. There was no movement. No stirring. No breathing.

Moving as if in a dream, Dana went around to the side of the bed and carefully drew the cover back. Tom Stein, his eyes open in death, the right side of his head and neck covered in blood, stared up at her.

She dropped the cover and stepped back, almost tripping over her own feet, stifling a scream that threatened to rise up in her throat. Her heart thumped against her ribs, and her stomach did a slow roll. She could smell something disagreeable, something rotten, but she forced it out of her mind.

Stay or go. She still had the choice.

But Tom Stein hadn't deserved to die that way.

The telephone was on the nightstand on the other side of the bed. She went around to it, got an outside line, and dialed 911.

Whatever she had become, she could not run away from this one.

5

Bill Lane's eyes were half closed as he sat back in his chair and watched the slow progression of photographs on the big screen. It looked as if he were sleeping, or about to drift off, but nothing could have been further from the truth.

He was a husky, thick-shouldered man, with dark, well-groomed hair, an honest if sometimes cruel face, and deep penetratingly blue eyes that could turn to ice if he felt he was hearing lies or what he called "bureaucratic bullshit." At forty-five he was a sharp dresser, his tastes running to British-tailored three-piece suits or Italian silk which draped nicely on his well-proportioned six four bulk.

A Rhodes scholar in comparative political systems, he'd gotten his master's degree from Harvard, and had joined air force intelligence in time to be kicked out of Vietnam when Saigon fell in '75. Three years later he'd joined NSA as an analyst and expert on Soviet Russia and the Communist bloc.

Six months ago, he and Tom Hughes, the closest friend he'd ever had, were assigned to work with the CIA and the FBI's Counter Espionage Division to ferret out a deep-penetration agent who operated somewhere at fairly high levels within the Pentagon. They believed he worked for the Ukrainian KGB, and it was because of him that Lane had killed two men. It was something he wasn't happy about, though he knew it had been necessary because the mole had already caused the United States at least as much harm as Aldrich Ames had in the eighties. Because of the man we'd almost gotten into a shooting war with Russia. Without Lane's intervention a lot of people would have lost their lives. That part, along with a number of other things he'd accomplished in twenty-some years, he was happy about.

A lot of years, a lot of water over the dam, he thought, watching the seemingly endless stream of faces on the screen. But he'd done a lot of good and significant work for the NSA and the CIA. Hughes had once paid him the ultimate compliment, telling him that he'd been one of the better front-line soldiers who'd helped win the cold war.

"All right, here they are again," Hughes said from the console above and behind him.

Lane opened his eyes all the way and focused on the 600-square-foot screen on which was displayed a full-color photograph of a group of men emerging from the front doors of what appeared to be a government building. The situation board, as it was called, dominated the wall of NSA's Crisis Management Center, facing a semicircular bank of communications and computer consoles rising four tiers above the central pit. The nation's crises were controlled from this room and those in the CIA, the Pentagon, and the White House.

"What's the date?"

"Six days ago. The twenty-second," Hughes said.

"Where?"

"The Council of Ministers building, Kiev."

Lane looked up at his old friend and grinned. "You never cease to amaze me, Tommy."

Hughes was a corpulent man, who stood something under five seven and tipped the scales at 275 on a good day, 285 after a long football weekend. He was not good looking: his skin was a mottled red as if his blood pressure was so high he was ready to explode, his eyes were almost always puffy and red-rimmed, and his round, pockmarked nose was almost always stuffed up. But he was as brilliant as he was kind. He'd earned his PhD at Georgetown University with a 4.0 average in Far Eastern Studies and languages (he read, wrote, and spoke eleven fluently). And his wife of twenty years and their six girls, two cats, one dog, and assorted gerbils, birds, and turtles adored him. In his home he could not lift so much as a finger for himself. Lane, who was Uncle Bill and godfather to the kids, knew in his heart that if the girls could eat, drink, and sleep for their father so that he would not have to be bothered with anything so mundane, they would fight among themselves for the honor.

Here it was a different story. As assistant director of NSA's Russian Division, Hughes did the lion's share of the work. If Lane, who technically was junior in the division, wanted Hughes to work twenty-seven hours a day, his friend would fit it in without a word of complaint.

Hughes liked to say that the difficult they could do immediately. It was the impossible that sometimes took a little longer.

"We got lucky this time. That's Lieutenant General Arkadi Sheskin, head of the Russian Federal Intelligence Service's First Chief Directorate, and Captain General Ivan Aleksei Lukashin, chief of the Ukrainian KGB's First Directorate, along with some of their staff."

"The enemies meet, but not on neutral territory," Lane said, studying the photograph. "But unless I miss my guess there's an old friend of ours in the back row."

"I wondered if you were too deep asleep to catch him," Hughes said. "Enhancing left upper center two hundred fifty percent."

The camera seemed to zoom in on a section of photograph above and left of center where they could just see the corner of a man's face, along with his shoulder and his right hand, raised as if he'd spotted the photographer and was trying to cover his face. Because of the extreme enlargement, the picture was grainy.

Lane sat forward. "Clean it up."

Hughes hit the proper keys and the image cleared somewhat, though not as much as they would have liked, and with the cost of fuzzing out the foreground. "That's as far as it'll go with the available data. We could extrapolate."

"Not necessary. It's Maslennikov. Question is, what was he doing in Kiev last week when we thought he was here in Washington?"

"And, has our boy returned to our blessed shores, or is he still ensconced in Kiev hobnobbing with the damned and infamous?"

Lane stared at the enhanced photo. "We had no idea that he was gone?"

"None."

"Which means he went to a lot of trouble to cover his tracks."

Hughes widened the picture to include the faces of the two generals. "Interesting company he keeps."

"What's our source on this photograph?" Lane asked. "Could it have been staged, or doctored?"

"Anything's possible, but I don't think it's likely. This came from Mrs. Katarian."

Joyce Katarian was the wife of an American businessman who'd worked with the Ukrainians for the past four years helping them redevelop their commercial airplane industry. Involved with a half-dozen relief agencies in Kiev, she had recruited herself two years ago by walking into the US Embassy and demanding to speak with a representative of the CIA. She figured the Ukrainians needed help with a lot of things, including protection from their own government. Her product, though not always as spectacular as this, was dependable.

"They called him back to ask his opinion about something," Lane said, looking up at Hughes.

"Maybe they sacked him."

"They didn't fire him."

Hughes was skeptical. "What makes you so sure?"

"In the first place, they would have simply put him on a plane back to Kiev with the explanation that his embassy assignment in Washington was at an end," Lane explained. "In the second place, had they fired him, he wouldn't show up outside the Council of Ministers building with his boss and his boss's Russian counterpart." He looked back at the photograph. "And in the third place, they have to know that we're getting close to finding their penetration agent, who is probably Maslennikov's star pupil."

"Do you think they're getting set to pull him out of the Pentagon?" Hughes asked.

"Either that or Maslennikov has been given a final assignment for his boy."

"A lot of ifs, William," Hughes cautioned. "A lot of long shots. We're not even sure that Maslennikov is an agent runner, let alone if the mole we've been chasing for the past six months is being directed by him."

"You might be right," Lane said, staring at the partially obscured figure behind the two generals.

"But you don't think so."

Lane shook his head. "We'll find out as soon as Maslennikov comes back here, especially by how he returns. For the moment he might not suspect we know he's missing. If his conference in Kiev was routine, he'll fly back to Dulles. If not, he'll sneak back in."

"There's a question if he's still in Kiev," Hughes said.

"When did that come up?"

"Just before you came down here. I sent the query out to all stations this afternoon, and we started getting responses around six. Maslennikov may have been spotted in Budapest thirty-six hours ago, then he disappeared again. But he hasn't come through Dulles yet, and no one is sure he actually left Kiev."

"What about New York, or maybe Miami, or Chicago?"

"The search program's been running for a half-hour now. I'm betting he came through Montreal via Paris, then by car to Burlington, Vermont."

Lane smiled. "If the girls ever find out how efficient you are, your free ride is going to come to a screeching halt."

"They'll never know unless you rat on me."

"It's a thought."

The familiar figure of Benjamin Lewis, director of NSA's Russian Division, stepped off the elevator and lumbered across the room like a bull elephant. He was a huge man, with thick black hair, a massive head that seemed too large even for his large body, and a barrel chest. His birth name was Lebedev. He understood the Russian mentality better than anyone in the Agency.

"What's happening in Kiev that has you gentlemen working overtime?"

"It's Colonel Maslennikov, in the back row behind Sheskin and Lukashin," Hughes said.

"That's a rare combination," Lewis said, staring up at the image on the big screen. "When was this?"

"Last week, but we think he's on the way back here."

"Good Lord, are they getting ready for something?" Lewis asked. "Something big again?"

"That's the sixty-four-thousand-dollar question," Lane replied. "One I'm going to ask him if and when he shows up in town."

Lewis studied the photograph with great interest. "Could be the break we've been waiting for."

"Our short list is down to eight people in five offices," Lane said. "We've started to lean on them, maybe something will shake lose when Maslennikov returns."

Lewis thought it through. "Okay, I'll take it upstairs. The director is starting to make noises. In the meantime, a friend of yours is here insisting on seeing you."

"Who is it?" Lane asked.

"Frances Shipley," Lewis said. "Something I should know about?"

"Or me?" Hughes asked innocently.

Lane had been divorced for over six years. Hughes and his wife, Moira, were after him constantly to find a good woman, settle down, and have a bunch of kids. Lane, who had come to prefer the peace and quiet of living alone with his black cat, Smokey, called it the "misery loves company syndrome," although at rare moments he could see their point. Frances Shipley and he had had a thing a few years ago when he'd been stationed in London. They were still friends, seeing each other from time to time. But coming here like this, unannounced, was not like her.

"I don't know, but I'll ask," Lane promised. "Where'd you put her?"

"In my conference room," Lewis said.

"Invite her for a late dinner," Hughes suggested. "I'll tell Moira to expect us in a couple of hours."

Lane ignored him, taking the elevator up to the third floor where the British naval intelligence officer was waiting for him.

She looked up from a series of photographs spread out on the table. Lane immediately recognized them for what they were. But his eyes were drawn back to the woman. Her coat was thrown over a chair. She wore a plain white silk blouse, a medium-short checked skirt, dark nylons, and high heels. On her slight frame the simple outfit looked elegant.

"You're even more beautiful than the last time I saw you . . . what, two years ago? And then you were nearly perfect," Lane said, crossing to her. They embraced warmly.

"Thank goodness for a man who's not afraid to compliment a woman for fear he'll be branded a sexist," she said, and she sincerely meant it.

"But I'm a raging macho chauvinist pig, and can't do a thing to change."

"Rather," Frances said, laughing lightly. "But you clean up nicely, and you do know how to order a decent bottle of wine."

Lane searched her eyes for a hint of trouble, a reason why she'd come down here from New York, but he could detect only her British steadfastness.

"This is not a social call," he said, looking at the satellite photos.

"No it's not, Bill. These came up earlier this evening, along with a twixt."

"Ours?" Lane asked, moving to the table and staring at the eight shots.

"Yes, but I have a problem with the analysis we were sent, so I thought I should come down to talk to somebody about it."

"Why me?"

"You're the only one I know here, and I can count on your either giving me a straight answer or telling me this is all we're going to get."

"Not my division, Frances."

"I know that."

Lane considered it for a second. "Okay, what am I looking at here?"

Frances handed him the message flimsy they'd received from NSA and then took him through the eight photographs, including the overlay she'd generated, and the conclusions she'd drawn.

"At the very least this was a violation of MEGAP," she explained. "We're putting together a team to check it out."

"Are you in on it?"

"Of course," Frances said seriously. "We leave for Tehran first thing in the morning, which means I have to take the shuttle back tonight."

"What do you want specifically?" If she wanted straight answers she would have to give some of her own, something Lane had absolutely no doubt she'd do.

"For starters, is there anything going on at Bandar-é Emān Khomeiní that we should know about before we go poking around?"

"Nothing I've heard about. Can you be more specific?"

"Nuclear-tipped subsea-launched weapons in Iran's arsenal?"

Lane whistled long and low. "Is that what you think?"

"I think it's a very real possibility that the jet attack on the oil rigs was nothing more than a diversion for a land assault on the base. But there was no significant damage, and no signs of any serious fighting. Which means an intel operation."

"A *possible* intelligence operation," Lane corrected.

"All right, possible," Frances conceded. "But everybody knows what's kept at Bandar-é Emān. The only question left is the nuclear one."

Lane started to object, although he felt that she was arguing a legitimate point.

"Hear me out, William. Assuming someone thinks something is going on there, and assuming the jet attack was diversionary, then it could be that a small team of commandos got onto the base."

"They had to get there somehow," Lane said. "Probably by sea. So what you want is our satellite infrareds. If they were dropped by boat, and then picked up, we'd catch the heat signatures. Might even tell us who made the attack. Are you thinking the Israelis?"

"My bet would be Iraq," Frances said. "Will you help?"

"Might not be a question of will, might come down to can. But I'll give it a try. How will I be able to get in touch with you?"

"Through my office at the UN. We'll set up a secure link as soon as we get to Tehran."

Lane looked into her eyes again, this time for another reason. "How about a long weekend when you get back?"

She hesitated uncharacteristically, then smiled. "I'd like that."

"Who is he?"

"A nice man, but we're just friends," Frances said.

"Take care of yourself over there, kid. They're a little touchy about women."

6

NORFOLK, VIRGINIA

The penetration agent got dressed in the uniform of a navy lieutenant commander and, pulling a courier's leather case on wheels, left his motel on Kings Highway, attached the base entry sticker to the lower left corner of the Corsica, and headed across town to the sprawling naval base. It was a few minutes before ten in the evening, and he was on schedule.

He checked his rearview mirror several times on the way over, but so far as he could tell he wasn't being followed. Nor did he believe he'd been followed out of Washington. Nothing that had happened so far this evening would have any effect on his mission. But by morning the situation would be different.

This was his last assignment in the United States. Even Mikhail had finally come to realize that the walls were closing in on them. He wasn't going to spend the next twenty years in an American jail because of bad timing, and because the Ukrainian KGB had not managed to catch any of the American spies working in and around Kiev who could be traded for his release. But this mission was important enough to carry out even though it would completely blow his Pentagon cover. It was the message his control officer had brought back from Kiev.

"We're not simply throwing away the good work you've done over the past year and half," Mikhail Maslennikov said, his coal black eyes flashing.

"I won't be able to return to Washington," Valeri Yernin told the older man.

"Of course not."

"Will I be returning to Kiev?"

"Not immediately. First you will go to Mexico City to turn over the data, and you will wait there for further instructions."

Yernin stared into the broad, squarely defined peasant face that radiated intense confidence. More than one of Maslennikov's field officers took comfort from that face. "Is this merely the first part of a new assignment?"

"All in good time, Valeri. Do this thing well, and believe that we will not allow your special talents to languish. On the contrary."

"As you wish," Yernin replied.

Norfolk Naval Base is the largest navy installation in the world, home to twenty-nine major commands and 120 ships, including the aircraft carriers *Roosevelt, Eisenhower, George Washington, America,* and *John F. Kennedy.* Even with the recent military cutbacks, there are nearly 100,000 active duty personnel here, along with 6,000 reservists, 125,000 family, and nearly 40,000 civilian employees. Because of the sheer size of the place, base security is lax.

At the main gate Yernin powered down his window and showed the SP Stein's ID card. The cop saluted and waved him through without question. He drove directly across base to a three-story complex that housed, among other commands, the Submarine Forces Atlantic Headquarters.

Traffic in town had been normal for this time of the evening, but on base it was light. He drove around back to a nearly deserted parking lot, where he parked the car in the shadows. He switched off the headlights and engine and sat for several seconds.

His window was still down, so he could smell the pungent odors of the bay and the tidal flats mixed with bunker oil and burned kerojet from the nearby air station. Out on the bay somewhere a boat sounded two blasts of its whistle. Another boat answered with the same signal.

He smiled in the darkness. No sweat, as the Americans liked to say.

The Commander, Submarine Forces, US Atlantic Fleet (COMSUBLANT) controlled the largest force of nuclear-powered attack submarines (SSNs) and nuclear-powered strategic ballistic missile submarines (SSBNs) in the world, with bases as far away as Sardinia. Between the small Mediterranean Sixth Fleet and the much larger open Atlantic's Second Fleet, thirty-eight SSBNs and forty-four SSNs were operational, or could be placed in operation on extremely short notice. It was an awesome force, even larger than the Pacific's Third and Seventh Fleets.

Besides the submarines home-based in Norfolk, there were submarine groups and squadrons at Kings Bay, Georgia, and Groton, Connecticut. But it was here at Norfolk where submarines were designed, built, and tested. Where the crews were operationally trained. And where the vast majority of the institutional infrastructure was located. If COMSUBLANT didn't know about it, it simply did not exist.

All of the fleet's business was managed by Computer Control, housed in a hardened subbasement beneath the headquarters building. Entry through the main doors was controlled by restricted pass, like the one Yernin had taken from Stein's body. But entry to the computers was restricted to personal recognition. It was the only real difficulty Yernin figured he would have to face tonight.

He checked the load on his Heckler & Koch, made sure the silencer was screwed tightly to the end of the barrel, and put the gun back in his case. He got out of the car and walked across the parking lot to the rear entry.

A security guard behind a glass booth watched as he passed Stein's security card through the reader. The door buzzed open and he stepped inside.

"Good evening, sir," the chief petty officer said, sliding the glass aside. "Computer center?"

"First elevator on the left. May I see your orders, sir?"

"Courier duty," Yernin said. He handed the SP a set of the orders that Maslennikov had supplied. He was delivering classified computer documents from CINCLANT Admiral Norbert Thompson at the Pentagon to COMSUBLANT Rear Admiral Donald Horvak.

The SP scanned his orders, his eyebrows knitting. "May I see your ID?"

"Sure." Yernin dug Stein's ID card out of his pocket and handed it over the counter.

The guard reacted, then hid his reaction as he looked up from the photograph on the ID card to Yernin's face, and then over at a monitor panel on his security board.

"There a problem, Chief?" Yernin asked, keeping the tone of his voice routine.

"Sir, I know Lieutenant Commander Stein. You're not him."

"What the hell are you talking about?" Yernin demanded. He opened his case, and before the guard could pull his gun, he pulled out the pistol, switched the safety off, cocked the hammer, and pointed it at the young man's face. "Okay, Chief, I want your hands in plain sight now."

The SP stepped back a half-pace, spreading his hands, palms out. The flap on his holster was open. His eyes darted toward a panel on his left. Measuring the distance. Calculating his chances.

"I'll kill you if you make a sudden move," Yernin warned. "Are you clear on that?"

The guard stiffened. "Yes, sir."

"I need a visitor's pass, and then I want you out of there. Right now. Over the counter." He stepped back to give the petty officer room.

The guard hesitated for just a moment before he eased a visitor's pass out of its slot on the main board in front of him. Then he jumped up on the counter, swung his legs over, and jumped down, using his left hand as a pivot while reaching with his right for the pistol at his hip.

Yernin moved to his right and brought the muzzle of the silencer up to the base of his skull. "Don't do it, Chief. I mean it."

The SP stopped dead in his tracks. "Okay, whatever you say."

Yernin took the pass from the guard, clipped it to his lapel, then glanced over his shoulder at the door. No one was coming, but he was pressing his luck. "Let's move it."

"Yes, sir, where?"

"The first empty office. You're going to call the computer center and tell them that we're on the way down."

"They won't let you in."

"That's my problem, Chief."

They started down the hall. If someone else came in, he was going to have to kill them as well as the guard and scrub the mission.

"There's a phone in here," the SP said at an office across from the elevators.

Yernin opened the door, and as he stepped inside the dark room he fired one shot point-blank into the base of the SP's skull. The noise seemed louder than it was, but anyone within fifty feet wouldn't have heard it or recognized the sound for what it was if they had. The force of the shot drove the dead chief the rest of the way inside.

"Too bad," Yernin said without feeling.

7

Lane had the full set of satellite images from the Persian Gulf incident, including the infrared shots, downloaded to his console from the National Reconnaissance Office over the objections of a very puzzled night supervisor. But senior NSA analysts were never denied any piece of information. Never.

The thirty-two separate images displayed in chronological order filled the Situation Board. Hughes came down from his console one tier up, a computer printout in hand, as Lane overlayed the infrareds with an outline of the coast and all the known man-made features in the coverage area. Next, he duplicated the heat signatures of the fifteen weapons strikes, laying them on top of one another so that they would cancel out. What was left were thirty-two images of the shoreline and immediate coastal waters minus the heat effects of the attack.

"What is this?" Hughes demanded.

"Someone hit the Iranian sub pens at Bandar-é Emān tonight, and Frances thinks it was the Iraqis."

"Whoever it was came by boat."

Lane had also picked out the strong thermal images of a boat lying nearly dead in the water about five kilometers off shore. It was too small to be a cargo vessel, and the heat images were far too strong, indicating two very powerful engines, for it to be a commercial fishing boat. Which left military.

He set the interrogation pipper directly over the strongest of the images, which showed up on photograph eighteen, and let the computer crunch the data to come up with a matchable outline that would conform to the probable engine sizes.

"The Iraqis don't have anything like that these days," Hughes pointed out. "Nor a port to launch it from."

"But they still have oil, which means they have friends."

The outline of the boat began to clear up a minute later, and within seconds the computer's recognition program kicked over.

"It's a Pchela fast-attack patrol boat," Lane said softly, and he gazed up at the satellite images. "How about that."

"Black Sea Fleet," Hughes said in wonder. "What the hell are the Ukrainians doing in that piece of water?"

"Working for the Iraqis."

"Okay, how'd they get there? Somebody would have taken notice somewhere along the line. They had to pass through the Bosporus, cross the Med, transit the Suez Canal, traverse the Red Sea, round two capes, and steam through the Strait of Hormuz. No mean feat."

"Maybe they went disguised as deck cargo," Lane said. "The real question is why are they helping Hussein?"

"How can you be so sure it was the Iraqis?"

Lane switched off one set of the duplicated weapons strikes, and the originals popped up. "Air-launched bombs, probably slicks, and maybe Maverick air-to-surface missiles. The Israelis might make a strike like that on their own, but they wouldn't work with the Ukrainians."

"Leaves Uncle Saddam," Hughes said. "But he doesn't have the jets."

Lane looked up at his old friend. "Would you bet your life on it, Tommy?"

"Moira would never forgive me," Hughes said. He nodded toward the big screen. "So let's say the Ukrainians are helping the RCC. Maybe trying to bring Uncle Saddam back to power. Everybody and his brother knows about Iran's little toys. This attack surely wasn't meant to do any real harm."

"I agree," Lane acknowledged. He stared at the satellite photographs. "Frances and her people think it was an intel operation."

"What were they looking for?"

"Nuclear-tipped cruise missiles."

Hughes leaned up against the console behind him. "I must say that your lady friend does think deep thoughts, William. Is she going to Tehran with this?"

"They leave in the morning," Lane replied distantly.

"The Iranians aren't going to take kindly to the UN poking around their precious secrets. All the less so if they've somehow managed to go nuclear. Is she aware that the Ukrainians might be involved?"

"Not yet. We'll get this up to her before they leave in the morning." Lane couldn't take his eyes off the screen.

"What else, William?" Hughes asked in concern. "What connections are you making?"

"The timing makes you wonder, doesn't it?" Lane asked. "Maslennikov shows up in Kiev and a few days later this happens."

"I don't get you."

"Maslennikov," Lane said, tearing his eyes away from the screen. "Before he became an intelligence officer he was a captain in the Soviet navy. A Kilo-class submarine captain."

A funny look came over Hughes's face, which was even more mottled than usual. He gave Lane the computer printout. "This came in when you were upstairs, I was trying to get a confirmation. Maslennikov is back."

"When?" Lane asked. The printout was a twenty-four-hour summary of an Immigration and Naturalization Service surveillance operation. Maslennikov's name showed up near the bottom.

"Yesterday afternoon. He was spotted at the embassy."

"Alone?"

"Yes, but like I said, William, there's no confirmation."

"He's back," Lane said firmly, a cold feeling at the pit of his stomach. He picked up his phone and called Joseph Bishop's home number. Bishop was assistant deputy directory of the FBI's Special Investigations Division. He was an old friend, and Lane's main contact at the Bureau. He was also chief investigating officer on the search for the penetration agent. He was a no-nonsense man who'd come up through the cops' ranks, starting in uniform on the streets of Portland, Maine.

The phone rang twice and Bishop's wife, Betty Lee, answered in her tiny down-east voice. "Hello?"

"This is a secret admirer, how'd you like to run away to Acapulco with me?"

She laughed. "Good timing. My bags are packed and Joseph is gone."

"Oh?" Lane asked, keeping his voice in check.

"They called him back to the office about an hour ago, and he left in a huff," she said lightly, but Lane could hear something in her voice. "You boys playing cops and robbers tonight?"

"Nope. Just wanted to buy him a beer."

"Call him."

"Will do, Betty Lee." Lane broke the connection and called Bishop's direct line.

The FBI cop answered on the first ring. "What?"

"Bill Lane."

"I was just about to call you. One of your boys broke loose tonight and murdered a navy lieutenant commander in a room at the Grand Hyatt. Hired a goddamned call girl to lure him there."

"Which one is it?"

"Gerald Isaacs. We got a good description from the girl. Name he gave her was Stewart Mann. Ring any bells?"

"No," Lane said. "What about the navy guy? Was he working on anything significant at the Pentagon?"

"Name is Thomas Stein. Possibly naval intelligence. We found some stuff on his body from Suitland. But his ID card was missing. We're checking out the rest of it."

"I'm at CMC. Send me whatever you come up with."

Bishop paused for a moment, and in the background Lane could hear the whine of a high-speed computer printer and the urgent voices of what sounded like a half-dozen people talking on telephones.

"You called here, Bill. What'd you want?"

"Mikhail Maslennikov got past your people last week and showed up in Kiev. But he came back yesterday."

"No proof that he's running Isaacs."

"The timing is interesting, wouldn't you say? Where's Isaacs now?"

"He took a cab over to the Holiday Inn on Thomas Circle, but nobody there saw a thing. That was nearly five hours ago."

Lane's jaw tightened. There was no use blaming Bishop, the man was the best there was. But this situation was getting out of hand.

"Send me Stein's package as soon as possible," Lane said. "And anything else you come up with."

"Will do."

Lane hung up the phone and stared at the satellite images on the big screen. There was a connection, though for the moment he couldn't imagine what it was.

"Pull out Isaacs's file," he told Hughes. "And better have a couple dozen copies of his photo run off."

8

NORFOLK NAVAL BASE

The computer center was enclosed behind a pair of unmarked steel doors watched by low-lux closed-circuit television monitors. Just inside the first door was a small anteroom where classified dispatches and materials could be transferred under secure conditions without compromising the security of the center itself.

Yernin stood beneath the television camera patiently holding up a copy of his orders as the security lock cycled.

A young petty officer second class with sand brown hair, his tie loose, his uniform shirt collar unbuttoned, let him in. His name tag said BOWMAN, and he looked like he was only fifteen or sixteen years old. "We weren't expecting anyone, sir," he said.

Yernin handed the boy a copy of his orders, and grinned. "Hell, I didn't know until after supper that I'd be driving all the way down here tonight. I'd like to get back around two. Heavy day tomorrow."

"Yes, sir," the young petty officer said. He logged in the orders. "What'd you bring us?"

Yernin reached down and opened his case. "Just the three of you here tonight?"

"Only two of us, sir. Not much traffic this time of the night."

Yernin took out his pistol and shot the petty officer in the middle of the face at the bridge of his nose. His head snapped back and he crashed to the floor.

First making certain that the outer door was locked, Yernin entered a five-digit code into the inner door's keypad. The sequence was changed every twenty-four hours. He'd gotten today's code out of the Pentagon's mainframe before he'd left his office. When investigators finally back-tracked, they would trace this incident to him.

But that would take time. And time was still on his side, although not by as large a margin as he might have thought.

Holding the gun at his side, he opened the inner door a crack and looked inside. A row of equipment, the gray, featureless back panels facing the door, blocked his line of sight into the computer center. But he could see that the room was very large, stretching more than thirty meters to the left and nearly that far to the right. The air smelled of electronic equipment, and he could hear the irritating high-pitched whine of several superfast printers spewing out copy somewhere within. There were no alarms so far.

He stepped inside, easing the door shut behind him, and moved silently to the right to the first break in the row of equipment.

A young petty officer was seated with his back to the door at a computer terminal ten meters away, his fingers flying over the keyboard. Yernin aimed the gun at the back of the man's head, steadying his hand on the edge of the equipment console, and waited for him to stop typing. If the operator was talking to someone, the interruption might create questions.

The petty officer hit a key, his screen went blank, and he started to turn around. "Mike . . ."

Yernin fired once, the shot catching the young man in the side of his head just above his right ear, driving him off his chair.

Yernin listened for several seconds, but still no alarms sounded. He sat down at one of the terminals, hit a series of keys, then Enter.

The US Navy's seal appeared on the screen, followed a moment later by the first instructions.

CINCPAC
RESTRICTED ACCESS
ENTER YOUR PASSWORD NOW

Yernin entered hep*@.#//.

WELCOME TO COMSUBLANT
NAVBASE NORFOLK
DO YOU WISH TO SEE A MENU?

Yernin typed NO, then entered another series of codes giving him direct access to the computer center for the Commander, US Submarine Forces Pacific Fleet, which was the twin of this center. Another series of keystrokes brought him further into the system, and when he had what he'd been sent to look for, he inserted a blank superhigh-density floppy disk into a reader and began copying the data.

The transfer would take ninety seconds.

Waiting several moments to make certain that the equipment was functioning properly, he took three of the fifteen one-pound bricks of P4 Semtex and three acid-timed fuses he'd brought with him out of his case. The first he placed at the base of the terminal he was using. He cracked the fuse at the eight-minute mark. The second he placed on one of the main memory units near the door, cracking the fuse at the ten-minute mark. The last he laid on the floor near the door.

When he got back to the terminal he removed the floppy disk, put it in his belt at the small of his back, then took a small answering machine from his case and brought it to a desk on the opposite side of the terminal where it would be well away from any blast damage. He disconnected the telephone on the desk, jacked it into the unit, and connected the device to the incoming line. He switched it to playback so that it would answer the phone after two rings.

He grabbed his case and went back to the door. He cracked the third fuse for zero delay, inserted it into the pale gray mass of the plastic explosive, and slid the brick in place on the floor, then shut off the lights and stepped into the anteroom, closing the door behind him.

The first security personnel who came into the dark room might step on the fuse if they were not careful, especially if they were in a hurry. The plastique would take out the door and whoever was nearby.

He stepped over the body, opened the door to the corridor, and walked back to the elevator. He pressed the call button and waited for the car to descend from the ground floor.

BASE SECURITY'S OPERATIONS READY ROOM

Petty Officer Janet Dagen waited until the phone rang ten times before she turned around.

"Lieutenant, I think we've got a problem," she called across the room.

The officer of the day, Lieutenant Earl Rowse, got up from his desk and came over. "What's up, Dagen? Somebody raising hell at the EM club?" Rowse was a tall, lanky man with a thick, bushy mustache and flaming red hair.

"No, sir. I can't raise security at Atlantic Fleet HQ number three entry."

"He probably took a hike to the head."

"Negative. I tried him twice in the last five minutes." She brought the phone line up on the loudspeaker. It was still ringing.

"Who's pulling that duty tonight?"

"Roy Llewellyn."

"Okay, Dagen. Try him on his walkie-talkie channel." Rowse figured that she was having a case of the jitters. Chief Llewellyn was her fiancé. They were getting married next month. A lot of kids in her situation got twitchy. He had, the month before he'd gotten married.

The petty officer cut the phone circuit and flipped a couple of switches on her console. "CINCLANT Base Three, this is Home Plate. Copy?"

There was a slight hiss on the speakers, but no response.

"CINCLANT Base Three, this is Home Plate, report status, please."

Still there was no answer. Llewellyn was a good man. He would not be goofing off or asleep over there. Either his comms equipment was down for some reason, or he was away from his post checking on something. Either way, Rowse didn't like it.

"Who's got duty at number one entry?" he asked.

"John Spires."

Rowse picked up the phone on the adjacent console and entered the number for Atlantic Fleet Headquarters main entrance. During the day there were three people on duty at each of three entries. At night only entrances one and three were manned, and each by only one person.

"Atlantic Fleet Headquarters Security, Petty Officer Spires. May I help you, sir?"

"This is Lieutenant Rowse. We might have a problem with the comms gear at entry three. Have you talked to Llewellyn tonight?"

"Not for the past couple of hours, sir. Do you want me to try to raise him?"

"Lock down your position and hustle back there. I want to know what's going on."

"Aye, aye, Lieutenant."

"Spires?"

"Sir?"

"Take your sidearm."

"Yes, sir. Stand by."

It would take a couple of minutes for the security cop to get across the big building to the rear entrance. Rowse patted his pockets for a cigarette, momentarily forgetting that he had quit eight months ago, and that the navy had banned smoking in all indoor spaces. Dagen handed him one of hers and held out a light.

"Thanks," he said. "Everything's fine over there. Roy is checking on something and he forgot to take his walkie-talkie."

"I hear you, sir." Something, some gut feeling, was telling her otherwise. Woman's instinct. Being pregnant, something no one but she knew about, did that.

"Lieutenant Rowse," Petty Officer Spires came back on his VHF Channel. "I'm at entry three. Nobody's here, sir. Llewellyn is gone."

"Is his position locked down?"

"Negative. Looks as if he just stepped away for a minute. Stand by."

Dagen looked up at Rowse, a worried expression on her face, her mouth turned down.

"Something's funny here, Lieutenant. The door into the booth is locked from the inside, but the glass is open. Llewellyn must have come over the counter."

"Check the head," Rowse said.

"Aye, aye."

Rowse was on his third tour of duty, but he was getting out. With all the cutbacks, the navy was getting tough. A little sparrow had told him that he was being riffed for lieutenant commander. Every department from admin to air ops was being downsized. It was just as well, though, because he figured he could do better in the civilian sector. Another full year of school and he'd have his law degree and be ready to sit for the bar exam.

"Okay, Lieutenant, he's not here," Spires radioed.

"Lock it down and get back to your own post. I'm sending somebody over."

"Aye, aye, sir. If he shows up I'll have him check in."

"Do that," Rowse said, and broke the connection. "Get over there and find out what the hell is going on."

Dagen jumped up and grabbed her uniform blouse. "Aye, aye, sir."

"Take it easy," Rowse said not unkindly. "The worst that's going to happen is I'll chew him a new asshole for not checking in."

"Gotcha."

She hurried downstairs to the parking lot, jumped into a Base Security jeep, and headed over to Atlantic Fleet Headquarters, a sick feeling at the pit of her stomach. She was nearly two months pregnant, and although she wasn't showing yet, she was having trouble with morning sickness, and with keeping her emotions in check. Sometimes she wanted to crouch in a corner and do nothing but cry. At other times she wanted to lash out like a raging banshee, in what she called her "superbitch" mode. And at still other times, like now, she was so beset with fears and premonitions of disaster that it was all she could do to hold herself together.

All of it was hormones, she told herself. Nothing more.

She had to smile thinking that the lieutenant wasn't the only one who was going to chew Roy a new asshole. She was getting pretty good at that herself. Wasn't right to scare a pregnant woman.

She pulled up at entry three in the rear of the headquarters building and raced up the walk, expecting to see Llewellyn through the glass. But the security booth was still empty.

She keyed the lockdown override with her master pass, yanked open the door, went inside, and checked the security booth's door. It was locked from the inside, just as Spires had reported.

It was hard to keep on track. She started down the empty corridor. It was a very big building. He could be anywhere, or nowhere. "Roy," she called his name under her breath.

He wasn't at his post, and Spires had checked the head. But if he was in the building she would find him. She would search the building systematically, room by room if need be.

She opened the door to the first office on the right, across from the elevators. Chief Petty Officer Llewellyn lay on his face in a puddle of blood, a small black hole at the base of his skull.

"Roy!" she screamed.

9

NATIONAL SECURITY AGENCY
FORT MEADE, MARYLAND

NSA's Special Operations Division had worked for the past six months under presidential order to try to find the penetration agent in the Pentagon. The roster had been narrowed to eight people, Gerald Isaacs one of them, though he'd not been at the top of the list.

When the official notification came via computer from the FBI that the suspect had disappeared and was probably responsible for the death of a navy lieutenant commander, the entire NSA team, along with a similar group of men at Langley headed by the CIA's chief counsel, Howard Ryan, were notified. Thus America's major law enforcement agency and two intelligence gathering organizations went into action. Lewis came down from his office on the third floor.

"What the hell is happening?" he asked Hughes.

"Looks like it's Isaacs, and he's on the move."

"I read the same thing. But have we gotten anything new on the naval officer he killed? Did he work at the Pentagon?"

"No. We thought he might be stationed at Suitland, naval intelligence. But now it looks like Norfolk."

"Doing what?"

"It's coming now," Lane said standing at a printer spewing out the lieutenant commander's personnel package. "Atlantic Fleet Headquarters, naval intelligence."

"He must have come up to Suitland for a briefing," Hughes suggested.

"What was he doing at the Grand Hyatt picking up whores?" Lewis demanded. "At this time of night."

"Happened this afternoon," Lane said absently, watching the stream of information the FBI was sending them. "He was probably on his way home, stopped in for a drink. Or maybe he just wanted to get laid. Such things do happen."

"Spare me," Lewis said dryly. He looked up at the situation board and stared at the thirty-two satellite images still displayed, a deep, thoughtful expression on his face. "The mole has been flushed. Means our job is finished."

Lane looked up at his boss. "That might be a little hasty, Ben. We flushed him, but he's still out there."

"From this point it's the Bureau's responsibility."

"His agent runner came back with a new assignment that was big enough for him to blow his cover. One dead so far, the bodies could start to mount up."

"Not our job, William," Lewis said sharply. "We're not cops. The last time you went running off, you almost got yourself killed. It's not what you get paid to do."

Lane tore off the fanfold still coming out of the printer, separated the last page from the rest, and handed it to Lewis. "Lieutenant Commander Stein worked in naval intelligence at Norfolk, all right. Specifically he was one of Don Horvak's people, boss of Atlantic Fleet submarines."

Lewis quickly scanned the information on the printout that identified Stein's unit assignment, then his eyes strayed to the satellite images on the situation board before returning to Lane. "What's your point?"

"Six days ago Maslennikov was recalled to Kiev in secret to meet with his boss and a high-ranking Russian intelligence officer. Less than six hours ago Iran's submarine base at Bandar-é Emān was attacked, maybe by Iraqis, but with the help of a Ukrainian gunboat. That was an attack against a base housing Russian submarines. Now, Maslennikov's star pupil kills a naval intelligence officer who's involved in submarine operations. Isn't all that just a little too coincidental for you, Ben?"

"Like I said, what's your point?"

"I know Isaacs. I came face to face with him at a Pentagon briefing about five months ago. He won't remember me, but I'll know him when I see him, no matter what kind of a disguise he's wearing."

"The FBI will catch up with him."

"They won't know the right questions to ask him."

"Then you can tell them," Lewis said, exasperated. "Better yet, you can be on the interrogation team."

"They won't catch him in time, because they don't know where he went tonight, or why he killed Stein."

"But you do?"

"That's right," Lane said. He handed Lewis a copy of Isaacs's file photo along with the photograph of Lieutenant Commander Tom Stein that the Bureau had sent over. There was more than a slight resemblance.

"Shit," Lewis said.

Lane sat down at one of the consoles and brought up long-distance information on a telephone line. In twenty seconds he had the number for Norfolk Naval Base Security Operations, and the call went through. It was answered on the first ring. Lane put it on the loudspeaker.

"Base Security, Lieutenant Rowse," the OD answered. He sounded harried.

"Lieutenant, this is Bill Lane. I work for the National Security Agency. I want you to call me back on AUTOVON so that you can confirm who I am."

"Look, I haven't got time to screw around. What do you want?"

"Have you got some trouble up there? Atlantic Fleet Submarine Headquarters?"

"Who the hell did you say you were?" Rowse demanded.

"Lane, NSA. You've got someone coming your way who's going to try to get into your fleet intelligence unit, or perhaps your computer center."

"Goddamnit," the lieutenant said. "I'll have to get back to you, Lane." The connection was broken.

Lewis stared up at the situation board again for a long moment. He shook his head in resignation as if he'd just made a decision that ran against his grain, then looked back at Lane.

"We'll chopper you two down there right now. In the meantime I'll warn the navy that you're on the way, and inform the Bureau what's going on."

"Tell them not to screw around, this guy is dangerous," Lane warned.

"Heed your own advice, William. I'll stay here and backstop you."

"You're a pearl of a fellow," Lane grinned. "Don't let anyone tell you different."

10

NORFOLK NAVAL BASE

Yernin was surprised that his luck had held as long as it had, although he was professional enough not to be disturbed when it ended. He'd hoped to be able to get off the base the same way he'd got on, without any further bloodshed. But he no longer thought it would happen that way.

He stood a moment longer at the elevator to convince himself that the controls had been locked out and the car recalled to the ground floor before he turned and walked to the stairs. Someone had already discovered the deserted security post and had started to lock down the building. Within a few minutes the entire base could be secured, and getting out wouldn't be so easy.

At the head of the stairs he studied the door lock and hinge mechanism. Taking a penknife from his pocket, he used the tip of the biggest blade to pry off the small end cap on the left side of the latch bar. As he expected, there were three wires leading from the mechanism back through the hinges and into the building's wiring. One would be a common ground, the second would activate an audible alarm in the corridor, and the third would light a position on an alarm panel somewhere here in the building, and possibly at a central security center elsewhere on base. The switching system was sealed so it couldn't be defeated.

There was no other way out except through the air-conditioning ducts, and that would take too long. By then the building would be completely sealed off, the base shut down. His window of opportunity for escape was rapidly closing.

The situation was irritating, for although he did not mind killing, it wasn't his style to spill blood unless it was necessary. Like a surgeon, his strokes tended to be precise.

Yernin pushed open the door with the briefcase, and an alarm horn shattered the silence, its high-pitched whooping echoing off the corridor walls.

Holding his pistol behind his right leg, he stepped out of the stairway directly into the barrel of a 10mm Colt automatic pistol held by a young man in uniform. Out of the corner of his eye he could read the man's name tag, SPIRES, and see his face. He was frightened.

"Jesus H. Christ, Spires, you scared the living shit outta me," Yernin shouted, falling back.

The petty officer hesitated a moment, not knowing what to expect, but definitely not expecting an officer who knew his name and acted as if he belonged here. It was a mistake, and all the opening Yernin needed.

He batted Spire's gun hand aside, and before the petty officer could react, he brought his own pistol up, jammed it into the young man's solar plexus, and fired once.

Spire's body hunched over, a surprised, hurt look coming over his face. "Shit," he rasped, and he slumped to the floor.

Yernin looked both ways down the broad corridor. No one was coming yet, though the alarm horn blared so loudly it was difficult to keep it out of his mind. But there was still time.

He stared at the petty officer's body for a moment. The boy was a soldier, but his death was a waste. Already the body count was impossibly high for such an assignment. The military police would demand civilian help, and very quickly every cop on the eastern seaboard would be looking for the killer.

He turned and headed toward the rear exit, checking his watch as he went. He'd been in the building less than ten minutes. It would take base security that much longer to secure all the gates leading off base. Once he got back into the city he could change his identity and lose himself.

No one here who'd seen his face tonight was alive. He meant to keep it that way.

A woman in uniform stepped out of the office across from the elevator where Llewellyn's body lay on the floor. "Freeze, you sonofabitch!" she shouted.

Yernin stopped short, then half-turned toward the woman. The girl was a petty officer. She held a standard-issue 10mm Colt automatic with both hands, her arms extended, her elbows slightly bent, exactly as she'd been taught to do. She could not have heard the shot, and if she didn't turn around she would not see her fellow petty officer's body lying by the stairwell door. Like Spires she was frightened, but there was something else in her eyes. A deep-seated, wild anger. Yernin guessed that the girl and the dead man in the office had been friends, or perhaps something closer.

"You weren't supposed to see that," Yernin said, motioning toward the office, his pistol concealed at his side. He had to shout over the noise of the alarm. "By the time I got to him it was too late."

A look of uncertainty crossed the young petty officer's face. Her name tag read DAGEN.

"Look, Dagen, has the building been locked down yet? Who's pulling OD tonight?"

"Who killed Roy?" the girl shouted hysterically.

"Whoever it was is probably still in the building. And unless you get a grip he'll get away. Now who's the OD tonight? I want you to raise him on your walkie-talkie. We're going to need more people over here on the double." Yernin started to turn away.

"Damn you, hold it right there! I want to see some ID right now!"

"Okay," Yernin said. The girl was confused but it wouldn't last. "I'll dig out my ID, but in the meantime call your boss, we don't have much time."

The young woman hesitated a moment, then shifted the gun to her right hand and reached for the walkie-talkie at her side. She had to look down.

Yernin brought up his gun and fired, hitting her in the chest just below her left breast, her legs collapsing beneath her.

He didn't think that anyone else would be popping out of the woodwork. Spires was probably the front-door man, and Dagen had been sent over to find out why the back-door guard wouldn't answer up.

But others were coming, and Yernin decided he was going to have to risk another half-minute to provide himself with a diversion. As long as the initial search was concentrated here, it would divert their attention away from the egress points off the base.

The girl had fallen facedown. Yernin turned her over on her back, then took a brick of Semtex from his case, set an acid fuse for zero delay, and shoved it into the plastique. He set the explosive on the floor and eased Dagen's body on top of it. When she was moved, the acid fuse would crack and the Semtex would blow.

Using the young woman this way would anger the naval authorities, especially those close to her, but angry people, even professionals, did not think clearly.

A jeep with base security markings on its side was parked opposite the back door. Yernin figured it belonged to the young woman he'd killed. He slipped outside and quickly crossed the parking lot to where he'd left his car in the shadows. He could hear sirens in the distance to the east. It would be base security in response to the alarm. But they were still far enough off that he could make a clean escape.

He tossed the case in the front seat beside him and headed west away from the sirens toward the Hampton Boulevard gate on the opposite side of the base from the gate he'd come through. A block later he switched on the headlights just as a base security patrol car, its lights flashing, came around the corner and passed him flat out in the opposite direction.

He checked his watch. In two minutes the first of the bombs he'd set in the computer center would go off. After that the naval authorities were going to find themselves with a lot of questions that had no immediate answers.

Four minutes later, Yernin came to gate 5 and prepared to stop, his right hand on the gun at his side, but the navy SP merely saluted and waved him through.

Yernin returned the salute and merged with traffic heading south along the motel row that served the base and its visitors, traffic once again picking up.

11

EN ROUTE TO NORFOLK NAVAL BASE

The Sikorsky SH-3L Sea King ASW helicopter touched down on the rooftop helipad of NSA's main administration headquarters, and Lane and Hughes were hustled aboard and strapped in by a dour-looking navy chief whose name was Paparella.

"You want down there right now, that right, sir?" he shouted over the noise of the rotors as he gave them helmets and showed them where to plug into the chopper's comms circuit.

"The sooner the better, Chief," Lane replied, donning the bulky helmet and snugging down his seat belt.

"In that case, hang on," Paparella shouted. He went forward and strapped in behind the pilot and co-pilot. A moment later the big helicopter lifted off with a sickening lurch. Dipping its nose, it gathered speed, and as it arched to the south, they could see the lights of Washington off to their right.

"When did you meet Isaacs?" Hughes shouted.

"I only saw him once at a briefing," Lane said. "Ben wouldn't have let us go if I'd told him the truth."

"Just great in light of the awful fact that I despise helicopters," Hughes said, clutching his attaché case to his chest. "These machines fall out of the sky with alarming regularity."

"Can you swim?" Lane asked his friend.

"If need be."

"Then you're in luck, Tommy. Some of our trip will be over water." Lane found the intercom switch and flipped it. "You guys copy me up there?"

Paparella turned around. "Five-by, sir," his voice came over their helmet earphones. "You okay back there?"

"Just peachy," Hughes said, keying his headset.

"What's our ETA at Norfolk, Chief?" Lane asked.

"Four-zero minutes, sir. We got a good tailwind."

"Can you raise CMC for me?"

"Can do, sir. Stand by and I'll bring it up on another channel."

A minute later Ben Lewis came on the line. "CMC."

"Okay, we're in the air," Lane told him. "Should be touching down in about forty minutes. Did you talk to Bishop?"

"Yeah, and he's pissed. His people are on the way down. He wants to know when and where you met Isaacs, and why the hell you didn't log it on an encounters sheet."

"No time for that now, Ben. Has Isaacs been spotted in Norfolk?"

"Might not be such a good idea sending you down there after all," Lewis continued. "If Isaacs recognizes you it might give him the edge."

"I'll recognize him first," Lane assured his boss.

"In any event it'll probably be all over by the time you get there. The navy thinks they've got him cornered. I talked to Captain Jensen, chief of Naval Intelligence Norfolk. He says Rowse is a good man, and he's got a good crew."

"Where'd they corner him?" Lane demanded.

"Atlantic Fleet Headquarters—"

"Where specifically, Ben? Is it anywhere near Fleet Submarine Headquarters Operations? Someplace where he could get his hands on submarine fleet data? Sailing lists, rendezvous station coordinates? Anything like that?"

"COMSUBLANT's computer center is there," Lewis replied. "But navy says the building's been locked down."

"Any casualties?"

"They didn't say."

"How about diversions? Accidents, explosions, power outages. Anything like that."

"Nothing like that," Lewis said. "Jensen would have made a point of it. He said that his people were on top of it. They had an intruder in fleet HQ, and they were taking care of it. Thanks for the help, but no thanks."

"I'll stand by on this frequency. I want you to raise Lieutenant Rowse and patch him over to me. He's probably outside Fleet Headquarters. I have to talk to him before anybody gets hurt."

"He's not going to want to talk to you—"

"Just do it. And as soon as you've patched him over, call Bishop again and tell him to put every asset he can field down there. Virginia Highway Patrol can help with the roads leading out of the area, and the Coast Guard can watch the bay and the rivers, but somebody's going to have to cover the airports."

"He's still on base."

"Don't count on it. He's had plenty of time to get in and get out with what he came for. I'm just trying to prevent anyone else from getting hurt. One dead lieutenant commander is enough."

"I'll see what I can do," Lewis said. "Stand by."

Lane sat back in his web seat and closed his eyes. It'd been a long day. Hughes stared at him curiously.

"You know this guy, don't you?"

Lane looked up. "He thinks he's a bloody hero, Tommy. The KGB trained all its people that way. Especially the ones they pulled up out of the sewers. Now he's got no home to go back to that's worth a damn, so that makes him a tragic hero. He's cornered and he's going to fight back. One last stand. It's the cowboy mentality, and the really stupid thing is that the silly bastards got it from us." Lane half closed his eyes again. "I never met Isaacs, but I've come across his type. I can still smell the stench."

"You think his coming down here proves there's a connection with the attack on Bandar-é Emān?"

"I don't know. But it's a thought."

"Wrong ocean," Hughes said. "The Persian Gulf is covered by the Seventh Fleet. Norfolk runs the Second and Sixth. Making any sort of a connection is a long stretch."

"It's something I intend asking Isaacs about. One of many things."

Ben Lewis came back five minutes later. "Rowse refuses to talk to you, he has his hands full. But someone will meet you when you touch down."

"What happened?" Lane asked.

"There've been two explosions in the computer center, and they've got casualties. They weren't being awfully specific, but they're out for blood and they're not going to want much interference from you. So stay out of the way until the Bureau shows up."

"Call Bishop and put out an APB on Lieutenant Commander Tom Stein."

"He's dead."

"Just do it," Lane said, and pulled the plug. Lewis would figure it out, and Bishop would know what to do. He unstrapped and made his way forward to the flight deck.

Paparella turned around. "Problem, sir?"

"The heat's just been turned up. We need to be on the ground at Atlantic Fleet HQ ten minutes ago."

"That'll cost you extra, sir."

"Put it on my account."

The chief grinned. "Will do." He turned to the pilot as Lane made his way back to his seat.

NORFOLK, VIRGINIA

Traffic was normal for this time of evening, and Yernin made good time across town. He drove with his window down to listen for sirens, but since leaving the base he'd heard nothing of the sort. By now both of the timed charges in the computer center had gone off, and it was likely that the booby trap beneath the young woman's body had been tripped. He could see the fear and anger in her eyes. She'd been crying, he thought, which reinforced his speculation that there'd been more than a casual relationship between her and the rear entry guard. It was the trouble with having women in the military; soldiers ought to be friends, not lovers.

A military staff car with base security makings on its door passed him, and his eyes darted to the rearview mirror to make sure he wasn't being followed. But this was a navy town, he told himself. At any given time there were bound to be plenty of military vehicles in the city. He allowed himself to relax a little.

Keeping to the main streets, his speed five miles per hour over the limit so that he would attract no attention, he got on Interstate 264, which roughly paralleled the Elizabeth River until it connected with Interstate 64 heading northwest back toward the base. A big green sign overhead gave mileages to a series of exits, the last of them Norfolk International Airport, four miles. He merged with traffic coming off the cloverleaf and increased his speed to just over sixty. His wasn't the fastest car on the highway, nor the slowest, but he kept to the center and right lanes as much as possible.

The one piece of bad luck this evening was the first guard he'd been forced to kill. The young man had known Lieutenant Commander Stein, a possibility which Yernin had thought would be unlikely. It made him rethink his immediate plans for getting clear of the city. There was a chance that Dagen had taken note of his car parked in the lot before she'd entered Fleet Headquarters. She might have called it in. The likelihood was slight, but he couldn't dismiss it. Although he might get out on the open highway, there was the possibility that he'd be stopped by the highway patrol.

He needed another diversion. Something to keep the authorities, naval and civilian, concentrated in one direction while he moved off to his intended escape route, a place that the American authorities would never think to look for him.

He took the exit to the airport four minutes later and followed the signs to long-term parking. Traffic back into the city was quite heavy. Yernin figured that one flight, possibly more, had just arrived. There were no cops, nor any unusual activity around the terminal that he could spot.

Taking a ticket from the automatic machine, he parked the Corsica between a pair of minivans so that it would not be conspicuous. With luck the car might not be noticed for several days. But if it was spotted within the next hour, it might help bolster the idea that he was still somewhere in the airport.

There wasn't much light. The car faced a one-meter-tall concrete divider. No one was coming for the moment. Yernin crouched beside the front left wheel and reached up into the wheel well, searching for and finding the front left spring and shock absorber. He molded a brick of Semtex around the base of the spring, cracked an acid fuse for zero delay, and inserted it into the plastic explosive so that the glass tip was wedged where the final coil of the spring attached to the frame. If they tried to move the car, the Semtex would blow.

Brushing himself off, he headed to the terminal with his overnight bag and case, tossing the car keys in a trash barrel by the elevators.

Although the departing gates had been busy, the terminal's main concourse and ticket counters were mostly empty except for a short line at the Delta counter and a slightly longer line at the US Air position. He walked over to a bank of television monitors that showed the departure times of Delta's remaining flights for tonight. He was in luck. There were three flights, one at 11:57 for Chicago, one at midnight for Miami, and a final flight at 12:22 A.M. for Montreal.

The Delta line was down to two people. When it was his turn, he laid Stein's gold Visa card on the counter. "I hope there's room on your Montreal flight tonight," he told the older woman clerk.

"I think there is, Lieutenant Commander," she said, entering the flight number and date into her computer. She looked up after a few moments and smiled. "Plenty of room. Will you be staying through a Saturday night?"

"I'll be coming back Sunday. Sometime in the afternoon, if you have it."

"No problem." She took his credit card and ran it through the reader. "Any check-on baggage?"

"None."

It took five minutes. When she was finished she handed Yernin his ticket and boarding pass in a Delta folder. "It's on schedule, leaving at 12:22 from gate 27B, that's the blue concourse to the left."

"Thanks, I'll find it." On the way across the main concourse he made sure that no one was taking any special interest in him. He took the corridor to the blue concourse, where he found an empty men's room on this side of airport security and locked himself in one of the toilet stalls. Working quickly, he changed out of Stein's uniform and donned a pair of light tan casual slacks, a soft pullover sweater, a green and yellow reversible windbreaker which he turned inside out, and a pair of Sperry Top-Sider boat shoes. His new papers, credit cards, family photographs, and press pass identified him as Tony Murdoch, a Reuters News Service reporter out of New York City, married with a wife and three children all back in London. He put on a baseball cap and square-rimmed glasses.

The remaining ten bricks of Semtex and acid fuses went into the overnight bag along with the pistol, two extra magazines of ammunition, a 9-inch stiletto, the computer disk, and his handheld micrologic computer. Stein's things went into the courier's case.

It had been less than ten minutes since he had walked into the terminal.

He went to the coin-operated lockers where he stashed the case, then crossed the main concourse to the front doors. He got a cab that had just left off a fare and ordered the driver to take him to the Omni Waterside Hotel.

Yernin looked through the window. In the distance, coming off the highway he counted at least four squad cars, their lights flashing, with more behind them.

They weren't escorting a VIP to the airport. They were looking for him. But how had they come this close so fast? It made no sense.

NORFOLK NAVAL BASE

"This is not looking good," Hughes said, peering out the side window as the Sikorsky dropped toward a landing.

"You're right," Lane agreed, watching from the other side. The sprawling Atlantic Fleet Headquarters building was lit bright as day by dozens of spotlights. Smoke poured out of the open rear door to the building, and glass littered the parking lot from what had obviously been an explosion inside. A perimeter had been set up thirty meters out with dozens of cars, trucks, and humvees, lights flashing, doors open, with hundreds of uniforms, navy, marines in combat fatigues and flak jackets, and what looked like civilian police crouched behind them. Several dozen soldiers were deployed on the roofs of adjacent buildings, and he counted at least six sharpshooters hunched behind trees and in other concealed positions. There were likely three times that many he couldn't spot.

Three groups of four soldiers hustled three body bags out the rear door and raced across the parking lot to the protection of the perimeter, where several ambulances waited.

The instant they were clear, two SWAT teams of six men each leapfrogged their way to the door and disappeared inside.

"If Isaacs is still inside, they're going to get hurt," Hughes observed.

"He's gone, but they're still going to get hurt," Lane replied.

The helicopter touched down on the street behind the parking lot, and even before the landing gear's shock absorbers had rebounded, Lane was unbuckled and headed out the door. He sprinted around the front of the chopper, crossed the street at a dead run, and made it through the first line of naval and marine security people before his way was blocked by a marine combat lieutenant in full gear. A staff sergeant and two corporals similarly equipped backed him up.

"Sorry, sir, but you'll have to remain here," the lieutenant said, his voice deceptively mild. He stood half a head taller than Lane, and looked like he ate raw meat for breakfast.

"My name is Bill Lane, I'm from the National Security Agency."

"Yes, sir. We were told to have you wait here until the situation is resolved."

"I have to talk to Lieutenant Rowse—"

"Sir, the lieutenant is busy just now."

Hughes came over from the helicopter just as two civilians made their way back from the front line.

"It's all right, Lieutenant, we'll take it from here," the older of the two men said. They wore dark windbreakers and baseball caps with FBI stenciled on the crowns.

The marine looked dubious, but he backed off. "Yes, sir. But these gentlemen are to proceed no farther than this."

"Right," the civilian said, and he introduced himself. "Dan Coniff, FBI Norfolk. This is my ASAC, Jim St. Clair. Mr. Bishop asked me to coordinate with you."

They shook hands.

"What's going on?" Lane demanded.

"Looks like they have Isaacs cornered in the computer center downstairs. The navy's taken a couple of hits, and they're understandably a little hot right now. As soon as they've bagged him we can go in."

Lane stared toward the lights and confusion across the parking lot. Smoke still came from the shattered rear entrance. "He's gone. Has an APB been put out?"

"It doesn't matter, Mr. Lane. Isaacs is still in the building," St. Clair said. He was a dark intense man with a nervous tic.

"How do you know that?"

"We talked to him."

"When? How?"

"About five minutes ago on the phone," Coniff said. "Right after his last booby trap went off. Christ, she was just a girl, not much older than my own daughter. He shot her to death, then wired a bomb to her body. So there's no way he's coming out of this one alive."

Lane was listening to the FBI agent, but he was working it out. Isaacs was too sharp to be cornered like this. He'd eluded detection by the Bureau, the CIA, and the NSA long enough to prove that. And he was here on direct orders from Maslennikov, who himself was no slouch. These guys were pros. They would have thought of everything, worked out every contingency.

"Sorry, but it's going to end right here," Coniff said. "And I can't say as I blame the navy."

"What'd he say?" Lane asked.

"Sir?"

"You said you talked to Isaacs on the phone. What'd he say? Did you tell him that he was surrounded, and that there was no way he was coming out of there alive without your help?"

"He wouldn't listen."

"Say again?" Lane asked sharply.

"He wouldn't listen to anything we said. He just made his demands and told us to call back when we'd done what he wanted."

Lane and Hughes exchanged knowing glances. "It was a tape recorder,

Coniff! A goddamned tape recorder! Which means he's not only long gone with whatever the hell he came here to get, but those SWAT teams headed downstairs are walking into a trap unless they're stopped!"

The truth of what Lane was saying suddenly penetrated, and Coniff was visibly rocked. "Oh, shit," he said, and he turned on his heel and headed toward the front line bulling his way past everyone in his path.

St. Clair started after his boss, but Lane stopped him.

"Do you know the local police and highway patrol?"

"Of course," the FBI agent said.

"Fine. You're going to ask them to set out a dragnet."

"Already happening—"

"We're going to tighten it," Lane said. "Right now."

12

In the darkness of the alley the cabby's eyes stared sightlessly out of the windshield at a flashing neon sign on a shabby hotel at the corner. His throat had been slit from behind, blood covered the front of his shirt. His body had been rifled, his money stolen, the wallet discarded on the seat next to him. His watch and wedding band were missing, as was the sterling silver rosary he carried in his jacket pocket.

This section of Norfolk was notorious for its crime. It was the crack cocaine center of the city, and even the metro police patrolled this neighborhood with extreme care, one eye always over their shoulders.

Very few ordinary people lingered on these streets, and those that did never stopped to ask questions, they minded their own business. Another body would surprise no one.

A streetlight cast Yernin's shadow down the sidewalk as he emerged from the alley and headed the way he'd come up Union Street. Most of the storefronts were either boarded shut or covered with metal security shutters. A bar across the street from the Seaway Hotel was the only other business establishment open on the block.

Someone was on his tail faster than he thought would be likely. The police cars arriving at the airport were no coincidence. It meant someone knew about him, knew what moves he was capable of making, and possibly even why he'd broken cover. There was only one man he could think of who was that sharp. He'd seen him only once, at a Pentagon briefing, but he never forgot the eyes, which looked like they had X-ray vision. His name was Bill Lane, and he worked for the National Security Agency's Russian Division. Yernin had been warned about the man, and he'd been waiting for Lane to show up for a long time. Maybe it was happening now.

He still had to get out of Norfolk but now he had no transportation, he was running short of time, and he was down to his last disguise and last set of identity papers and credit cards. He couldn't afford to use those foolishly. Nor could he kid himself into thinking that the normal routes out of the city would not be covered. Airports, bus depots, ferries, and highways would be watched.

The solution to all three of his problems presented itself when a customized pale yellow Cadillac Coupe de Ville with gold trim and a gold radiator grille pulled up at the curb half a block away.

Yernin stepped into the shadows of a doorway as a very tall black man dressed in a yellow suit and a wide-brimmed yellow hat unfolded from the backseat of the car. He reached inside and pulled a struggling young woman out of the car, slapped her across the face a couple of times, and dragged her inside an apparently deserted building.

Yernin could see a driver behind the wheel, but nobody rode shotgun. The street was deserted for the moment. He took out his gun, checked the load, and, keeping it out of sight at his side, headed toward the car, his movements unsteady as if he were drunk or high on drugs.

The driver watched him come up the street and pass, then turned away indifferently. He was a very large man with a thick neck and double chins. He wore a metallic silver jacket with a black shirt underneath and a multicolored knit cap.

Yernin turned suddenly, crossed to the car, jerked open the back door on the driver's side and slipped inside, tossing his bag on the seat and placing the muzzle of the Heckler & Koch against the back of the man's head as he closed the door.

"Motherfuck . . . what the fuck you think you doin'?" the driver shouted, rearing back as he reached inside his jacket.

"I'll kill you," Yernin warned.

The driver stiffened, then looked up at Yernin's reflection in the rearview mirror. "That'd be the worse fuckin' mistake of your fuckin' life, motherfucker. What you want?"

"Drive."

"Like shit . . ."

Yernin cocked the hammer, the ratchet noise very loud. "Drive," he repeated calmly. He met the driver's eyes in the mirror. "We just want to give your boss a message."

"All right, my man. Give me the message and I'll pass it along."

"If he comes out of that building I'll put a bullet in your brain. Then I'll open the door and kill him. Next week I'll come back and give the message to whoever took over."

"You're motherfuckin' crazy," the driver said.

Yernin forced a laugh. "Yes. I am."

The driver hesitated a moment longer, then slammed the car into gear and took off. "Where we going'?"

"Richmond," Yernin said.

"Shit," the driver replied. "Is this what it's all about, my man? Ain't no need for a turf war, 'cause I got some major shit I could tell you."

This car would be missed in the next few minutes. But Yernin doubted that its owner would file a stolen vehicle report with the police.

The driver glanced nervously in the mirror, misinterpreting Yernin's silence. "Shit," he said softly, figuring for the first time that he was in some serious trouble.

NORFOLK NAVAL BASE

"Stein has been spotted at the airport," Hughes shouted down from the helicopter's open door.

Lane watched the Norfolk SAC Dan Coniff and a naval officer emerge from the blown-out rear door of Atlantic Fleet HQ and start across the parking lot. They were arguing about something. Members of the SWAT team that had gone in earlier came out of the doorway. Then a dozen navy personnel in blues went inside.

Smoke still swirled around the shattered entryway. Blood streaked the light green walls just inside the corridor and out onto the stairs. It was a petty officer's body that Isaacs had booby-trapped. The marine sergeant who'd turned her over was killed in the blast. There was plenty of blood to go around. The smell of death lingered in the air along with the acrid odor of explosives.

"It was Semtex," Lane said. He recognized the smell. "Tell them at the airport to watch themselves. He's probably laid other traps."

"He's booked a flight to Montreal which doesn't leave for another hour and a half," Hughes said. "He could be hiding out there, changing his identity, thinking he could somehow get past the cops. He might not even know we're this close behind him."

"We're nowhere near him, Tommy," Lane said. "He's no longer Stein. By now he's taken a new identity."

"He's got to get out of the city somehow, he has to know somebody is looking for him."

"That's right. Which means he has a plan. All we have to do is figure out what it is, and get one step ahead of him."

"Easier said than done, William."

Lane looked up at his friend. "It might help if we knew what he got here."

"Assuming he was successful."

"He was." Lane turned back as Coniff and the navy lieutenant whose name tag read ROWSE came over. Rowse was red in the face from exertion, and he was clearly so angry that he was having trouble keeping it in check. He wasn't a very bulky man, but Lane wouldn't have wanted to tangle with him just now.

"Are you the guy from NSA who tried to warn us?" he asked dangerously.

"That's right. Name's Bill Lane." He stuck out his hand but the lieutenant ignored it.

"I've got six good people dead in there, one of them a woman. Why didn't you get your act together sooner so we could have had a fighting chance?"

"I called you the minute I figured it out. Nobody screwed around, Lieutenant. But this guy is a pro."

Rowse's face darkened further. "God help the son of a bitch when I come face to face with him. Dagen was just a kid. She and Llewellyn were getting married next month. Now they're both dead. It's her body plastered all over the walls in there."

"It'd help if we knew what he came down here for," Lane said.

"Doesn't matter, Mr. Lane," Coniff broke in. "I just got word that the Bureau's Counter Espionage Division is taking over. We'll handle it from this point."

"Is Bishop on his way down?"

"Yes, sir. He should be here any minute now. I talked to him, and he said to tell you that we're taking it from here, unless Isaacs gets out of the country. In that case the CIA will handle it."

"How about in the meantime?" Lane asked, making an effort to keep his patience. The SAC was merely following orders.

"I don't follow you," Coniff replied uncertainly, but then they could hear a helicopter coming in from the north, and he looked relieved. "That'll be Mr. Bishop."

"What about the meantime? Do we let Isaacs slip through our fingers without trying to nail him?"

"Everything is being done that can be done," Coniff said, officiously. "The local cops are cooperating with us. He won't get out of the city."

"Expand the dragnet all the way back to Washington, now, while we still have a decent chance."

"There's no way he's heading back to D.C. It'd be crazy."

"Are you willing to bet someone else's life on that?" Lane demanded.

"He got into the computer center," Rowse said. He was starting to calm down, to think it out instead of simply reacting. "If he knew the proper passwords he could have come up with the sailing orders and patrol stations for every submarine in the Atlantic Fleet."

"How long did he have?"

"A couple of minutes. Maybe as long as ten."

"Couldn't he have gotten the same information using the computers in the Pentagon?" Hughes asked from the open hatch.

Rowse shook his head. "The center is isolated to prevent anything like that from happening. We learned the hard way a few years ago when some hackers in Amsterdam got into the DOD's system."

The incoming helicopter touched down on the street thirty yards away, and Joe Bishop jumped out. Coniff trotted off to intercept him.

"Can we find out what information he got from the computer?" Lane asked.

"Under ordinary circumstances I'd say yes. But besides the explosive device we found and disarmed just inside the inner door, he set off two others down there. Did a lot of damage. I don't know if we'll ever be able to figure out what he was after."

"Pacific Fleet submarine headquarters has a similar computer center, don't they?"

"Out in Honolulu."

"Is it isolated like this one?" Lane asked.

"I imagine it is," Rowse replied.

"But is it isolated from this center as well? Or is there cross talk between the two commands?"

"I don't know," Rowse shrugged.

"Find out," Lane said, as Bishop and Coniff came over. The Norfolk SAC didn't look happy.

"Dan filled me in," Bishop said. "What's your thinking?" He was a short man, with thick shoulders and deep-set hooded eyes that sometimes made him look like an Eastern European king.

"It's a safe bet Isaacs got what he came for, and he's got a good plan to get out of here."

"The airport was just a diversion?"

"I think so," Lane said. "He was too open about his moves, figuring it might slow us down. Keep us searching in the immediate area, which would give him a chance to slip away and head off in a different direction. He has to pass on his information."

"To Maslennikov?" Bishop asked.

"It's possible."

"Maslennikov is gone."

"Where?" Lane demanded.

"My people tailed him to Mexico City."

"Then that's where Isaacs is headed," Lane said. "Expand your dragnet now."

"I think you're right," Bishop said. He turned to his Norfolk SAC. "Get on it, Dan. Use the comms gear in my chopper. Have Sal do an all-points fax of Isaacs's picture and description."

"I was just about to suggest it," Coniff said, avoiding Lane's eyes. "He won't get far, I'll guarantee it."

RICHMOND, VIRGINIA

The Checker cab pulled up with a squeal of brakes in front of the Amtrak station in the heart of downtown. Yernin paid the cabby and jumped out.

The place looked nearly deserted, but unless his train had departed early for some reason, he had a few minutes to spare.

"Who're pickin' to win?" the cabdriver shouted after him.

"The Bills," Yernin called back as he headed into the depot.

There'd been police activity on Interstate 64 a few miles outside Norfolk, but it had thinned out almost immediately, and no one had bothered to stop them. His hijacked Cadillac driver had asked no further questions during the ninety-minute drive, and when they pulled into the parking lot of what appeared to be an abandoned shopping mall on the outskirts of Richmond he didn't seem surprised. Merely resigned. Yernin ordered him out of the car, and a few yards away, just as the man started to plead for his life, he put a bullet into the back of his skull.

He'd left the yellow Cadillac in back of City Hall, turned his windbreaker right side out, and caught the cab in front of a Howard Johnson's two blocks away.

The big clock in the main arrivals hall of the old, ornately designed depot showed five minutes before twelve when Yernin crossed to the stairs and took them down to the tracks two at a time. The station smelled of stale cigarette smoke and booze as well as neglect, dirt, and age. Twenty-four hours ago when he'd made his round-trip reservations, the Amtrak clerk in Baltimore told him he was lucky. He'd gotten the last first-class compartment in any train heading down to Miami.

"I hope you already made your hotel reservations," the clerk warned. "Super Bowls pack 'em in down there. Second time in five years."

"I'm staying with friends," Yernin had mumbled. That afternoon he bought a Super Bowl XXXIV reversible windbreaker.

Nobody would think to look for him here, because in general when Americans thought of travel they thought in terms of cars or airplanes. Very seldom did they think of trains. Especially these days when Amtrak was on the verge of bankruptcy. A train filled with football fans would provide even better cover. He figured he would be safe.

Trackside there was a big commotion as the conductor busily hustled the last of a couple of dozen drunken fans aboard, so no one noticed Yernin climbing into the last car and finding his way to his compartment.

13

NORFOLK NAVAL BASE

One of the computers printed passenger lists for public conveyances departing from a two hundred mile radius of Norfolk. At first nobody paid any attention to the dense stream of type.

Since most public transport systems shut down around midnight, and usually before one in the morning, they were forced to consider four possibilities. Either Isaacs was holed up somewhere in Norfolk; or somewhere nearby waiting until morning to make his way south; or he was already aboard some public transportation; or he'd left by car.

His green Corsica, booby-trapped, had been found at the airport, and so far no cars had been reported stolen or missing between 10:30 P.M. and now except for a cab. But that had been found in a tough section of downtown, the driver murdered and robbed. It was such a common crime that no one linked it to Isaacs.

Lane suddenly realized that they were going about their search all wrong. He walked over to the computer spewing out passenger lists and ripped off the fanfold, gathering up at least twenty feet of printout. "He's either in here someplace, or we can quit and go home."

They'd taken over Base Security Operations Ready Room, turning it into a mini crisis management center. Everybody was in a dark mood. Hughes and Lieutenant Rowse had set up secure communications and computer links with Ben Lewis at the CMC in Fort Meade, as well as with the FBI's Special Operations Center and the CIA's Operations Room at Langley. Bishop and Coniff, huddled together at one of the consoles across the room, looked up.

"You have to give these kinds of things more time, Mr. Lane," the Norfolk SAC said pompously. "In my experience, if you allow the street cops the room to do their jobs, they'll work out just fine for you."

Bishop came over. "What have you come up with?"

"He had a plan to make his rendezvous with Maslennikov in Mexico City, and he's sticking with it."

"Maybe he switched cars and disguises and headed down Interstate 85 or 95," Bishop said.

"Too dangerous. If he was stopped for anything he'd have to suspect it was because we were onto him, and he'd have to shoot his way out. He'd be no better off than he was earlier tonight."

"That's a little thin, isn't it?" Coniff asked.

"On the surface, yes," Land admitted, holding his temper in check. Coniff was a fool, and he was doing more posturing for his boss than any real police work. "But if he's out there in a car there's nothing we can do to catch him from here. It'll be up to the highway patrols in forty-eight different states. If he did take a plane or a bus or whatever, he's already aboard and heading south. Means his name will be on one of these lists."

Coniff's lip curled. "Come on now, Mr. Lane, you don't think he'd be stupid enough to buy a ticket under his real name, or even under Lieutenant Commander Stein's name . . ." He trailed off when Bishop shot him an ugly glance.

"Maslennikov came back less than thirty-six hours ago with Isaacs's orders," Lane said. "Assuming we're guessing right about that part, then Isaacs may have booked his transportation sometime within that time period. Single traveler, heading south, sometime between . . . let's say 10:30 P.M. and 12:30 or 1:00 A.M."

"We can start with Norfolk and work outward," Bishop said.

"That's what I thought," Lane agreed. He handed sections of fanfold to Bishop, Coniff, Hughes, and Rowse, and took a section for himself over to one of the consoles. He sat down, put his feet up, and started down the list. In this case he was looking at Greyhound bus bookings from a half-dozen stations starting in Norfolk and working south toward Emporia on US 301 and I-95.

Hughes stumbled onto it in the first five minutes. "What name did that call girl say Isaacs used?"

"Stewart Mann," Bishop said, looking up from his reading.

"It seems Mr. Mann is a football fan."

Lane went over to where Hughes was set up at one of the tables, his section of fanfold spread out. "What'd you find, Tommy?"

"An S. Mann booked a round-trip first-class compartment on Amtrak to Miami. Left Richmond at midnight."

"Super Bowl," Rowse said in wonder.

"When did he buy his ticket?" Lane asked.

"Yesterday morning through the Amtrak office in Baltimore, with a Visa card under the name Stewart Mann."

"He made a mistake."

"Looks like he did at that, William," Hughes said, sliding over to a computer console. The navy rating moved aside to let him in.

"Can I help with something, sir?" the young petty officer asked.

"I have to log onto a civilian network."

"Sorry, sir. But that won't happen with this system."

Hughes got an outside telephone line, hit a few keys, and then pulled up an Internet program. Within ninety seconds he was into Amtrak's routing system. A real-time map of the eastern seaboard routes showed on the monitor.

"They probably didn't teach this in tech school," Hughes said kindly.

"No, sir," the kid replied, impressed.

The Silver Meteor enroute to Miami was approaching the North Carolina border. Its next scheduled major stop was Fayetteville, 150 miles south.

"We'll meet the train there," Lane said, stabbing a finger at the small city.

"The Bureau will take care of it," Coniff said.

"Yes, we will," Bishop told his Norfolk SAC. He winked at Lane. "Your chopper or mine?"

"Mine," Lane replied. "I've got a zippy crew."

"I'm coming with you," Rowse said.

ABOARD THE *SILVER METEOR*

The train was utter bedlam. Starting in New York City, the Super Bowl–bound passengers had been drinking all evening, and few of them showed any signs of tapering off. It was party time. And when football fans partied, *everybody* partied. Aboard a train there were no responsibilities. No one had to be the designated driver, there was room to move around from car to car, each of which had its own noisy group, and, best of all, you could sleep when you wanted to sleep, eat when you wanted to eat, and crash if you had to crash. It was the ultimate pregame tailgate party.

Yernin stood at the window in his dark compartment watching the occasional light pass his window. They were twenty miles south of Richmond, but instead of settling down as he thought he would, he was becoming increasingly nervous.

He had an almost overwhelming urge to get out of his compartment. It was a feeling bordering on claustrophobia. He did not want to jump to any conclusions, but over the twenty-five years of his career he had come to understand his gut feelings and then had come to rely on them. One of his instructors at KGB's School One outside Moscow had warned him to listen to his inner voices after he had separated the real concerns from the paranoia.

The police had showed up at the airport much too fast for mere happenstance or luck. The authorities were looking for a man posing as Lieutenant Commander Stein. It meant that Stein's body had been discovered at the

Hyatt. Probably because the whore had gone to the police after all. They would have discovered that Stein's ID card and security pass were missing. Combined with the trouble tonight on base, it seemed that somebody bright had put it together.

Bill Lane. The National Security Agency analyst who had come up against General Normav and won. Maslennikov had given Yernin ample warning about the man. But since Lane had probably been given the assignment to ferret out the mole in the Pentagon, he'd been an untouchable until now. Assassinating him would have led the authorities to redouble their efforts in finding the penetration agent.

"If Lane catches your scent, he won't let it go," Maslennikov had said. "He'll keep coming until he's successful or he's dead. So if you do finally come up against him, and there's nowhere for you to run, kill him."

Yernin's eyes narrowed. There was no reason to think Lane had traced him this far this fast, yet the longer he was aboard, the more unsettled he became.

He had thought of everything, though not killing the whore had been a mistake. He could see that now. Because of her they'd traced his movements as Stein to the navy base and then to the airport. But everything else had gone according to plan.

Then he had another thought. It suddenly came to him that the name Stewart Mann was the problem. The whore knew him by that name. And he'd made the train reservations under that name. It was an amateur's error. One that had apparently nagged at his subconscious from the moment he'd seen the police cars converging on the airport.

If someone was coming, and now he thought that was a possibility, he would need another diversion. One that would be so big and splashy it would draw the authorities for miles around away from the manhunt.

One that would buy him some time.

He taped four bricks of Semtex to his midriff, then pocketed the micrologic computer and a remote firing fuse. He taped the floppy disk to his left calf, reloaded his Heckler & Koch with a fresh magazine, then stuffed it in his belt at the small of his back. Working by penlight in the dark compartment, he removed the covering plate from the light switch beside the door, ran a pair of wires from the hot side and the ground to an acid fuse, which went into the last six one-pound bricks of explosive. These he placed under the pull-down bed. Then he replaced the switch cover.

When he was finished he made certain that the wires would be hidden from anyone coming into the compartment. When the light switch was thrown, the plastique would blow, taking out the entire car.

Before he stepped out into the noise and confusion of the corridor he once again examined his reasons for abandoning the safety of his compartment, and reviewed his contingency plans for getting to Mexico City if he had to get off the train before Miami. If he was pushed to it, a great many people aboard this train would die or be injured tonight. But there was no help for it. Jumping off the train now would not only be risky, it would be unnecessary. Yet he did not want to be cornered in his compartment. He needed freedom of movement.

Out in the corridor he had to shoulder his way through a group of noisy revelers, then past a couple who were passionately embracing in the corner before he got outside to the connecting platform between cars. Four men, all of them smoking, were arguing about the point spread. They automatically stepped aside without looking up for Yernin to pass.

The next car forward was just as noisy and crowded as his.

The third car forward was the dining car, crammed wall to wall and end to end with bodies. The noise, heat, and smoke were intense, but nobody paid him the slightest attention as he pushed his way through. He was just another football fan.

The final two cars were coach class and just as crowded as the others. Loud music played from a portable stereo in one of them and couples were trying to dance in the narrow aisle. Somebody handed him a beer.

The last two connecting platforms were empty, as was the final one between the forward-most coach-class car and the rear of the second of the two diesels pulling the train. The door to the back catwalk of the engine was locked, however.

First checking to make sure that no one was coming, he screwed the silencer on the end of the gun barrel and shot out the door lock, careful to do as little visible damage as possible. Next he shot out the single overhead light, plunging the connecting platform into darkness.

He slipped outside, the noise and wind terrific. He untaped the Semtex from his middle, retaped the four bricks into one mass, and inserted the remotely fired fuse into the plastic.

Jumping across to the rear catwalk of the big diesel, he lay on his stomach just above the rear wheels and jammed the bomb between the engine's lower frame and the upper support structure of the wheel assembly. When he triggered it, the force of the blast would take the entire wheel assembly off, derailing the engine and pulling the passenger cars off the track one at a time.

He got up, jumped back to the coach car, and went inside, where he leaned back against the rear bulkhead in the darkness. He would wait here until it was time to leave. Somehow he didn't think he would still be aboard when the train reached Miami. *If* it reached Miami.

EN ROUTE TO FAYETTEVILLE, NORTH CAROLINA

Bishop shoved his headset back. "A cabby in Richmond thinks he might have picked Isaacs up at the HoJo and taken him to the Amtrak station." He had to shout over the noise of the helicopter rotors. "He says he remembers him because he told the cabby he was rooting for the Bills, but he was wearing a Packers jacket."

"Once he gets to Miami he'll be tough to stop," Hughes pointed out. "There are lots of ways to Mexico City from there."

They were over the outskirts of Fayetteville. The train wasn't due for another twenty minutes. Which gave them plenty of time to get their people in place and settled down so that Isaacs might not notice anything out of the ordinary.

"Right," Bishop agreed. "Which means we get aboard the train, isolate him, and take him out at the next stop, which is Dillon, South Carolina, fifty miles away. Gives us a little less than an hour to corner him. My people will be standing by, along with the South Carolina Highway Patrol and Rowse's people. We shouldn't have too much trouble."

"Do that and somebody else is going to get hurt," Lane said.

"No place for him to go."

"At the very least he'll blow the train, and then get away in the confusion."

"He's a spy, not a mad man," Bishop argued.

Lane turned his ice blue eyes to his FBI friend. "What's the body count so far?"

Bishop shrugged. "I see your point, but we're not going to let him get to Miami. Maybe we can get the other passengers off, a few at a time."

"They're on the way to the Super Bowl, I don't think they'll cooperate."

"Maybe we can disconnect the cars one at a time, so if he tries something it won't involve the entire train," Rowse said.

Lane nodded. "We might get away with something like that once, but no more."

"Well then, what do you suggest, Mr. Lane?" Coniff piped up.

The helicopter's rotors changed pitch as they started down for a landing in the parking lot down the street from the depot.

"You and I will be the only two to board the train," Lane told Bishop.

"And me," Lieutenant Rowse interjected. "I've got a stake in this."

"Then what, William?" Hughes asked, giving his friend a worried look.

"I'll show him the error of his ways."

14

ABOARD THE *SILVER METEOR*

Yernin watched from the darkness of the connecting platform as they came into a fairly good-sized town. He figured it was Fayetteville, and when they eased into the station his guess was confirmed by the sign over the trackside platform.

A dozen people waited to board, most of them dressed in Packers green and yellow. He studied their faces, and the way they waited for the train to come to a complete stop. It was late, but they were keyed up for the trip to Florida. They looked as if they'd been partying all night, just like the other fans already aboard. They would fit in well.

The doors to the middle three cars opened, and boarding steps were put out. Yernin watched as the football fans clambered aboard, laughing and shouting and good-naturedly jostling each other.

All except three of them in line for the car farthest back.

Yernin pressed his cheek against the window so that he could see down the length of the train. Three men, none of them dressed as football fans, climbed aboard. Moments later the train jerked and headed out of the station, pulling away from the bright lights.

He continued to watch out the window, and as they cleared the end of the depot, he saw at least three police cars parked along the street between the buildings, and then the train angled away into the switchyard.

He stepped back into the darkness, his left hand going to the calculator in his pocket. He had only to push the square-root key, which was the lowest button to the left, and the explosives over the diesel engine's wheels would blow.

Not everybody he'd seen aboard the train was dressed in football colors, but most of them were.

Nor were all of them drunk, and boisterous, though most of them were.

The three men he watched boarding the train wore dark jackets, which was about all he could tell from the distance and angle. But they'd not behaved like everybody else. As if they were not a part of the crowd.

It might be nothing, but Lane or somebody had traced him to Norfolk and to the airport. It was possible that they'd traced him here under his Stewart Mann work name. From what he knew about Lane, the man was certainly capable of doing such a thing.

He was ready for just such an eventuality. But he wanted to be sure before he took such a drastic action. Killing without good reason was not only foolish, it was dangerous.

He opened the door, left the safety of the connecting platform, and pushed his way to the end of the coach car to the next connecting platform. He closed the door behind him and shot out the overhead light.

The train was already out into the countryside, the view out the windows pitch-black. Yernin opened the door and stepped into the next coach car just as the bathroom door opened and a man came out. Yernin had to move aside.

The man gave him a bleary-eyed grin. "Next," he said, and he headed down the aisle. A woman so drunk she could barely walk staggered up the aisle past the man who happily patted her on the rump, but she didn't notice or didn't care. Her attention was focused on Yernin standing at the bathroom door.

"You goin' in, or just waitin' for company?" she asked, with a goofy, unfocused look.

Yernin realized she was trying to flirt with him. She was wearing a wedding ring. He wondered where her husband was.

The door at the far end of the car opened and he got a brief glimpse of a man in a dark jacket before the crowd moved in. But the man was familiar. One of the three who'd boarded the train? If so it meant they'd divided their search. He was running out of time and maneuvering room.

"What's it gonna be, sweety?" the woman asked.

Yernin smiled at her. "After you," he said. He took her by the arm, shoved her into the bathroom, and stepped in behind her. As he was closing the door he got another look at the man in the dark jacket, and he recognized him. It was Bill Lane. He was sure of it.

"Hey, not so rough—" the woman protested.

Yernin locked the door, then pulled the woman to him. She tried to pull away at first, but then pressed her body against his, moving her hips and pelvis suggestively.

"What about your husband?" Yernin whispered, slipping the stiletto out of its sheath beneath his left arm. He couldn't have her chasing him through the train.

"He's already passed out." She turned her face up to his.

Still holding her with his left hand, he moved aside and plunged the stiletto into her chest beneath her left breast, angling the blade upward so that it penetrated her heart.

Blood gushed out onto his hand and wrist, but then her heart stopped and she slumped to the floor.

Yernin washed her blood off his hands and the stiletto, then propped the woman on her knees in front of the toilet, her head lying on the toilet seat as if she were throwing up. Next he wiped the blood off the floor with a handful of paper towels, then checked out the window to see where they were. But the night was black, except for a green signal light they passed. He estimated they were moving about fifty miles per hour and accelerating slowly. If he jumped from the train now he would hurt himself. He would have to time his departure for when the train slowed for a sharp curve or a bridge. Amtrak rails were so bad, deceleration was required by law.

Lane was a NSA analyst, not a field officer. But Maslennikov had warned him that the man had a habit of showing up at the wrong time and wrong place. He had been targeted by several field-hardened KGB hitmen and he had killed them. Because of Lane, General Normav's carefully crafted operation during the joint U.S.–Ukraine war games in the South Pacific last year had unraveled at the seams. Kiev was still embarrassed by the setback.

"Do not underestimate this man," Maslennikov said.

Whether or not he killed Lane now, he still needed a diversion. If one of the other two men who'd boarded the train tried to search Yernin's compartment, he might trigger the explosives. And if Lane were still aboard when the Semtex over the locomotive's wheels went off, he would probably be killed or injured. Especially if he was close to the forward end of the train.

Yernin figured that would be the best-case scenario. It would take the authorities a long time to dig through the wreckage before they could know what was going on.

He needed to isolate Lane in the connecting platform between the forward coach car and the diesel engines, and kill him.

The train was packed, and Lane took his time moving forward through the cars. He did not think Isaacs would recognize him if they came face to face, but he wasn't sure, so he took care to pretend he was just another football fan in no particular hurry. He wasn't eager to engage in a shootout in the middle of a crowd, he just wanted to establish that the man was aboard.

If they could isolate him to one car, more of Bishop's people could be brought aboard at Dillon, and by the time they reached Miami this afternoon they would be in better control of the situation.

Isaacs was ruthless, but Lane didn't think he was desperate enough to commit suicide. When he realized that the odds were severely against him, he would give it up.

The man was probably a Ukrainian. And Lane understood them as well as anyone could understand a people. Ukrainians were not fanatics. They did not believe that the way to salvation was through sacrificing one's own life.

Isaacs might be on his guard, but by now he would have to believe that he was home free. That he would get off the train in Miami, lose himself in the crowd, and make his way to Mexico City with whatever he'd gleaned from the navy computer center.

But a man like Isaacs would have contingency plans. He had the backing of the Ukrainian KGB, and it was pretty good these days. In some ways even better than the old Soviet Union's KGB because it wasn't so administratively top-heavy.

Lane extracted himself from a group of Packer fans who'd tried to draw him into an involved discussion about Bart Starr and pushed his way to the front of the coach car, opened the door, and stepped onto the connecting platform, his shoes crunching on broken glass.

The ceiling light had been smashed or shot out, leaving the small space in darkness, the floor littered with glass.

Lane stepped aside so that his back was against the bulkhead, not the door, and transferred his 9mm Beretta automatic from his shoulder holster to his jacket pocket. If need be he would kill the man. Providing he had a clear shot, and there were no alternatives.

He checked the window into the car he'd just left, and then the window into the next car forward. Football fans. A few of them curled up in their seats, trying to get some sleep under impossible conditions, but more of them partying. A beer keg was set up between the last row of seats and the restroom. A half-dozen men were gathered around it, drinking beer out of big plastic mugs with the Buffalo Bills insignia.

Isaacs had been here, and he was still somewhere close. Lane could almost feel the man's presence in the air, he could almost smell the stench of death. He'd shot out the light so that whatever he'd done here would not be observed . . . from where? Outside?

Lane checked the exit doors on both sides of the car; they were locked. There were lights in the distance, but the countryside was mostly in darkness. There was nothing to see.

Isaacs may have stood here as the train pulled into the station at Fayetteville. What would he have seen? Something to warn him off? It was possible that he'd gotten off the train while it was still in the switching yard, but somehow Lane didn't think so.

Lane had another thought. Isaacs had booby-trapped his way out of the navy computer center in an effort to slow down his pursuers. He'd also booby-trapped the car he left at the airport. It was his style. There was no reason to think he would do anything different now. The surest way to stop a train was by stopping its engines. The big diesels pulling it.

He left the connecting platform, pushed his way through the crowded car, and peered out the window into the forward connecting platform. It was dark like the last one.

Making sure no one was paying any attention to him, Lane took out his gun, opened the door, and stepped gingerly onto the connecting platform, his shoes again crunching on broken glass. Isaacs had been here as well.

The exit doors on both sides of the car were secure, but the lock on the forward door had been shot out. Lane cocked his gun, then opened the door and, keeping low, darted across to the locomotive's rear catwalk. The noise from the wind and the big diesels was terrific, and he had to brace himself against the swaying motion. But he was alone.

If Isaacs had set explosives to take out the diesels, he would have done it here. Somewhere very close.

The train began to slow down, its brakes squealing. Pocketing his gun and holding onto the safety railing, he leaned out as far as he could, but there was little or nothing to be seen forward. The train was decelerating for some reason, possibly for a road crossing in some small town, or perhaps for a sharp curve or a bridge.

Something was about to happen. Lane could feel it in his gut.

It suddenly struck him that Bishop and Rowse had not been sufficiently warned about booby traps. They could be walking into a trap. Isaacs could have set more than one.

Lane jumped back across to the coach car and onto the dark connecting platform. He was about to yank open the inner door when a hand shot out of the darkness and the muzzle of a silenced pistol was jammed into the base of his skull.

"Mr. Lane, I presume."

It was Isaacs. Lane recognized the voice from surveillance tapes he'd listened to. He willed himself to relax.

"Mikhail has gotten you into some deep shit this time, comrade," he said in Russian. "No way out."

"In this case it's no way out for you or the two men who boarded the train with you," Yernin replied in English. "You shouldn't have come. Because of you even more people will get hurt tonight."

"There's no reason for it," Lane said. The exit door on the left side was ajar. Isaacs had shot out the lock during the time Lane had been on the locomotive's rear catwalk. "The countryside is crawling with cops looking for you. How far do you think you'll get?"

"As far as need be, because all those policemen will be busy attending a train wreck."

The train continued to decelerate. Either Isaacs had set a timer on the explosive charge somewhere aboard the diesels or he had a remote-control device. In either case, as soon as the train slowed enough for him to get off safely, he would jump. And he was right about one thing. Forced to deal with a train wreck, the police would have no choice except to abandon the search for a spy in favor of helping the victims.

"You won't get off this train," Lane said.

"I think I will."

"You're forgetting something."

"What might that be?" Yernin said, with little or no concern. He was waiting for the right moment.

"We know about Mexico City—"

An explosion somewhere toward the rear of the train caused all the cars to lurch sharply forward against their couplings. Lane ducked away from the barrel pressed to his head and used the train's momentum to slam his shoulder into Isaacs's chest, shoving the man against the forward bulkhead with enough force to drive the air out of his lungs.

Isaacs's pistol discharged. The bullet ricocheted off the floor, a fragment of the steel-jacketed shell hitting the side of Lane's head. A billion stars burst in his brain, his legs momentarily buckling beneath him.

Yernin pushed away from the bulkhead, stepped to the side, and jammed the barrel of his pistol into Lane's sternum.

"*Spasiba,*" he said. Thanks.

Lane grappled for Isaacs's gun hand, jamming his thumb in front of the ejector slide, preventing it from firing as the Ukrainian pulled the trigger.

"You're welcome, you son of a bitch," Lane said. He smashed his right fist into Isaacs's face, once, twice, and a third time, again forcing the man against the bulkhead.

Yernin was a man driven by purpose. He yanked his gun back and fired, the snap shot plucking at Lane's coat collar.

The door to the forward passenger car slammed open as Lane batted Isaacs's gun hand away and dropped a roundhouse right into the man's rib cage.

Isaacs cried out in pain and rage as he dropped to his knees. He looked up as several men crowded through the doorway. "Help me," he cried out. "He set another bomb!"

"Son of a bitch," one of them shouted. They grabbed Lane and yanked him backward off his feet. Something hard smashed into the back of his head, forcing him to the floor; his gorge rose as his stomach did a slow roll.

Through a thin veil of haze he saw Isaacs grinning in triumph, and then they hit him in the back of the head again and everything momentarily went fuzzy.

For several long seconds he crouched in a kneeling position, his forehead resting on the dirty floor, his stomach turning over, his head spinning. There seemed to be a lot of noise and activity around him, and a sharply cold wind roared through the small compartment.

Isaacs had set the explosion at the back of the train, and a lot of people were probably hurt. Maybe Bishop or Rowse were in the middle of it.

Lane looked up. The exit door was open. Isaacs had jumped. That thought crystallized in his head. He pushed himself up and staggered to his feet. Someone grabbed him by the shoulders and slammed him roughly against the bulkhead.

"Where is it, you bastard?"

It was his worst nightmare: standing by while someone innocent was about to get hurt. His mother hadn't been able to defend herself against his father. *His father.*

"The bomb! Where did you hide it?"

Lane focused on the bleary-eyed man holding him. He was very big, and he was angry and frightened.

"You son of a bitch!"

Lane shoved him aside with one hand and pulled the emergency cord with his other. "Get everybody out of the first two cars, and brace for an explosion," he shouted thickly.

"What the fuck?"

"The diesels are set to blow! Now do it!" Lane shoved the man's hand away and stumbled across the compartment and out the forward door.

If the train had been booby-trapped to jump the tracks, the explosives would have to be set over the engine's wheels.

He staggered across to the diesel locomotive and dropped to the deck. Hanging over the edge, he grappled in the spaces above the wheels.

The train was slowing down, the wheels squealing, sparks flying from metal protesting against metal.

The explosives would have to blow at any second, before the train's speed completely bled away, if they were to be effective.

Lane's numb fingers brushed against a puttylike mass jammed up between the engine's frame and a steel cross-member above the wheels. He pried it away, then scrambled to his knees and tossed it out into the darkness.

As he turned away to shield his face and eyes, a huge fireball blossomed behind them.

For a long time he remained crouched against the side of the diesel, his stomach still turning over, his head spinning.

"You okay?" someone shouted from behind.

Lane looked up. The bleary-eyed football fan from the connecting platform stood braced in the doorway, his eyes wide.

"I'll take the Pack and give you six points for ten bucks," Lane shouted. "Is it a deal?"

PART
TWO

15

Strong lights bathed the four great submarines and the half-loaded missiles, as if dark, malevolent gods were watching over their machines of destruction. The Russian-built subs, each nearly as long as a soccer field, floated low in the black water, ready at a moment's notice to submerge and go forth to rain destruction on the unsuspecting.

Very few people got this far, but those who did were awed by the potential for death waiting only for the orders to attack.

The sub pens had been evacuated, and all work had been halted after the incursion, except for cleaning up the battle debris. A tall, slender man dressed in plain army fatigues with no markings emerged from the shadows and moved slowly along the quay behind the submarines. A Glock 17 pistol was strapped to his hip. It was 1:30 in the morning.

He stopped at the stern of each warship and turned his black eyes to the markings on the sails. When these machines surfaced, there could be no doubt to which country they belonged. Rafsanjāní's people had insisted on painting the flag of Iran just below the bridge. It was a foolish act, he thought. Submarines were meant to be creatures of the depth, creatures of stealth and hiding, not ships that so openly advertised their countries of origin.

Their technicians had been in the process of loading a cruise missile aboard one of the boats. It hung in its chain fall directly over one of the hatches. The intruders had come this far. They'd seen this much.

He turned to look up at the catwalk twenty-five meters above. They'd seen the missile, but from that high vantage they would not have been able to tell what type of warhead it was equipped with, nuclear or high explosive. No way to determine which without a closer examination.

Amin Zahedi turned his gaze back to the poised missile. No secrets here for which to mount a suicide mission. Every intelligence service in the world knew about Iran's submarines. And most knew that although Iran wanted nuclear weapons, she didn't have them yet. But the attack was drawing the piranhas. Already the infidels were gathering.

"This is war," General Mohammed es Sultaneh, director of SAVAK, Iran's Secret Service, told him yesterday. "A jihad because we have enemies not only in the West, but here among us. Our own brothers."

"They didn't do any real physical damage," Zahedi pointed out. "Beyond that they can cause us no lasting harm."

"Except that this incident has once again focused attention on us," General Sultaneh said. "Can you be sure of the results?"

"I'll personally make sure the UN team sees only what we want them to see, General," Zahedi replied, his thoughts at that moment elsewhere. The strike on the oil platforms was just a diversion. They knew that much, as they knew that the ground attack had involved only two men, one of whom had been killed above the sub pens. The other one had cleverly escaped, and he was probably trying to get . . . where?

The intruder had been to the sub pens and seen with his own eyes the cruise missile. The question was what conclusion he was drawing and what information he was trying to deliver to his masters. Did he believe that the missile was equipped with a nuclear weapon?

"Their aircraft's radar codes were American," the general said. "But there are no aircraft carriers in the northern Gulf at this moment, nor did the jets come from Saudi Arabia or Turkey."

"Israel?" Zahedi asked.

The general spread his hands. "It is up to you to find out for us. Speedily and discreetly."

And then what? Zahedi wondered.

Unlike many of his countrymen, he was not a fanatic, though he was a believer. He'd been educated at UCLA, so he'd lived among the infidels. They were not the Satans that His Holiness Grand Ayatollah Hajj Sayyed Rūhollāh Mūsaví Khomeiní had claimed. But America was the strongest nation on earth, and unless Iran learned to deal in moderation with them it would be Iran, not the infidels, who would perish.

It was not a view he shared openly.

Now the UN Peacekeepers had invaded the sanctity of their borders again because of the Middle East General Accord on Peace.

Someone came out onto the catwalk and called his name. He looked up. It was his partner, Fazolleh Eghbal.

"The UN team is at the front gate, Amin."

"Is there trouble?"

"Plenty," Eghbal said, his voice echoing in the great hall.

"I'm coming up," Zahedi said.

It was about power, he thought. The current struggle in the parliament was centered around control of this installation. At the moment the Islamic fundamentalists held the upper hand. The base commander was a mullah, a religious cleric, and his authority was strong. The division was tearing their country apart. The UN's coming here wouldn't help, especially if something happened to one or more of the team members while they were on Iranian soil.

Frances Shipley stood with Terrence Reilly beside the lead blue-and-white UN van trying as best she could to hold her anger in check. They were surrounded by at least fifty armed and nervous soldiers, young boys most of them, and four Muslim clerics in robes and head coverings. The others on the UN inspection team had returned to the two vans when the situation at the main gate began to get difficult.

Frances was requesting entry to the base in the name of the UN-administered MEGAP, while the mullahs, one in particular, were denying them permission. When Frances refused to turn back, demanding to speak with the base commander, more soldiers had materialized.

"How dare you refuse to let us pass," Frances said, her hands on her hips. Like the others in the UN party, she wore combat fatigues, her trousers bloused in her boots. "You will open these gates immediately, or produce your commanding officer. We have passes signed by your Department of State in Tehran." That part was a bluff. They'd been all but ignored in the capital city.

"This is not Tehran," the lead mullah said, glowering at her. "Cover your hair, and don proper clothing before you come to me. Have you no respect for our faith?"

"Let me speak with your commander."

"I am the commanding officer here," the old cleric said.

Frances guessed he was about sixty, his long beard and thick eyebrows shot with gray. "This is a military installation, but you are a civilian," she said. She turned to one of the soldiers, who had lieutenant's bars on his collar. "Who is your commanding officer? We wish to speak with him."

The young man glanced apologetically at the mullah. "Madame, the mullah is our commander. He is Ali Ghavan es Razmaregh, mullah of the mosque in town."

"Since when does a cleric take charge of a submarine base?" Frances shot back, realizing as she spoke that she'd gone too far. Reilly took her arm and pulled her back.

"What do you know of this base, you harlot spy?" the mullah raged. "I'll place all of you under arrest, and we shall see what respect you'll show after three months in the darkness! The Koran has laws for trespass and spying, and for women who are nonbelievers! *In sha'Allah*."

"Frances," Reilly warned in her ear. "Sometimes retreat is a better part of valor, darlin'."

The night was dark, the sky partially overcast, so the strong lights of the base obscured the countryside behind them. The Zagros Mountains to the north and even the town of Bandar Ma'shur, which had been renamed Bandar-é Emān Khomeiní, were lost in the haze. The navy installation was on full alert. Beyond the gates they could see hundreds of soldiers guarding buildings, and every intersection they could see was blocked by tanks. Machine-gun nests had been placed on many of the roofs, and sharpshooters were stationed behind sandbagged barriers all along the perimeter fence.

"We're sorry, Excellency, but we have been ordered by the United Nations to find out who attacked you," Reilly said politely. "If it was Saddam Hussein's forces, as we expect it may have been, then sanctions will be tightened."

The mullah turned on him. "We do not want you here," he said angrily. "Leave now."

A jeep pulled up inside the gate and two men dressed in plain army fatigues got out and started over.

"Perhaps if you would be so kind as to check with your superiors in Tehran, Excellency, this misunderstanding could be cleared up," Reilly patiently suggested.

"By God and the Prophet, go back where you came from or we will blow you to hell! *In sha'Allah.*"

"That won't be necessary, Commander," the taller of the two men in fatigues said. "I will take full responsibility for our friends from the United Nations."

"They do not belong here," the mullah replied, sharply.

"They're here to help, not to interfere. And they have been expected." He turned to Frances and Reilly, a hint of amusement on his face. "Though not in the middle of the night."

"We're on a very tight schedule," Frances said. He looked like a younger, slimmer version of Omar Sharif, his eyes were sparkling. The mullah, although dangerous, was nothing compared to this one, she thought. "We'd like to be back in Tehran within thirty-six hours."

"Naturally I will do everything within my power to help you. I'm Colonel Amin Zahedi, chief investigator for the Department of Defense. This is my assistant, Lieutenant Eghbal."

They shook hands.

"We don't mean to cause you any trouble."

"Very well. But I don't think it's such a good idea to inspect the damaged oil platforms in the dark. Morning would be better."

"I agree," Frances said. "Right now we'd like to inspect the base."

"I forbid this," the mullah roared.

Zahedi ignored him. "Why?"

"We have evidence that you were attacked," Frances said.

"Yes? What evidence is this?" Zahedi asked, mildly surprised. The mullah was fuming.

"There was a power failure. The base was blacked out shortly after the attack began." Lane's message before they'd left New York had confirmed that the power station had been damaged, along with the telephone exchange and a back gate. The most stunning news of all, however, was that of the Ukrainian patrol boat that had apparently dropped off the ground attack forces. It definitely pointed toward Saddam Hussein.

"Two fighter aircraft came out of nowhere, so the power was shut down to make the base less of a target," Zahedi said. "It was Mullah Razmaregh's quick thinking that saved us."

"No stray hits in the darkness?" Reilly asked.

"None that I'm aware of." He turned to the cleric. "Your Excellency?"

"We suffered no damage," the mullah replied dourly.

"In any event it would have been futile for them to have hit this base," Zahedi said.

"How so?" Frances asked.

"You are aware of what is kept here?"

"Take care that you do not go too far, Colonel," the mullah warned.

"Yes, we are," Frances replied.

"Then perhaps you are aware of our security measures. The boats are kept in hardened enclosures. Quite impossible to inflict any serious damage on us from the air."

The mullah said something to him in Farsi that Frances didn't catch. Zahedi replied harshly, and waited for the cleric to respond. But the mullah turned away in disgust.

"From the air," Frances prompted, looking for a reaction, but Zahedi kept a poker face.

"Yes, from the air."

"But not from a ground attack," Reilly said. "Perhaps you were infiltrated."

Zahedi considered it. "I see. The jet attack as a diversion so that a force of commandos could fight their way onto the base. Perhaps down to the submarines to do—what? Plant bombs? Sabotage?"

"Something like that," Frances said. The son of a bitch was more than dangerous, he was smooth.

"Would you like to see our submarines? All four of them are here at present."

Again there was another rapid-fire exchange between Zahedi and the cleric. This time when it was over, the mullah turned on his heel and he and his three fellow clerics climbed into a staff car and drove back inside. The lieutenant and his troops, however, remained.

"How long will it take for you to get authorization from Tehran?" Frances asked. "And then from the base commander; he doesn't seem pleased."

"I'll show them to you now, if you'd like. Or if you wish to return to your hotel and get a good night's sleep, I promise you the full tour in the morning. You'll see more then."

"Now," Frances said, calling what she figured was his bluff.

Zahedi smiled. "You and Captain Reilly will be the only ones allowed inside. Your other team members will remain here. No photographic or electronic equipment will be allowed. And you will submit to a search of your person."

"Understood," Frances said.

"There are no female personnel on this base to conduct a search of you," Zahedi warned.

"Shall we get on with it, Colonel?" she said.

They went back and explained to the others what was happening, then followed Zahedi through the open gate and climbed into his waiting jeep. Eghbal drove them across the base to the administration building above the sub pens. There was activity everywhere, but no evident battle damage.

They were taken into a conference room, a half-dozen nervous soldiers crowding in with them. Eghbal ran an electronic wand over their bodies, and Zahedi patted Reilly down.

When he was finished, Frances spread her legs, stretched out her arms, and looked directly into his eyes, daring him to hesitate. But he didn't. He frisked her as completely and professionally as he had Reilly. When he was finished he stepped back.

"Satisfied?" Frances asked wickedly. The guards were practically licking their chops.

"Yes," he said brusquely. "Now you will be shown our submarines and then returned to the main gate."

They were led to the end of a long corridor, down a flight of stairs, then out onto a narrow gallery that looked down into the sub pens. The Russian-built warships lay low in the water, apparently undamaged. As the first Westerner to see them here, like this, it gave Frances an odd, twitchy feeling. They were not weapons of defense.

"May we go aboard one of them?" she asked.

"No," Zahedi said.

"Can we go down to the docks?"

"That won't be possible at this time," Zahedi said. "But as you can clearly see, if there was a commando raid here it was quite unsuccessful."

"When will the next patrol begin?" Frances asked.

Zahedi looked at her coldly. "If you have seen enough, we will take you back."

Frances took a long last look at the four submarines waiting in their pens. Waiting for what? she wondered. And how long would they remain here, dormant? It was axiomatic that weapons of offense would sooner or later be put to the use they were intended for.

On the way to their hotel in Bandar-é Emān, Frances sat back in the darkness lost in thought. The Iranians were lying about something. Either the Ukrainian-backed attackers did get onto the base before they were repulsed, as the satellite photographs suggested, and/or the Iranians knew who their attackers were and what they were after.

"That was something, darlin'," Reilly said. "You pushed the bastards to the wall and they backed down."

Frances looked up. "Yes, but what are they hiding?"

"What do you mean?"

"What they showed us tonight was extraordinary, Terry."

"You bet."

"But it was a trade-off. They showed us something we didn't expect to see, in trade for hiding something they didn't want us to see. Considering what they did show us, what they're hiding must be important."

"What do we do about it?" Reilly asked.

"I don't know," she said distantly.

16

Sunday traffic was in full swing. The overcast was getting darker, dropping along with the plunging temperatures as a cold front swept down from Canada. Three to four inches of snow was forecast, and everyone was praying for it to hold off at least another few hours.

Lane rode alone in the backseat of a Capital City cab only vaguely aware that they had passed through Chevy Chase on the way to the National Security Agency's Fort Meade complex. He'd been lost in thought since the cabby had picked him up in front of the hospital.

He still had a blinding headache from injuries he hadn't even felt on the train—a slight concussion—and although the doctors wanted to keep him for another twenty-four hours of observation, they said the effects of a bullet fragment in his skull plus the two solid blows with a whiskey bottle would pass with time. Provided he didn't do something stupid, like put his head in the way of another solid object.

He'd made a series of mistakes, one of which had cost Lieutenant Rowse and seven civilians their lives when Isaacs's booby-trapped train compartment had exploded.

Bishop, whose left arm was broken in the blast, had taken part of the blame for not warning the lieutenant. There was plenty of it to go around, but Lane wondered if it would make any difference to the man's widow. He doubted it.

Staring at the heavy traffic on the roadway above as they passed beneath I-95, Lane turned his thoughts to Isaacs and how he was going to catch him. It wasn't going to be easy because he'd come up against the man once and lost. Now he was going to have to convince a lot of skeptical people that he knew what he was doing.

Isaacs had been an effective agent for several years, and he'd managed to elude detection for the past six months even though he'd been the object of a very intensive search. If he had not surfaced, it might have taken them many more months to finally catch up with him. The part that was going to be more difficult was that after all this time they still didn't know his true identity. Nor did they know what assignment Maslennikov had brought back from Kiev for him. Knowing either might be a big help.

Lane disliked bullies. Because he'd been big for his age as a child, the toughest kids would pick him out for a fight. But he usually managed to walk away. The only time he ever raised his fists in anger was when he saw the bigger kids picking on the smaller, weaker ones. He'd never been able to stand that, and there'd been more than one kid who'd suddenly found himself flat on his back with a bloody nose and a few battered ribs.

Isaacs was a bully. Killing the young woman and then booby-trapping her body at the naval base had been an unnecessary act of savagery. One that the Ukrainian was going to pay for.

"You got a pass or something?" the cabby asked as they turned off the main highway and pulled up at the busy east gate.

"Yeah," Lane replied, digging it out. All but the tallest antenna masts and satellite dishes scattered throughout the installation were hidden in the thick woods. But there was no mistaking the purpose of the electrified double chain fence topped with rolls of razor wire, or the serious-looking armed guards at the gatehouse.

He rolled down his window, showed his Level One pass, and the guards waved them through. The cabby followed the winding road up to the east door of the vast administration and operations building.

"Go back to the gate the same way you came up," Lane said, paying the fare. "You wouldn't want to make them nervous."

"No, sir."

Lane waited until the cab was gone, then went inside where he had to step through an electronic scanning arch before he was allowed to proceed. It was only 6:00 but already the building was settling in for the swing shift.

Ben Lewis, his tie loose, his shirtsleeves rolled to the elbows, charged down the corridor like a one-man freight train. Although he was a big man, his step was light, and Lane often thought that in his day the Russian Division chief would have made a hell of a linebacker. He looked haggard, though, as if he'd not slept in a couple of days. And he didn't seem happy to see Lane.

"What are you doing here, you damn fool?" he demanded harshly. "The hospital said you checked out against their advice."

"You're a paragon of warmth," Lane said. "What's the word on Isaacs? Have Bishop's people caught up with him?"

Lewis's face darkened when he was frustrated or angry, and now he looked like a ripe plum with bushy eyebrows. "No, but it's no longer our problem or theirs."

"What are you talking about?"

"The CIA has it. He was spotted in Mexico City."

Lane gave his boss a sharp look. "He killed a lot of good people. We could have done better."

"As of three this afternoon the number was up to eight civilians dead and sixteen injured aboard the train," Lewis said heavily. "Three of the sixteen aren't expected to make it. But your quick action saved a hell of a lot more than that, so don't beat yourself up about it."

"It's not going to stop."

"For you it is."

"I'm not going to back off."

"That's exactly what you're going to do. The CIA is watching the Ukrainian embassy in Mexico City. The moment Isaacs or Maslennikov moves they'll be on top of him."

"Then what?"

"It'll be up to them. I've got another job for you."

"I have a splitting headache, there's a ringing in my ears, and I think I'm starting to see double." Lane grimaced. "I don't think I'll be able to tackle anything new for at least a week."

"Bullshit. You dug yourself a hole with your own curiosity. Don't tell me that you're not interested in what happened at Bandar-é Emān. We're talking about two of your favorite subjects—Ukrainians and women."

"I see your point," Lane conceded cheerfully. He'd managed to bring Lewis around. "Frances must have received my book cable. Has she found out anything, or are they giving her the runaround?"

"A little of both. Your lady friend pushed them to the wall, but instead of kicking the UN team out of the country, they were shown the submarines. All four of them in their pens. Stopped them in their tracks."

"Did they see any damage?"

"Nothing obvious. But the fact they were shown anything was extraordinary. Means the Iranians are worried big time. I took this upstairs, and Roswell took it over to Roland Murphy at Langley. The White House was briefed, and Bill Townsend is briefing the president in the morning." Townsend was the president's national security adviser, and a straight shooter. Thomas Roswell was director of the national security agency.

"Sounds like the Iranians aren't the only ones worried."

"The Iranians have submarines and the Ukrainians have nuclear missiles," Lewis said tiredly. "We'd like you to find the connection."

"They're enemies."

"For the moment."

"That can change," Lane agreed. "Like the kids used to say: Shit happens."

Lane promised to go home, but as soon as Lewis left, he went into the CMC. Tom Hughes was seated at one of the computer consoles on the top tier, a cigarette burning in an ashtray filled with butts at his elbow, a half-empty Styrofoam coffee cup next to it. He looked more worn out than Lewis.

"If Moira finds out you're smoking again she'll kill you," Lane said.

"If she finds out that I didn't stop you from checking out of the hospital she'll kill us both."

"Then we better not tell her."

Hughes looked up from the steady stream of data crossing the screen and scowled. "You look worse than I feel. How are you, William?"

"I've felt better, but I'm okay."

"No lie?"

"No lie, Tommy."

Hughes looked skeptical, but he nodded. "Ben wants us to backstop the FRIFINTEL operation in Iran. Isaacs was apparently sighted in Mexico City. No mean feat, considering the circumstances. The Bureau is hot for his blood."

Lane perched on the edge of the adjacent console. "I think we should do exactly what Mr. Lewis wants us to do."

"You mean find out who attacked the sub base?"

"We know who, Tommy. Question is why."

Hughes grinned wickedly. "Gosh, in order to do that, we'd have to find out why a former Ukrainian sub commander ordered his agent in the Pentagon to steal something from the Atlantic Fleet Submarine Headquarters computer system."

"You catch on quick, kemo sabe." Lane motioned toward the computer screen. "Come up with anything yet?"

"The navy is cooperating, and that's the first step. I'm trying to put together what he could have done in Norfolk's computer center that he couldn't have done in the Pentagon's."

"Did he gain access to the Pacific Fleet's computer system?"

"I'm still working on that part, William. But I did find out that both systems do cross-talk on a regular basis. Which means if he knew which buttons to push, he could have gotten anything out of Honolulu that he wanted."

"Without their knowing about it?"

"I'm looking for backtraces now. But I can't be sanguine. It's like searching for a needle in a haystack when we don't know for sure it's there, and even if it is, what it looks like."

"Sounds like a piece of cake."

"Any chance I could talk you into going home for a few hours?"

Lane glanced down at the big screen in the pit. "Isaacs is a KGB-trained Ukrainian, which means he's in our computer somewhere."

"Along with several hundred thousand others, provided we didn't miss him, provided they didn't do plastic surgery on him, provided he might have been born in this country."

Lane shook his head. "He's no amateur."

"So what?"

"He's a professional, Tommy. Means he has experience. Which also means he's left a track, and I'm going to find it."

MEXICO CITY

Yernin stared at the montage of photographs showing one man in various scenes around Washington, D.C., outside the White House, outside the NSA's Fort Meade complex, outside an apartment building in Georgetown, and another series shot outside a heavily guarded bunker on Do Pai island in Rio de Janeiro's outer bay. He'd slept less than four hours in the past forty-eight, yet each time he closed his eyes he saw the same face, and he would awaken in a cold sweat. They should not have found out about the train so fast.

"What are you doing here at this hour?" Mikhail Maslennikov demanded. It was past two in the morning.

"I want to go back and finish the job," Yernin answered simply. He was seated at a conference table in the KGB's *referentura* section of the Ukrainian embassy on Avenida Eduardo, a few blocks from the Palacio Nacional.

"Finish what job?"

Yernin looked up from the photographs to his control officer's serious face. "This one knows about me. He will figure out what I got from the computer center and will ruin everything."

Maslennikov picked up one of the sheets of photographs and studied it. "Why didn't you kill him when you had the chance? I warned you about him."

"It was a mistake. One I would like to rectify."

"No."

Yernin's temper flared, but he held himself in check. He was not used to failure. The Semtex beneath the wheels of the locomotive should have derailed the train. From the time he jumped until he picked himself up, got clear, and pushed the button was less than ninety seconds. He closed his eyes and Bill Lane's face was there. Somehow Lane had figured out what was about to happen, searched for and found the explosive plastique, pried it loose, and tossed it away.

Maslennikov laid the sheet of photos back on the table. "The entire operation was a mess. Fifteen people killed, more injured. Every military and civilian law enforcement agency in the United States is looking for you. They have your photograph, and they have the willingness to bend their own rules in order to apprehend you."

"The photographs are of Isaacs and Stein."

"Lane saw your face. Undoubtedly he's provided an accurate description."

"Then I will change my appearance again. It is nothing . . . "

"It is everything," Maslennikov retorted coldly. "I should have you sent back to Kiev. They are in desperate need of fresh volunteer work crews at Chernobyl."

"You'd be throwing away my talent," Yernin said calmly.

"Perhaps an out-of-control talent."

"I think not, and neither do you, Colonel. You did not expect me to make it this far because the odds were against me. I did not fail the primary mission."

"No," Maslennikov admitted. "And you will not fail when you're given the second, more important, half of this mission."

"Lane will have to be dealt with."

Maslennikov tapped a blunt finger on the pile of photographs. "Where did you get these?"

"By facsimile transmission from our Washington embassy."

"The traffic will have been monitored."

"I ordered it encrypted and sent with the daily congressional report."

Maslennikov studied his star agent for several seconds. "You won't fail me."

"No, sir," Yernin said.

"When the time is right I will give you Mr. William Lane if you still wish to kill him," Maslennikov said. "Now get some rest, you'll need it." He turned and left the room.

Yernin's eyes once again went to the photographs. Killing Bill Lane would have nothing to do with desire, he thought, but everything to do with necessity.

17

TEHRAN

Iraq maintained an embassy in Iran despite the disastrous eight-year war in which hundreds of thousands of Iranians were killed by Saddam Hussein's forces. Even though Hussein was no longer in power, and the embassy was in disarray, the place was heavily guarded by the Komīté, the Iranian Revolutionary Guard Corps.

The movements of every person even remotely connected with the diplomatic mission were closely monitored around the clock. No one in Tehran doubted that many of the diplomats in residence still owed their allegiance to Hussein. Even the interim ambassador was not allowed to come or go unchecked.

All electronic traffic to or from the building was recorded, decrypted if necessary, and analyzed. Food and all incoming supplies were searched, as was everything outgoing, including garbage. At irregular intervals each day the embassy's telephone and electrical service were interrupted for up to two hours at a time. Anti-Iraq sentiments continued to ride high in Tehran.

Surveillance operations were directed from a command center on the top floor of an apartment building across the busy Valī-yé Asr Street from the embassy. It was noon, and most of the staff had left for lunch.

Amin Zahedi studied the front entrance of the embassy through 25 × 100 binoculars on a tripod by the window. His eyes were gritty from lack of sleep, but the big glasses were so powerful he could read the brand on the package of cigarettes one of the guards pulled from his pocket. They were Marlboros. If the man's supervisor caught him, he'd be in trouble.

He'd sent Eghbal back to SAVAK headquarters this morning to make sure that the surveillance operation on the UN Peacekeepers team was running as planned. He didn't want them moving around the country without escort, especially not the woman. Their files identified her as a British Secret Intelligence Service agent. Her presence was troubling.

In the meantime Zahedi proceeded on the theory that the intruders at Bandar-é Emān were Iraqi, and that the survivor might try to make it to his embassy for help. It was the best they could come up with for the moment. SAVAK and regular army troops were scouring the countryside, and the border was sealed as tightly as any border that cut across difficult terrain could be. The embassy was their only remaining option.

The young technician at the telephone console held up a hand. "Colonel," he called.

Zahedi went over and plugged in a spare set of headphones.

"... *no one of that name here. Who is calling, please?*" a man was saying in Arabic.

"*Tell him that Jamal is here with a very important message for a mutual friend. It would benefit all of us, you as well as us. Do you understand this?*"

"*No, I do not. And if you do not immediately identify yourself I will hang up.*"

The telephone call was incoming to the embassy. The man calling was under a strain, Zahedi could hear it in his voice.

The technician was on another line speaking in low tones with the telephone exchange. Traces still had to be done manually, which meant that someone had to physically inspect hundreds of relays, buried in row after row of equipment racks to come up with the number.

"*I was sent here on an extremely important diplomatic mission,*" the caller said. "*One that will fail unless what I've learned gets back to the proper authorities.*"

"*What authorities? I'm aware of no special mission,*" the embassy official replied cautiously. "*Perhaps it would be for the best if you came here and presented your information in person.*"

"*That's not possible.*"

Telephone numbers in Tehran consisted of six digits. The technician had jotted four numbers on a pad, his pencil poised to write the fifth.

"*There is nothing we can do for you even if this is a legitimate call for help, and not some trick by the SAVAK.*"

"*The fact that I know Mustafa al-Bakr's name must mean something, you fool.*"

Zahedi pressed the earphones tighter. Until recently Bakr ran Iraqi secret service (Mukabarat) operations here. He'd hung on after Hussein's fall by promising allegiance to the new coalition government. But forty-eight hours ago he'd suddenly been recalled to Baghdad. The caller didn't have that information.

The technician wrote the fifth number.

"*There is no one at this embassy by that name,*" the official insisted.

"In any event, if you did know that such a man were here, you would not have tried to make contact on an open line."

"Traitor," the caller snarled, and the connection was broken.

"Hell," Zahedi swore under his breath, and he pulled off the earphones.

"Just a minute, Colonel, I have the sixth number," the technician said. He wrote something on the pad, then looked up in wonderment. "It's a telephone box downstairs. Directly across the street."

Zahedi rushed to the binoculars, released the elevation and azimuth brakes, and pointed the glasses down at the street. It took a moment to find the telephone booth, but when he did he was in time to see a tall, well-built man dressed in Palace Guard camos step away from the phone, hesitate a moment, then head east.

At that moment Eghbal pulled up in his Peugeot.

Zahedi grabbed his coat and pounded downstairs, intercepting his partner on the way up. "He was in the phone booth across the street!"

"Alone?" Eghbal demanded, falling in behind Zahedi.

"It looked like it."

On the ground floor an old woman dressed in black stepped back into her doorway as they rushed past her and out onto the busy street to the car.

"He's big, dressed in Guard camos," Zahedi explained, jumping in the passenger seat. He got on the radio as Eghbal pulled away from the curb and made a dangerous U-turn in traffic.

"Control, this is Zeta One Mobile."

"Go ahead, Zeta One Mobile."

"We've flushed Starlight intruder. He's on foot headed east from the Iraqi embassy. We need backup now!"

"The first units will reach your position within three minutes."

"Subject is male, heavily built, height one meter ninety, weight approximately one hundred kilos. Dressed in Guards Camos, possibly officer's shoulder boards. Presently he's heading east on Valī-yé Asr. We're in pursuit."

"Ana af-ham," Understood, the dispatcher said.

"That him?" Eghbal asked.

They'd reached the Valfajre-8 Shipping Company on the corner in time to see the tall man in camos duck down one of the side streets that led into a section of the city that was a rat warren of commercial buildings, shops, and stalls crowded into a maze of narrow, dark alleys. It was a perfect place in which to get lost. The man was not stupid.

"That's him! Pull up here," Zahedi ordered. "Subject has just entered Bahjat Ābād," he told dispatch. "We're going in on foot, so tell them to watch for us. Have units blocking Kheyābūn-é Ostād Motahharī to the north, Hāfez and Lārestān to the west, and Mīrzā-yé Shīrāzī to the east."

"Will do."

They'd found the jeep he'd used to get off base fifty kilometers north of Bandar-é Emān, and so far as they'd been able to determine, only one man had escaped. But he was very good to have come this far.

Zahedi pulled out his gun and crossed to the narrow side street, motioning for Eghbal to back him up on the left. The crowd began to scatter when the people saw the two armed men coming their way.

Within ninety seconds the street was deserted. A smoke pall hung over the two- and three-story buildings from the charcoal braziers shopkeepers used for warmth and cooking. A red silk scarf billowed gently in a doorway halfway down the block, and behind them they could hear the traffic noises on the main thoroughfare. But here the silence was eerie.

The man they were following was gone. But he hadn't enough time to get to the end of the block in the short interval since he'd turned down this street, which meant he was very close.

Zahedi pointed to the roofline and then to himself, then motioned for Eghbal to stay put. The only way out of here was across the roofs.

"Watch yourself, Amin," Eghbal warned.

Zahedi scurried across the street and entered a two-story building through a narrow doorway behind a coppersmith's stall. The building smelled of cooked lamb, cinnamon, and charcoal. He took the dark stairs up two at a time, switching the Glock 17's safety off. Killing the intruder would do them no good, they needed him alive to answer some questions. But Zahedi did not want to charge blindly into a trap and get shot to death.

He hesitated at the head of the stairs just below the door to the roof. The building was still except for a radio or television playing martial music very softly.

Cautiously he eased the steel door open, held for a moment, then ducked through the doorway, rolling left as he hit the tar and gravel.

A shot was fired from behind him, the bullet kicking up stones two centimeters from his head which cut his cheek and opened a shallow gash in his forehead.

Zahedi turned over, brought his gun around, and in one smooth motion fired a snap shot at the figure of a man disappearing behind a concrete cistern. Then he scrambled to safety in the doorway.

In the distance he could hear a lot of sirens.

"It was skillful of you to have made it this far from Bandar-é Emān, but your journey ends here," Zahedi called in Arabic. "You will not be considered a coward if you choose to save your life by surrendering."

The cistern was about one meter tall and eight or ten meters on a side, isolated in the center of the roof. From Zahedi's vantage point he covered every possible escape route. By now the intruder would have to know that he was cornered. It was possible that he was willing to die rather than be captured. A lot of Saddam Hussein's followers were fanatics, preferring death over dishonor. But some kinds of death were less preferable than others. Since the eight-year war, Iraqis and Iranians alike were frightened by an ugly weapon that both sides had used to terrible advantage.

"Lieutenant Eghbal, can you hear me?" Zahedi shouted.

"Yes, I can hear you, Colonel," Eghbal called from below on the street. "Is everything all right?"

"I have this godless dog cornered, but he refuses to surrender. Bring up the gas masks."

"Yes, I understand."

Zahedi trained his pistol on the far corner of the cistern, pausing a moment for what he was saying to sink in.

"Bring up the gas canister. The Sarin."

The intruder suddenly leaped away from the cistern, firing as he came, the bullets smacking into the steel door and door frame. Zahedi took deliberate aim and fired two shots, the first catching the big man in the leg above his right kneecap, the second hitting him in the right hip, knocking him down.

Before the intruder could bring his gun around, Zahedi raced across the five meters of open roof and shot the pistol out of his hand at point-blank range.

The intruder cried out more in rage and frustration than in pain, and glared up at Zahedi. "You think you have won, but you have not," he said through clenched teeth.

"We'll see," Zahedi replied tiredly. "But for you this has been the easy part." Not that the rest would be easy for anyone, he thought. He despised what was coming next with everything in his being, even though he understood its necessity.

The prisoner's wounds had been tended to and the bullets removed so that he wouldn't bleed to death. But his hip was broken and Zahedi had not allowed the doctors to set it. Nor would he allow the administration of morphine. As a result the man's pain was blinding.

He'd been moved directly from the hospital to a basement interrogation room in the Aliens' Bureau of the Ministry of Foreign Affairs, which was housed in a squat, unattractive concrete block building two kilometers northeast of where he'd been captured. The entire wing of the basement was heavily soundproofed. What went on down here was not for outside ears to hear.

His fingerprints and photograph were matched in SAVAK's files, identifying him as Colonel Jamal el-Kassem, formerly an intelligence and special operations officer in Hussein's Second Armored Division, one of the few units to distinguish itself in Iraq's adventures in Kuwait, and since 1993 a special field operative for the Mukabarat. He'd disappeared from Baghdad when Hussein and his followers had run to the desert, and it had been presumed that he would turn up sooner or later.

Kassem, dressed in white hospital pajamas, was strapped in a wheelchair, his arms and legs restrained so that he could not move to ease his pain. When Zahedi came in he looked up with wariness, but also interest, in his intelligent eyes.

"Good morning," Zahedi said. He placed several file folders on the small steel table, then sat down across from the Iraqi. There were no other furnishings in the concrete box of a room. The only light came from a bulb recessed behind steel mesh in the ceiling.

Kassem said nothing.

"So, you know about our submarines, Colonel Kassem. Quite a price to pay. Your two jets were shot down by Allied forces west of Qar and your friend, Lieutenant Midafi, was buried this morning on one of our gunnery ranges in the desert. No honor in his death."

"*In sha'Allah,*" Kassem responded softly.

It was the first crack in the Iraqi's armor. From reading his dossier, Zahedi figured the man would be tough. "If you are a true believer, I think you might be the first Princeton graduate to actually look forward to martyrdom. But of course neither of us believes that to be the case. Which means that we will spend some time together. How long that might be will depend upon your strength and the inventiveness of me and the doctors."

"It will be a waste of time."

"How so?" Zahedi asked conversationally.

"Since you know who I am and what I have done, you must know that my mission was unsuccessful. But if you wish me to confess something, I will do it. Anything you wish." Kassem managed to return Zahedi's smile, and he was rewarded by a brief look of irritation that crossed the Iranian's face.

"The problem is what to do with you when we are finished here. Since you do not work for the current legitimate government of Iraq, we can hardly turn you over to them. Nor will we arrange for you to be returned to your unit hiding in the desert with the criminal Hussein. You have murdered any number of our soldiers, but a public trial would be an embarrassment to us. We should be able to protect our borders and especially our military installations with more efficiency. And believe me, a simple execution would satisfy no one in my government."

"It would not do for you to anger the mullahs," Kassem said.

"Which leaves me with few choices," Zahedi replied dryly. "I can walk out of here and instruct my people that you are not to be disturbed for the next seven days. For any reason. Your dying would not be so pleasant."

"I've faced worse."

"Or I could loosen the straps holding your arms, leave a loaded pistol on the table, and walk out of here with the same instructions to my people."

"In exchange for what?"

"The truth."

"We came to sabotage your submarines, and we nearly succeeded."

"Our submarines are no threat to Saddam Hussein."

"Revenge," Kassem said. "You cannot imagine the hate and bitterness."

"Religious zeal?"

A thin smirk curled Kassem's mouth. "Something like that."

Zahedi opened one of the files and took out a typed transcript. " 'I was sent here on an extremely important diplomatic mission. One that will fail unless what I've learned gets back to the proper authorities.' " Zahedi looked up. "That was meant for Mustafa al-Bakr, a former Mukabarat officer."

"That was a coded message for my rescue."

"You came to Bandar-é Emān not to sabotage our submarines. You came to gather intelligence. And since the entire world knows about our submarines, the only question remaining is the nuclear one. Do we have nuclear cruise missiles aboard our submarines? Now that, my dear colonel, is the sort of information that Hussein could use. It would give him a strong position from which to bargain with the United States."

"If that was our mission, we failed."

"I wonder," Zahedi said thoughtfully. "The question is who helped you and why."

"We had no help."

"You came by sea. Hussein has no boats and no coastal access."

"We came by rubber raft. You must have found it."

"Launched from where?"

"Fao."

"I think not," Zahedi said. "Let's make it the first truth that we'll seek." He went to the door and opened it. "It is time for Dr. Kalud."

18

The navy never slept, and Tom Hughes used that fact to his advantage, cajoling sleepy midshift ODs into cooperating with him until Honolulu's Pacific Submarine Fleet's computer center was open to him from front to back like a can of sardines.

> WELCOME TO COMSUBPAC
> NAVBASE PEARL HARBOR
> DO YOU WISH TO SEE A MENU?

He tore his eyes away from the computer screen in time to see Lane rise from his position in front of the big screen three tiers below and head for the men's room. It was after three in the morning, and they'd operated all night on little more than caffeine, nicotine, and leftover adrenaline from the near miss. Hughes was not worried about himself, but he could see that his friend was suffering from the effects of his injuries. Lane needed bed rest, and he needed it soon or he would collapse.

But it wouldn't happen, Hughes knew, until they found what they were looking for.

He turned back to the keyboard, brought up the menu, and, beginning with Seventh Fleet submarine sailing and station keeping orders, dipped into the highly sensitive top-secret data pool. He was looking for several things at once. First, he wanted to know if getting into the navy computer center was possible without raising any alarms. So far he'd experienced no real difficulties. Second, he wanted to know the extent of the information available. Often, even in this computer age, highly classified information was not put in data files, but instead was written by hand in a paper file that one or two people were responsible for. The information was much easier to control that way, and there was a clear chain of responsibility to follow should there be a leak of any kind.

But the entire Seventh Fleet's submarine operations were in the electronic files. It meant that someone possessing a copy of the data—something Hughes figured could have been transferred onto a floppy disk in the ten minutes they thought Isaacs had been in the Norfolk center—would be able to pinpoint the exact location of every ship or sub anywhere in the Pacific. That included the Persian Gulf.

Last, he looked for frequency-of-use indicators. It was a new navy program called "data streaming." Information was assigned a series of numbers that indicated how often the data was called up for use. The files most frequently visited were assigned top priority within the computer's mainframe. Depending on the sensitivity of the material, access procedures were streamlined for this kind of most-used data. The least-used files were relegated to much slower programs that sometimes were stored on old-fashioned tape reels that had to be retrieved by hand.

Submarine station keeping and sailing information would be of the first, most-used variety. That meant access would be streamlined, but it also meant that each file or broad spectrum of files would be countered. That is, each time the file was used, it got a time and date stamp. This would allow analysts to review their data-streaming program on a regular basis.

Getting to this data-streaming information, however, was even more difficult than accessing the files themselves, because the information was used only by analysts.

Twenty minutes after he'd begun, however, Hughes found what he was looking for.

Unmindful that Lane had returned to his console below and brought up a rapidly shifting stream of photographs on the big screen, Hughes stared at the data he'd uncovered.

Three nights ago at 0333 GMT, which was 10:33 P.M. Norfolk time, a data transfer was made to Lieutenant Commander Thomas Stein showing the dispositions of every submarine and sub hunter controlled by COMSUB-PAC for the next ninety days.

It was the connection Lane had feared. The attack on Bandar-é Emān. And the Ukrainians were behind it.

Lane sat at his console watching the rapid-fire stream of photographs being displayed on the screen towering over the pit. He'd pulled up Isaacs's photograph from Pentagon employee records, had added a few changes based on his eye-to-eye contact with the man aboard the train, and had set NSA's powerful recognition programs to work.

He'd been at this part of the task for eight hours, dredging up file photos of every Soviet Russian group in the Agency's vast archive. Counting individual faces . . . many of them in group photographs, many in panoramic shots of mass gatherings ... the numbers were in the tens of thousands, and probably more than a hundred thousand.

Many of the photographs were blurred, imperfect images taken from Russian television broadcasts. Several series had been lifted from aircraft surveillance flights over Afghanistan and from former Warsaw Pact countries. Some had even been lifted from high-resolution satellite images; faces raised to the sky, as if the subjects knew the satellites were overhead in space and were posing for the cameras. One of the men, a Soviet Missile Service colonel, his shoulder pips clear, was even smiling. "Take my picture, you bastards, but you'll never beat us," he seemed to be saying.

Several times during the long search, the computer automatically stopped and zeroed in on a face. But each time, after a series of operator-directed enhancements, Lane was able to determine that the man he was looking at was not Isaacs.

The work was frustrating because of the vast number of photographs, and because there was no guarantee that Isaacs's face was anywhere within their files. He was a professional, presumably trained by the Russians in the seventies or eighties—judging from his age, which Lane thought was in the forties—and the old KGB had been very careful to shield its top agents from this kind of record.

It was also frustrating because despite the powerful computer recognition program, the machine could still miss Isaacs. Combined with Lane's exhaustion, the chances for success were slim.

But he'd seen the look in Isaacs's eyes. He'd read the reports about the young woman he'd shot to death and whose body he'd booby-trapped. She'd been pregnant. That final act of savagery had gained Isaacs no more than a few minutes. It was a horrible image that would stay with Lane forever.

At 3:45 A.M. he got lucky. A series of photographs taken just before the bombing of the marine barracks in Beirut showed two clear images of Isaacs. Even without computer enhancements Lane knew he'd found his man. And his dossier, though scant and incomplete for the past five years, was in NSA's files.

Valeri Fedorovich Yernin was born on December 19, 1957, in the small town of Nosovka a few miles northeast of Kiev, the capital of Ukraine. His father was an engineer at the Tupolev factory, and had been sent to "count the birches," as they say, in Siberia for some transgression against the state. During his ten-year sentence, he met and married Valeri's mother, a sloe-eyed Siberian beauty from Irkutsk on Lake Baikal's south shore. In 1960 he brought his wife and three-year-old son back to Chernobyl, where he got a job on the nuclear reactor project.

Valeri did extremely well in school, especially in mathematics, physics, and foreign languages, most notably German, French, and English, until his mother died when he was sixteen. That year ended in disaster for the Yernins. Valeri was branded an "incorrigible" and his father was sentenced to twenty years in Siberia for telling his co-workers that he thought the Soviet Union would not survive until 1984. It was a line from Andrei Amalrik's book that had landed the dissident writer in Siberia as well.

Young Valeri refused to return to Siberia with his father, so he ran away to Moscow and tried to join the air force. He wanted to fly jets. A friendly recruiter urged him to finish his schooling and go on to Moscow State University, which he did. In his second semester he got into a fight with one of his professors, and he killed the man with his bare hands, even though the professor had been the amateur all-Russia boxing champion four years in a row. This feat, plus his obvious intelligence and the fact he had no relatives other than a father, impressed the KGB, which decided it would groom Valeri for its own uses.

He finished college in an accelerated program in 1977 and went directly into the KGB's School One outside Moscow. He was taught everything the service knew, from armed and unarmed combat—he became an expert at every weapon he ever handled, especially the stiletto—to codes, electronics, and American idiomatic English, which he studied in total immersion courses from men and women who'd lived in the United States undetected and had returned to tell the tales as instructors.

In the eighties, he participated in dozens of kidnappings, murders, and car, bus, and airplane bombings, mostly in the Middle East. He gained such a reputation that although the CIA and a dozen other intelligence services around the world knew about his exploits, nothing could be proven. A British Secret Intelligence Service officer summed it up in 1991 by admitting that even if they had the proof, trying to arrest Yernin would cost them plenty in casualties. Maybe too many casualties. Yernin had earned the nickname "the Surgeon" not only because of the precision of his killing skills but because of his apparent total detachment and lack of feeling. Several passengers on the *Achille Lauro* who'd come face to face with him and were lucky enough to survive the encounter all told the same story: "He was a man without a soul. You could see the lack in his eyes."

Lane had looked into Yernin's eyes, and he knew exactly what those people meant.

After the collapse of the Soviet Union, Yernin surfaced briefly in Kiev but then disappeared. It was assumed at the time that he'd been shot trying to escape to the West, just as his father had been shot to death in 1987 for trying to escape Siberia.

"Is that him?" Hughes asked from behind.

Lane looked tiredly over his shoulder at his old friend. He was having trouble focusing. "Valeri Yernin."

"According to our files, he's dead."

Lane shook his head. "Not yet, Tommy. But he will be." He looked up again at the photographs on the big screen, then made a gun with his thumb and forefinger and pointed it at the screen. "Bang," he said.

19

THE WHITE HOUSE

The incident at Bandar-é Emān had not yet hit the media, but everyone in the know figured it would only be a matter of time before CNN would get wind of the fact that a UN Peacekeeping team was in Tehran. The ubiquitous blue and white vans were a red flag to journalists. The presence of the UN meant trouble, and where there was trouble there was a story.

William Townsend had been the president's national security adviser since the election. Born in Omaha, Nebraska, he graduated summa cum laude from the University of Wisconsin at Madison and served in the marines in Vietnam, where he was wounded twice and won the Medal of Honor. After the war he got his graduate degree in political science and international policy from Harvard, where he met the president, who'd been a draft dodger. Despite their obvious differences they'd become respected opponents. Townsend had worked for the US Senate, the House, the State Department, and the UN in advisory capacities until Matthew Reasoner's election, when he was tapped for the job of deputy assistant to the president for national security affairs.

It was precisely 9:00 A.M. Monday when Townsend entered the president's study, not quite sure how the president would react to the latest problem. Townsend could read his boss on many issues, but this one was virgin territory in part because the president himself had no clear policy. Hell, Townsend had to admit, they were all groping around in the dark ever since the second Gulf War. Bush had settled nothing in the first conflict, and his successor had done little more than kick Saddam Hussein out of Baghdad, but not out of real power, in the second. Islamic fundamentalists—especially the Hezbollah—wanted to be left alone. Plain and simple. Just as it was plain and simple that the West could not keep its hands off the Middle East because of one overriding factor: oil.

"Good morning, Bill," the president said, looking up from his desk and flashing his winning smile. "How's the world treating us this morning?"

"Good morning, Mr. President. There was a problem in Norfolk Friday night that might be related to the jet attack on the Iranian submarine base." Townsend handed the briefing file to the president.

"Another terrorist attack here, on American soil?" the president asked sharply, his smile replaced by a fierce expression.

"There was some damage and unfortunately a number of deaths and injuries, but I don't think we can call this incident a terrorist attack. It was worse than that, with a very ugly potential."

The president studied his NSA's face for a penetrating moment. Townsend was not given to melodrama; if anything, his character was unemotional. "Get yourself a cup of coffee," the president said, and he opened the briefing file to the first page and began reading. The report, which ran to nearly ten thousand words, consisted mostly of dry facts, drawing very few conclusions and speculating on almost nothing. It was Townsend's style. The thrust of the report, however, was crystal clear: Some people were beginning to take seriously the possibility that Iran had acquired nuclear-armed cruise missiles for its submarines. What wasn't so clear was who those people were, or why they wanted the information, although Saddam Hussein's loyalists helped by Ukrainians was a strong possibility.

"What's the latest from Baghdad?" the president asked when he was finished.

"If you mean Hussein, Mr. President, he's still moving around in the desert. Every day more and more of his loyalists are joining him. But short of all-out day-and-night raids on every square foot of desert, we may never find him. And if we're talking about a Ukrainian connection, we still haven't come up with any direct evidence."

"Only the patrol boat offshore on the night of the raid," the president said. "What happened to the boat? Surely it couldn't have disappeared like those jet fighters."

"We found six boats so far—" Townsend said, and the president interrupted.

"According to your report all of them belong to the Iranian navy. Did the Iranians stage a raid on their own facility?"

"That is a possibility we considered. There are a number of serious faction fights going on between the religious right and Rafsānjaní's moderate government. But the CIA's and NSA's best estimate is that the patrol boat was picked up by a cargo vessel and has been hidden on deck under tarps or perhaps some kind of false superstructure. There are dozens of boats plying the Gulf at this moment that could do the job. Two of them are Ukrainian, as a matter of fact. But short of boarding them at sea, something I don't think you want to authorize our navy to do, we have no way of telling for sure."

"Hussein does not have access to those resources," the president said.

"The jets might have been his. They used an old navy transponder code, which they could have gotten from one of our downed pilots in the last war."

"Okay, assuming they were Hussein's people, what exactly were they after, Bill? Sabotage or information?"

"If Hussein could bring us proof that Iran's navy has gone nuclear, he might think we'd cut him some slack."

The president sat back and gave his NSA the famous Reasoner grin. "The hell of it is, we *would* cut him some slack."

Townsend said nothing.

"Have we heard anything from Hussein's people?"

"Nothing."

"Anything from the UN team in Tehran?"

"Nothing of any value, other than the fact that they were shown the submarines in their pens."

"How are you reading that?" the president asked directly.

Townsend shrugged. "They're probably hiding something."

"Like what?" the president demanded.

"Could be nuclear weapons," the NSA replied grudgingly. He was on shaky ground now. "But if that's true, then the UN team is in big trouble. Probably more trouble than they know."

"If you're right, we're all in trouble," the president replied thoughtfully. "It'd be ironic if Hussein and I had the same goals here."

"An irony that hopefully will never be tested in the public forum," Townsend said seriously.

"Can we send the UN team any help?"

"As a matter of fact, the National Security Agency is working on it. You might recall Bill Lane, who worked on the Pit Bull project last year."

"He's the one who saved our bacon."

"Yes, sir. Well, he's been involved in looking for the penetration agent in the Pentagon."

The president's jaw tightened.

"The Ukrainian agent," Townsend said with emphasis.

"You mentioned the connection with the attack on Bandar-é Emān."

"The agent broke cover Friday, killed a navy lieutenant commander here in Washington, stole his security pass, and made his way into the Atlantic Fleet's submarine forces computer center in Norfolk. He killed six people down there before he made his way to Richmond where he boarded an Amtrak train bound for Miami."

"What'd he get out of the computer center?"

"Unknown to this point, but Lane and his people are working with the navy on it. There's a possibility that the penetration agent linked up with the Pacific Submarine Fleet's computer center in Honolulu. He would have had access to sailing orders for the Seventh Fleet, which covers the Persian Gulf."

The president put up a hand. "Wait a minute. This sounds like an Iranian operation. Sailing orders for our submarines and submarine hunters in the Gulf would be of more interest to the country with its own submarines than to Hussein."

Townsend sighed. "Like I said, Mr. President, we don't have enough information to come to any firm conclusions at this time. It could be anybody's ball game."

"What about the penetration agent?"

"He escaped. We think he made it to Mexico City."

Recognition suddenly dawned in the president's eyes. "The explosion aboard the Amtrak train in South Carolina. It was no accident."

"No, sir. That was the story released to the media. Isaacs—that's the name he used—booby-trapped the train. At least nine people were killed. But if it wasn't for Lane, there would have been many more casualties."

"Then Lane is the man for the job," the president said decisively.

"What job exactly is that, Mr. President?" Townsend asked mildly.

The president leaned forward for emphasis, his eyes narrow and cruel-looking. "Finding Isaacs," he said in a low, menacing voice.

"It may be impossible to arrest him off American soil," Townsend said, looking the president directly in the eye.

"I didn't say anything about arresting him."

"I understand."

"Do you, Bill?"

"Perfectly, Mr. President," Townsend said.

"Very well. Then Mr. Lane is to be given anything he wants, anytime he wants it, with no questions asked."

"Yes, sir," Townsend said. He rose and headed for the door.

"Wish him luck for me," the president said.

When Townsend got back to his office, he had his secretary place a call on a secured line to Tom Roswell at the National Security Agency.

"I just briefed the president," he said. "Has there been any progress overnight?"

"Nothing significant. We're still analyzing the infrared satellite images. But Bill Lane came back to work. He checked himself out of the hospital last night."

"Was that wise?" Townsend asked. He'd been apprised of Lane's injuries.

"Wise or not, it's typical of the man."

"The president is concerned. He'd like Bill to head up the team to find Isaacs and figure out what's going on. Am I correct in thinking that he has a personnel connection with one of the FRIFINTEL team members in Tehran now?"

"Frances Shipley. From what I gather, they're old friends. She came down here the night before last to ask for his help."

"She's a British intelligence officer, isn't she?"

"That's right."

"You allowed Lane to give her NSA information?"

Roswell chuckled. He and Townsend went back to the old Senate Subcommittee on Intelligence together. They and their wives played bridge and tennis together, and as often as possible the two men snuck away for a round of golf.

"Bill more or less runs his own shop downstairs."

"Is he fit for duty?"

"So far as I know, he is."

"Then get him started as soon as possible. He can have anything he wants within reason. The president wants an early resolution."

"I'll convey the president's wishes to him."

"You'll order him—"

"You've never spent any time with Bill Lane, have you?" Roswell said, cutting the president's national security adviser short.

"No," Townsend admitted.

"Like I said, I'll convey the president's wishes to him."

GEORGETOWN

Lane woke from a deep dreamless sleep. His body ached and his head threatened to blow apart. For the first moments he was disoriented, until he realized that Tom Hughes was standing at the foot of his bed holding a steaming mug of coffee, a worried look on his mottled face.

"Did Moira and the girls finally kick you out?"

"It speaks," Hughes said, bringing the coffee around as Lane shoved the covers off and sat up.

"Did you go home and get some sleep?" Lane asked, gratefully taking the mug.

"I got a couple of hours. Roswell called, asked me to fetch you back to work."

"The big dogs are finally interested." Lane looked at his watch. It was a little after 5:00. "When did he call?"

"I think it was about ten this morning." Hughes said grinning. "What with family problems and one thing or another . . . well, sorry I'm late."

Lane got up and took a cigarette from a crumpled pack on the dresser.

"Bad habit," Hughes observed.

"The worst," Lane agreed, lighting the cigarette. "Let me guess, the president was briefed, and he and Townsend decided that I was the man for the job. I'm to be given anything I want within reason, but I'm not to be coddled."

"I never could keep a secret from you."

"They want me to get Isaacs, and they want me to find out if Iran has gone nuclear."

Hughes got serious. "You can turn it down."

Lane headed for the bathroom. "Not a chance, Tommy. When do I leave?"

"The Blackbird is out of mothballs and standing by at Andrews. It'll take you as far as Riyadh. From there you go commercial, Iran Air. I'll catch up with you tomorrow."

"You're staying here," Lane said.

"We're a team," Hughes argued.

"That's right. I'll be in the field with my ass hanging out. I'll need a good backstop. Somebody who's not afraid to pull a few chains, take a few shortcuts. Can you think of anyone else who fits the bill?"

"Yeah, but it'd be a waste of my time. I never win an argument with you."

Lane grinned. "That's because I'm more afraid of Moira and the girls than I am of SAVAK."

20

RIYADH, SAUDI ARABIA

The Saudi Arabian capital was spread like a handful of jewels tossed onto a black velvet cloth. The predawn winter air over the desert was crisp and crystal clear. Coming in for a steep landing at the Allied-Saudi Air Base thirty miles north of the city, the SR-91 delta-wing Blackbird reconnaissance airplane was all but invisible to observers on the ground. The rubber-coated titanium fuselage and wings were nearly radar-invisible as well.

The 3,000-mile-per-hour-plus aircraft had made the 7,200-mile Washington-to-Riyadh trip in something under four hours, which included midair refueling 300 miles east of the Azores. She carried only one passenger in addition to the pilot, and Lane hated every trip he ever made aboard the cramped, uncomfortably cold machine, which wasn't equipped with any creature comforts—not even a bladder bag.

Lane tried to get some more sleep on the way over, but his brain wouldn't shut down. He kept thinking about Petty Officer Dagen and her unborn child, and the cold, dead emptiness he'd seen in Yernin's eyes. He looked out of the canopy as the land rushed up to meet them.

To the north and west the great, nearly featureless desert stretched nine hundred miles to Israel and the Mediterranean. Nothing out there except a few wandering bedouins and oil. Yet these lands had been fought over for thousands of years. More than oil had flowed on the desert. The blood of countless millions had soaked the sands and would continue to do so for the foreseeable future.

Israel had tactical nuclear weapons. If Iran managed to acquire a few of her own, the deadly Middle East equation would once again change for the worse. This time when the holocaust came the piles of incinerated corpses would contain as many Arabs as it would Jews.

Except for a few scattered dim lights, the air base was in darkness. The white and green rotating tower beacon wasn't lit, nor were the runway lights on. The Blackbird's pilot followed an invisible electronic beacon that would guide him, if need be, all the way to touchdown in zero-zero conditions. Lane figured his situation was the same except he had no electronic beacon to guide him, though he knew what he was going to do and exactly how he was going to do it.

A team, probably Iraqis, had come ashore at Bandar-é Emān, and under cover of a jet attack had probably gotten into the base, possibly as far as the submarines. They had come for the same information that Lane now sought.

Lane would have no air cover. But he was going to have to do the same thing the Iraqi team had done. See with his own eyes what secrets the Iranians were hiding at the sub base.

Problem was that the SAVAK would expect something like that and would be waiting for him.

Two hundred feet from touchdown the airstrip's lights suddenly came on directly in front of them. The pilot's approach had been so precise that he did not have to alter course. The touchdown was smooth, and as soon as the big plane came to a halt at the end of the runway, the lights went out again.

A dark blue Mercedes station wagon, headlights off, emerged from the darkness as the Blackbird's canopy opened, letting in the cold desert air and a myriad unrecognizable smells. Lane unstrapped, shook hands with the pilot, retrieved his small zippered bag from behind his seat, and climbed down to the tarmac.

A short man with hooded eyes and thick black hair waited by the car. "Welcome to Saudi Arabia, Mr. Lane. I'm Walt Zimmerman, chief of CIA Station Riyadh." They shook hands.

"You have a package for me?"

"Yes, sir. In the car, with instructions. The rest of your equipment is waiting near Bandar-é Emān."

"Did your people have much trouble setting it up?"

Zimmerman looked at him coldly. "You could say that. But now we've got about one hour to get you over to King Kahlid International. Your Iran Air flight takes off at seven sharp—more or less."

"Did you get word to the UN team that I'm on my way in?" Lane asked as they climbed into the car.

"I think it got through, but I'm not sure," the COS said. They headed away from the supersonic jet. "It's a little chaotic up there just now. Word is SAVAK got its hands on one of the squad members who hit Bandar-é Emān."

"Any chance of us getting to him?"

"Hell, I don't know, Lane. We've got our own problems right here in River City. The Saudis have decided that they've had about all of us they can take. They're making serious noises about kicking our sorry asses out of here and taking their chances with the Iranians."

"Submarines and all?" Lane asked.

"Right. It doesn't make sense to me either. But they're figuring that with the Iranians they'd be dealing with fellow true believers, not infidels."

"Is there going to be a problem getting me in place?"

"Shouldn't be. The cover we've fixed up for you is a good one. Your name is Marshall Prentice, and you work for the US Economic Development Agency. You're coming to Tehran because certain business interests are worried about the current embargo negotiations, and they're getting nervous that the UN Peacekeepers will screw them up. It's in your package on the backseat. You can look it over on the flight up. Take a taxi from the airport to the Laleh International—the old Intercontinental Hotel. We've booked you a suite for the week. It's the same hotel that the UN team is staying at." Zimmerman glanced over at him. "From that point you're strictly on your own."

"How about a car?"

"Best we could do was a Fiat. Legitimate plates, but we stayed away from a diplomatic series. It might have caused too many complications if you were to be arrested. Keys and papers are in the package. Car's parked a half-block from the hotel."

"Do I have a contact in Tehran?"

Zimmerman looked sharply at him this time. "Do you need one? Because if you do, it could screw the pooch. SAVAK might swallow your meeting with the UN team. But if it gets wind of the fact that you're also meeting with one of our people—and let me tell you that most of our people up there are on SAVAK's short list—the entire situation will fall apart. Especially when you disappear. A ton of bricks would fall on your head. I shit you not."

"Good point," Lane conceded. "In the meantime let me give you a suggestion."

"What's that?" Zimmerman asked crossly.

"Don't count on winning the Agency's Mr. Congeniality award this year."

TEHRAN

"What is the purpose of your visit to Iran, Mr. Prentice?" asked the plain-clothes airport customs official holding the passport Lane had been given.

"Business," Lane replied evenly.

His single nylon bag was open. Two uniformed customs officers spread his things out on the counter and went through them.

"Are you here in an official capacity for your government?"

"Not exactly."

"Yes, what does this mean, not exactly?" the stern-faced official asked.

Although the rabid hatred for America had faded over the past few years, and several American companies were starting to explore business opportunities in the country, American presence was barely tolerated.

Lane leaned closer conspiratorially and made a gesture of ensuring that no one else was within earshot. "Certain corporations have asked for our help. It's a matter of interference, you see."

The unimpressed official waited.

"There is a team of United Nations investigators here in Tehran at the moment. I don't suppose I have to tell you that."

The customs officer stiffened slightly. Lane had his attention now.

"I was sent to . . . liaise with them. Make sure that they stick to . . . business . . . and leave *business* alone, if you catch my drift."

"How long will you be in Iran?"

"Two or three days." Lane shrugged.

"Do not stay any longer than necessary, Mr. Prentice," the customs official warned. He stamped Lane's passport.

When he had his bag, Lane went outside and caught a taxi for the forty-minute ride into the city. Tehran was a large, filthy, overcrowded, polluted metropolis that was, even after two decades, still an Islamic revolutionary city. Soldiers armed with submachine guns seemed to be stationed on every street corner, and Islamic Purity Patrols were everywhere.

The Laleh International, or more properly the Hotel-é Lālé-yé Bein-ol-melalī, was housed in a reasonably modern thirteen-story building in the heart of downtown at the edge of a large park containing what looked to be a couple of museums.

Although his reservations were good, his flight had been late taking off from Riyadh. Counting the delay here at the airport and the taxi ride in, it was nearly eleven by the time Lane got up to his surprisingly spacious and clean rooms.

He showered and changed into a clean shirt before he called Frances Shipley's room. She wasn't in, nor had he expected she would be. But the desk told him that Ms. Shipley and some of the other UN officials were presently dining in the hotel's Rôtisserie Française restaurant on the thirteenth floor.

It took him under five minutes to find the three bugs: one in the sitting room, one in the bathroom, and one over the king-sized bed. He disabled them, put on his bush jacket, and went up to the restaurant.

Frances, wearing a long khaki skirt and a soft contrasting gray and white thick shawl-necked sweater, the sleeves pushed up to her elbows, sat at the table near the window with three men, all of them dressed in UN Peacekeepers winter undress blues, their boots bloused.

Ignoring the maître d', Lane crossed the busy restaurant to their table. At the last moment Frances looked up. He shot her a warning look, then broke out into a broad grin.

"I don't know if you remember me, Ms. Shipley. I'm Marshall Prentice.

I'm with the US Economic Development Agency. I think we met at your embassy in Washington last year."

She recovered almost instantly, though not quickly enough to escape a searching look from the huskily built man directly across the table from her. Lane took him to be military.

"Of course," Frances said. "Fancy meeting you here."

"Well, it's not a coincidence," Lane said. "Business, I'm afraid. Duty calls and all that."

Frances introduced her team members, the one across the table Terrence Reilly, a fellow American. They shook hands.

"Would you care to join us for lunch, Mr. Prentice?" Reilly asked.

By the look in his eyes and the way he watched Frances, Lane figured he was the one she was involved with at the moment. He approved of her choice, because Reilly looked solid, and she never picked stupid men.

"I'm sorry, no," Lane replied. "Busy schedule."

"Duty calls," Reilly said.

"Exactly," Lane agreed. He turned back to Frances. "But if I could have just a few minutes of your time, Ms. Shipley, I'd be ever so grateful."

"Now?"

"If you don't mind."

"Don't wait lunch for me," she told her companions, who rose as Lane held her chair.

She followed him across the restaurant to elevators which they rode down to the eighth floor in silence. When they entered his suite, he held a finger to his lips, and then took her into the bedroom. He closed the door, and she came into his arms.

"There were bugs in here. Could be some I missed," he whispered in her ear. Her body felt wonderful against his.

"Clever boy," she said, snuggling closer. "What are you doing here?"

"Helping you, on the president's orders."

She looked up into his eyes, her lips parted in a half-serious, half-questioning smile.

He shrugged. "We don't want to disobey the president of the United States, do we?" he asked softly.

"Heaven forbid," she replied.

He pulled her sweater over her head and tossed it aside. She undid her skirt and let it fall around her ankles to the floor. Then he lifted her and carried her to the bed. It had been entirely too long since they'd been together.

"Duty calls," he said tenderly.

21

Dusk had settled over the Iranian capital city, and with it sharply colder temperatures, a thick lowering sky, and a light snow. Traffic was desultory, and one by one charcoal braziers were lit on street corners to ward off the chill, but they accomplished little more than adding to the already heavily polluted air.

Amin Zahedi hunched up the sheepskin collar of his coat as he waited patiently in the doorway of a closed shop across the street from the complex that once held the US Embassy but now housed the Revolutionary Guards Computer Training Center. The events of the past twenty-four hours were nothing short of confusing. General Sultaneh was pressing for answers that Zahedi did not have.

Jamal el-Kassem's revelations in the interrogation unit were troubling in that Zahedi wondered if his own government was lying to him. It was a mistake to believe everything that a prisoner under torture might say. Yet the Iraqi's final confession had a ring of truth to it. At least the prisoner had firmly believed that he'd seen a nuclear missile in the sub pens.

It was a question of balance of power. Between the mullahs and the moderate right here in Iran, and between Iran and the new puppet government of Iraq. Which country would become the dominant power in the region? Rafsānjaní's government was being squeezed like never before in the UN. There'd even been talk of increased sanctions, which had everyone worried. They all remembered the privations under the Ayatollah Khomeiní's regime.

Kassem had admitted that he'd been sent to Bandar-é Emān to confirm the existence of nuclear weapons aboard the submarines. This information would be used by Hussein as a bargaining chip with the Western alliance.

Zahedi watched the traffic for a moment. A man in an olive drab parka, the hood up, walked past the computer complex without stopping. He turned at the corner and was gone.

The Iraqi admitted that he'd seen a nuclear-tipped missile being loaded aboard one of the submarines in the pens before the trap had been sprung and his partner killed.

Zahedi had seen that same missile poised above the submarine's forward loading hatch, but it contained only a conventional warhead. If it was the *same* missile the Iraqi had seen.

"Maybe we do have nuclear missiles," Eghbal said. "Listen, Amin, it is none of our business." He grinned. "But it would teach the bastards a lesson."

There was a pattern, but to this point it made no sense. It was like looking at the pieces of a complicated puzzle knowing they could be put together, but not knowing what the final picture should look like. With this puzzle a wrong move could be deadly.

The Iraqis had come searching for nuclear weapons, as had the UN Peacekeeping team. And this afternoon an American claiming to be from the US Economic Development Agency had shown up. He'd checked into the same hotel where the UN team was staying, and he had met with the woman team leader.

Zahedi lit a cigarette. The man had taken her to his room where they made love. It was all on tape, indistinct because only one bug embedded in the ceiling had remained operative, but oddly upsetting to Zahedi because he had touched her body. He had felt her womanhood. And listening to the tapes two hours ago, he'd been erotically stimulated. It had disturbed him.

A black Nissan Sentra pulled up a half-block away and doused its lights. A man got out of the passenger side, looked back the way they'd come, then started toward Zahedi, his stride purposeful. He was dressed in a dark jacket, a dark watch cap on his head. He looked neither left nor right; in any circumstances this was no place for anyone to be curious, especially not an American.

As the man passed the doorway, Zahedi fell in beside him. "Thank you for meeting me like this, Mr. Summit," Zahedi said in English.

"I'm armed, so if this is some kind of a trap, I'll blow you away first," the American, Bradley Summit, warned. He was assistant chief of CIA operations for Tehran, working out of the American Interests Section three kilometers from here.

"This is no trap. I'm quite alone, I assure you."

When they were safely around the corner, away from the former US Embassy and possible surveillance by the Revolutionary Guards, Summit pulled Zahedi into the shadows.

"All right, pal. You got me here, now what do you want?"

The Nissan cruised slowly around the corner and parked across the narrow street from them. The driver once again shut off the headlights.

"I have something to give you."

"In trade for what? Are you defecting?"

"Hardly," Zahedi replied. "I would like some information."

"About what?"

"The real reason the UN's intelligence team is here in my country."

"What makes you think that I'd know something like that, or tell you if I did?" the American asked. The CIA was very circumspect in Tehran, in part because of the ruthless way Iran dealt with foreign spies and in part because they strongly suspected that SAVAK had most of them spotted. Both governments were reasonably tolerant of each other's operations so long as no one did anything foolish or spectacular.

"An assistant chief of station would know."

"I don't know what you're talking about," Summit said without missing a beat.

"Last week two Iraqi intelligence officers working for Saddam Hussein came ashore at Bandar-é Emān to spy on our submarine base. One of them was shot and killed in the submarine pens and the other was captured this morning several blocks from here. You can have him in trade for the information I want."

"Is this an official request?"

Zahedi shook his head.

"Like I said, pal, I don't know what the fuck you're talking about. So if you'll excuse me, I'm outta here."

The American started to leave, but Zahedi roughly grabbed his arm and stopped him.

"The man is Colonel Jamal el-Kassem. Do you know this name?"

The American CIA officer showed no reaction.

"At least report my request to your superiors."

"Yeah, right," Summit said sardonically.

SAVAK HEADQUARTERS

At seventy, Mohammed es Sultaneh was an erect, stern man, with thick, unruly gray eyebrows, huge gnarled hands, and a severely square face framed by the head wrap he always wore. He held the rank of general in the army and had distinguished himself in the war of aggression against Iran. He was also an *imam,* which was a religious title of high esteem, and a *hojatoleslam,* which was an even higher title given to religious scholars. But he was also a worldly man, and ran Iran's secret intelligence service with an iron fist.

Not surprisingly, he was still in his office when Zahedi came back from his meeting with the Summit. "Vigilance never sleeps, Colonel. What progress do you have to report?"

"The attack was definitely directed by Saddam Hussein," Zahedi said. "Our prisoner admitted that he'd be sent to confirm the existence of nuclear weapons aboard our submarines."

"Then his mission was not a success," General Sultaneh suggested softly.

"He believes differently, Excellency."

"So apparently does the United Nations. Has their true mission been revealed?"

"I think so."

The old man sipped a glass of sweet *cha*. He looked over the rim at Zahedi, his gaze penetrating. It was said that what Sultaneh did not see, was not there.

"We have submarines, and now the world believes we have nuclear missiles. It would make Iran a very powerful nation. A true rival, finally, for the Zionists in Israel. But it places us in a very dangerous position. Do you see this?"

"Sometimes perception is more important than truth," Zahedi replied. He felt that he was treading on dangerous ground.

"What is your perception, Amin?"

"Your Excellency?"

"Do you believe your government is lying to you in this?"

Zahedi hesitated.

"Come now, the truth is most important to an intelligence-gathering agency. Without truth we are not able to make important decisions. Our predecessors learned that."

"I don't know. But I am conducting my investigation as if we have a very important secret that must be safeguarded at all costs."

"A wise attitude," Sultaneh said sagely. "What about the United Nations team? How soon will they leave?"

"They have seen the base and the submarines with their own eyes. For now they are being bogged down in discussions with our Departments of State and Defense. One would hope that they'll soon realize that there is nothing here for them."

"And the newly arrived American, Mr. Prentice?"

"He's almost certainly an American intelligence officer. We're watching him."

"Indeed," the SAVAK director said. He handed Zahedi a file folder. "His actual name is William Lane. He is a top analyst for the American National Security Agency."

Zahedi opened the file, which contained several photographs of Lane and a brief dossier describing his most recent assignments with the Agency.

"As you see, Mr. Lane is an NSA Russian expert."

Zahedi looked up from the file. "What's he doing here?"

"It is for you to discover. But one would assume that he has brought information vital to the UN team concerning our Russian-built submarines."

"The nuclear question again."

The general sipped his tea. "We live in a difficult world. The old alliances, which seemed at the time to be dangerous, were safe by comparison to the dangers we face now. We cannot trust anyone, and yet we cannot exist alone, as fervently as we would wish it."

"No, sir."

"For instance: By your recent actions at Bandar-é Emān, you have angered the mullahs. It places you in a precarious position."

"I must be allowed to do my job unhindered—"

The old man held up a hand for silence. "For the moment you have my complete faith and confidence. I will shield you from any unpleasantness. But you must not fail, nor must your investigation be prolonged."

"I understand, Your Excellency."

"I hope you do," the general said. "Find out what these people want, and then rid Iran of them."

"Yes, sir," Zahedi said. At the door Sultaneh stopped him.

"Did you learn anything this evening from your meeting with Mr. Summit?"

Zahedi was taken aback. He'd told no one about it. "No, sir," he said evenly.

"You will make no further attempt to treat with the infidels without first informing me."

"Yes, Your Excellency."

"Go with God."

"*In sha'Allah,*" Zahedi replied softly and he left.

MEXICO CITY

A biting wind blew across the square in front of the Palacio Nacional, people on foot bending into it. Valeri Yernin sat alone at a window table in a nearby restaurant sipping a martini as he waited for his lunch to arrive. It amused him to be surrounded by government officials, powerful businessmen, and international journalists, many of them American, some of them probably CIA agents. He was one of the most wanted men in this hemisphere, yet he was beyond reach because he was smarter than they were. He'd slipped out of the embassy unobserved. He was sure of it.

His ebullient mood was tempered, however, by his failure against Bill Lane. It was difficult to believe that the man had found and disposed of the bomb aboard the locomotive so quickly.

And he was soured somewhat by Maslennikov's hesitancy to move forward with the project. He'd been told everything last night, and now he found it difficult to contain himself. Waiting was useless, a waste of his time and energies.

His dispassion had given way to hate, a new emotion for him, and one that he rather enjoyed.

But Mikhail had promised him revenge.

The waiter came with a telephone and plugged it in at Yernin's table. "There is a call for you, señor," he said politely, and left.

A couple of people in the room glanced over in idle curiosity, then turned away.

He'd not given his name to the maître d', nor did anyone know he was coming here for lunch. It had been a spur-of-the-moment decision. He studied the other diners, and the two exits from the room, but there was no sign that he was being set up. Nothing untoward. Nor did his highly developed sixth sense give him any warning.

He picked up the telephone. "*Sí*," he said.

"Leave enough money to cover your lunch, then get up from your table and leave the restaurant immediately," Maslennikov instructed.

"That might direct too much attention my way."

"Turn left toward the cathedral, you'll be picked up by a man wearing a green cap driving a brown Mercedes." The connection was broken.

Maslennikov was having him watched. It was not only surprising, it was irritating. Yernin put down the telephone, left a few hundred pesos, and walked out of the restaurant. Turning left, the wind at his back, he headed toward the looming cathedral, wondering why Maslennikov had taken such extraordinary measures to get him out of there.

He decided that something had come up, something so compelling that his control officer was willing to break a fundamental rule of tradecraft: Never do anything to bring attention to yourself or your fellow operatives.

At the corner, a brown Mercedes diesel driven by a thick-necked man wearing a green baseball cap pulled up. Glancing at his own reflection in the car's windows, Yernin made sure that he'd not picked up a tail, then climbed into the backseat.

Maslennikov, a look of expectancy on his broad Slavic face, was hunched in the corner. "Drive," he told the driver.

They pulled away and headed past the cathedral toward the Avenida Rio Consulado, the ring highway looping around the city. Traffic was heavy, and the air quality today was poor; a yellow haze hung over the city, totally obscuring the mountains.

"What do you think you were doing back there?" Maslennikov demanded.

"Having lunch. Has something happened?"

"By leaving the embassy you may have jeopardized the mission. I thought I made it clear."

"I do not wait well."

"Nor do you follow orders."

Yernin looked at his control officer. "You didn't go to these lengths to offer me a schoolboy's lecture. Now, what's happened?"

Maslennikov seemed to come to a decision. "You're leaving Mexico now. Your things are in the trunk, along with a package of materials you will study enroute."

"Where am I going?"

"Tehran."

"What about the mission?"

"It's developing, but first you are being granted your wish."

"Bill Lane?"

"Da," Maslennikov replied. "Before Kilo Option fully develops, you are going to kill him."

"What is he doing in Iran?"

"He is a brilliant, dangerous man, Valeri. Somehow he has made the connection between what happened in Norfolk and what happened at Bandar-é Emān. If he figures it all out, we will be in trouble."

"I understand," Yernin said absently. He was thinking ahead.

"This time killing Lane will be your only mission. Do not fail me."

Yernin met his control officer's eyes. "I won't fail."

22

"Go home," Lane said.

Reilly laughed and glanced at Frances, but her expression was dead serious. "We have a job to do here."

They were having dinner in the hotel's other good restaurant, the Tiare Polynesian. The room was crowded and the noise level was sufficient that Lane didn't think there was much chance that their conversation could be overheard by anyone seated nearby. Nonetheless they were circumspect. It was a way of life in Iran, especially for Americans. There was little doubt that they were being watched by SAVAK, and it was possible the Iranians had acquired the electronic filtering technology to cut through background noise.

Lane had taken Frances for a walk away from the hotel this afternoon where he'd explained something of his assignment to her, and what he expected of her team. He didn't tell her about Yernin or the trouble in Norfolk, because the UN's mission here was simply to find out who had attacked Bandar-é Emān and why.

She was not overly anxious to go along with him, because as she said, she too had a job to do that was of interest to the entire United Nations, not just the United States. But she agreed to brief Reilly, who was the team co-leader.

"What is it exactly that you're trying to tell us, Mr. Prentice?" Reilly asked.

"You've done your job here, now go home."

"We're not finished."

"Yes you are," Lane said. He signaled the waiter for their check. "From this point forward no one in Iran will give you any help. You're going to get the runaround. And eventually they'll kick you out at gunpoint."

"It's been done before," Reilly admitted.

"We're already getting the runaround," Frances said. "We spent the day at the Department of Defense and got nowhere. But we can't just pack our bags and leave."

"Why did you come here in the first place?" If by chance SAVAK could hear what they were saying, it would expect something of substance.

The question surprised Reilly, but he was enough of a professional not to be thrown off stride. "We're investigating the attack on Bandar-é Emān."

"That's three hundred fifty miles away. What are you doing in Tehran?" Frances shot Lane a questioning glance. She was confused. "Our jobs."

"Bullshit," Lane said amiably. "My guess is that you screwed something up down there which will make it difficult for the rest of us to do any business here." The waiter came, and Lane handed him a gold Visa card. "All you're doing now is irritating people. On both sides of the ocean. You're not going to find out anything else. So why not go?"

"It doesn't work that way, Mr. Prentice," Reilly said, giving Lane a hard look.

"Oh?"

"You've heard of MEGAP, I presume?"

"The region is at peace, unless you're trying to make this another Bosnia."

"The attack on Bandar-é Emān was hardly a peaceful gesture."

"Have you found out who the attackers were?"

"Saddam Hussein's people. And we have the proof."

It was news to Frances, and she looked questioningly at Reilly. "We're not certain of that, Terrence."

"Yes we are."

Lane watched the interplay between them. He didn't want to think it was a power struggle, unless he had misjudged the man. He made a slight gesture toward the door which they both caught. "Then you've found what you came looking for, so get the hell out and leave the real work to us."

The waiter came with the charge slip, which Lane signed. "I need a little fresh air, it's starting to smell like crap in here."

Understanding dawned in Frances's eyes. "I resent that."

"Tough shit," Lane replied. He got up and headed for the elevators.

"All you give a damn about is money," Frances called loudly after him.

A number of people looked up, hostile expressions on their faces. Foreigners were nothing but trouble.

"What else is there, sweetheart?" Lane replied without looking back.

He picked up the tail, two men in dark gray windbreakers, the moment he left the hotel and headed into the big park that fronted on Kheyābūn-é Hejāb Street, the same place he'd taken Frances. The evening was damp and cold. A light snow surrounded the occasional streetlight with a gauze curtain. Tehran was a foreign city, its streets and buildings, its sounds and smells alien, of a different time, an ancient, violent time.

Frances had picked up on the hidden meaning behind his gesture and five minutes later she and Reilly caught up with him in the park. No one else was around except for the two SAVAK legmen lurking somewhere behind them in the shadows. For the moment he figured they were safe from eavesdropping.

"Sorry about that there, but we're not supposed to be friends," Lane said.

"I'd hate to be your enemy," Reilly said ruefully. "But Frannie gives you high marks, and that's good enough for me. I assume that everything said back there was for SAVAK's ears."

"Right. We have a tail."

"I know."

"You said that you had proof that Saddam Hussein's people attacked the sub base. Are you talking about the Iraqi prisoner SAVAK captured?"

Reilly was stunned. "How the hell did you find out so quickly? The embassy just got the message to us."

"The CIA briefed me before I flew in. Can we get to him?"

"The Agency guys here think it's a setup," Reilly responded.

"Was that the call you got from Brad Summit before dinner?" Frances asked. She seemed slightly irritated.

Reilly nodded. "He said that he had contact with a SAVAK colonel who told him that they'd captured one of the attackers. Offered to trade him for information about us."

"What sort of information?" Frances asked.

"The real reason we're here, among other things. He identified their captive as a Mukabarat colonel loyal to Hussein."

"But Summit didn't go for the trade?"

"Like I said, darlin', he thinks SAVAK is playing games. It's possible that the attack was actually staged by the Iranians themselves to cover some sort of an operation that's about ready to take place."

"Was he more specific than that?" Lane asked.

"No," Reilly said. "It was a courtesy call on his part. He told me that we'd better watch ourselves. When SAVAK starts making these kinds of moves, something is about to come down." Reilly looked bleakly at Lane. "Matter of fact, he gave me the same message you did: Get out of Iran while the getting is good."

"Did he give you a name?"

"Colonel Jamal el-Kassem. He disappeared into the desert just after the war."

The snow had intensified, muffling all sounds. They stopped. Lane lit a cigarette while surreptitiously looking back the way they had come for any signs of their tail. But he saw nothing in the darkness.

"All that's left is the nuclear question," he said. "Frances has already given me the layout of the base and sub pens. So what's next on your agenda? Are you going to call for backup from New York?"

"We're thinking about it. Sooner or later the Iranians will have to cooperate with us."

"Only if they don't have nuclear weapons. Otherwise it'll never happen."

"Then you agree with Brad that we really should leave?" Frances asked.

"I want you to pack up and pretend as if you're getting set to go. But tomorrow I want your team to start making as much noise as possible. Hit every government department that has even a remote connection with the submarines, with the military, or with their State Department. Even SAVAK if you can pull it off."

Frances eyed him dubiously. "Why am I getting the feeling that I'm not going to like what's coming next?"

Lane studied the path behind them. Then he turned back to Frances. "If I can prove that they've loaded nukes aboard their submarines, will you take your team home and turn the entire matter over to the Security Council?"

Frances's eyes narrowed. "What are you going to do?"

"I asked you a question."

"We'll go," Reilly said. "But there can't be any guesswork, they either have the nukes or they don't."

"Will you take my word on it?"

"Yes."

"Do you know Tom Hughes?"

Frances nodded.

Lane gave her Hughes's secure number. "If I'm not back in twenty-four hours, I want you to tell him that I need help."

"You're going to Bandar-é Emān."

Lane grinned. "It's a dirty job, but somebody's got to do it."

"You'll never get past their security," Reilly warned.

"I'm not going to have to see the weapons with my own eyes to find out if they have them."

"Then how the hell are you going to know for sure?"

"Easy," Lane said. "I'm going to swim into the sub pens and put a Geiger counter on the hulls."

Back at the hotel, Reilly and two of the FRIFINTEL team members set up a compact white-noise generator in one of the rooms after disabling the bugs they found. For the moment they figured they would be secure from SAVAK interference.

When he was certain they were ready, Reilly sketched the overall config-uration of a Kilo-class submarine, with its pressure hull, inner hull, and most of the important compartments and machinery spaces, for Lane.

"Without knowing what kind of radiation-detection device you've been supplied with, all I can advise is to crank the sucker wide open and hope for the best. The Russian-made SS-N-fifteen and -sixteen series don't leak a significant amount of radiation unless they're mishandled pretty badly. What you'll be picking up is something only slightly above background noise. But you should be able to see the peaks at the forward hatch where they load the missiles, and in the torpedo room where they'd be stored."

"Could there be anything else aboard that might cause similar readings?" Lane asked.

"The boats are diesel-electric, so there shouldn't be any radiation sources other than weapons," Reilly said. "Not to put too fine a point on it, it doesn't matter what type of nuclear device they're carrying."

"You know a lot about the navy for a marine."

"I've always loved ships, it's just that I hate water."

"Look, you don't have to do this, it's our job," Frances said from across the room.

"There's something else going on that I'm working on."

"What?"

"It'll hold until I come back," Lane said.

"What is it?" she said sharply. "Our arses are on the line here as well as well as yours."

"Later, Fran. You're going to have to trust me on this one."

She wanted to argue, it was clear on her face, but she bit her tongue. "Twenty-four hours."

"How are you getting down there?" she asked.

Lane said nothing.

After a moment she came over and gave him a hug. "Be careful, William."

"You too," he said.

At the door he shook Reilly's hand. The marine captain gave him an odd, questioning look.

"Later," Lane said, and Reilly knew exactly what he meant. Now was not the time to discuss their mutual interest in Frances.

Outside, he picked up the same tail as before. This time he wasted no time losing them, and within twenty minutes he was back at his car parked on a side street a half block from the hotel and headed through the city to the southern highway that led to the city of Qom in the mountains, from where all roads led to the Gulf.

Iran maintained some of the best roads in the Middle East, and despite the snow he was able to make excellent time. The Fiat was in good condition, the tires new and the engine in tune. Three jerry cans of gasoline were wedged in the trunk, and starting out with a full tank of gas, he figured he'd be able to make it to the Gulf and back without having to stop.

Very few cars or trucks were on the road between Tehran and Qom, and south of the mountain city of 170,000 the highway was deserted. On the high desert plains villages were tiny, few and far between. No prying eyes. No one to see and report the small car speeding through the night. And because of the overcast skies he was even safe from satellite observation.

He was as utterly alone and isolated here as he'd ever been in his life. Almost as far away from civilization as if he'd been at the bottom of the ocean in the Mariana Trench, while above and all around him a tempest raged.

At midnight Lane stopped at the side of the road to urinate. It had stopped snowing, but the sky was still covered with thick black clouds.

He turned off the Fiat's lights, and when his eyes were fully adjusted to the darkness he scanned the horizon for 360 degrees. There were no lights in any direction. The only signs of civilization were the highway and the telephone poles that followed it.

The wind was biting; it penetrated his light jacket and seeped into his bones. Back in the car, he turned the heater to full blast and floored the gas pedal. He wanted this night's work to be finished. Even Tehran, at this moment, seemed like a safe haven.

His mind drifted back to the moment on the train just before he blacked out. He'd looked into Yernin's eyes and had seen the triumph in them. But there'd been something else—or rather a lack of anything else. Looking into the Ukrainian's eyes was like looking into the eyes of a dead person.

He would come face to face with the man again. Of that he was certain, although he did not know where or when it would be.

Darkness surrounded him, and he willed the little car to go even faster. It was all he could do for the moment.

23

BANDAR-É EMĀN

Lane stood out of the bitter wind in the shelter of an abandoned stone hut one hundred yards from the beach and watched the lights of the naval base a half-mile to the west. There'd been no traffic on the roads leading here, nor was there any now except around the base perimeter.

Through binoculars he saw what appeared to be a changing of the guard at the main gate. Even from this distance it was clear that they were serious. When the canvas flaps of the troop transport were pulled back, the soldiers spewed out, rushed into formation, and crisply came to attention.

The same thing was happening at various other points around the fence. If they'd maintained this level of security in the first place, the base would never have been penetrated, at least not with the apparent ease with which it had been done. It was like locking the barn door after the horse had run away.

He looked again toward the highway from the mountains to the north. Still no lights, no sign that anyone had followed him from Tehran. But no one expected him to be here tonight. Long ago he'd learned that you could almost always get away with the unexpected.

Almost always.

The Fiat was parked behind the partially tumbled-down stone hut. It would be safe there until first light. Until then no one passing on the road could see it.

Lane took a small shovel from the trunk, went inside the hut, pulled a piece of corrugated iron and some other debris away from the northwest corner, and began to dig. Within a couple of minutes he uncovered two large olive drab canvas duffel bags that the CIA's Iranian contact had buried here for him, pulled them out of the hole, and dragged them over to the open doorway facing the sea.

The equipment Zimmerman's people had dropped here was of Russian and Israeli manufacture, so that if it was discovered the Iranian authorities might not suspect an American operation. It wasn't much of a subterfuge but, as the Riyadh COS had unnecessarily explained, there was no love lost out here for Americans. The scuba gear was an Israeli Mark-VI mixed gas rebreather that, unlike the old-styled oxygen rebreathers, could be used safely below twenty feet while still leaving no telltale trail of bubbles. The wet suit was Russian and fit poorly, as did the fins and mask. But the Russian-made Geiger counter sealed in a waterproof case was one of the best available anywhere, its sensitivity at least three times that of a comparable American unit. The literature had come across Lane's desk a couple of years ago when the piece of equipment had been snagged during an operation at Chernobyl. Lane liked toys, especially well-made toys.

He stripped down to his underwear, then pulled on the wet suit, and stashed his clothes in the Fiat. He figured he had two hours to get into the sub pens, take his readings, and get back out. He wanted to be on the road no later than 3:00 A.M. Even that would be cutting his return to Tehran very close.

He stuffed his pistol inside his wet suit, donned the rebreather, and, keeping low, rushed down to the stony beach where he pulled on his fins and mask and entered the cold, dark waters of the Persian Gulf, no one there to see him off or wish him luck.

The thought crossed his mind that if he died here tonight, no one would ever know what really happened to him. But then, he grinned behind his face mask, it'd save on funeral expenses.

Fifty yards offshore, he turned back to look at the stone hut and the road behind it. He could barely make out the glint of stray light reflecting off the Fiat's front bumper, but the highway was still deserted. The only lights came from the offshore oil platforms. From here he saw no signs of damage from the raid, nor was it obvious that the shoreside installation was anything but industrial—something to do with the pumping, refining, or handling of oil.

Lane took a compass bearing to the sub pen, submerged to a depth of ten feet, and kicked off toward the west, nothing visible in the nearly absolute darkness.

"You don't have to do this." Frances's face swam into his mind's eye. She was concerned. She didn't scare easily, nor did she respect those who did. It was one of the reasons Lane admired her. One of the reasons he'd almost asked her to marry him two years ago. But he'd seen fear in her eyes last night.

Something, some barrier, had turned him away from making the proposal. There was more for him to accomplish, more for him to do without the added concerns—baggage, he'd once called it—of a committed relationship.

He grinned again behind his face mask. He didn't want to deprive Tom

Hughes of the pleasure of matchmaking, an endeavor Lane wholeheartedly supported.

Frances had been right when she agreed that he was a macho pig. He was. And as long as he could get away with it, he was going to continue to enjoy his role to the hilt.

He swam steadily, but without overexerting himself, using his powerful leg muscles to propel his body through the frigid water. He checked his compass often; nevertheless, he briefly surfaced twice to make sure of his bearings. An unknown current could have pushed him off course. Or a two- or three-degree error in his compass could have put him ashore too soon, or angled him away from the base, out toward the oil platforms.

But the second time he surfaced he was near enough to the sub pen doors to see the weld joints holding the high-tensile steel plates together. A small patrol boat started away from the docks with a angry roar and headed directly toward him.

Slipping underwater again, Lane angled sharply down, heading deep as fast as he could pump his legs.

Seconds later the patrol boat passed above and behind him, and as he slowed down to catch his breath his fingertips brushed the lower lip of the steel doors.

Sinking a couple of feet lower, he swam beneath the doors, then headed forward while angling slightly upward, the surface of the water twenty feet above glowing with an ethereal light.

Despite his exertions, the cold of the Gulf water seeped into his bones. The wet suit was barely adequate to ensure against hypothermia, but without it he would not have gotten half a mile.

He stopped dead in the water, hanging in the division between the pitch-darkness below and the eerie glow above, and held his breath, suddenly aware of a dull throbbing noise. It was impossible to pinpoint the direction of the low-pitched sound, but he could feel the vibrations through the water.

It was as if an engine were running somewhere near. A very large, very powerful engine slowly turning a propeller. A boat's propeller. A submarine's screw.

He backed up a few feet as a second low-pitched throbbing sound, this one farther off to the right, joined the first. Moments later a third engine started, and finally a fourth, the water around him vibrating.

The engines aboard all four submarines had been lit off. Which meant what? They weren't going out on patrol. Not at this hour of the night, certainly not all of them at the same time.

They were expecting an intruder. Someone in scuba gear to swim in under the blast doors to sabotage the submarines by placing explosives on the hulls. By running the engines they would create a backwash to force the saboteur to swim closer to the surface and away from vital below-the-waterline mechanisms.

"Be careful," Frances had warned him.

But that wasn't possible. Being careful and conducting a covert operation were by definition mutually exclusive.

He floated motionless for a moment, listening to the deep-throated engine noises, feeling the vibrations against his body, imagining the gigantic nine-blade propellers turning over, ready to suck a man to his death into their vortices. But the answer to Iran's nuclear question came down to here and now.

Lane held the Geiger counter up to his face mask so that he could read the illuminated dials. He flipped on the power switch, centered the background radiation indicator to zero, and set the sensitivity control to maximum. If there were nuclear weapons of any sort aboard these submarines, their presence would show up on the dial.

Tightening his grip on the Geiger counter, he kicked his fins and started slowly toward the source of the noise while heading just as carefully toward the surface.

The illumination around him increased rapidly, and suddenly the hull of one of the submarines loomed up out of the distance, the water at its stern roiling, as if it were a pot of boiling water on the stove.

Lane angled to the right, away from the worst of the prop wash, until he could make out the hull of another submarine twenty yards away. The water at its stern was agitated from its rotating screw, but between the two boats, equidistant from both propellers, the water was reasonably calm.

He swam about five feet beneath the surface through the middle of the calmer water until he was forward of the after hydroplanes, and clear of any danger from the prop wash, then he angled back toward the submarine's hull.

You should be able to see the peaks at the forward hatch where they load the missiles, and in the torpedo room where they'd be stored.

He held the Geiger counter two inches away from the sub's hull and, keeping his eye on the radiation indicator, started forward toward the bow.

Nothing happened. The dial remained pegged at zero, normal background level.

He stopped to readjust the background setting to make certain he wasn't making a mistake, and started forward again. Reilly had warned that if nuclear weapons were aboard the submarines, the radiation levels would be extremely low. Barely above background noise.

But he was picking up nothing. If the Geiger counter was correct, and if the Iranians hadn't gotten smart and added extra lead shielding around their torpedo storage spaces, there were no nuclear weapons aboard this submarine.

He would check the others, and then get the hell out of here. He was beginning to feel spooked.

He turned away from the bow of the first submarine and headed for the second when something splashed in the water above him. He looked up in time to see a pair of thick ropes or wires sinking toward him.

Wires, the thought crystallized.

Battery cables.

Something like a battering ram slammed into him, causing every muscle in his body to contract violently, ten billion fireflies exploding in his head, a gigantic hand pressing down on his chest, stopping the flow of air to his lungs, grasping his heart in an excruciatingly painful grip.

A moment before he lost consciousness he remembered seeing the same thing happen to a pond of fish when someone tossed in a pair of electrical cables. The fish hadn't had a chance.

24

NATIONAL SECURITY AGENCY
FORT MEADE, MARYLAND

It was a few minutes before eight Tuesday morning when Tom Hughes parked his Range Rover in his slot and took the elevator up to his third-floor office. He'd spent a restless evening here at the complex, and a sleepless night at home with Moira and the girls fussing over him.

They hadn't heard from Lane yet. Communications in and out of Tehran were spotty at best. And no one wanted to upset any applecarts just yet by shouting something from a rooftop for everyone to hear. Still, Hughes was worried. Something in his gut told him that all wasn't right with his friend.

Switching on his lights, he laid his briefcase down on his desk, took off his jacket, and sat down. His office looked out over the operations center, which was starting to come up to speed for the day.

The hand-delivered night reports were already on his desk, and the summaries of electronic activities over the past eighteen hours were available on his monitor as soon as he was ready for them.

By ten he needed to have his first read on the overnights ready for Ben Lewis, who would in turn kick everything upstairs to Director Roswell.

Bertie Drogan, the day shift comms chief, came to the door. "Glad you're here. You've got an incoming that I was about to transfer."

Hughes looked up. "Is it Bill?"

"No, it's a woman. Maybe Frances Shipley. The call originated from Tehran."

"I want an exact ID and location. We've got her voice prints on record. I want to make sure she's not under duress."

"Gotcha."

Hughes picked up his secured line, which scrambled telephone signals both ways even though one side of the conversation came from a nonencrypted phone.

"Yes?"

"Tom Hughes?"

"That's right. Who am I talking to?"

"Frances Shipley. Do you know who I am?"

"Yes, I do," Hughes said. The woman was under pressure, he could hear that much in her cultured voice. But he didn't think she was speaking with a gun at her head. "Are you calling from a secure place?"

"For the moment it is. But this phone line is undoubtedly being monitored."

"It's all right, I have a back scramble on you, so we can talk. Are you calling about our mutual friend?"

"He should have been back by now, but there's been no word."

"He gave you this number to call under a certain set of circumstances?"

"Yes. He told me to call you if he wasn't back within twenty-four hours. It's nearly five in the evening here, and he left early last night."

Drogan came to the door.

Hughes held a hand over the telephone and gave the comms chief a questioning look.

"It's Frances Shipley. She's under strain, but I'd say she's not being forced to speak."

"Is her line being monitored?"

Drogan nodded. "We're handling it okay. She's at the Laleh."

"Mr. Hughes?" Frances said.

"I'm here. I was just checking on something. Now I want you to tell me everything you know. Did William tell you where he was going and why?"

"The base at Bandar-é Emān. He was going to check for radiation."

"Did he have any trouble in the city?"

"Not that I know of. But we have a tail here, and all our rooms are bugged, so once he left I had no way of knowing for sure."

"How was security at the base?"

"Very tight. The faction fight between the mullahs and the SAVAK was evident, Mr. Hughes. And if Bill is caught up in the middle of that, he won't have a chance."

"I understand. Did William give you any other instructions? Anything he wanted you to do, or anything he wanted you to tell me?"

"Just that if he wasn't back within twenty-four hours I was to call you because he needed help."

"What else?"

Frances hesitated a moment before answering. "He told me, all of us, to get out of Iran."

"Why?"

"Because we're in danger."

"Have you come up with any indications, no matter how slight or fanciful, that Iran has got nukes aboard their subs?"

"No."

"Any chance you'll come up with anything like that in the near future?"

"No."

"Anything that you or your team can do right now to help William?" Hughes asked relentlessly.

"No, goddamn you," Frances flared. "But I won't simply abandon the man."

"I suggest that is exactly what you must do, Ms. Shipley," Hughes advised gently.

"No—"

"Please listen to me, because he is my friend too. If he *is* in trouble, we'll take the steps to get him out of there. Something you and your team are simply not equipped to handle."

"I don't like it," Frances said in anguish.

"Neither do I. But getting yourself and your team into trouble would do nothing but compound the issue."

"I could speak with my government."

"And explain to the Iranian government why a British intelligence officer working for the UN is attempting to help an American intelligence officer doing something illegal in their country."

Frances was silent for an interminable second or two. "I see your point."

"Get out of Iran as soon as possible and let me attend to William's rescue." Hughes forced a chuckle. "Assuming, that is, that the guy needs any rescuing. I've seen him do some amazing things."

"I hope you're right," Frances replied solemnly.

So do I, Hughes thought, but he didn't say it. "Call me when you're out, dear."

"You may count on it, Mr. Hughes," Frances said, and she hung up.

Hughes put the phone down. He and William had discussed this possibility and their options, none of which was wholly satisfactory. But the prize was worth the gamble.

He met Ben Lewis in Thomas Roswell's office. "It's about as bad as it gets," he told them.

"Have a seat, Tom," Roswell said. "Have we received word about Bill Lane?"

"Indirectly," Hughes said, settling heavily. "I just got a call from Frances Shipley, with the UN team over there."

"She's the one who brought the discrepancy in the Bandar-é Emān strike photos to our attention, isn't she?" the NSA director asked Lewis.

"Yes, sir. She's a very capable woman. British intelligence."

Roswell turned his penetrating gaze back to Hughes for a moment, then opened a desk drawer and switched off the room's recording devices. Next he phoned his secretary and instructed her that they were not to be disturbed for anything short of a national emergency. He looked like McNamara, square-jawed, thick eyelids, and heavy black hair. In personality and temperament, however, he was anything but a politician. He directed the NSA with as firm a hand and as strong a grasp of geopolitical realism as any man who'd ever sat in his chair, or in the chair of the director of the CIA in Langley, and he didn't care about popularity polls.

"All right, lay it out for us," he said.

"It's possible that William has been arrested by the Iranian authorities. SAVAK, hopefully, but possibly the religious leadership at Bandar-é Emān."

"How certain are we?"

"We think he started out for the base. According to Commander Shipley, those were his plans. He instructed her to call me in the event he didn't return within twenty-four hours. He hasn't shown up, so she telephoned. The call was secure."

"He made no other rendezvous or contact points? Nothing by radio?"

"No, sir. Nothing. The presumption is that he's been arrested."

"Or killed," Lewis added.

"No," Hughes interjected sharply. "Not killed. They would have made something out of it. A dead body is only as useful as the publicity it generates. Whereas a live body is a strong negotiating element."

"Which is why you're here. To ask that steps are taken to negotiate his release—if he has been arrested, and if he is not dead."

"We sent him, Mr. Director. On the president's orders," Hughes flared again.

Roswell's gaze never wavered. "He understood the odds. And you know how long it took for us to secure the release of the hostages in the eighties."

"They didn't know as much as Bill Lane, if you want to reduce it to those terms. They got the publicity, deservedly so, but William could cause this agency, and certainly this administration, a great deal of harm that might take years to recover from."

Lewis tried to interrupt, but Roswell held the Russian Division chief off.

"Point taken, Tom. What do you suggest we do? Send in the marines?"

"If need be."

"Or something else?"

Hughes girded himself, thinking of Moira, which always gave him strength.

"I mean no disrespect, Mr. Director."

"None taken," Roswell replied evenly.

"What were your plans in case William's mission ran into trouble?"

A niggling smile played at the corner of the director's mouth. "Take advice from my staff, and make my recommendations to the president."

Hughes glanced at Lewis. His boss was nonplussed. But he'd never known Lewis to back down when his support was needed. Like now. His expression at the moment, however, seemed to be saying: You've got the rope, careful you don't hang yourself with it.

"Assuming William is alive, and until I see his body with my own eyes I'll assume he is still alive, then he is definitely a negotiable commodity. His value to the Iranians, of course, will depend upon two things: Have they equipped their submarines with nuclear weapons, and has William discovered this fact?"

"If both conditions have been met, then Lane would be better off dead—in the Iranians' view," Roswell said.

"Not if our offer to them for his release is so compelling they couldn't possibly turn it down."

"What might that be, Tom?" Roswell asked mildly, his eyes hooded now.

"The raid on Bandar-é Emān was not staged by the Israelis. We know this for a fact. Either it was ordered by Tehran for some as-yet-unknown purpose, or it was ordered by Saddam Hussein."

"To what end? He didn't hurt the Iranians."

"For the same reason we sent William; for the nuclear question. If Hussein has the information, he could use it to bargain with us. And probably be successful."

"And if it were an Iranian disinformation plot?"

"Then William's incursion wouldn't be so meaningful. The key is Saddam Hussein."

"We're listening," Roswell prompted.

"SAVAK undoubtedly knows who they've got by now. They know who he works for and what he does. If he got into the sub pens and got close enough to the submarines to check them out with a Geiger counter—which I'm sure he did—they know he's good at what he does." Hughes hesitated for a brief instant. "They would know that whatever assignment he was given, he'd carry it out with great zeal and professionalism. If he set out to do something, anything, he would have a very good chance of succeeding."

"Get to the point."

"Something that we and the Iranians would most like to see now, and in fact would like to have seen for several years, William can give them."

The director's office was silent. Outside, the morning was gray. It promised to snow again.

"Saddam Hussein," Hughes said.

Roswell looked puzzled. He spread his hands. "What?"

"If the Iranians release William, his next assignment will be to assassinate Saddam Hussein."

TEHRAN

Frances Shipley sat with Terry Reilly at a window table in the hotel's Tiare Polynesian restaurant staring out at the smoldering city thirteen floors below. The Iranian capital in winter always seemed to be on the verge of an all-out conflagration. Smoke rose from tens of thousands of charcoal braziers, and there seemed to be a deadly air of volatility hanging over the vast metropolis, ready with the slightest spark to send them into instant firestorm.

They were leaving in the morning. The final warning from Tom Hughes coming on the heels of Bill Lane's disappearance convinced even Reilly that it was time to bail out. Frances didn't want that. None of them did, but she especially felt as if she were deserting Bill.

"Bloody hell," she murmured.

Reilly reached across the table and covered her hand with his. "I know, darlin'. But staying here won't help him. We can pull a lot more weight across the border."

Frances looked into his intelligent, loving eyes. He was a good man, and it'd been grand with him. But seeing Bill again in Fort Meade had rekindled feelings she thought she'd buried long ago. She cared for Reilly. But she knew now that she was in love with Bill Lane. And had been from the first day she'd seen him.

Reilly read something of that from her eyes. "He's a big boy. He can take care of himself. And now that his people know he's in trouble, they'll send help."

Frances looked bleakly at him. He was trying to help, she knew that. But it didn't stop her from being sick with worry. Lane was a macho pig and a son of a bitch. But he was her son of a bitch, and she was sorry she'd let him go.

What if he was dead? She turned that thought over in her mind as she looked down again at the city. No, she thought. Somehow, by whatever telepathy, she knew for certain that Lane was alive, but in trouble.

Part of her wanted to remain in Iran, to return to Bandar-é Emān and demand Lane's release. But another, more intelligent, part of her knew that Reilly was right. They could do more for Lane from outside Iran's borders.

The restaurant was crowded, the hum of conversations creating a pleasant undertone. It suddenly stopped.

"Shit," Reilly said half under his breath.

Frances turned around as six men, two of them in civilian clothes, the other four in uniform and armed with rifles, came across the restaurant. They looked serious.

Reilly got to his feet.

"Captain Terrence Reilly?" one of the civilians asked stiffly.

"What do you want?" Reilly replied evenly.

"Are you Captain Reilly?"

"Yes."

The civilian turned his gaze to Frances. "Are you Commander Frances Shipley?"

"Yes, I am," Frances said, rising. "Who are you?"

"You and your team are under arrest. Please come with us without trouble."

"I want to know who the hell you are before we go anywhere. Are we being kidnapped? We're here under the authority of the United Nations—"

"You are here spying on Iran for the United States," the civilian shouted, spittle flying from his lips. He pulled out a pistol. "You will find out soon enough who we are."

"Easy does it," Reilly said holding his hands up palms out. "Where is the rest of our team?"

"They are being taken into custody at this moment."

"May we be allowed to contact our embassies?"

"It is not permitted."

"Sanctions," Frances said, looking the Iranian in the eye.

"What?"

"We came here to help, is this how you repay us?" She glared at the man. "Maybe another few years of international sanctions will get your attention."

"Either come with us now, or we'll shoot you right here," the other civilian said emotionlessly.

Frances glanced at Reilly, who gave her a smile. "All right," she said.

Yernin sat at the corner table in the Tiare Polynesian with Aleksandr Sorokin, a Ukrainian intelligence officer working in Iran under double cover as a Russian journalist. Neither the Iranians nor the Russians knew his true identity.

They watched as the two UN inspectors were led away. Since Lane had disappeared, the woman was to have been Yernin's lead.

"Who was the man with her?" Yernin asked.

"An American marine captain. He's on the FIRFINTEL team with Commander Shipley," Sorokin replied without hesitation.

Yernin gave him a penetrating look.

Sorokin pursed his thick lips. "I'm a journalist. It's my job to know things. You would be surprised what the FIS pricks tell me." The FIS was the renamed Russian KGB.

"Did you recognize the Iranians?"

"SAVAK. But I would like to have been a little bird over there to hear what that was all about. They didn't seem very happy."

"Have we got anybody inside SAVAK?"

"We don't, but my Russian friends do. I think I can find out why they're pissing around with the UN. Should have just kicked them out."

"I want to know about Lane," Yernin corrected the portly intelligence officer.

Sorokin glanced at the doorway. "Do you think that Lane has been arrested, and has implicated the UN team?"

"He hasn't been seen since yesterday, and now this," Yernin said thoughtfully. "If there is a connection, I want to know about it. That and about Bandar-é Emān."

"There has been no word as yet, Colonel," Sorokin admitted uncomfortably. Yernin's reputation, as shadowy as it was, demanded a great deal of respect and even more caution. He was to be told the truth, no matter how disagreeable. "In fact, our resources down there are not good just now. Even since the . . . incident. The stupid bastards let themselves walk into a trap."

"We didn't stay to help. Instead we turned tail and ran."

"We'll find out about the UN team."

"And about William Lane, and about Colonel Kassem," Yernin said. "Within the hour."

Impossible, Sorokin wanted to say, but he swallowed it. Instead he nodded. "I'll see what I can do, Colonel."

"Yes, you will," Yernin said.

25

THE WHITE HOUSE

Thomas Roswell had been in service to his country nearly forty years, since the halcyon last days of the Kennedy administration. During that time he'd been involved in a number of operations of a questionable nature.

But he'd never been faced with anything like this, though a couple of his predecessors at Fort Meade and even more over at Langley had gotten their hands plenty dirty. From Allende to the Bay of Pigs and back, a lot of those deals had gone sour, burning the participants.

This had all the earmarks of just such a disaster. But he couldn't duck the issue, or even pass the buck. It was his man over there, and his president who'd asked for a solution to a tough problem.

It was 10:00 A.M. The president had agreed to see Roswell immediately. He waited in the Oval Office with his national security adviser, Bill Townsend. They'd been deep in conversation, seated opposite each other on the couch, and they looked up with odd expressions on their faces when Roswell was shown in. Where Roswell was the perfect spymaster, precise, always acting close to the vest, Reasoner was the consummate politician, hale, hearty, and well-met. Normally the two attributes were like oil and water, but Roswell got along with this president much better than most.

"The situation in Iran is beginning to get ugly, Mr. President," Roswell began.

"You wouldn't have come over here this morning if it wasn't important, Tom," Reasoner said. "Coffee?"

"No thank you, Mr. President."

Reasoner exchanged glances with Townsend. He motioned for Roswell to have a seat in one of the wingback chairs.

"Do you have something for me to look at?"

"Not at this time," Roswell said pointedly. "I don't think this should be in writing. At least until a decision is made. And maybe not even then."

"Bill Lane?" Townsend asked.

Roswell nodded. "We think he's been arrested for espionage at Bandar-é Emān. We've intercepted a number of military communications between the submarine base and Military Command Center in Tehran which seem to indicate that there is a struggle going on between the religious leadership and the secular arm of the government for his custody."

"Did he find out what he was sent for?" Townsend asked.

"We've had no communications from him since he left the States. But the CIA tells me that he picked up a cache of equipment that was left for him near the base." Roswell passed a hand over his forehead. "The car he'd been supplied with in Tehran was gone."

"Anything by satellite?" the president's NSA asked.

"It's overcast throughout the region. Even infrareds are not being given a high degree of reliability."

"So you're saying that to this point we have learned nothing definite about the submarines," Townsend said. "The nuclear question."

"That's correct, sir," Roswell replied directly to the president.

"Presumably there's been no contact between Lane and the Ukrainian agent—" Townsend stopped in midsentence because of the suddenly tense expression on Roswell's face.

"The man's name is Valeri Yernin. He was in Mexico City, but we think he may have left there. Possibly to Damascus via London. We're not certain about that."

"Tehran?"

"Possibly. But the timing might have been too tight for Yernin to have been involved in Lane's arrest. Besides, if Yernin's in Tehran, he'll be under cover. The Ukrainians are not welcome there. Only the Russians are."

"Acting as a Russian would be easy for him to pull off." Townsend sat forward. "Are you reading this the way I am, Tom?"

"Providing Yernin is in Tehran—"

"Come off it," Townsend interrupted. "The evidence is more than circumstantial that Yernin's people knew that Bill Lane was in Iran. And Yernin was sent to kill him."

"Means we have another leak, is that right, Tom?" the president asked.

Roswell nodded. "I would say under that set of circumstances it's possible."

"Who's in the loop?" Townsend asked.

"On the substance of why I'm here this morning, only Ben Lewis, who is the head of our Russian Division, and Tom Hughes, who is Lane's immediate supervisor. On Lane's mission in Tehran, a lot of people in my shop as well as over at Langley are in the know."

"It's a start," Townsend said. "Were you informed about the UN team?"

"No, what is it?"

"They were arrested by SAVAK, on charges of espionage."

"Christ," Roswell said to himself. It was unraveling even faster than he feared it would. Hughes had warned them it would go like this, and that they'd have to run like hell to catch up. "This won't be another long, leisurely hostage crisis, Mr. Roswell," Hughes had cautioned.

"The lid is being kept on it for the moment, but all hell is about to break lose."

"Fight fire with fire," Roswell muttered.

"What?" the president asked.

"Mr. President, Bill Lane was arrested because he tried to find out if Iran has equipped their submarines with nuclear missiles. The UN team has been arrested because they—at least some of them—helped him. It means if we want them released, we'll have to negotiate his release."

"Negotiate is the operative word here, Tom," the president warned. "I'll be goddamned if I'll send in the marines for him. That cost Carter his job."

"Yes, sir. But the Iranian government won't give him up so easily."

"So we have to offer them something they can't refuse," Townsend said, fascinated now. "We have some of their people in prison."

"Terrorists," the president interjected.

"Yes, sir," Townsend said. "We also have a few billion dollars in Iranian assets on hold here we might be able to release. Or part of them."

The president was eyeing Roswell. "I don't think that'll be enough. Do you, Tom?"

"No, Mr. President."

"But you have something in mind."

"Yes, sir."

"Something I'm not going to like very much. But we made the first move and lost, didn't we? So now we pay."

"We can't leave him there. He knows too much."

"So I'm told," the president said dryly. "What do we do about it, Tom?"

"I need your authorization to call General Mohammed es Sultaneh and explain our position to him. He's director of SAVAK, but he's a respected mullah as well, so he's able to see both sides."

"You're going to ask him to release Bill Lane, an American intelligence agent who has probably learned Iran's most precious state secret?"

"Something like that."

"Why should he do that for us? In fact why should he even take your call?"

"He'll take my call because he's expecting it, Mr. President. He's not a blind fanatic. He knows we want Bill Lane returned to us. And he knows we'll either try to grab him by force or try to negotiate. The first has undoubtedly been prepared for. Now he's waiting for the second. And as for why he'll do it for us, he'll have nothing to lose once I explain our offer."

"You're not asking me to call Rafsānjaní directly," the president said.

"No, sir, because we can't take this any higher than SAVAK."

"One secret agency to another."

"Yes, Mr. President."

"But you want me to know what you're going to do."

Roswell nodded.

Reasoner looked at his national security adviser. "I asked for this, didn't I?"

Townsend didn't answer; none was expected.

"Go ahead," the president told Roswell.

"SAVAK will release Lane because we have proof that Saddam Hussein staged the raid on Bandar-é Emān to steal one of the submarines and a nuclear missile, and use it to attack Tel Aviv so that Iran would take the blame."

"Jesus Christ, is that true?" Townsend demanded.

"No. But it's what SAVAK wants to hear. Once Lane is released, our plan is for him to enter Iraq, infiltrate Hussein's desert hideout . . . and assassinate the man."

The president looked incredulous. "You can't be serious."

"Yes, Mr. President, I am serious about promising Sultaneh such a thing. But Bill Lane's real mission will be to act as bait for Yernin, who will come after him. When that happens we'll . . . take care of the man. In the meantime both you and Rafsānjaní will have deniability. No one in his right mind would believe that the United States and Iran could work in collusion on an assassination plot."

"Do you think it'll work?" Townsend asked, his voice hushed.

"I don't see that we have any other choice."

"Tom," the president said.

"Sir?"

"Don't ever run for public office."

"No, sir," Roswell said. "Do I have your authorization?"

"You don't need it," Reasoner said evenly. "Because what you're about to do will never have happened. It couldn't have happened. As you say, no one in his right mind would believe it."

"Yes, Mr. President." Roswell rose to go. At the door the president called to him.

"Wish Bill Lane good luck for me, Tom."

"Will do, sir."

NATIONAL SECURITY AGENCY
FORT MEADE, MARYLAND

Tehran was eight and a half hours ahead of the U.S. eastern seaboard, which by the time Roswell got back to his office put the time there at around eight in the evening. It was known after several years of intercepts

that General Sultaneh kept late office hours, rarely leaving SAVAK headquarters before ten in the evening, so the timing of the call would be perfect.

But Roswell hesitated a half-hour, bringing up Sultaneh's extensive file
on his monitor. "You can't be serious," the president had said to him.
Even now he didn't know if this insanity could be considered serious. He
doubted it. But since the Wall had come down and the Soviet Union had
collapsed, it seemed as if all the old rules of engagement—secret as well
as open—had completely changed. No one knew anything for sure any
longer.

While he stared at Sultaneh's image on the monitor he had NSA's computer find the SAVAK director and dial his blind number. The call was
connected after the third ring, but Sultaneh didn't answer until a full three
seconds had passed.

"This must be Mr. Thomas Roswell of the American National Security
Agency," Sultaneh said in English, his voice low, authoritative, unhesitant.

"How did you know?" Roswell asked, deciding not to be coy or indirect
with this man.

"Because my equipment can only tell me that this call has originated
outside Tehran, and my recording devices have been rendered inoperable
by some means. Your agency, Mr. Roswell, is the only organization in the
world with that capability."

"You have one of my people."

"Yes, we have your Mr. William Lane, in Iran illegally under a false
identity, defeating and crossing security barriers to spy on one of our
military installations. Crimes punishable by death. *In sha'Allah.*"

"Only in times of war."

"Iran is at war, Mr. Roswell. The jihad. We are fighting for our lives;
for a culture, need I remind you, that was already a thousand years old
by the time your country was born."

They were even. He'd admitted to the SAVAK director that NSA was
spying on Iran. And the old cleric had admitted that Lane was alive. It was
a start.

"I would like to offer you a trade, General," Roswell said.

"I will not bargain with you like a common street merchant. But say
your piece, I will listen."

Bullshit, Roswell said to himself.

"I have some intelligence information that is of great interest to your
country that I would be willing to share with you."

"In exchange for what?"

"Your goodwill."

Sultaneh chuckled. "Your proposal is as inventive as your technology."

"As you may be aware, the United States maintains a constellation of
three intelligence-gathering satellites in geosynchronous orbit a little over
twenty thousand miles above your head. These satellites are capable of
monitoring telephone conversations, military communications, television

and data broadcasts, and just about anything else that generates an electrical signal of any kind."

"I understand this," Sultaneh said, and Roswell could hear the old man's consternation. What he was being told was nothing new or startling, but that an American even admitted the satellites' existence, let alone bragged about them, was vexing.

"These satellites are also capable of sending us real-time television images that are often clear enough that we can read the print on a newspaper."

"They cannot see through concrete, or even clouds."

It was Roswell's turn to chuckle. "I won't get into that, General. Suffice it to say that we monitored the attack on your naval installation at Bandar-é Emān. The complete attack. The jet strikes on your base and offshore oil platforms. The LAW rocket strikes on the concealed air vents supplying your power station, as well as the small strike force that was set ashore. I'm told that you captured one alive. Congratulations."

"Yes."

"He is an Iraqi intelligence officer, working directly for Saddam Hussein. It speaks well of your people that you caught him, and that you have come that far with your investigation. But I am willing to tell you that we have proof that the attack on your naval installation was directed by Hussein, and we know why he attacked."

"I am still listening."

"Hussein meant to steal one of your submarines and use it to launch a nuclear strike on Tel Aviv while blaming Iran for the attack."

"Don't take me for a fool, Roswell. Only two men came ashore. One was killed on the base and the other we arrested."

"A capable submarine crew, trained by officers of the Ukrainian Black Sea Fleet, stood offshore waiting for the signal to come in."

"Impossible."

"I have proof, which I can transmit directly into your computer terminal through this line. Right now."

Hughes had set up the "evidence" using satellite data and images from the attack plus digitally generated images that showed soldiers aboard a freighter several miles offshore from the base. Some of the soldiers were in the process of donning wet suits and scuba equipment. All of them were heavily armed, and in Iraqi uniforms.

"What do you want?" Sultaneh demanded.

"Mr. Lane's immediate release, along with the release of the United Nations inspection team which your people are illegally detaining."

"Impossible."

With three keystrokes Roswell captured the computer terminal on the general's desk and began transmitting the images.

"I'm breaking the connection," Sultaneh warned.

"We have a common enemy. He is Saddam Hussein. It would be better if he were dead. Killed by a capable assassin. No one would mourn his loss."

"You are insane! An infidel!"

"My president knows nothing about this. I am doing this because Lane is my friend."

"No."

"He will do it for me."

"You are lying."

Roswell hesitated a beat, allowing more of the digital images he was sending to appear on Sultaneh's screen. "Perhaps I am."

"They will be executed in the public square."

"You would not risk the economic sanctions that would be placed on Iran. It would be much worse than before. Rafsānjaní's government would place the blame at your feet. And the mullahs would not thank you. Those submarines are heathen inventions. Satan's tools."

"You can do nothing. You are incapable of this act."

"There is the nuclear genie, *Hojatoleslam* Sultaneh. Once that knowledge is let out of the bottle, life is never the same."

"It is Iran's business . . ."

"It doesn't matter, *Imam*. If the world believed Iran had acquired nuclear weapons, then its relationship with Iran would be changed forever. Can your people stand up to such a thing? I think not."

"Where is the freighter at this moment?" Sultaneh asked after a moment.

"Somewhere in the Gulf. I'm not sure."

"Under what flag does she sail?"

"Ukraine."

"What name is this ship?"

"I won't give you any further information until Lane and the others are released. Unharmed."

"No."

"You have twenty-four hours. In the morning this will go to the White House, and will be made public almost immediately. The outcry will be great."

"It is of no consequence."

"Hussein's raid on Bandar-é Emān will be made public in Iran as well as the rest of the world." Roswell lowered his voice. "You cannot believe the strange bedfellows we Americans have cultivated to gain our ends."

"Infidel!"

"You already said that," Roswell replied. *"In sha'Allah.* Shall all of Iran be martyrs to the cause?"

26

The room was long and narrow, the floor, the walls, and the ceiling made of bare concrete. As through the last three interrogation sessions, Lane was seated naked on a metal stool in front of a long table behind which sat five Muslim clerics.

As best as he could determine, it was sometime in the evening of the second day of his capture, although he might have been unconscious for much longer than he thought. He felt like hell, because of the concussion he still was recovering from and from the effects of his treatment.

They had not hit or tortured him, but they had denied him any sleep by keeping him in a cell so small he could not lie down. Strong lights and harsh, very loud music continuously battered his senses, and each time he squatted in the corner and shut his eyes, his cell door clanged open and guards hustled him out into the corridor where he was made to do calisthenics while being sprayed with ice-cold seawater.

He was also denied food and drink other than tepid water and a thin gruel of brown rice with bits of vegetables. He had to relieve himself in a metal bucket chained to one corner. It had not been emptied since he arrived, and the stench in his airless cell was horrible. Worst of all, however, to his mind, was not being able to clean himself, to bathe or wash his hands and face, although the seawater sprays were better than nothing.

Of the five men in robes and head wraps, the one seated in the middle was the oldest, his long beard and thick eyebrows shot through with thick tufts of gray. His eyes were deep and wide-set, his features craggy. Lane figured he was in his sixties, and was probably the base commander that Frances told him about.

He searched his memory for the man's name. Frances said he was a strict traditionalist and therefore rabidly anti-Western, which made him dangerous. He would not respond to logic, and probably not to threats.

It was something like Razmaregh, he thought. Mullah of the mosque in Bandar-é Emān.

The cleric looked up from the file he'd been reading, the corners of his mouth downturned in a scowl. "You are an infidel. A nonbeliever, this much we understand clearly. And for this you deserve the death penalty. What we want to know is why you attacked this base twice in less than one week."

"I didn't attack you," Lane replied softly, willing his body to relax. Sitting on the stool was a relief. "May I have something to eat?" By now Frances would have called Hughes. Help was on the way.

"No," the mullah said. "The jet airplanes were American, as were the ground weapons. Are you denying this?"

"Saddam Hussein's people attacked you."

"Do you think we're stupid?" the base commander shouted.

Lane managed a slight smile, a couple of obvious comments coming immediately to mind. "I'll let you be the judge of that, Imam Razmaregh."

The mullahs were stunned that he knew the base commander's name. Razmaregh jumped up and snatched a pistol off the table, fire shooting from his eyes. He pointed the gun at Lane's head. "Lies!"

"SAVAK captured one of them in Tehran. Even tried to sell him to the CIA."

Keeping the pistol pointed at Lane's head, the old religious leader made his way around the table. "You won't leave this room alive, unless you tell us what we must know."

"Saddam Hussein sent his people here with the help of the Ukrainian KGB to find out if you had equipped your submarines with Russian-made nuclear cruise missiles. Apparently they were unsuccessful, because one of them was killed here, and the other captured, as I said, in Tehran."

The base commander's mouth was open, his teeth black and half rotted out of his head. He stank of strong body odor.

"I was sent by my government for the same reason. We've known about your submarines for a long time, but we weren't sure about the nuclear question." Lane looked up into the old man's eyes. He was seeing double again, and he had a blinding headache. "Now we are. So you should put me on the plane back to the States. You have nothing to hide. No nukes. Nothing showed up on my Geiger counter."

Razmaregh deliberately brought the muzzle of the gun to Lane's forehead. It was an old US military .45, the bluing gone in spots. It would be inaccurate as hell much beyond ten or fifteen feet, which was no comfort at this moment.

"Talk to me, spy."

"The truth?" Lane asked.

"*Aywa.*" Yes.

"I do think you're stupid."

The mullah pulled the hammer back.

"Your Excellency," one of the men at the table said softly.

"If you were smart you'd realize that you could use this situation to your advantage. Killing me will gain you nothing."

The mullah's gun hand shook.

"SAVAK would have a very good case for your removal. One less voice for Allah."

"Don't speak his name in my presence," the cleric screamed. He slashed the barrel of the pistol against Lane's head, opening a three-inch gash in his cheek and causing a billion stars to burst in his head.

With his strength almost gone, Lane managed to bat the old man's gun hand away and drive to his feet, shoving the cleric backward. He hooked his right foot behind the man's right leg, pulling him off balance, and as Razmaregh went down, he grabbed the automatic.

The other men at the table scrambled to their feet, but none of them was armed.

The door slammed open and two soldiers carrying Kalashnikov assault rifles crowded in.

Lane turned unsteadily on his heel and fired four shots in rapid succession, the first two hitting one of the soldiers in the chest, knocking him backward into the second guard. His next two shots took the second guard in the face and throat. Both soldiers were dead or dying before they hit the floor.

Razmaregh grabbed Lane by the leg and tried to bring him down, but Lane hit him in the side of the head with the butt of the .45. The cleric's eyes rolled up into the back of his head and he fell back, momentarily stunned.

Lane looked up at the four mullahs at the table. One of them hastily shouted instructions into a telephone. They stared at him in fear.

"You people wouldn't know objective truth if it bit you on the ass," Lane said.

He sprinted drunkenly across the room to the fallen guards where he exchanged the .45 for one of the Kalashnikov rifles and an extra magazine of ammunition.

The corridor was clear for the moment. But sirens started to wail, and from somewhere to the right he could hear shouting, and the sounds of dozens of footsteps pounding in his direction.

He turned left and headed down the corridor in a dead run, no idea where he was or where he was going.

Or how he was going to get rid of his headache and his double vision.

SAVAK HEADQUARTERS

Zahedi stood in front of General Sultaneh's desk, his hands behind his back like a schoolboy, scarcely believing what he was hearing.

The general was on the speaker phone with a highly agitated Razmaregh who was screaming about a major crisis. The American Bill Lane had somehow managed to escape minutes ago, killing two soldiers in the process and actually laying his hands on the person of the imam himself. For this the infidel dog would die.

"No," the general said. "Listen to me, my old friend. We need this infidel alive more urgently than dead. He is like a very hot and dangerous flame burning on a cold night with summer not in sight. He has singed our fingers, Imam, but as much as our very instincts cry for us to extinguish him, we must not."

"I do not understand, Your Excellency. He is an infidel spy. He has murdered young boys."

"Yes, he is an unbeliever, but he has not been shown the way."

"No," Razmaregh cried in anguish.

"You will capture Mr. Lane, but you will not harm him. I am sending Colonel Zahedi by helicopter to take charge of your prisoner. I expect him to be in your control, bathed, clothed, fed, and ready for transport. Do I make myself clear?"

Razmaregh made a strangling sound. "I will try."

"I should hope so," the general said. "You have work to do. I suggest you get on with it, Your Holiness."

Sultaneh pushed the disconnect button. For a moment he stared at his hands, but then he looked up into Zahedi's eyes.

"As I was saying, Colonel, we are getting our wish. We are finally going to get rid of Mr. Lane and the meddling United Nations team of spies."

"But he penetrated base security, almost certainly with the technical advice and assistance of Commander Shipley."

"You're probably right."

"It means they know—"

"They know what, Colonel?" Sultaneh asked gently, like a father might ask a son. "That we have four operationally ready submarines? You yourself showed two of the UN spies our boats."

"The nuclear question."

"Those submarines are not equipped with nuclear missiles. The Iraqi infiltrators got no proof. The United Nations spies can prove nothing. And Mr. Lane gathered no information. We have nothing to hide."

"Yes, Your Excellency."

"You have done your job. All that remains is for you to fetch Mr. Lane from Bandar-é Emān. Bring him back here, and make sure that he and the entire UN team are aboard the first airplane out of Iran."

"Yes, Your Excellency."

"This task will be accomplished by morning."

There was more. Zahedi could feel it. "Then what, General?"

Sultaneh smiled, but there was no warmth in the expression. "Then your real job will begin."

"Am I to know what this job will be?"

"Not yet, my son. But suffice it to say when Mr. Lane leaves Iran, it will not be the last time you see him."

TEHRAN: *PRAVDA'S* OFFICES

Yernin turned off the recorder after listening to the taped telephone conversation between the director of SAVAK and the mullah in charge of the navy base at Bandar-é Emān.

"This answers one of your questions," Sorokin said respectfully. "But for the moment it seems as if the Iraqi they captured has disappeared. I think it's possible they killed him."

"Never mind about him," Yernin said. "What's happening with Lane? Why are they bringing him back here? Why not simply kill him? Something is going on that we don't know."

Sorokin spread his hands.

"Why hasn't a continuous tap been maintained on Sultaneh's telephones?"

"It'd be too dangerous, Colonel. We'd be discovered."

"There are methods."

"With proper budgets. It's expensive."

"Can we monitor SAVAK radio frequencies?"

"Most of the time."

"Then we can find out when and where Lane will be arriving with this Colonel Zahedi?"

"Almost certainly."

Yernin eyed the obese man with disgust. "Can you supply me with a couple of shooters?"

"Killers?"

"Yes. Someone reliable. Someone expendable."

Sorokin shuddered. "I think so."

"Very well. I'll kill Mr. William Lane before he leaves Tehran, and you and your shooters will provide my diversion."

27

The alarm hadn't spread to the sub pens yet. The four boats lay low and quiet in the water. Strong lights bathed the huge cavern, casting strange shadows on the docks, the walls, the catwalks, and the submarines themselves.

Armed guards were stationed on the dock at the bow of each vessel, but so far as Lane could tell there was no activity aboard the warships.

He crouched in the darkness behind a pile of steel plating and welding equipment thirty feet from the water's edge on the western side of the facility. His head was pounding and his legs were rubbery. The nearest guards were sixty feet away, but they were looking in his direction, making it impossible for him to reach the water.

He had formed his plan on the way through the facility, when he'd found out that he was still in the submarine command center. Taking the base commander hostage would have done no good because the man was a Muslim cleric. A revolutionary soldier in Iran's jihad against the West. It meant that the old man would rather die a martyr than let himself be used that way. His troops would understand and respect this.

But one of their submarines was a different story. Another mullah could always be found. But an operational sub was a very expensive item. One that, given the present world climate, the Russians might not be able to replace.

Lane tightened his grip on the assault rifle. There were a lot of ways to permanently wreck a submarine, especially if it was loaded with operational weapons—specifically high-explosive torpedoes.

But any method he could think of depended upon getting aboard one of the subs. Something that was seemingly impossible at the moment.

If he opened up on the two nearest guards with the Kalashnikov, they wouldn't have one chance in a hundred of surviving. But the shooting would bring the other guards down to the docks, and he'd be bogged down in a firefight that he could not win.

He needed a diversion. Something to attract the guards' attention toward the opposite direction.

He crawled to the end of the pile of steel and edged around the corner. He was still in the shadows, but now he was much closer to the two soldiers guarding the nearest submarine. They were talking about something, and laughing, still facing the direction Lane would have to go in order to get aboard the boat.

A diversion was provided for him when sirens began wailing, echoing off the walls and high ceiling of the cavern.

The two guards spun around, bringing their weapons up.

Lane leaped to his feet and, keeping low, raced across the dock to the two soldiers. He smashed the butt of the heavy Russian assault rifle into the skull of the first guard. As the second man started to turn back, Lane kicked him in the back of the legs, and when he went down, hit him square in the jaw with the rifle stock, knocking him unconscious.

No one noticed the commotion.

Lane crossed to the edge of the dock in four steps and raced out onto the finger pier, keeping the hull of the submarine between him and the concentration of soldiers at the opposite side of the cavern.

The forward loading hatches of the sub were closed. Only the escape trunk was open aft of the sail. The conning tower hatch was probably open to provide ventilation below. He needed to secure both entrances to the submarine before the soldiers got to him.

A neat trick, he thought, if there were crew aboard. Their best intelligence guesstimates were that trained crewmen were so few in Iran's navy, unless the submarines were being prepared for a mission they were guarded but not manned.

But that was just a guess. Nothing more.

Conscious that his bare white skin stood out in sharp contrast against the submarine's black hull and deck, Lane took only a second to make certain no one was in the escape trunk before he scrambled down the ladder. He pulled the hatch closed and dogged it, then climbed the rest of the way down into the stores room just aft of the crew's main mess, which in turn was aft and below the control room and attack center beneath the conning tower tunnel.

He stopped to listen for several seconds to let his heart slow down. He was having trouble keeping on track. The submarine was deathly still except for the faint whir of ventilator fans. The air smelled of cloves and some other spice on top of diesel oil. He closed and dogged the inner hatch, sliding the locking bolts in place so that the hatch could not be opened from above.

The interior of the submarine was dimly lit. Lane hurried through the empty crew's mess and noiselessly took the ladder up to the control room. Because of the darkness he almost missed the man standing below the tunnel, looking up into the sail. The conning tower hatch had to be open, because Lane could hear the sirens outside.

The man was an officer with silver pips on his uniform shoulder boards. Sensing a motion behind him, he turned suddenly as Lane made it all the way up through the hatch and swung the Kalashnikov up.

"I hope for your sake, pal, that you speak English," Lane said.

The officer stared at the naked apparition standing in his control room pointing an assault rifle at him. The sight was almost impossible to believe. But he nodded. "Yes, I speak some English."

"Who else is aboard this boat?"

The officer shook his head. "There is a crew of fifty-five men and officers."

"How many are aboard tonight? Right now?"

Understanding dawned in the man's eyes. "Ah, I see. No, there is no one here. Only me"—he stopped himself in midsentence, suddenly realizing what was happening—"and ten armed soldiers," he finished lamely.

"Nice try." Lane grinned tiredly. "Now listen carefully, because you're going to have to get this right when you tell it to your people."

Another connection was made in the officer's mind. "You're the American spy who we caught yesterday."

"That's right. Once you leave this boat I'll lock the conning tower hatch. The other hatches are locked as well. I'm going to set a torpedo to explode on my command unless my demands are met."

"Impossible," the officer said.

"The torpedo will be in one of the tubes, armed, but with the outer doors closed. I will be in the attack center where I'll press the fire button."

"But that would cause the torpedo to launch, and explode in its tube," the Iranian said. "Destroying this boat, and killing you in the process."

"*In sha'Allah,*" Lane replied. "Get the hell off my boat."

The officer hesitated, one ear cocked to the open hatch above.

"Now," Lane said. "Or I'll kill you."

The man backed up and reached for the ladder. "How will we know what you want?"

"I'll call you on one of your radio channels. Go!"

"You allowed this man to do what?" Zahedi demanded of the base commander.

"You will take care how you speak to me, Colonel," Mullah Razmaregh said, his words much harsher than his tone. He was a frightened man.

"He murdered two of your personal guards, disabled two others, and hijacked a submarine, all of that in the middle of a full-base alert, and all of it while not wearing a stitch of clothes, and after little or no sleep for nearly two days and little or no food."

"If I am allowed to do my job he would be dead by now," the cleric complained.

"If you had done your job in the first place we would not be at this point."

"We can force one of the hatches . . ."

"He will destroy the submarine."

"He's not capable."

"If he says he can do it, I believe him. He is a capable man. He's been aboard all night. Plenty of time to prepare some nasty surprise for us."

"An infidel!"

Zahedi turned and studied the submarine at the end of the quay. "Yes, an infidel."

"Death to—"

"No," Zahedi interrupted, turning back to the mullah. "There are other plans, Your Excellency. Let SAVAK deal with him and you may continue your excellent work administering to the needs of this installation."

"Are you suggesting that we meet his demands, and contact the American Interests section in Tehran?"

"No need for it," Zahedi replied. "He *radioed* his demands to you."

"I don't understand."

"He didn't use shore-link telephone. He used a radio frequency that his agency regularly monitors. They know by now where he is and what is happening here."

The mullah looked stunned.

"This is my job now, Your Excellency. I'll handle it."

Earlier the periscope had raised two meters out of its shaft, and it was presumed that Lane was watching them. Zahedi grabbed a walkie-talkie, stepped away from the hastily erected sandbag barrier, and, keeping his hands in plain sight, walked alone down the dock.

Fifty meters from the submarine, the periscope turned toward him. He stopped and raised the walkie-talkie. "Bill Lane, can you hear me?"

"Yes," Lane's reply came immediately.

"I'm Colonel Amin Zahedi. I was sent from Tehran to bring you back to the airport where you and Lieutenant Commander Shipley and the others on the UN team are to be deported."

"Come aboard. We'll discuss it."

"As you wish."

Zahedi walked the rest of the way to the submarine, jumped aboard, and entered the boat through the conning tower hatch left slightly ajar.

"Lock it," Lane instructed once Zahedi was inside.

He complied, then climbed down into the control room. Lane, dressed in a crewman's coveralls, short boots on his feet, was seated at the chart table, a .45-caliber pistol from the boat's weapons locker on the table within easy reach. A bandage covered the gash on his cheek.

"You gave us all a merry chase, Mr. Lane. One for which the base commander would like to see your head on a pike."

"Who sent you?" Lane asked directly.

The identity of SAVAK's director was a closely guarded secret in Iran. "General Sultaneh," Zahedi said without hesitation. "He and Thomas Roswell spoke about you at some length. It was extraordinary."

"You said the UN team is to be deported. Why?"

"They have been arrested and charged with espionage. May I sit down?"

"No."

"It seems as if everyone knows that we have submarines, that we do not have nuclear missiles aboard them, and that Saddam Hussein ordered the attack on us to steal one of our boats and use it under cover of our flag to attack Israel. Fanciful, but deadly if his plan had succeeded." Zahedi shrugged. "You're a spy, but the secrets we were trying to guard are no longer secret. Detaining you, and the others, and putting you on trial would result in nothing but sanctions against us."

"What else?"

"We want our submarine back, and you gone from Iran."

Lane smiled tiredly. "I'm supposed to lay down my weapons and walk out of here with you, that right? Nothing will happen to me, except that I'll get booted out of the country?"

"Something like that," Zahedi answered.

"From the airport at Tehran?"

Zahedi looked at his watch. "A flight leaves at eight this morning. Gives us just enough time to chopper you up there."

"No," Lane said. "One of our aircraft from Kuwait City will be sent to Tehran within the hour to pick up the UN delegation."

"Impossible."

"When I have confirmation that they are safely out of Iran, a helicopter from the guided-missile cruiser *Mississippi*, which at this moment is less than one hundred miles from here, will come to pick me up."

"Such incursions into our airspace will not be allowed."

"I suggest you try for it, Colonel." Lane motioned toward the bank of radio equipment on the forward bulkhead. One of the transmit lights glowed. "Everything we've said here has been transmitted. My people are monitoring this channel."

Zahedi had to smile. The infidel was good. "I'll see what I can do."

"I'll be here," Lane said.

TEHRAN

Yernin watched from the second-floor window of his apartment off Nōfl Lōshātō Street around the corner from the Russian embassy as Sorokin got out of his car and came in. There was something about the way the portly man moved, the set of his shoulders, his bowed head, that was bothersome.

Something had gone wrong, and the instant Sorokin appeared in the doorway Yernin knew that it was bad. He worked to control his temper.

"Lane isn't coming back here," he said. He took a miniature tape recorder from his jacket pocket and clicked it on.

"*One of our aircraft from Kuwait City will be sent to Tehran within the hour to pick up the UN delegation.*"

"*Impossible.*"

"*When I have confirmation that they are safely out of Iran, a helicopter from the guided-missile cruiser* Mississippi, *which at this moment is less than one hundred miles from here, will come to pick me up.*"

"Who is the man speaking with Lane?"

"Colonel Amin Zahedi. SAVAK. He'll get what he wants. Lane is definitely leaving Iran this morning, but not through Tehran."

"I will go to Kuwait City."

"I have the shooters. Shall we go after Commander Shipley and the others?"

Yernin looked at him and shook his head. "Your excellent work on this mission is completed, Aleksandr Nikolaevich. We shall have no further contact."

"Very well, Colonel," Sorokin said with relief. "I am happy that I was able to be of some assistance."

Yernin turned away, and after an awkward moment Sorokin let himself out.

28

Lane stood braced against the periscope column as Colonel Zahedi came down the quay. The SAVAK colonel carried a walkie-talkie and a bundle of clothing.

The soldiers had been moved out of the submarine docking cavern ten minutes ago. Since then there'd been no activity until Zahedi's radioed message that he was on his way back.

Forty-five minutes earlier, Lane had spoken briefly with Frances aboard a navy VC-10 Gulfstream jet which had just cleared Iranian airspace and was minutes away from touching down at Kuwait's International Airport.

He heard the strain in her voice, but she assured him that all was well, and wished him good luck.

He turned away from the periscope and took a microphone down from the overhead. "*Mississippi*, this is Lane. Copy?"

"Lane, this is Navy zero-one-six-zero, inbound your position. What's your situation?"

"I'm still aboard the sub. What's your ETA and where will you set down?"

"We're about twelve minutes out. We're touching down right above you on the roof. We're a LAMPS II Seasprite."

"If I'm not in sight when you come in, don't land. Turn around and get the hell out of there. Copy?"

"Yes, sir, we copy," the navy helicopter pilot replied. He sounded young. "But we've been ordered to extract you at whatever costs. The *Mississippi* is standing by. Her weapons radars have your position illuminated."

"Mr. Lane will be in position on time, and you will be unchallenged," Zahedi's voice broke in.

"Who's on this frequency?" the pilot demanded.

"SAVAK," Lane replied. "Do whatever you need to do."

"Roger."

Lane replaced the mike, then went up into the sail and undogged the hatch.

Zahedi came aboard and tossed the bundle of clothes on the weapons plot table. He was glaring.

"We're not going to start a war over you, Mr. Lane. You're not that important to us."

"That's nice to hear," Lane said. "Put the radio down, turn around, put your hands above your head on the bulkhead, and spread your legs."

Zahedi complied. Lane stuffed the pistol in the belt of his coveralls and quickly frisked the SAVAK colonel. The man was unarmed.

"I suggest you hurry if you want to make your rendezvous."

"Stay there," Lane said. He laid the gun on the weapons plot table, took off the boots and coveralls, and quickly got dressed in his own, dark clothing. His wallet and other personal things were there, as was the Beretta and spare magazine.

"Are you ready?" Zahedi asked.

"So far you've done everything right, Colonel. But you're going to be a very dead man at the slightest hint of trouble."

Zahedi looked Lane in the eye, and nodded. "Don't come back to Iran. Next time the advantage will be mine."

"You're not a mullah, and unless I miss my guess you were educated outside of Iran. So how do you swallow all of this?"

"Is that what you want? To get into a religious debate with me?" Zahedi asked angrily.

"Next time," Lane said.

Zahedi shook his head. "There won't be a next time if I can help it." He motioned toward the hatch above.

"After you."

Zahedi climbed up the ladder and ducked through the hatch. He moved several feet away so that Lane wouldn't feel crowded.

"We have seven minutes," he said.

Lane remained in the protection of the submarine's superstructure for a half-minute. The cavern was well lit, but there were deep shadows everywhere. A hundred marksmen could be hidden and he wouldn't see them.

But like the man said, they weren't going to war over him.

"Okay," he said.

Zahedi jumped down to the finger pier first, and Lane came directly after him, narrowing the gap between them to an arm's length before they reached the quay.

"We'll take the weapons loading elevator to the ground floor, and then the stairs to the roof," Zahedi said. "The route is being guarded but no one will interfere with us unless you make a stupid move."

They headed down the quay and Lane thought he might have spotted one or two marksmen up in the catwalks, but he wasn't sure. In any event it wouldn't matter. If they wanted to stop him, there was nothing he could do.

The big freight elevator was open and waiting when they reached the end of the quay. At the top they took a broad corridor to the stairway, pairs of armed soldiers stationed at intervals of thirty or forty feet.

Two stories up, a steel door opened onto the roof of the administration building. The helicopter landing area was on the west side, away from the communications antennae. Lane took the walkie-talkie from the Iranian.

"Navy zero-one-six-zero, this is Lane. I'm on the roof."

"Stand by, we're two minutes out."

"Roger."

"Is it so important that we don't have an atomic bomb?" Zahedi asked.

"Very," Lane replied. It was tough to pick out the helicopter's navlights against the rising sun and the backdrop of the oil platforms out to sea. But he spotted the red and white lights moving fast and low across the water.

"Doesn't Iran have the same rights as other nations? France? China? Russia?" Zahedi demanded.

"Your government supports terrorists."

"It is a means of defense—"

"Bullshit, pal. Terrorism against innocent people is no defense against anything. It's plain and simply mindless violence."

"Like Hiroshima or Nagasaki?"

Lane studied the man. "You're better educated than that. You can come up with something a little more original. Or maybe I've misjudged you after all."

"Heathen."

"The word is infidel," Lane shot back. "Are you aware that more people have been killed in the name of religion in the past two thousand years than for any other single principle? Or don't you care? Don't you people read your own Koran, which preaches nonviolence?"

"Don't presume to teach me my faith."

"Faith my ass. I'll bet you a hundred to one that you're a nonbeliever."

They could hear the incoming helicopter now.

Zahedi glanced out to sea. "If I see you in Iran again I will kill you." He looked at Lane as if to memorize his face, then turned and walked away.

"We have you spotted," the chopper pilot radioed.

"Roger, Navy. You're clear as far as I can tell," Lane answered.

He watched Zahedi go back into the building. He had a feeling that he'd be seeing the SAVAK colonel again, sooner or later. Probably sooner.

A half-minute later the Kaman SH-2F LAMPS helicopter touched down with a tremendous roar in a flurry of dust. Lane scrambled aboard and the chopper lifted off with a sickening lurch, swooped to the right, and dove for the water, the pilot firewalling the throttle to make all possible speed.

FAILAKA ISLAND
OFF THE COAST OF KUWAIT

The safe house was on the site of a fourth-century B.C. Greek garrison of Alexander the Great's. The two-story building itself had housed the island's administrator and his family before the first Gulf War. After the second war it had been abandoned, although the eight-mile-by-three-mile island was Kuwait's most important archaeological site, and parts of it were still visited. Since the destruction of the second Gulf War was greater than that of the first, Kuwait was putting all of its rebuilding efforts into the necessities of here and now. The past would be taken care of later.

The emir, Sheikh Jabir al-Ahmad as-Sabah, and his family owed the United States a large debt of gratitude. So the island had been used as a forward listening post and radar site, as well as a small emergency air force base. Those facilities were closed now, but if trouble were to come again, they could be up and fully operational with units from nearby Saudi Arabia within six hours.

Security around the island was provided by patrol boats and surveillance units from the *Mississippi* or whatever other US cruisers, battleships, or aircraft carriers were on patrol in the northern Gulf. And there was always at least one major US flag vessel in the region.

The chopper that had come for Lane had flown weapons-light with extra fuel tanks to give the 445-nautical-mile machine an extra margin of safety. It touched down fifty yards from the safe house a few minutes before ten in the morning. Already the sun was heating up the desert island for what promised to be a beautiful, cloudless day.

"Thanks for the lift," Lane shouted up to the pilot.

"Glad to oblige, sir," the young man replied with a grin. He gave Lane the thumbs-up sign, lifted off, and headed back to his ship in the Gulf.

Lane watched, shading his eyes against the glare, until the chopper was out of sight. When he turned, Hughes was there, a lopsided grin on his pudgy face.

"Moira and the girls have been beside themselves with worry, William."

Lane grinned tiredly. "Sharing state secrets with your family, Tommy?"

"Don't have to. They're mind readers. Are you all right?"

"I've been better, but I suspect I'll live."

"Good. It'll save a lot of bothersome paperwork if you do."

They headed up to the house, which sat on a low rise overlooking the open Gulf to the east. A fair wind was blowing, and whitecaps marched steadily into the bay below.

"Frances is here," Hughes said.

"How is she?"

"Mad as hell, but she wanted to stick around to see you. We sent Captain Reilly back with the others." Hughes eyed his friend shrewdly. "Is there something going on between Frances and Reilly, or was it just my imagination?"

"I think they're friends. Why?"

"He wanted her to return with him. They got into a row over it, but the lady was adamant."

"Has she contacted her own people yet?"

"No. She insisted on seeing you first. Something we should know about, William? Because we've got plenty for you to chew on."

"Let's wait so I only have to tell it once," Lane said.

29

FAILAKA ISLAND SAFE HOUSE

Inside the front hall they were met by two security guards, one of them an American from the National Security Agency, but the other a Kuwaiti from the Special Palace Guard, which was the emirate's secret police.

"Are you armed, Mr. Lane?" the tall, heavyset American asked politely.

"Two automatics. One the CIA supplied me with, and the other I lifted from an Iranian submarine."

"If you'll just leave them here, I'll take care of them, sir."

"Sure." Lane turned over the weapons and the two men moved off. He glanced up to the head of the stairs.

Two other guards, one of them big and bulky, the other small and dark, probably another Kuwaiti, were watching. They were armed with Mac-10 compact submachine guns. Whatever was going on here was no mere debriefing.

Hughes followed his gaze. "Security's tight. Roswell's people insisted on it."

"Did he come over with you?"

Hughes nodded. "He and Frances are waiting for us in the library. But we'll get you something to eat first. They'll understand."

"Who else is here?" Lane asked.

"Just the guards."

"Who else knows that Roswell came to talk to me?"

"Only the president and Bill Townsend."

"Short list, Tommy."

Hughes looked uncomfortable. "I'll let him tell you about it."

Lane studied his friend's face. "No problem, kemo sabe. I'll eat later."

"Shit," Hughes said.

Lane and Hughes went back to the huge, palatially appointed Arabic library where NSA Director Thomas Roswell and Frances waited.

"Hello, Bill," Roswell said. "We're happy to have you back in one piece. Are you all right?"

"I feel like hell, but I'll survive, sir."

Frances was seated in front of the fireplace. She got up, and stood shivering as if she were in pain.

"We'll make this initial session brief so that you can get some rest. Then we'll pick it up again later tonight or tomorrow morning."

"William?" Frances said in a small voice.

"I wouldn't have gotten out of there without your help, Frannie. Thanks. I owe you one."

She wanted to go to him, but she restrained herself. The effort showed on her face. "I got you into it in the first place. Least I could do was blow the whistle."

He winked at her, then turned back to Roswell. "The Iranians have no nukes aboard their submarines, but they're ready, willing, and able to get them."

Roswell motioned for them to sit down. "I understand that you spent a night aboard one of their boats."

"They weren't happy about it. But if they had stopped to think about what I was getting into, they might not have been so ready to let me out of there."

"What did you find, specifically?"

"About half the charts, manuals, and orders are in Farsi and Arabic, but the rest are in Russian, which I read. Their torpedo tubes can accept the new SS-N-sixteen, but unless they were carrying nuclear weapons they wouldn't need blast range charts and radiation detection equipment. Both of which I found aboard."

"What else?"

"Two of the torpedo storage racks were empty. The top two. Which I took to mean that they were getting ready to load something."

"No residual radiation to suggest those racks might have held nuclear missiles?" Hughes asked.

"Not a trace, Tommy. Or anywhere else aboard the boat for that matter."

"Any indications of a timetable for when they might get such weapons?" Roswell asked, his eyes glittering.

"Not that I saw."

"Did you bring any of that material out with you?"

"I didn't think it wise under the circumstances," Lane said.

"You're right, of course. Still, some hard evidence would have been helpful."

"You'll just have to take my word, Mr. Director," Lane bridled. His nerves were raw.

"I didn't mean it the way it sounded, Bill," Roswell apologized. "But the fact of the matter is that some hard data *would* be helpful."

Lane nodded his agreement.

"Did you see any evidence of the faction fight between the religious right and the secular moderates?" Frances asked.

"I met the base commander you warned me about. But it was a SAVAK colonel who got me out of there. Name of Zahedi."

"Amin Zahedi," Hughes interjected. "He was educated in the US. UCLA. A real moderate, and with any luck he'll go places unless they kill him first."

Lane shot his friend a sharp look. "What are you telling me, Tommy? That this was a setup?"

"Yes, it was," Roswell said. "Hughes came to me after Commander Shipley called, and I took it to the White House. I was authorized to pull a few strings to gain your release. Which I did."

"What strings?" Lane demanded.

"Later," Roswell said.

Lane glanced at Frances. "If you're trying to keep her out of the loop, I think it's a little late."

"I disagree."

"Send her out of the room, if you want, but I'll tell her later."

"No."

"Yes, I will, Mr. Director. Because it was her life on the line back there."

"In that case she would have to remain with us until the mission fully develops," Roswell said carefully.

"Valeri Yernin may have followed you to Tehran," Hughes said. "It means he's stalking you."

"And Commander Shipley, unless she's cut out right now," Roswell warned.

"If he tracked me that far, then he knows about Frances by now," Lane said resignedly. He turned to her. "You're going to have to stick around. Can you pull that off without causing too much of a fuss?"

"Not as a prisoner," she said after a beat. "I think that I could be temporarily assigned to your shop," she told Roswell.

"You would be better off out of this," the NSA director cautioned. "It could get sticky. And besides, I'm not sure that I could authorize placing you in the loop."

"Without her you don't have me," Lane said.

Roswell sighed deeply. "Why do I have the feeling that I've just been railroaded?"

"Go with the flow, sir," Hughes advised solemnly. "I've been doing it for a long while now. And after the first couple of times it doesn't hurt so bad. Honest."

Roswell nodded. "I'll see what I can do."

"What strings?" Lane asked.

Roswell looked at him bleakly. "I telephoned General Sultaneh, director of SAVAK, and told him we wanted you back."

"That was inventive."

"He agreed."

"Apparently he did," Lane said. "What was the offer? That I assassinate Saddam Hussein for them?"

Roswell was startled. "Why, yes, that's exactly what I offered him."

It was late. They had agreed that Lane needed rest, and Roswell needed time to arrange a transfer for Frances from the SIS. They would start again in the morning.

A light sea breeze had picked up, and the evening had become chilly. Lane stood at the open window of his second-floor bedroom smoking a cigarette and looking out to sea at the lights.

This part of the Gulf was especially busy with oil platforms and offshore loading facilities. He could pick out the slow-moving lights of surface ships, some of them undoubtedly military, as well as the strobe lights of commercial and military aircraft. This was a busy, tense section of the world. Soon to be made even more tense if Roswell's insane proposal were for real.

"Don't let them make you do it," Frances said from the open door behind him.

He saw her reflection in the mirror above the bureau beside him.

"I might not have the choice," he replied softly. He could smell her delicately clean feminine scent.

"We're the good boys and girls. We don't do things like that, William."

"Should we have sent an assassin in 1938 to kill Adolf Hitler? Knowing what we know now? Would our hands have been dirty or clean?"

He turned to look at her. She wore one of the white terry-cloth robes every room was supplied with. Her skin was luminescent in the starlight. "Could we have lived with our consciences?" he asked.

Frances closed and locked the door, then came across the room to him.

They looked into each other's eyes, until Lane pulled her to him, and she came willingly.

"Oh, hell, William, I was afraid for you."

"It's okay."

"For the moment. But if they want you to kill Hussein you'll do it for them."

"I don't think it'll come to that."

"But if it does you won't walk away from it."

"Probably not, Frannie. But that's who I am. Can't change a leopard's spots."

Frances looked up into his eyes again, hers glistening in the soft light. "I love you."

He put a finger to her lips. "Later, when we have more time." He carried her to the bed and laid her down. He opened her robe, the sight of her body exciting him as it always had.

Later, he said to himself and he went into her arms.

30

Before breakfast, Lane and Hughes went for a walk down a stony path to the beach. The sun was coming up but the morning was still cool. The air smelled of a combination of seawater, oil, and refinery gas. It was the smell of money. Kuwait still had the richest oil deposits of any country in the world.

"No one believes we're serious about this assassination scheme, but we're all acting as if it's going ahead," Hughes said.

"Why the big lie, Tommy? If the press gets on to it, there'll be hell to pay."

"There're already a lot of puckered cheeks over at the White House. But how did you figure it out?"

"It was the only way of getting me out of Iran not in a body bag." Lane stopped his friend. "Okay, nobody believes I'm going to kill Hussein, yet they let me out of there. What's going on?"

"I wanted to eliminate some possibilities. The raid could have been staged by the Israelis, or even by the Kuwaitis, or by any number of anti-Iran factions. Maybe even by SAVAK in an effort to loosen the mullahs' grip on things."

"Either the Iraqis staged the raid for the reasons we told the Iranians. Or the raid was a big fake to make us think Iraq was after them. I don't know which is worse."

"Valeri Yernin is the key," Hughes said. "If we can get to him, we could find out for sure."

They started to walk again, and Lane lit a cigarette. Hughes declined.

"They knew I was coming. They were waiting for me in the sub pens."

"Was anything disturbed at the equipment drop?"

"Not that I could see. But there could have been surveillance on the drop point."

"They would have arrested you then and there. Which means they didn't know the location of your equipment cache, but did know that you were coming."

"Who knew besides you?" Lane asked.

"Ben Lewis and Roswell."

"How about the president's national security adviser?"

Hughes nodded his head sadly. They both knew where the conversation was leading. "What about your side of the world? Was there anyone other than Frances and Captain Reilly who knew your timetable?"

"No."

"Could SAVAK have eavesdropped?"

"It's possible but not likely," Lane said. "We took a lot of precautions. We got rid of the bugs in the hotel room, and Reilly set up a white-noise generator while we went over the layout of the subs and the base."

"How about Reilly?"

"Check his record."

"Already have," Hughes said. "He's as innocent as a newborn babe."

"Doesn't leave much, Tom."

"Yeah," Hughes replied.

They stopped at the edge of a low limestone cliff overlooking a small bay. As far as they could see in every direction were oil installations. The shipping traffic was particularly heavy this morning.

"This is a bad one, William," Hughes warned. "I have a terrible feeling in my gut."

"What's Roswell going to tell us?"

"I don't know. He hasn't shared his great wisdom with me." Hughes looked at his watch. "Speaking of which, it's time."

"I'm counting on you to backstop me, Tommy."

Hughes nodded. "I'll be there, William."

THE SAFE HOUSE

The wind had started to pick up again as Lane and Hughes trudged up the path from the sea to the safe house. A different pair of guards, one American and one Kuwaiti, checked them in, and they went back to the study.

Roswell was speaking on a telephone that was connected to what looked like a laptop computer that in turn transmitted an encrypted wireless signal to the roof where several small satellite dishes were positioned.

He waved them to the couch and chairs in front of the fireplace without interrupting his phone call. He was speaking, they could see his lips moving, but they could not hear his voice. A soft hiss came from the handset, and Lane recognized it for what it was: white noise, which effectively blocked his words from anyone else within earshot.

He hung up after a minute. "Have you two had breakfast yet?"

"No," Lane said.

"Well, it'll have to wait. I'm leaving in a half-hour and there're some things I need to get straight with you first."

"Where is Frances?" Lane asked.

"Commander Shipley will *not* be included in our discussions for the time being. Not until her service agrees to detach her to us. Something, frankly I don't think they'll do. In fact it's likely that she'll be recalled from her job with the UN. She was supposed to be there under cover."

"She may not want to go home," Lane said.

"Be that as it may. She's a British citizen, not an American. So there's nothing I can do. In the meantime you two have a job to finish."

"First I'll need to make sure that she's protected."

"That is her government's responsibility."

"I don't go any further until I have your word that she'll be taken care of," Lane said sharply. "She saved my life, and we are not turning our backs on her."

Hughes grinned sheepishly. "I'm sorry, sir, but I'm going to have to request maternity leave. I think Moira is pregnant again. And I'm going to have to be with her."

Roswell studied them. "Ben Lewis said you might try to pull a stunt like this."

"I don't know what you're talking about, Mr. Director," Lane said innocently.

"I could fire you."

"Yes, sir. But at least provide the three of us with transportation back to the mainland so we can get to the airport."

Hughes looked at Lane, who grinned. "We could take the ferry, William. That way we wouldn't be a bother to the director."

"Good idea. I'll tell Frances."

Roswell threw up his hands. "He also said that I would lose." He smiled wryly. "She can remain here, under guard, until your mission is resolved. Afterwards it'll be up to her and her government. I won't interfere."

"Fair enough," Lane agreed. "But you're not serious about sending me after Hussein, are you?"

"Of course not. But all of us are going to operate as if this were a legitimate mission in progress."

"Did General Sultaneh believe you?"

Roswell shrugged. "He arranged for your release. Which means he's hoping that we'll keep Hussein's fanatics at bay long enough."

"For what?"

"For Iran to fully develop its nuclear program. We believe that the Russians may be on the verge of selling them nuclear missiles."

"Chernenkov's people?" Lane asked. Captain-General Vasily Chernenkov was a fanatical right-wing military commander who wanted to overthrow the democratically elected government, replacing it with a Stalin-type dictatorship with himself in the top spot. He was popular in Russia with only a small faction of the military and some ex-communists. But he did have nominal command of a nuclear battalion in the southeast. By supplying Iran with nuclear weapons in secret, Chernenkov could later make a strong case for a preemptive strike against Tehran. He would be seen as a strong military leader, and a hero of the Soviet peoples who helped save them from a nuclear terrorist threat from the south. Lane had outlined the possibility six months ago.

"Reasoner is finally taking your suggestion seriously."

"Maybe all of this is a disinformation plot after all," Lane suggested.

"I thought it was possible until your old friend Valeri Yernin moved from Mexico City and showed up in Damascus, then Tehran. If your analysis of the satellite photos over Bandar-é Emān was correct, and the Ukrainian government is indeed on Hussein's side, that definitely makes you a threat."

"The key is Yernin," Lane said tight-lipped. "I have a score to settle with him anyway."

"You'll be killing two birds with one stone when you go after him. If you can stop him, it will hurt Hussein. And no matter what, it'll convince Iran that we're serious about keeping nukes out of the region. Serious enough to go after anybody who tries to introduce them. Ukrainian or Russian."

Another thought suddenly occurred to Lane. "What else did you and General Sultaneh agree to?"

"It was his suggestion, after the fact, and it made sense to me," Roswell said uncomfortably. "I told him that Yernin might be in Tehran. The general called, and told me that two SAVAK officers were killed trying to arrest a man fitting Yernin's description. So he is keen on catching up with the man."

"We'll send them the autopsy photos and DNA results after Yernin is dead."

"The CIA will help you with this," Roswell continued, ignoring Lane's remark. "In addition we have ten of our people here, and the Kuwaiti Special Palace Guard has agreed to cooperate. They have no love lost for Hussein, of course. But they're not exactly buddies with the government in Tehran either."

"What was the general's suggestion?"

"That you're to have help catching Yernin."

"Someone from SAVAK?"

"Primarily an observer," Roswell said. "Unless for some reason you need to go back into Iran, then he'll act as your liaison."

"I see," Lane said.

"You don't have to take this assignment, William," Hughes cut in. "We're analysts, not cowboys."

Lane could see the lack of human warmth in Yernin's eyes, and he thought about the young Wave's body the Ukrainian had booby-trapped in Norfolk. It hardened his resolve.

"Step away from it," Hughes warned.

"Can't do that, Tommy." Lane looked bleakly at his friend. "I'm in for the duration."

Hughes gave a little shrug. "Me too."

31

The Iranian legation was housed in a sprawling concrete-block building behind a white wall in Kaifa, a neighborhood beyond the second ring road on the way to the international airport.

Lane took a cab to within a couple of blocks, then made a pass on foot, watching for any signs that he was being followed. As far as he could tell there was nobody behind him, not even the Kuwaiti Special Palace Guard that Lane figured would keep close tabs on him. Kuwait owed the United States a great debt of gratitude, but it didn't stop them from being nervous that Americans were conducting operations on their soil. Nor was Yernin behind him, though he could practically smell the man's presence in the air. It was the stench of death.

His jaw tightened and his eyes narrowed thinking about the Ukrainian. Yernin had had help before and he would have it again, because there was probably another leak in Washington. Somewhere at high levels. Possibly in the CIA.

"They were waiting for you at Bandar-é Emān, Bill. Which means they were tipped off ahead of time," Roswell had agreed.

"Points to the CIA, or someone on the UN team," Lane replied. "We have to find the one with the most to gain."

"That could take a while," Hughes said glumly. "But we don't have the time."

"However it happened, your arrest put us behind the eight ball," Roswell continued. "We had to get you out of there, whatever it took to do it."

"We could ignore the Iranians," Lane suggested.

"I think you'd rather have the lion facing you than sneaking up behind you."

"I'm not going to spend much time protecting whoever they sent. If he gets between me and Yernin, I won't hesitate to shoot."

"It's up to you make him understand that," Roswell had said. "But keep your ears open."

He approached the embassy from the opposite direction, waited for a break in traffic, then crossed the street to the front gate where he rang the bell.

"*Balé*," yes, said a voice that came from a speaker grille set above the button.

"William Lane. I believe I'm expected."

"One moment, please."

Amin Zahedi, wearing a khaki uniform without insignia of rank, opened the door a minute later.

"I see," Lane said, not really very surprised. There was always a symmetry to field operations.

"I don't like this any better than you do. But I have my orders, as I expect you do."

"Right," Lane said.

He followed Zahedi to a windowless room at the rear of the embassy compound, barren of any furniture except for cushions around a low table on a worn Persian rug. The Iranian motioned for Lane to sit, and then poured them scalding hot tea in glass cups.

"This room is safe from *inside* ears as well as outside," Zahedi said.

"When did you get here?"

"Last night."

"Were you briefed?"

"Only in the most general terms," Zahedi answered, sipping his tea. "Our first objective is this Ukrainian assassin, Valeri Yernin. He killed two of my people in Tehran, and then disappeared like a will-o'-the-wisp."

"Who knows why you're here besides the general?"

Zahedi hesitated.

Lane sat forward to emphasize his point. "Don't lie to me, Colonel. My life may depend on it."

"It works both ways," Zahedi shot back.

"Who else knows why you're here?"

"My partner and no one else. Are you really going to make an attempt on Hussein's life, or was that merely a sham to gain your release?"

"It was a sham. You would have killed me otherwise."

"Amazing," Zahedi said. "You might not walk out of this embassy alive."

Lane smiled. "You should have searched me first."

Zahedi's control was very good. He said nothing.

Lane was impressed. "Tell me about the Iraqi colonel you captured."

"He was looking for evidence that our submarines were armed with nuclear weapons. He found nothing."

"Did he get that information back to Hussein?"

"We don't believe so."

"Where is he now?" Lane asked.

"Dead."

Lane considered the Iranian's answer. "You people might not have nuclear weapons aboard those subs yet, but you're getting ready for them. Where are the missiles coming from?"

Zahedi's jaw tightened.

"The Russians? Chernenkov?"

"I'm just a colonel, not a politician. You're asking me to tell you something that I do not know."

"Hussein's people know, or at least suspect as much. That's the reason they mounted the raid. With Ukrainian help."

"We've had trouble with the Ukrainians in the past," Zahedi admitted. "The incidents are increasing in frequency."

Lane managed a smile. "Interesting combination: The Ukrainians helping Iraq, and the Russians helping Iran. I don't see much of a difference. It's the jihad. In the name of Allah you can do anything you want, including state-sponsored terrorism. Forgive me if I don't shed a tear when one of your bases is attacked."

Zahedi was seething. "Why are you here, infidel?"

"Because my boss gave your boss his word."

"Get out now, while you still can. Or I will kill you myself."

"You may try, Colonel, but I don't suggest it, because just now I'm in a particularly bad mood. I'm after a man who is worse than all of you put together. And if he gets his way, the entire Middle East will be at war within ninety days."

Zahedi was brought up short, his anger draining away. "That's a very specific timetable. Where did you get it?"

"Yernin worked as a deep-cover agent in the Pentagon for two years. Last week he walked away from his job, broke into a navy computer in Norfolk, killing a lot of people in the process, and stole sailing orders for all of our warships and submarines operating in this hemisphere. Sailing orders for the next ninety days."

"Why would he want such information?"

"A good question," Lane said. "It's your turn. They were ready for me at the sub base. How did they know I was coming?"

"General Sultaneh told them."

"How did he know?"

Zahedi looked tired. "I don't know."

Lane waited.

"I swear by Allah that I do not have an answer to that question. The general has many sources that he shares with no one. Not the president, not even the mullahs."

Lane had a nasty little thought, but he put it aside for the moment. "What orders were you sent here with?"

"That I am to cooperate with you so far as that's possible," Zahedi replied, a troubled expression on his face. "The general didn't think that your people were serious about an assassination attempt. But we are anxious to track down this Ukrainian who is helping Hussein. Especially after he killed two of our own people."

"Then what?"

Zahedi shrugged. "Find the connections between the raid on your navy computer and the raid on our submarine base."

"I wonder," Lane said guardedly, the same errant thought as before crossing his mind.

Zahedi was watching Lane. Something suddenly dawned on him. "You have met this Ukrainian before. You've had contact with him. And lost."

Lane nodded.

"But he is afraid of you. That's why he came to Tehran. It was to find you, and kill you."

"I think so."

"Do you think it's simple revenge?"

Lane shook his head. "He's under orders and he considers me a threat to his operation, whatever that might be."

"So you're to be the bait with which we will catch this man," Zahedi said. "A dangerous game, which makes, as Americans say, for strange bedfellows. Do you have a plan?"

"Yes."

Zahedi waited a moment. "Well?"

"If I tell you, and if it backfires, it'll mean that you're a part of the leak. In which case I'll kill you."

"I understand," Zahedi said softly.

"I sincerely hope so."

FAILAKA ISLAND SAFE HOUSE

Hughes sat on the small balcony that looked toward the northeast as he smoked a cigarette and listened to Arabic music playing on the radio in his bedroom. He sipped a glass of ice-cold white wine, all the more pleasurable because it was illegal here. This time of the day, noon, was by tradition his.

Moira and the girls respected his time-outs, as they called them, and so did his superiors at the Agency, because very often during these times he came up with amazing insights. When they were working on a particularly vexing problem, Lane would send him away to be by himself.

Hughes was an intellectual. Or that's what others called him, and he accepted the label because to him it simply meant that he had the ability to figure things out. To see relationships where the connections were often deliberately hidden or disguised. To come up with leaps of intuition, fitting apparently unrelated facts together in new and novel ways.

But he was also a pragmatist. Even in this business, situations and people were often exactly what they seemed to be. And his practical self was telling him that Lane was placing himself in unnecessary danger.

Yernin could be dealt with at the diplomatic level. The relationship between the United States and the Ukraine was close enough that if President Reasoner told President Borodin what we knew about Yernin and demanded that the man be recalled, it would happen. No one would get hurt. No one would be placed in danger.

Lane didn't see it that way. Hughes could just imagine what was going through his friend's mind. Lane was seeing the horribly devastated remains of the young, pregnant woman whose body Yernin had booby-trapped. It was a sad business that Lane took personally.

The cellular telephone in his pocket rang. Hughes put down his wineglass and answered it.

"Yes?"

"Sir, this is Special Agent Verplank. I'm calling from position Charlie." That was one of the observation and listening posts around the island that had been set up to monitor traffic in the air or on the water that approached within one mile of the island.

"Go ahead," Hughes said. He felt a strong premonition of disaster.

"We have a possible problem out here that I'm going to need your authorization to pursue. There is a forty-foot pleasure boat that has been cruising back and forth about a mile and a half out for the past hour or so. They're scanning us electronically, and we've spotted someone with binoculars on deck watching us."

"Who owns the boat?"

"It's a rental, apparently hired by a crew from CNN. If that's the case, and the news network is on to us, we better do something."

"I see your point," Hughes said. "Have they made any attempt to come closer?"

"No, sir. I'd like to send a boat out there to find out what's going on."

"Hold for a bit. I have a friend with CNN in Atlanta. I'll call him and find out if anything is going on out here."

"Yes, sir."

"In the meantime, keep a sharp lookout, and inform the other positions."

"Will do, sir."

32

ON THE DESERT
SOUTHWEST OF BAGHDAD

Saddam Hussein entered the receiving chamber in his bedouin tent. They had moved a hundred kilometers across the desert to this wadi in the middle of the night, and the strain of the move and of the long exile showed in his dark, puffy features.

The men in the room stood for him, and waited respectfully until he had taken his place alone on an overstuffed tattered brown couch. He smiled and raised his hands together to them.

"I hope all is well with my friends this morning."

His cousin, General Riza Nuri al-Tikriti, who was minister of defense, nodded. "All is well with us, Dear One, but you look tired. You should rest."

"There will be time for rest when I reenter Baghdad to take my rightful place in the presidential palace," Hussein said. "Which will be very soon if certain operations are carried out successfully."

Of the five men seated around him, only General Nuri was a relative. Some of Hussein's other relatives had defected to the West in '95, and he'd ordered some of the remainder to be executed. Those who were left were ultra-loyal.

Of the others at this meeting, the short, thin, extremely intense Abdel Aref was minister of propaganda, and a useful tool, though not to be trusted too far. Ali Sidqi, who looked like a French banker with a badly made toupee covering his baldness, was minister of foreign affairs. Unlike Tariq Aziz before him, Sidqi was a very convincing liar. And the portly, always secretive Rashid Emir, with his expensive tastes in cognacs, and taste in young boys, was chief of the secret service—the Mukabarat. Hussein overlooked his infidel tastes in liquor because of his dedication and loyalty.

Hussein turned his wide, dark eyes to the fifth man, the most enigmatic, and therefore the most useful or possibly the most dangerous. "Congratulations on your intelligence coup in the United States, Valeri Fedorovich."

"Thank you Mr. President," Yernin said pleasantly. He hid his true feelings of loathing. It was possible, after all, that Iraq would play a vital role in Ukraine's future.

"I have brought you together to tell you about these certain operations which will, with the assistance of the government of Ukraine, not only return me to the capital, but bring our beloved country back to its rightful place among the nations of the world."

Hussein motioned to his Mukabarat director. Rashid Emir got ponderously to his feet and went to an easel at the end of the chamber. He flipped the cover sheet back to reveal a montage of photographs of Iran's submarine base and the four warships with their dozens of support vessels.

"Bandar-é Emān Khomeiní," Emir said. "Iran has taken delivery of the last of four submarines from Russia, and the latest intelligence report suggests that the crews are operationally ready. I sent a penetration team of two very brave men to this base to gather information vital to our plan. One of the men was killed outright, but the other learned what he'd been sent to find out, and made his way to Tehran where he managed to send us a message before he was captured. I'm told that he died of his wounds while in a SAVAK prison. Be that as it may, I have learned that Iran has in its possession at least one Russian-made nuclear missile. They probably have more. And this desperate situation facing us must not be permitted. If we strike now, decisively and with imagination, power will be ours."

"We can send saboteurs to the base and sink the boats where they're docked," General Nuri blurted. "It would teach them that they cannot take advantage of us in our presently weakened condition."

"Which might result in an attack directly on us out here in the desert," Ali Sidqi warned. "I think this time that the Western alliance might do nothing to stop such an attack. In fact, it would be to their advantage for Iran to finish us off once and for all."

"Don't be an old woman," General Nuri shot back.

"They have the strength. By destroying their precious submarines we would give them the will for such an expedition." Sidqi twisted his mustache unconsciously. "Perhaps they would salvage a nuclear missile and use it against us."

"Is that a possibility?" Hussein asked.

"No, because they do not have nuclear missiles yet, though their submarines are equipped for them," Yernin answered. His jaw ached and his mouth was pulled down in a scowl.

All eyes turned toward him.

"Colonel Kassem gave his life for that information," Rashid Emir said.

"He was wrong. An American intelligence officer, aided by members of a United Nations spy team, discovered that fact."

"Yes, we know about this team because of your good work, Colonel Yernin," Hussein said. "In fact, we have traced William Lane and Frances Shipley to Kuwait. Neither of them will spy again."

"Is that for sure, Mr. President?" Yernin asked.

"Yes," Hussein replied. It was clear he was disappointed, as he went on doggedly. "Even now my operatives are closing in for the kill."

"It will be a suicide mission," Abdel Aref warned darkly.

"In sha'Allah," the deposed Iraqi leader replied indifferently. "Can we be certain that Colonel Kassem was wrong?"

"Yes, Your Excellency," Yernin said. "Though under certain very precise conditions, something might be arranged."

Hussein's eyes sparkled. "We will not sink the submarines, General Nuri. I have another plan, which it seems may be rescued by our Ukrainian friends."

They all waited expectantly, though Yernin knew what was coming.

"We will steal one of their submarines out from under their noses, in such a way that the West will believe that the warship is sailing under Iranian orders, with an Iranian crew, to an Iranian purpose."

"Even if that is possible, Dear One, of what use would it be to us?" Abdel Aref asked. An operation without propaganda value was worthless in his view.

Hussein smiled slyly. "Israel used great restraint during the first war to liberate our homelands in Kuwait by *not* using weapons of mass destruction against us after we attacked them with our scud missiles. We could return the favor by attacking Iran the moment it attacks Israel."

"Are you suggesting that we use the Iranian submarine to attack Israeli shipping? Perhaps their navy?" General Nuri asked. "We do not have a trained submarine crew."

"A submarine crew will be made available to us from the Ukrainian Black Sea Fleet," Hussein said. "Is this not correct, Colonel?"

Yernin nodded absently as he took his thoughts several steps ahead of what Hussein was outlining for his exile cabinet.

"If our friends from Kiev can also supply us with nuclear missiles, we will attack Tel Aviv and Haifa. It would be not only the end of Israel, but the effective end of Iran as well."

Abdel Aref went positively radiant. It would be the perfect propaganda coup. "The Americans constantly crow about a dominant, stabilizing force in the region. At one time it was us. It could be us again."

"Maybe another shah would be put in place in Tehran," Ali Sidqi suggested.

"The war and the downfall of Rafsānjaní and his henchmen will occur so fast it will catch everyone off guard," Aref bubbled. "Remember that the attention of the entire world will be focused on the poor Zionists. The primary objective of the United States and the other Western allies will be to protect their Jew friends."

"The risks are too great, Dear One," Sidqi pleaded. "If that submarine were to be captured, the Ukrainian crew would not accept responsibility. As Abdel suggested, the primary objective of the Western alliance would be to protect their ally, Israel. The submarine would be hunted down and killed. There would be no place for it to go. They would be trapped in the Mediterranean Sea."

"Is this correct?" Hussein asked Yernin.

"Unfortunately yes," Yernin said, still thinking it out. "But there may be another way for you to achieve your objectives."

Hussein clapped his hands. "There is always a path if we put our best minds to it."

"If the blame falls on us, the Western allies will not hesitate to annihilate Iraq," Sidqi argued. "Men, women, children. Everyone."

"*In sha'Allah,*" the Iraqi leader whispered.

"Even you, Dear One," the minister of propaganda suggested.

Saddam Hussein was insane. Yernin had suspected it, but now he was convinced. All of them lived in a fantasy world. Their time had come and gone, never to return. They were men willing to make desperate gambles no matter the outcome. They wanted to win at all costs. If they were to be defeated, they were willing to take the entire region with them.

So be it, Yernin thought. "We may not have to strike Israel," he said.

"Now you are making sense," Sidqi said, relieved.

"But we will supply you with a crew, and we will supply you with nuclear missiles."

"Why?" the minister of foreign affairs sputtered.

"To make a nuclear attack."

"On whom?" Hussein asked, his eyes glinting like polished obsidian.

"On your most hated enemy, Your Excellency," Yernin replied. "In the meantime I will go to Kuwait to make sure that Lane and the woman are killed."

33

KUWAIT INTERNATIONAL HOTEL
KUWAIT CITY

"We're not going to crowd him," Lane instructed the dozen NSA special agents and Kuwait Special Palace Guard security people gathered in his fourteenth-floor suite. "That means no one in the lobby. He'd spot your people right off the bat."

"You're the boss," NSA agent in charge, Cal Trilby, said. "But if he's as good as you say he is, you'll be placing yourself in an unnecessarily risky position."

The hotel was across from the US Embassy on Arabian Gulf Street in the section of the city known as Beneud Al-Gar. It was a favorite haunt of Western VIPs and journalists. Lane had registered this morning under his own name without trying to conceal his presence. The other rooms on the fourteenth floor were either empty or occupied by security people. A helicopter and pilot were stationed on the roof.

"It's Yernin who'll be putting himself in risk. Because if he gets this far, this floor becomes a killing ground."

"Don't we want him alive, sir?" one of the Kuwaitis asked.

Lane turned his steel blue eyes to the man. "That would be nice. But if you give this guy half a chance, if you hesitate for just a fraction of a second, if you don't kill him the instant you see him, he'll kill you."

He looked at the others, including Zahedi, who stood by the window uneasily listening to Lane's instructions.

"I've seen what he can do. If he thought that taking out this entire hotel was the only way to get to me, he'd do it."

"What's his beef with you, Mr. Lane?" Trilby asked.

"Let's just say that I got in his way before, and I'm in his way now and he doesn't like it."

"If he's got some agenda, wouldn't it be better if we did take him alive?" Trilby persisted. "I heard that Norfolk wasn't very pretty. I for one would like to talk to him."

Lane nodded. "Okay. I wanted to see only one body bag going out of here. But I'd like to have a chat with this guy myself. Alone, in an empty room. So if your people want to do it your way, I won't interfere."

Trilby and the others looked uncomfortable.

"We're going to give him seventy-two hours. If he hasn't shown up by then, we'll have to think of something else. He might not take the bait, or his people here might already know what precautions we've taken."

"How?" Trilby asked.

"We might have a leak."

The NSA agent gave Lane a very hard look. "Just great. Means we've lost our advantage."

"Fourteen to one are pretty good odds," Lane said quietly.

"From what you say and from what I read, he's faced worse."

Lane hated maneuvering people, but in this case it had been necessary for their survival. "You have a point. So we're going to change plans in midstream, and nobody outside of this room will know about it."

It occurred to Trilby that they'd been had. He grinned sheepishly. "They said you were good, Mr. Lane, but they were wrong. You're better than that."

"I went up against this guy once and lost, so hold your praise until afterward."

"What's the plan?"

"We'll go with the assumption that he already knows that we've laid a trap up here for him. So we're not going to hide a thing. We'll lock out the elevators from this floor, and station people at the stairwell doors, as well as the elevator doors in case he stops one of the cars on the fifteenth floor and climbs down."

"The man's not a fool. What makes you think he'll try for you if he knows it's a trap?" Zahedi questioned.

The Kuwaitis were especially nervous having the Iranian officer here. But they all regarded him with respect. They'd seen his impressive file.

"Because he's arrogant, and because he knows he can even the odds," Lane explained.

"How?" Trilby shot back.

"I don't know yet," Lane admitted. "But if he shows up, it'll mean he has a plan."

"If it was me I'd cut the power and phones to this floor," Zahedi said.

"That's a start," Lane agreed. "We'll station a man in the basement where the power and telephone distribution equipment is probably located."

"How about the roof?" Trilby suggested. "If he could get that far and take out our chopper pilot he might be able to rappel down to us. It's only five floors."

"Put an extra man up there too."

"Air-conditioning ducts, service elevator, pipe and cable runs?"

"You have the manpower."

"We'll have to call in some extras—"

"No," Lane interrupted. "No calls out of here. No one can know what we're doing."

"But it'll leave this floor practically unguarded," the NSA special agent protested.

"You're right, and he'll know it," Lane said. "When he has all of your people spotted, he'll make his move. Colonel Zahedi and I will be waiting for him."

"You're setting yourself up as bait," Trilby said. "But we'll have every possibility covered. He'll never get to you."

"Yes he will," Lane said. "Because he's already figured out a way in here that we haven't come up with."

"He won't get in here unless he's invisible," Trilby said, exasperated.

"Then maybe that's what he'll do."

ABOARD THE FAILAKA FERRY

The ferry was ten minutes late leaving the island dock for the mainland, and the handful of passengers who'd come over to see the sights were getting restless.

NSA field operative George Straite and his Kuwaiti partner, Ibn Salem, due to escort the last load back to the mainland, waited at the rail. Straite smoked a cigarette as he peered at the pilothouse on the upper level.

There was no one up there that he could see. He hadn't paid much attention to the crew, but he didn't think the pilot had gotten off.

"Is there something wrong?" Salem asked respectfully. The NSA field officers were better than any of the CIA bunch he'd worked with in the past. Sharper, more professional. Although he did not like foreigners in his homeland, he was learning a great deal about security procedures that would one day stand him in good stead with his superiors. He wanted eventually to head the Special Palace Guards, a position of great importance and respect.

"We're late, and no one seems to be minding the store."

Salem's eyes followed Straite's gaze to the pilothouse. "A mechanical problem?"

"Maybe." Straite flipped his cigarette into the water and leaned his beefy frame out over the rail so that he could see the stern of the boat. The car ramp was up, but the line tenders stood idly by waiting for orders.

They'd wanted to close the island to any public traffic, but the Kuwaiti government wouldn't bend that far. Instead they'd offered security help all over the island, as well as aboard the ferry, which made the one-hour trip four times a day. The hovercraft that had also serviced the island had been discontinued after the war. Private watercraft or aircraft were forbidden to approach within the one-mile exclusion zone.

Straite looked at his partner. "Cover my back while I go up and take a look."

"It's probably nothing."

"Yeah," Straite said. He went upstairs to the empty open deck, then took out his pistol and climbed the ladder to the pilothouse deck, his movements surprisingly light and graceful for a man of his size.

The pilot lay facedown in front of the control panel in a pool of blood, the back of his head wet, his hair matted around a small black hole.

"Shit," Straite swore. He scrambled down the ladder and took the stairs to the main deck two at a time.

"What is it?" Salem asked, alarmed.

"The pilot is dead," Straite explained, keeping his voice low so no one else could hear him. He didn't want a panic among the passengers. "Radio the house and tell them we're on the way back."

Salem keyed the walkie-talkie as he fell in behind Straite, who headed toward the stern where they could get off the boat.

"Abel unit, this is Baker Three, incoming with a red star express." It was the code phrase for imminent trouble.

"Roger, Baker Three, understood. Do you need any help?"

"Negatory," Salem radioed, using the American vernacular even though he recognized the voice at the house as a fellow Kuwaiti security officer. "We're coming in. Watch yourself."

34

KUWAIT INTERNATIONAL HOTEL

Valeri Yernin, dressed in a shirt and tie and a dark windbreaker, listened on a telephone in a room at the end of the corridor from Lane's suite. The handset was connected to the line through a sophisticated processor that allowed him to hear what was going on in any room on this floor.

A toolbox marked AT&T KUWAIT sat on the floor at his feet. He'd snuck into the hotel through a basement service entrance and hidden himself on the fourteenth floor early this afternoon, as soon as he learned that Lane was laying a trap instead of remaining on the island with Frances Shipley. It had taken him nearly four hours to set everything up for his countertrap, and he'd almost been caught. He had to take a lot of chances, but the prize was worth it.

Yernin had heard everything said in Lane's suite, and he knew with a sickening feeling that he would be hard-pressed to get out of here in one piece, let alone make an attempt on Lane's life.

To this point Maslennikov's source had been infallible. But Lane's last-minute change in plans had come as a complete, disturbing surprise. Perhaps he had underestimated the man after all.

Maslennikov had given him fair warning. Twice. But the American was nothing more than an analyst. A desk jockey. An observer, not a field man.

Still, Lane had come close to ruining everything on the train from Richmond. And he'd gotten surprisingly far in Iran for someone who was supposedly nothing more than an academic.

The stairwells were being watched now, as were the elevator shafts and pipe and cable runs that connected the hotel's services to each floor.

But Lane's security people were watching for someone to get onto this floor, from either above or below, not get off.

Killing Lane here and now would be desirable. But if he could get to the woman and kill her, or even hold her hostage, Lane would drop everything and come after him. Men driven by such passions usually were prone to big mistakes. Fatal mistakes.

However, if a shot were to present itself to him, he would not hesitate to take it. His primary goal before anything else was to kill Bill Lane.

Making his decision, he entered a code on his laptop processor that automatically routed a telephone call from his room through the switching network downstairs to a repeater somewhere in the city that in turn relayed his call to a transmitter on a specially scrambled radio frequency. The call bypassed the hotel's switchboard, its point of origin masked.

The connection was made in under five seconds. He pushed a talk button.

"Units one through four, are you in place? Overseer requests."

"*Āywa Wāhad.*" Yes one.

"*Āywa Itnīn.*" Yes two.

"*Āywa Thalātha.*" Yes three.

"*Āywa Ārb'a.*" Yes four.

"Remain in position. I'm coming over in a chopper. Do you understand?"

"*Āywa,*" the one he recognized as the group leader, Captain Ahmad Barzani, replied tersely. The Mukabarat field leader was a capable man with a lot of imagination. His troops loved him. He would do as he was told so long as it was practicable, though he would not risk his command. There were too few of his people left.

"If I'm not there within twenty minutes, proceed with your primary mission."

"As you wish, *In sha'Allah.*"

Yes, pray to your God, Yernin thought. In the end it may be all that is left for you and the madman you choose to follow.

He broke the connection, then hit a series of keys on the processor, which would block all calls to or from this floor.

Next he screwed the silencer on his gun, checked the load, and made sure he had two extra eighteen-round magazines of 9mm ammunition in his jacket pocket, and the nine-inch stiletto under his left arm.

Finally, he hit another series of keys on the processor unit, punched in a thirty-second delay, and touched the Enter key.

A signal was sent to the electrical distribution system in the basement where the main circuit breaker relays were put on hold for thirty seconds before they would shut down.

He turned off the room lights, listened a few moments at the door, then unlocked it and eased it open a crack. One man stood at the stairwell door at the end of the corridor. No one else was in sight.

Yernin turned back and glanced at the processor's luminous screen. The unit counted down past ten.

At zero the lights throughout the hotel went out, plunging the entire complex into darkness for a few seconds before emergency lighting would take over everywhere except this floor.

Yernin stepped out into the pitch-black corridor and, trailing his left hand along the wall silently, made his way to the stairwell door.

He stopped, sensing that someone was very close ahead. It was aftershave lotion, and some other smell. Gun oil, Yernin thought. His sense of smell was sharp.

"Charlie, watch yourself back there," a voice came from a radio less than one meter from where Yernin stood.

A tiny red light winked on at about eye level. It was the walkie-talkie's transmit light. The stairwell guard was holding it up to his mouth.

"I can't see a thing," the guard whispered.

"The emergency lights will be on any second."

Yernin crouched down and aimed up and to the left of the red light. He cupped his left hand over the gun's receiver to catch the spent shell, and fired. The sound of the silenced shot was soft, certainly not audible from much more than a few meters away. But the guard grunted loudly, and fell backwards into the stairwell.

Yernin jumped over the guard's body, tossed the hot shell casing down to the next landing, picked up the walkie-talkie, and silently took the stairs up, two at a time.

"We're coming out," Lane shouted, racing down the still dark corridor from his suite. Something was wrong with the emergency lights.

He and Zahedi had been studying the hotel's engineering diagrams, which one of the Kuwaiti security people had supplied. When the lights went out he rushed to the door and tore it open but hesitated on the threshold. Anyone moving around out there would be a target.

Zahedi was behind him, his gun drawn, when they heard the noise at the end of the corridor and recognized it for what it was.

"Trilby," Lane shouted.

"At the elevators," the NSA special agent answered.

"Everybody else stay in position," Lane shouted. "Someone call for backup."

"Phones are out," one of Trilby's men shouted from the right.

Keeping low, Lane zigzagged from one side of the corridor to the other as he ran, trailing first his left and then his right hand against the walls to guide him.

Coming around a corner, he skidded to a halt and fell back, Zahedi right on top of him. The west emergency door was open and lights were back on in the stairwell.

From where Lane crouched he could make out the figure of the downed security agent, his legs holding the door open.

Trilby came up behind them a second later. "The Ukrainian's on this floor!"

Something didn't set right with Lane. "Maybe," he said, studying the open door. "He didn't come past you?"

"Not unless he was a ghost," Trilby replied.

"Maybe not a ghost, but he was invisible," Lane said. Something still nagged at the back of his head. "Start your people checking the rooms one by one, and tell them to be careful for booby traps."

"Right," the NSA special agent said, falling back.

"He might still be in the stairwell," Zahedi suggested.

"Cover me," Lane instructed, and before the Iranian could object, he dashed to the end of the corridor, keeping low and zigzagging.

At the door he flattened himself against the wall, took a quick look inside the stairwell, then ducked back.

The downed agent had been shot just below his jaw, the bullet probably crashing directly into his brain, killing him instantly. He'd been shot by someone standing below him. On the landing.

He looked back at Zahedi, his eyes straying to the emergency lights near the ceiling. Why weren't they working?

Holding his Beretta in both hands, he spun around the corner into the stairwell, jumping over the special agent's body. He swung the gun in a tight arc down the stairs, then spun on his heel and covered the flight up.

Nothing moved. Nor was there any indication that anyone had come this way except for the dead man.

"Lane?" Zahedi called softly.

Lane gestured for him to hold back. Something wasn't right here, damnit. He felt like an absolute fool for not seeing what it was.

He moved down to the next landing, swinging his gun in a tight arc. As before, there was no movement.

Turning to start back up, his eye strayed to a shell casing lying on the floor. He picked it up. Standard 9mm. Same caliber Yernin used in Norfolk, which meant nothing. Except that the casing was on the lower landing. Meant Yernin stood down here and fired up at the guard. Meant he could have used night vision goggles.

Meant he knew the lights were going out and how long they'd stay out, because he'd engineered it that way.

It struck Lane all at once. If Yernin had engineered the lights to go out, it meant he'd had a head start. It meant that, once again, someone had fed him information.

Lane raced up the stairs to the fourteenth floor. The emergency lights still hadn't come on.

Yernin had been here on this floor sometime this morning, or maybe early this afternoon, *before* Trilby and his people showed up. The dead guard and the shell casing on the landing were a ruse.

Yernin had waited for them. But something happened to make him change his mind. So he'd shot the guard and gotten out.

It meant that somehow he'd overheard the briefing Lane had given the others in the suite.

"Are the phones still out?" Lane demanded as he raced down the corridor.

"So far as I know," Zahedi said.

"In here," one of Trilby's men shouted from one of the rooms.

The curtains had been thrown back. The light from outside was enough that they could see the laptop computer.

"It's hooked to the phone line," the agent said. "But the program running now is apparently holding back electrical power from this floor."

Trilby came pounding up the corridor. "He's not here," he shouted, pulling up short at the open door.

"He was here all along," Lane said. "And he heard that we were changing plans, so he got out."

"I've got a man in the basement. Maybe he can intercept the son of a bitch before he gets out of the hotel." Trilby pulled the small walkie-talkie out of his pocket. "Stewart, do you copy?"

"Roger."

"Yernin's on his way down. Get up to the west stairwell door in the lobby as fast as you can. If you see him, shoot to kill. We'll be right behind him so look sharp."

"Roger that. I'm on my way."

Lane was staring at Trilby. "Do all your people carry walkie-talkies?"

Trilby nodded. "Us and the Kuwaitis."

Lane pushed past the startled special agent and went back to the stairwell where he quickly searched the dead agent's body.

The others followed him.

"He knows everything," Lane said.

"Sir?" Trilby asked.

"He took this man's walkie-talkie."

Trilby looked at his own radio. They'd been outmaneuvered.

Lane grabbed the walkie-talkie from the agent and keyed the transmit button. "Yernin, you bastard, I'm coming after you. Just you and me. You name the spot."

There was nothing but the soft hiss of a dead channel.

"Yernin, I'm coming," Lane said in Russian. "We know what you took from the navy's Honolulu computer."

"Fuck you," Yernin's voice came from the tiny speaker, his transmission distorted.

It sounded to Lane like the Ukrainian was inside a waterfall.

Yernin keyed his radio again. This time he merely laughed. But again they heard the waterfall distortion.

"Where is he?" Trilby asked.

The special agent who'd discovered the processor on the phone shrugged. "Wherever he is, it's windy."

"The roof," Lane said. He bolted up the stairs in a dead run, the others directly behind him.

* * *

NSA Special Agent Dan Restormal took a couple of steps toward the rooftop door and started to raise his walkie-talkie when a thunderclap burst inside his head.

Yernin slipped out of the shadows behind the helicopter, yanked open the passenger-side door, and climbed inside.

The pilot reached for his gun, but Yernin placed the muzzle of his pistol against the side of the man's head.

"You have less than thirty seconds to start this machine and get away from here before I kill you. Twenty-five, twenty-four, twenty-three . . ." Yernin started the countdown.

The pilot was convinced. He flipped on the master switch, auxiliary fuel pump, turbocharger boost pump, and then turned the key. The Jet Ranger's engines spooled up slowly, the power indicators finally rising to the green.

Still holding the gun to the pilot's head, Yernin watched the west stairwell door.

"You're running out of time."

The door started to come open.

Yernin slid the window back and got off two shots, then turned back to the pilot.

"Lift off or die. Now!"

The helicopter lurched off the roof, then dove over the edge toward the east as it picked up speed. The last Yernin saw of the rooftop, the stairwell door was coming open again and several men were piling out.

35

Night had already fallen by the time George Straite and Ibn Salem reached the safe house from the ferry.

On the way up they were stopped twice for identification; once on the road leading up to the house, then at the hundred-meter perimeter.

Hughes and Dick Scott, who was the number-two man in the NSA special detail, waited at the front door.

"The ferryboat pilot was shot to death, but apparently none of the passengers saw or heard a thing," Straite told them. "I figured we'd better get back as soon as possible. Is everything okay here?"

"I don't know," Scott said. "We spotted a big powerboat in the bay this afternoon. Supposedly rented by a CNN crew. But Mr. Hughes called a friend of his at CNN. It's not theirs."

"It was the *Natalee,* a forty-five-footer, Kuwaiti registry," Hughes said. "White hull, blue canvas on her superstructure. Did you see anything like that in the harbor?"

"No, sir," Straite said.

"Well, she's gone now."

"I might have believed it was nothing, until the incident on the ferry," Scott admitted. "I've doubled up the outside positions, but we're getting stretched pretty thin."

"How about Mr. Lane and our people at the hotel?" Straite asked. He was getting a creepy feeling between his shoulder blades. They all were.

"We can't get through to them," Hughes said. "Problem with the phones. The CIA is sending someone across the street to the hotel to find out what the hell is going on. So for the moment we're on our own."

"What about the navy?"

"They're standing by," Scott said.

"For how long?" Straite asked.

"Until we don't need them any longer," Hughes shot back.

"Sorry, sir. I just wanted to know how to pace my people. They can't all work twenty-four hours a day."

"I just don't know," Hughes admitted. He went to the window and looked outside. "But my gut tells me whatever it is will happen sometime tonight."

"Good enough for me, sir," Straite said. "Now if you'll excuse us, we have work to do."

"Better send for a new ferryboat pilot. I'd rather not have those passengers wandering around the island."

The last of a series of four clicks sounded in Captain Ahmad Barzani's ear where he lay with the three other men in his squad a few meters from the inner perimeter checkpoint. It meant that the other three Mukabarat commando units were in place around the island.

They were dressed head to toe in black ninja night-fighter bodysuits, their faces blackened. They were equipped with night vision goggles which made the night seem like ghostly day, giving them the advantage over the American and Kuwaiti guards. The only weapons they carried were suppressed .22-caliber automatic pistols with folding shoulder stocks, scopes, and sixty-round magazines. Since most security people wore Kevlar body vests, Hussein's special commando units were trained to make only head shots. Their Ukrainian instructors were the best, and tonight's assault team was the crème de la crème.

They had come over from the mainland a few at a time aboard the ferry, while out in the bay a cruiser provided a diversion for them. The only mistake so far had been killing the ferryboat pilot. But the man had apparently once lived and worked in Baghdad, and had recognized one of Barzani's team members.

Unfortunately it had drawn the American and Kuwaiti officers aboard the ferry back to the house, and now the island's defenders were alerted that something was about to happen.

"In sha'Allah," Barzani whispered to himself. If it was Allah's will that they all die here on this godforsaken rock, then so be it. Each of them had a price on his head with the puppet government in Baghdad. They would die here sooner, or home later; it did not matter. Martyrdom would be theirs.

Barzani motioned for his number two, Mubarak al-Hadr, to look at the checkpoint where two men leaned against a humvee parked across the narrow road.

Hadr studied the situation for a second, then turned back and nodded.

Barzani motioned for Hadr to take out the guard on the right, on three.

Again Hadr nodded. He brought his weapon up, centered the scope on the head of the man to the right, a Kuwaiti, and made his count. "One . . . two . . . three."

He fired at the same moment as Barzani, the shots barely audible as soft pops. Both guards crumpled where they stood, neat round holes in the exact centers of their foreheads.

Barzani keyed his walkie-talkie once, indicating to the other teams that he had taken out his objective. Within the next five seconds the other teams responded in kind. The inner perimeter around the house had been secured.

"Get one of their walkie-talkies," he told Hadr.

Hughes went to the upstairs sitting room where Frances Shipley, dressed in a robe, stood at the window watching the lights out at sea. A fire burned in the fireplace, and the Gallic singer Enya's voice came from the stereo. The scene was domestic and Western, anything but Arabic. Which was at the heart of our troubles out here, Hughes thought.

"Close the curtains and step away from the window like a dear, would you please?" Hughes said.

She turned, startled, and let the heavy curtains fall back. "Do you think Hussein has sent his assassins here?"

"It is a distinct possibility."

"Tonight? This moment?"

"Unfortunately, yes. There was an incident aboard the last ferry. The pilot was killed."

Her gray-blue eyes narrowed. "Has Bill been informed?"

"There's a problem with the telephones at the hotel. Nothing uncommon. But we've asked the CIA to send somebody over to check it out."

"Have you called for the navy to backstop us?" Frances asked.

"We don't think it's necessary yet. No reason to get anybody riled up. But they're standing by, so if we should need help it's not far off."

"Coming after Bill and me is not simple revenge," she said. "We're interfering with their plans somehow, and they want us stopped."

"I agree. But I think that if we can sting them by eliminating their mentor, Comrade Yernin, it might give them pause."

Again her eyes narrowed. "But we are in this for revenge, Thomas? Is that what you're saying?"

Hughes gave her a sad look. "William is a man with an extraordinary sense of honor. Right versus wrong. Good versus evil."

"He's no Boy Scout," Frances flared.

Hughes smiled. "Heaven forbid. But Valeri Yernin has to be stopped. William has set himself to do it."

"It'll get him killed."

"Perhaps it will," Hughes replied coolly. "In the meantime I thought it best that you be forewarned. I suggest that you get dressed. I assume you can handle a gun?"

"Yes."

"When you're ready join us downstairs, I'll have one for you."

She stopped him at the door. "Tom?"

He turned back. "Yes."

"It's just that I love him," she said.

Hughes smiled gently. "I know, dear. So do I."

36

KUWAIT INTERNATIONAL HOTEL

On the roof, Lane and the others watched the helicopter turn north, directly across Kuwait Bay, and hit the deck so that it skimmed the surface of the water. Then its lights went out and they lost it in the confusion of the lights on the ships and oil platforms out there.

"The border with Iraq is less than fifty miles away," Trilby said. "They can make it in twenty minutes unless we ask the air force to shoot it down."

"The pilot would be killed," one of the special agents said.

"Yernin will kill him anyway," Trilby replied bitterly.

The inside information Yernin was getting was good, almost too good, Lane thought. Very few people had known the setup at the hotel. Yet the assassin had found out soon enough to beat Trilby's people. Yernin knew that Lane would be here just as he knew that Frances was at the island safe house.

"Is this operation over with now?" Zahedi asked with a smirk. "Are you going to let him go?"

"He's not going to Iraq," Lane said, turning toward the stairs. Someone was on the way up.

"He'd be a fool to try anything else," Trilby said, but then a funny look came over his face. "Failaka? Do you think that the son of a bitch is going to the island? He'll be dead meat once he sets down."

"He has help," Lane said.

Two men in suits came through the door, paused to take in the situation, then approached Lane and the others.

"One of you guys named Lane?" the taller, darker of the two men asked.

"Me," Lane said.

"Tom Hughes asked us to check out what's going on. The hotel's phone lines are down, all the power was out, and there's a dead guy with National Security Agency ID down on the fourteenth-floor landing."

"Did Hughes say that he needed help?"

The man shook his head. "No. But when we tried to confirm who the hell he was, we couldn't. He's on Failaka, we got that much, but the phones out there are dead too. What the hell is going on? Nobody said anything to us about any operation."

"I'll explain later," Lane said. "I assume you're CIA. Do you have access to a helicopter, and I mean right now? Something with radio gear we can raise the navy on?"

"Hold on, cowboy. We're just embassy security from across the street. How about some ID?"

"I'm Bill Lane and I'm with the National Security Agency, as are some of these gentlemen. Some of the others are Kuwaiti Special Palace Guard officers. And this gentleman"—Lane pointed to Zahedi—"is a colonel in the Iranian secret service. What's more, I'm not a cowboy, and unless you move your ass, some friends of mine might get hurt. And I would take that personally."

The man's eyes went wide. "You're *that* Bill Lane," he said. "I didn't know." He stuck out his hand. "Chad Thomas."

He motioned to the other man. "My partner, Art Hager."

Lane ignored the outstretched hand. "Can you get us a chopper?"

"Five minutes," Hager said. "Right here be okay?"

"That'll do," Lane said.

Hager stepped to one side and said something into a lapel mike.

"Mr. Lane, are you expecting an attack on our sovereign lands?" one of the Kuwaiti officers asked suddenly. He did not look happy.

"It's possibly already in progress. Someone may have come ashore on Failaka."

The Kuwaiti's jaw tightened. He glanced at Zahedi with hate. Not many people in Kuwait liked the Iranians.

"Would they be Iraqis? Saddam Hussein's terrorists?"

"It's likely."

"Why wasn't my government informed of this?"

"You're here. You must have been told something."

The Kuwaiti glanced at Zahedi again, then at the others. "Our part in this operation is over. Take your helicopter to Failaka and evacuate your people—all of your people—immediately out of Kuwait. I don't care where."

"You don't have the authority," Trilby sputtered.

The Kuwaiti puffed up. "I am an Al-Sabah. My uncle is the emir. You will all leave my country before this night is over."

He and the other Kuwaiti security people stalked off.

"That one will cause you trouble," Thomas cautioned.

Lane stared at him. "It won't matter if everyone on the island is already dead."

FAILAKA ISLAND

The helicopter pilot was very good. He managed to hold the machine barely two meters off the surface of the water at full throttle all the way across from the mainland.

They approached the island from the southeast, which put them on the opposite side from the house and ferry dock. There was a surveillance post on the coast, but Yernin was certain that Barzani had taken it out by now.

He switched the helicopter's radio to Captain Barzani's frequency.

"Unit One, what is your situation? Overseer requests."

"We're inside the inner perimeter."

"Is it safe to land?"

"Yes. But you will alert the house."

"That doesn't matter. Cut their power and wait for me, I'll be there in two minutes."

"Very well." Barzani's disgust was evident in his voice.

Yernin smiled to himself. The captain's day of atonement and martyrdom would probably come a lot sooner than he expected.

"Set us down on the road below the house," he shouted to the pilot.

"I don't know what you're talking about," the young man said. "What house?"

"The safe house where Commander Shipley is staying."

"Who's that?"

"Your courage is as remarkable as your flying skill, young man, but unless you have a death wish you will do as I say."

"You'll kill me anyway, you son of a bitch."

"No, I won't," Yernin said convincingly. "Because I don't know how to fly one of these things, and I need you to take me and the woman off the island."

"I don't believe you."

"What other choice do you have?"

The lights in the house went out at the same moment Captain Barzani heard the distinctive noise of an incoming helicopter. They had their assignments. But the Ukrainian's coming here jeopardized the entire mission. If the US warships in the Gulf were alerted when their radars detected the helicopter, none of his people would leave this island alive.

But, Barzani sighed in resignation, the man was in charge, he had the ear of Hussein himself, and he was good. The best.

Barzani brought his gun to his shoulder and studied the front of the house through the scope. They had taken out eleven American and Kuwaiti guards so far, leaving only those inside the house alive.

They'd also taken out the phone lines to the house, as well as the two satellite communications dishes that had been set up in back.

Sooner or later the navy, the Kuwaiti authorities, or the CIA would show up out here to investigate. But unless there were more defenders inside the house than Barzani figured on, the operation would be completed within minutes. And hopefully Yernin's action at the hotel was providing them with a diversion.

A face appeared briefly in the window to the left of the door. Barzani tightened his aim and waited patiently.

The helicopter touched down at the end of the road a hundred meters below, the noise even at that distance distracting.

The face appeared again at the window. Barzani centered the crosshairs on the bridge of the pale, ghostly nose, certain it was a man and not the woman, and touched off a shot.

Something very hard slammed into Barzani's left shoulder, breaking his collarbone and spiraling down through his lung and toward his heart. He was shoved over on his back.

Over him, Hadr and the two other men in his squad laid down an overlapping pattern of fire on the front of the house that lasted for an intense three seconds.

Unless whoever had fired the returning shot that had hit Barzani had gotten immediately out of the way, he was now dead. Barzani marveled that he could still think that clearly.

"Captain, can you move unaided?" Hadr's face was above him.

Barzani wanted to tell his assistant squad leader that of course he could not move unaided, he was mortally wounded. But although he could think the words, he could not speak.

The Ukrainian was suddenly there. "Can he move?"

"No," Hadr said.

Yernin looked up toward the house. "Kill him," he ordered indifferently.

Hadr hesitated.

Yernin shrugged, his eyes empty as his soul, pulled out a big silenced pistol, pointed at Barzani's face, and fired.

37

FAILAKA ISLAND

Dick Scott and Ibn Salem were dead. George Straite lay slumped in a corner by the door holding his left hand to his neck, blood streaming between his fingers.

He was beyond help and he knew it. But he could hold a gun for a little longer.

Hughes stood at the base of the stairs, his pistol trained on the front door. Frances was a few stairs up, her pistol aimed at the door as well.

They'd heard the helicopter land a few minutes ago. At first Scott hoped it was Lane or some other reinforcements. But they'd mistakenly checked out the windows and paid for the error.

Now someone was outside, on the porch.

Straite heard the noise, and he urgently waved Hughes and Frances upstairs. He would provide them with at least a small delay. It was all he could do.

Hughes cocked his head, and raised his pistol, but Straite grinned resignedly and motioned again for them to get upstairs.

Hughes started up when a fusillade of bullets ripped into the front of the house, like hail on a tin roof.

A moment later someone broke through the door at the rear of the house, and a flash grenade went off with a boom that shook the entire structure.

Straite managed to get off a couple of shots down the hall toward the back as Hughes and Frances raced silently upstairs. At the top, Hughes looked back. The last he saw of Straite were bullets slamming into his already dying body, shoving him up hard against the wall. It was an image he knew he would never forget. But it would be one of the few things that he would not share with Moira.

Grabbing Frances's arm, Hughes hustled her down the nearly pitch-black corridor to the narrow stairs that led to what had been servants' quarters on the third floor.

"Did you manage to contact the navy?" she whispered urgently.

"Unfortunately not, dear. The bad guys took out our comms links as well as the telephones before I thought it was necessary to call the cavalry."

"But you warned Bill?"

"I called the CIA and they promised to speak to him. When he tries to call here and can't get through he'll know that something is wrong."

The front door crashed open, and they heard the footsteps of at least a dozen men below, but eerily no voices, no shouted commands. They were obviously a well-trained, well-motivated force.

"Then we'd best hold out that long," Frances said, a determined set to her eyes.

One hell of a woman, Hughes thought. "If it's clear in back, you should be able to climb out the corner window onto the upper wall. From there, with any luck, you can make it into the rear courtyard and lose yourself somewhere on the island. These people aren't going to stick around very long."

"I won't leave you."

"Don't be a fool. It's you and William they want, not some old carcass like me."

"They'll kill you."

"Not if I give up first and promise to tell them all my tedious little secrets." He grinned at her. "You'd be amazed, my dear, at how inventively long-winded I am with the proper motivation."

Someone started up the stairs.

"Bloody hell," Frances whispered. She reached up and kissed Hughes lightly on the lips, then turned and hurried noiselessly upstairs.

Hughes shut the stairwell door, then hurried across the corridor and ducked into the sitting room. A few embers still alive on the grate cast a red glow in the room.

He stuffed his 10mm Colt automatic into the cushions on the couch, grabbed the glass of wine Frances had been drinking earlier, and sat down. He crossed his legs and leaned back.

He heard them at the head of the stairs. There were at least four of them, maybe five. They checked each of the four rooms, then suddenly a figure dressed all in black, night vision goggles covering his eyes, appeared in the doorway.

"*Masa' al-khair,*" Good evening, Hughes said pleasantly in Arabic.

The night fighter pointed his small-caliber automatic pistol directly at Hughes's head.

"Wait," someone in the corridor ordered.

The night fighter stepped aside, and a tall, well-built man wearing a dark jacket over a white shirt and tie appeared.

"Ah, Valeri Yernin. *Dabry vyecher,* good evening."

"Who are you?" Yernin demanded.

"Thomas Hughes, Russian Division, National Security Agency. I believe we have a mutual acquaintance."

Recognition dawned in Yernin's reptilian eyes. "You work with Bill Lane."

"Yes. And he and some other people who'll be along shortly will take exception to what you and your Iraqi friends have done here this evening. You might take this opportunity to get out while the getting is good."

"Bill Lane is dead. Where is Commander Frances Shipley?"

A strong hand clutched at Hughes's heart, but he refused to let it show. He smiled instead. "I don't think that's likely."

Yernin raised his pistol. "Where is she?"

"Since you put it that way, she's in the basement, hiding like a little mouse."

Something flickered across Yernin's expression. "I don't believe you. Tell me the truth or I will kill you."

"You'll kill me now or later, it doesn't make much difference, except that your superiors would vigorously disapprove of your wanton wastefulness, my boy."

"What are you talking about?"

"NSA's Russian Division includes Ukraine. You'd be surprised at the stuff we know about you and your control officer Mikhail Maslennikov. For instance, we know that on January 22nd he had a meeting at the Council of Ministers' headquarters in Kiev with Lieutenant General Arkadi Sheskin, who heads the First Directorate of the Russian FIS, and Captain General Ivan Lukashin, chief of your own First Directorate."

Yernin was thunderstruck. Hughes didn't think the man had ever experienced such an emotion. He wanted to shoot Hughes so badly his gun hand shook. His eyes, which had been devoid of emotion, were suddenly filled with hate. And fear.

"I'll ask you for the last time. Where is the woman?"

"In the basement, like I said. I put her down there when we lost contact with our people on the outer perimeter. But you won't find her in time."

Again something flickered across Yernin's face. Uncertainty.

Yernin stepped aside and motioned with his gun. "You'll show me. If we don't find her I will kill you despite your knowledge." The Ukrainian assassin's eyes were neutral again.

"I see," Hughes replied. He put his glass on the end table, debated reaching in the cushions for the pistol, then got to his feet. "Actually I feel somewhat sorry for you, my dear boy. Because when you are gunned down like the rabid dog you are, no one will mourn your passing."

"Move," Yernin said, when they both heard an incoming helicopter.

* * *

They came in directly from the southwest over the empty ferry dock. The *Mississippi* agreed to send help. But it would take their SEALs thirty minutes to reach the island by chopper.

They had tried to reach Hughes or anyone else on the island by radio with no results. The *Mississippi*'s electronic counterintelligence unit confirmed that all comms links with the island were out. There were no electronic emissions of any nature detectable at the moment.

The entire island was dark, and they almost missed the helicopter parked on the road below the house. Lane spotted it first.

"There," he shouted to the ARAMCO pilot the CIA had commandeered. "Set us down behind the ridge on the other side of the chopper."

"Yes, sir."

"Look," Chad Thomas said, pointing to something lying on the ground beside a humvee parked on the road.

They were coming down and sideslipping toward the ridge, but Lane caught a quick glimpse of two bodies on the ground and a third in a ditch closer to the house. The black form was outlined against the lighter-colored sandy soil.

"Your people?" Thomas asked.

"I think so," Lane replied, tight-lipped. "Set me down here, then fly around to the back of the house and drop the others off," he told the pilot. "When you've done that you can get out of here. This isn't your fight."

"I hear you," the oil company employee said, only too happy to comply.

"I'll come with you," Zahedi said.

"No. I want you to go with Thomas and Hager. You guys are going to provide a diversion until the navy arrives. So spread out."

"What about you?" Thomas asked. He and his partner weren't happy, but they were along for the ride.

"I'm going to make like a ghost and scare them to death."

The others looked at him like he was a crazy man. But no one offered any objections.

Lane took out his Beretta, checked the load, and checked to make sure he had two extra magazines of ammunition in his jacket pocket. The instant the helicopter touched down behind the ridge, he shoved the hatch open, jumped out, and raced around the hill toward the ditch in front of the house.

Behind him the chopper lifted off and headed to the west, giving the house a wide enough berth to be safely out of range of any small arms ammunition.

The ground was rocky and uneven, forcing Lane to slow down; a broken ankle now would be a death warrant. He was sick that Frances and Hughes were both inside the house, which had obviously been assaulted by a large and clearly well-trained force. At least two perimeter guards were down, and all the comms gear was out. Which meant it was possible that all their security people on the island were dead.

His speculation was partially confirmed a hundred yards from where he was dropped off when he came upon two more bodies. Both men had been shot precisely in the middle of their foreheads with small-caliber guns. Probably high-powered .22-caliber night-fighter stealth weapons. It fit with what he'd spotted lying in the ditch by the house.

At the end of the ridge, Lane scrambled down into the ditch, and on hands and knees crawled the last seventy or eighty yards to the black-clad body he'd spotted from the air.

The man had taken a hit high in the shoulder, and another at point-blank range into his right eye, shattering the lens in his night spotting goggles.

Flattening himself as low to the ground as possible, Lane peered up over the edge of the ditch. The front of the house had been shot up, all the windows shattered. The front door was open, and Lane spotted what he took to be a body lying in the hall.

Nothing moved in the night. The wind had died to a zephyr, and the sounds of the helicopter had faded to the west. For the moment he could have been utterly alone on an alien planet.

Lane took off his jacket, then undressed the dead night fighter. The only thing he could not work out was how the force of commandos expected to get off the island under the noses of the US Navy, the Kuwaiti military and Special Palace Guards who watched their borders like hawks, and the US Air Force which had fighter-interceptors stationed nearby in Saudi Arabia.

Lane was not overly squeamish by nature—though from time to time Hughes accused him of being a neat freak—but he had a momentary shiver of revulsion as he donned the blood-soaked night fighter bodysuit, pulling the hood over his head. He stuffed his Beretta in the belt at the small of his back and the extra magazines in one of the zippered leg pockets.

He checked the load on the dead man's .22-caliber autoloader. The magazine was nearly full. Then he put on the ruined night vision goggles. Surprisingly, the left eyepiece still worked.

He looked at his watch. If the navy SEALs were on schedule, they would be showing up in fifteen minutes. It was possible that Yernin's commandos monitored the navy's frequency, so they too might know the timetable.

The distinctive sharp crack of M-16 fire suddenly broke the silence of the night. Zahedi and the others were starting their diversionary attack.

He cocked an ear. If there was any returning fire, it came from silenced weapons, because he could hear only the American assault rifle fire.

Clutching his left shoulder with his gun hand, he struggled to his feet as if he were a man mortally wounded who, by dint of great spirit, had willed himself to rise so that he could help his brothers repel an attack at the rear of the house.

The attention of those in the house would be focused toward the back, but Lane didn't fool himself by believing lookouts hadn't been posted in all directions. Guns would be trained on him now, but the men would be having second and third thoughts, seeing what they took to be a ghost. Their own comrade brought back from the dead.

"*In sha'Allah,*" Lane whispered, not meaning any blasphemy. But it *was* only God who knew the outcome.

He staggered through the open gates into the outer courtyard, and headed directly for the front door.

Something moved at one of the windows, but then was lost in the shadows.

Lane lowered his head, lurched to the left, then, regaining his balance, trudged the rest of the way to the house and stepped inside to the front hall.

Scott and Straite were both down with multiple gunshot wounds to their heads and bodies, as was one of the Kuwaiti Special Palace Guards. Frances and Hughes were nowhere in sight, one small thing to be thankful for.

One of the night fighters stood halfway up the stairs staring down at him in obvious shock; another similarly clad man flanked him, left of the doorway. He too seemed stunned.

Lane grunted in pain, lurching left again. The commando by the window said something in Arabic that sounded like *Barzani.*

"Same to you, pal," Lane said. He fired two shots into the commando's chest and face, then, feinting back to the right, continued to bring the silenced .22 stealth weapon up and around, firing four more shots, two of which hit the man on the stairs in the neck and face before he could fully react.

Two men appeared in the back corridor knowing something was happening in the front of the house, but not sure what it was.

It was all the advantage Lane needed. Switching the .22's fire selector to full automatic, he emptied the big magazine down the corridor, taking out both men.

He tossed the weapon aside and grabbed the gun and one of the flash grenades from the downed man by the window. He pulled the pin, tossed the grenade down the back corridor, and, before it went off, grabbed a second grenade, pulled the pin, and launched it up the stairs.

The grenades went off within a couple of seconds of each other. Several men at the rear of the house began screaming in agony. The second floor was silent.

Lane took the stairs up two at a time. A commando was down in the corridor, blood oozing from his eyes, nose, and ears.

A second night fighter, his hood off, his face smeared with blood, stood in the doorway of the sitting room. His weapon up.

For an instant, the commando was stunned into immobility.

Lane shot him twice in the neck and face. And he went down without a sound.

The screams downstairs were stifled, and the house was deathly still for the moment. Lane started down the hall just as Tom Hughes came out of the sitting room and stepped over the body of the night fighter. When Hughes saw what he took to be another commando, his expression darkened.

Lane said nothing, although his heart immediately lightened seeing his old friend alive and apparently unhurt.

Yernin stepped out of the sitting room, looked at the apparition standing in the corridor, and immediately raised his pistol to Hughes's head.

"Since you're not one of us, you must be Bill Lane," he said.

Keeping the .22 stealth weapon aimed in Yernin's general direction, Lane pulled off the ruined goggles, tossed them aside, and pulled off his hood.

"About time you showed up," Hughes said, grinning with relief. "I was beginning to think that I was going to have all the fun myself."

"Where's Frances?"

"She's safely out of reach of these scum. I heard shooting in the back. Did you bring the navy?"

"CIA. But the navy's on the way."

"They'll be here in twelve minutes to be precise," Yernin said. "And the helicopter you arrived in holds only four people plus the pilot. So I don't think we have to worry about being overrun."

"I personally took out six of your people, and I don't hear much shooting going on at the moment."

"It doesn't matter, we have time."

"For what?" Lane asked coldly.

"A trade. My life for your friend's life."

"Tom signed on the same dotted line as every soldier does."

Yernin laughed. "I don't believe you would throw away your friend's life simply to kill me."

Lane cracked a smile. "Don't count on it."

Yernin looked at Lane, the flat expression in his eyes again. "What will my death gain you? It's nothing more than politics."

"It's murder," Lane retorted. "Did you know that the young woman at Norfolk whose body you booby-trapped was pregnant?"

"She was a soldier. The same as all of us. She signed on that dotted line."

"What about the people on the train? What army were they with?"

"If you hadn't pushed me, they would not have died," Yernin said indifferently. "But we're not here to discuss the past. We're here to discuss our future."

Lane shrugged. "Go to hell."

Yernin was irked. "Then it becomes a queen's gambit after all."

"You're forgetting one of your choices."

"What's that?"

"Give up and I promise you safe passage back to the States where you'll stand trial. It's the only deal I'm making."

A sudden, urgent look came into Hughes's eyes. He looked at something over Lane's left shoulder.

"It is you who has run out of choices," Yernin said in triumph. "Kill him," he instructed someone down the corridor.

Lane dove to the left, pointing the stealth weapon over his right shoulder and spraying the corridor behind him while keeping his eyes on Yernin.

The Ukrainian brought his pistol around to bear on Lane, but before he could take proper aim and fire, Hughes shoved him against the wall, then sprinted back into the sitting room.

Lane had just enough time to feel slightly disappointed that his friend had run for safety, but glad that he had done so, when two bullets slammed into his right hip and leg from behind, knocking him to the floor.

He rolled over on his back and sprayed a long burst at the two commandos firing from a low crouch. Both of them went down at the same moment his .22 ran out of ammunition.

Dropping the weapon, he rolled back onto his stomach as he snatched the Beretta from the belt at the small of his back.

Yernin had recovered and he fired three shots at Lane's still-moving figure at the same moment Lane pumped four shots down the corridor, one bullet smacking into Yernin's shoulder, the others going wild.

Something hit the back of Lane's head and he went down, still conscious but momentarily unable to move.

Something brushed past him, and with a supreme force of will he managed to lever himself over to his side in time to see Yernin reach the stairs.

"Yernin," he croaked.

The Ukrainian turned in surprise, hesitated, then fired two shots over Lane's head.

Answering fire came from the sitting room door, one of the shots hitting Yernin in the left leg.

Yernin staggered back, fired a third shot down the corridor, and Hughes cried out in pain and crashed to the floor.

Lane managed to bring his gun up even though he was seeing double and he couldn't keep his balance. The house was spinning as if it were caught up in a funnel cloud.

Yernin shifted aim directly at his head.

Lane squeezed off a shot which hit Yernin's already wounded left shoulder, shoving him against the railing at the head of the stairs. The next two shots went wild. The fourth hit the Ukrainian in his left side, and the fifth hit him in the side of the face at the base of his nose, sending him crashing down the stairs.

Lane pulled the trigger one last time at the retreating figure, but the hammer slapped on an empty chamber.

He slumped down on the floor, conscious of movements downstairs, and then the sounds of at least two heavy choppers coming from the southeast. The navy, finally, he thought.

"Tommy?" he said, painfully turning over.

Hughes, a 10mm Colt automatic held loosely in his right hand, sat on the floor, his back against the doorjamb, a silly grin on his face. He held his side where he'd been shot.

"Gee, that was fun. Think we can do it again soon?"

Lane smiled. "Only if you promise not to tell Moira that I almost let him kill you."

"It's a deal," Hughes said, but Lane only heard part of it before he passed out.

38

It seemed to Lane that he had lived in a fog for days, possibly weeks. At first there'd been bright lights, and loud noises, jarring sensations, deep-throated vibrations. Those gave way to distant dreams, faces swimming overhead, poking and prodding. Someone speaking his name. He wasn't glad when it ended until he opened his eyes and saw a pretty face.

"You're beautiful," he mumbled.

The nurse, whose name tag read KRAUS, flashed him a bright smile. "Welcome back."

"Will you marry me?"

"They said you were tough, but nobody warned me that you were a flirt." She laughed. "How do you feel?"

"Hungry," Lane said. "Tom Hughes, the man I was brought in with, how is he?"

"Just fine, waiting for you to come around. And so is Commander Shipley."

"Was she hurt?"

"She's fine too," nurse Kraus reassured him. "The only reason she's still here—by the way you're at the air force hospital in Ramstein—is because of you."

Lane allowed himself to relax a little. "How long have I been here?"

"You've been sedated for two days. The doctor didn't want you moving around. One concussion on top of another is bad for the health."

"I couldn't agree more, Ashley my dear," Hughes said from the doorway. "But the boy has the unfortunate habit of sticking his nose in bad places."

Lane turned his head so that he could see for himself if his old friend was truly okay. Hughes, dressed in a hospital gown and bathrobe, sauntered into the room. He carried himself a little stiffly, but he looked good. Lane allowed himself to relax even more.

"Raise me up a little, please," he told the nurse.

"I will not," she said.

"Better do it, Ashley, otherwise the lad will crawl out of bed and do it himself."

"Oh, all right." The nurse raised the head of his bed six inches. "That's it for now or else the doctor will have my hide."

"And a fine hide it is."

"God protect me," she moaned. "I'll tell the doctor you're awake and then get you something to eat."

"Thank you."

She flashed him another big smile, and left.

Hughes closed the door and pulled a chair over to the bed and sat down. "How are you feeling, William?"

"I'd have a tough time finishing nine holes of golf."

"The doctor says you'll recover fully." Hughes cocked an eye. "I didn't know you played golf."

"I don't," Lane said. "Frances is okay?"

"I sent her out a back window and over the courtyard fence when the situation started to heat up. She bumped into Chad Thomas and his partner, and helped out with the diversionary attack." Hughes shook his head in admiration. "That's one tough lady."

"Is she still here?"

"She was recalled to London this morning to talk to her superiors. But she promised she'd be back as soon as possible."

"We got beat up pretty badly, Tommy."

"Yes, we did," Hughes said solemnly. "But we stopped them. The body count of the bad guys was up to thirteen as of this morning when they pulled another one out of the bay."

"How about Yernin?"

Hughes's expression darkened. "His body hasn't turned up yet, but it will. He was hit too badly to have gotten very far. I saw that much with my own eyes."

"He might have had help. There might have been some of them still alive downstairs."

"The SEALs met no resistance. I think they were a little disappointed," Hughes said. "It's my guess that Yernin and whatever was left of his force somehow made it to the water's edge, where they had hidden rubber rafts, and headed out to sea. They were supposed to rendezvous with a private cruiser, but they never linked up because we found the cruiser at a covered dock in Al-Khiran. That's about fifty miles south of the island. So whatever happened, they were stuck out there. And later that night they got some pretty heavy weather."

Lane was skeptical.

"He'll show up," Hughes said.

"I believe he will," Lane replied softly. "But not in the way you think."

The door opened and Frances, dressed in a skirt and blouse, her coat on her arm, breezed in. She tossed the coat aside, came over to the bed, and gave Lane a kiss.

"God, I'm glad to see you," she said, a catch in her throaty voice.

"I was worried about you," Lane said, relieved.

"I can see when I'm no longer needed," Hughes said, getting up. He put the chair back, and looked down at Lane. "The boss sends his thanks for a job well done, and says you can take as much sick leave as you need. The world's problems will have to wait."

"Funny thing," Frances said. "My boss told me the same thing. And it just happens that a friend of mine has lent me her house outside of Saint-Tropez."

"The things a man has to do for his country," Lane sighed.

"I'll take that as a yes," Frances said, looking into his eyes. "Close the door on the way out, would you, Tom," she said and she came gently into Lane's arms.

FAILAKA ISLAND AIR FORCE BASE

It was night again when Yernin hobbled painfully out of his room onto the gallery overlooking the hangar floor twenty meters below. His entire left side was numb, and almost useless. But from where the bullet had gone through his face, shattering his upper teeth and breaking his left and right cheekbones, a living hell of intense pain radiated into his neck, down his spine, and around to his chest.

Once again he'd been defeated at the hands of Bill Lane. But once again he had survived, and hate burned even more strongly in his body than did the pain from his wounds.

It was a feeling that would sustain him through everything that was to come, including the humiliation of defeat when he would be denounced by Saddam Hussein, as well as his own control officer.

His right hand gripped the railing tightly, making his knuckles white.

A dim light flashed briefly behind one of the mothballed helicopters that the US Air Force stored here, and Lieutenant Hadr stepped out. He spotted Yernin on the gallery above, and gave him the thumbs-up sign. It meant the helicopter was ready to fly.

But not yet, Yernin told himself. They would wait for several days until everything on the island quieted down. Search parties still roamed the island's beaches and cliffs looking for more bodies. Their communications, which had been nonstop for the first forty-eight hours, had begun to slow down.

They'd searched this base the first thing this morning, but Yernin and

Hadr had remained in hiding in the honeycomb of limestone caves that connected the house with the base.

The existence of the subterranean passages and the hidden opening in the bowels of the ancient house were known to the archaeologists, and of course to Kuwaiti security. But in the aftermath of the action, nobody thought of it.

For the moment they were safe, Yernin thought, shuffling back into their quarters. When the search died down, he and Hadr would fly the helicopter across the border using up-to-date naval transponder codes, which were another bit of intelligence he'd gleaned from Honolulu's computer.

Time now to recover, he told himself, lying down on the cot. He touched the bandages wrapped around his face.

There would be time later to kill Bill Lane.

Time, he thought as he drifted off to sleep, to put his own plans into action.

PART
THREE

39

THE FRENCH RIVIERA

Lane pulled himself out of the long, narrow lap pool, grabbed a towel, and stood at the low stone balustrade at the end of the patio as he dried himself. From here he could see across the bay to the pretty town of Beauvallon, and beyond it Sainte-Maxime. The morning was a little cool, but the rising sun felt good on his body.

The place that Frances's mysterious unnamed friend had lent them for as long as they wished was more like a small villa than an ordinary house. Perched atop a high promontory above the Mediterranean, only one narrow road led down to Saint-Tropez. The hills and cliffs were so steep that any off-road approach would be extremely difficult at best, so he and Frances had felt reasonably secure for the past five weeks.

He'd taken his recovery slowly at first, content just to walk around the expansive house. But after the first week he started doing laps in the pool in the mornings and afternoons. Before lunch he ran down the road then back up. Just a hundred yards the first few times, until yesterday when he'd run nearly five miles round trip carrying a thirty-pound sack of stones on his back.

"His penance," he called it, for nearly getting himself killed twice.

Once a week a British doctor, another of Frances's friends, came down from Nice to see him. Two weeks ago he smiled and shook his head.

"I suppose telling a man like you to take it easy would be an exercise in futility," the doctor said.

"Rather," Frances agreed.

Rising to go, the doctor shook Lane's hand. "I shan't be back unless you break a leg or something. You're healing quite remarkably well without me." He glanced at Frances and grinned. "Must be the water . . . or something."

She returned his warm smile.

Later that afternoon when they were making love in the big four-poster bed, Lane looked down at her beautiful body.

"Is this the 'or something' the good doctor was referring to?"

"Hmm," she purred. "Rather."

He touched the still-tender patch at the back of his head. In twenty or thirty years the two concussions he'd suffered would probably cause him problems. Double vision, nausea, and perhaps difficulty in maintaining his balance. If he lived that long.

They hadn't found Yernin's body and had given up the search. But according to Hughes, five days after the attack someone stole a Cobra helicopter from the mothballed air base on the island. The machine had shown up on the black market in Basra, so the official line was Kuwaiti entrepreneurship. It happened all the time. After all, if you couldn't steal from friends for profit, then who could you steal from?

"The thing was that they knew the current transponder codes. Something Yernin could have gotten out of Honolulu's computer," Hughes said.

"Means he's still on the run," Lane replied thoughtfully.

"Watch yourself, William," Hughes warned, his voice low. "It's getting strange around here."

"What do you mean?"

"Hard to say, but Ben Lewis is almost always gone, no one has seen Roswell in days, and no one is talking. It's un-American keeping secrets in a place like this," Hughes quipped. "When are you coming back?"

"Would they accept my resignation?"

"Not likely."

"I'll be back in a few days, Tom. In the meantime, run a search program in Kiev in case our friend shows up there."

"Already up and running."

"Nothing yet?"

"Nada."

"How about Baghdad and Basra?" Lane asked. "Are we coming up with any hard intelligence on Hussein's whereabouts?"

Hughes hesitated uncharacteristically. "Officially no. But I caught a glimpse of a National Reconnaissance Office printout addressed to us— Roswell specifically—from one of their KH-series birds. Looked to me like a section of real estate southwest of Baghdad, complete with bedouin tents."

"Not unusual."

"Except that bedouins as a rule don't use satellite communications dishes."

"I see what you mean," Lane said. "Keep your eyes open. I'll see you next week."

"Take care, William."

"Will do."

That was three days ago. Ever since then he'd expected someone to show up here, so he wasn't surprised when he heard a car starting up the switchbacks on the road below. It wasn't the Peugeot Frances drove. He recognized that engine sound.

He went inside and threw on a pair of slacks, a light V-neck sweater, and a pair of moccasins.

Frances had driven up to Nice to do some grocery shopping at the *Supermarché,* and wouldn't be home for another couple of hours. If she returned early she would see the car in the driveway and take the proper precautions.

He took out his Beretta 9mm, checked the action, and went outside around front where he took up a position by the stone fence. From there he could see the road to the right and the turnabout and parking area to the left.

Only a few people knew that he and Frances were here. Although he'd not shared with Hughes his hunch that there must be a leak at a high place in the NSA or the CIA, his suspicions had deepened the more he thought about the coincidences leading up to his arrest at Bandar-é Emān, the incident at the hotel, and the attack on the island.

Someone who had known his moves had transmitted them to the enemy. Paranoia? He thought not. Someone on his own side wanted him dead.

He stepped a little farther into the shadows beneath the grape arbor as a dark blue Renault with deeply tinted windows topped the hill and came through the gate, parking in the turnabout.

Ben Lewis levered his bulk out of the small car and studied the front of the house as if he were looking for something. He wore an open collar shirt and an ill-fitting brown checked suit. He seemed nervous.

Lane stuffed the pistol in the waistband of his slacks at the small of his back, stepped out of the shadows, and walked up to the driveway. Lewis turned around, startled.

"I heard the car, but I had no idea who was coming," Lane told the NSA Russian Division director.

"You look better than I thought you would. How are you doing?"

"I've felt worse."

They shook hands.

Lewis glanced again at the house. "Is Commander Shipley here this morning?"

"She's shopping," Lane said. "Won't be back for another couple of hours. Any word on Yernin's whereabouts?"

"He's either back in Ukraine or hiding in Iraq. But we figured out how he escaped."

"He took the helicopter from the air force base."

"Yeah, but the best part is the limestone caverns beneath the house. The Greek garrison used them for storage. Thing is that the cave system connects with the air base."

"Nobody knew this?" Lane asked sharply.

"The archaeologists did, and so did Kuwaiti security," Lewis shrugged.

"But no one thought of it." Lewis looked at the house a third time. "Can we get out of the sun? I'm hot and tired and I want a drink."

"It's only nine thirty in the morning."

Lewis grinned ruefully. "I'm suffering from jet lag. Besides, the hour of the day never stopped you."

"True," Lane said, leading the way.

Lewis wasn't himself, and there was an oddness between them. They'd known each other for years, but for the first time Lane could not read the man. Lewis was hiding something.

They sat in the shade by the pool. Lane brought out a bottle of Jack Daniel's and two glasses and poured them each a shot. Lewis downed his immediately, and Lane poured him a second.

"There was a lot of blood in the cave," Lewis said. "But by the time they get a hundred yards, where they hid in one of the side chambers, the blood has stopped."

"They?"

Lewis nodded ponderously, the small whiskey glass lost in his meaty paw. "He had help. We found a second set of footprints in the dust. Same pattern sole as the other commandos wore."

"Iraqi?"

"Almost certainly, although none of them carried identification. It was a pretty expensive operation for them. Hussein doesn't have that many troops left. Meant he wanted to stop you in the worst way."

"Pretty expensive for us too, Ben," Lane reminded him. "Starting with Lieutenant Commander Stein, and including Norfolk, Richmond, the train, the two men at the hotel in Kuwait City, and then the island, the body count is high."

"Would have been higher without you," Lewis said, looking Lane directly in the eye. "The president knows what happened out there, the risks you took, and he sends his sincere appreciation."

"It's not over."

"No," Lewis said glumly. "In fact it's just beginning. It's the reason I came." He looked up from his drink. "Have you been watching the news? Tom says you always refuse to when you get like . . . this."

"No news, just music."

"How about Commander Shipley?"

"What's happened, Ben?"

"There's been a massacre at a place called Nukhayb in the Syrian desert about a hundred fifty miles southwest of Baghdad. Twenty-five hundred men, women, and children were gassed to death with Sarin eighteen hours ago. We don't have all the details yet, but it was almost certainly done by Hussein's troops. The story is that the townspeople refused to house some of Hussein's people so he retaliated."

"Just like Hamma in Syria," Lane said. "He's made his point. He still has weapons of mass destruction and he's not afraid to use them. He wants to be back in Baghdad." He focused on Lewis. "What are we going to do about it?"

Lewis shook his massive head. "The Western alliance is sick of the fighting. So long as Hussein confines his antics to within Iraq's border, we're going to stay out of it. At least that's our official position. The only one we can take under the circumstances. OPEC is threatening to cut back on oil deliveries to us if we make any overt military move out there. Meanwhile Sirak's new government in Baghdad is screaming bloody murder. They want our help and want it now."

"We're not interested in a blockade for fear that OPEC would carry out its threat?"

"No, the president would never authorize such a move. Cowboy tactics, he'd call it. The situation is too explosive, and the stakes are going to take another quantum leap soon."

"Something else happened?" Lane asked, his cool blue eyes steady now that he knew why Lewis had come to see him.

"Two subsea SS-N-sixteen nuclear missiles have disappeared from the Black Sea Fleet's stockpile at Sevastopol. Nobody knows where or how, nor can they pinpoint the date closer than two weeks ago."

"How'd we get this information?"

"Joyce Katarian."

"Then the information is solid, but those missiles could be anywhere by now."

"That's what we figured."

"They wouldn't do Hussein any good out in the desert even if they could get them there."

"Technical Services says they can be modified to launch from a land-based facility," Lewis said. "They've got a ten-thousand-mile range. Intercontinental."

"They'd have to be programmed first."

Lewis looked startled. "That's true."

"Do we know if those particular missiles still held specific target programs?"

"According to the last SALT treaty, all their missiles, and all our missiles, were targeted harmlessly out to sea."

"If you believe that, I have some land three hundred miles due east of New York City I'll sell you."

"We can try to find out," Lewis said lamely.

Lane fixed his penetrating gaze on the Russian Division director. "Let's cut to the chase, Ben. Why'd you come to see me? What is it you want?"

"Roswell sent me to talk to you. No one else knows a thing for the moment. Not even the president or his people." Lewis met Lane's gaze. "Even Tom Hughes isn't in the loop this time."

"I'm listening."

"Saddam Hussein is a madman, and he won't stop until he's regained power, probably embroiling the entire Middle East in a war the region would take fifty years to recover from." Lewis wiped a hand across his sweaty brow. "Maybe longer if his people are smart enough to drop the missiles down a couple of oil shafts in Kuwait, or maybe Saudi Arabia. It would contaminate oil in the region for ten thousand years."

"The Syrian desert is a big piece of real estate. Lots of places for him to hide."

"We know where he is," Lewis said softly.

"How?"

"The National Reconnaissance Office found what they believe is his camp."

"You're a little far afield from the Russian Division, aren't you, Ben?"

"I'm in because of the Ukrainian connection."

"If we know Hussein's whereabouts, why don't we take him out? One stealth bomber could make a surgical strike. We nearly did it with Gadhafi and we didn't have such sophisticated equipment."

"This administration doesn't do things that way."

"Bullshit, Ben. You came here to ask me to sneak into Hussein's desert camp and assassinate the man. What's the difference, except that I'd probably not make it back out of the desert alive?"

"You're deniable," Lewis said.

Lane sat back. "Ah, a refreshing dose of honesty. If I try but bungle it, the White House can claim I was unhinged because of what happened in Kuwait."

"Something like that."

"What if I succeed? How do I get out of there? Hitchhike?"

"In that case we'd get you out. There'd be so much confusion in the aftermath that it would be relatively easy to extract you."

Lane got up and walked over to the edge of the patio. The morning mist was finally beginning to burn off, revealing the vast Med which seemed to go on forever.

"We can set you down on the desert within ten miles of his current camp. We can give you all the equipment you need, radios, GPS navigators, weapons, land mines, LAWs rockets, whatever."

Ever since he was a kid, Lane had hated war and violence; he'd joined the military because he figured they were the only class of people who could hate war more than he did.

When he got out of the service he hid himself behind a desk under the guise of analyst. If killing had to be done, he'd be the man to tell them who, when, where, how, and most importantly, why.

"Nobody knows all the details except us, and no one ever will," Lewis assured him. "But the president believes in you, and so does Roswell."

Lane thought of a line he'd read years ago when he was in school. He forgot where it came from but the sentiment had stuck with him.

It is only those who have neither fired a shot nor heard the shrieks and groans of the wounded who cry aloud for blood, more vengeance, more desolation.

He could feel Lewis's eyes on his back, staring at him, waiting for an answer.

"All right," he said.

"You'll cross the border from northern Saudi Arabia. We'll brief you in Riyadh."

"I want Tom in on this."

"Absolutely not," Lewis said harshly.

"Tom will backstop me or I won't go," Lane replied without turning.

Lewis capitulated after a hesitation. "But the British will be kept out. That means Commander Shipley."

"Agreed."

A chair scraped against the tile, and Lane sensed that Lewis had gotten up. "I'll see you Wednesday."

"Okay," Lewis said.

After a few moments Lane heard the car start up and head back into town, and then the hilltop was silent again except for birdsong.

He remembered the end of the quotation from school. It had been presented at a military academy's graduation in Michigan in the late 1800s. It was just as true now as it had been through the ages.

War is hell.

40

Lane, carrying the heavy bag of stones on his back, made it to the bottom of the hill and was halfway back up when he heard the Peugeot start up the switchbacks.

The noon sun was hot for this time of the year, and the air desert dry this far above the sea. He pushed himself to the limit. The strain on his muscles felt good to him. It was as if he were punishing himself for agreeing to go ahead with something that went totally against his grain.

The sounds of the car came closer, and Lane tried to go faster, as if he could outrun it; the human body versus the machine.

It wasn't possible, he knew. Human flesh was frail after all, the heart easily stopped with just an ounce of steel-jacketed lead and a few grains of smokeless powder.

Not much with which to end the genius of, say, an Einstein or a Mother Teresa. Or the evil of a Hitler or a Hussein. Who made the choices? And who could say if the choices once made were the correct ones?

"Cute buns," Frances yelled from the open car window as she passed, and disappeared around the next switchback above.

He waved and smiled, but it didn't help his morose mood. Since his divorce, he had avoided serious entanglements. Frances was a trained British secret service operative, yet he thought of her more as a woman than as a spy who knew how to use a gun. He thought of her more as a woman, smaller and weaker than he was, with needs and desires different than those of a British navy commander. Feminine. Soft. Rounded.

He strove to protect her, not nurture her as a partner in the business. If he were to continue on his present course, could he afford the luxury of such a relationship? Or would thinking about her take away his edge? It happened in the sixties and seventies during the height of the cold war when both sides were burning up agents almost as fast as they could be produced and shoved out into the field. Those with wives and families back home seemed more susceptible to capture than loners. But the family men seemed better able to resist their interrogators than the single men. It was a trade-off.

She was waiting for him by the pool when he reached the house. She'd changed into a bikini, and had laid out an ice-cold crockery pitcher of sangria and two glasses. She looked as if she'd been lounging around the house all morning instead of shopping in the heat.

"What about the groceries?" he asked at the patio door. Given the circumstances, the mundane concern seemed silly.

"The stuff that'll rot is in the fridge, the rest can wait," she said brightly. "Take your shower and come sit down, I have something to tell you."

"Important?"

"Yes," she said. "Now, shoo."

Lane took a cool shower, then put on a pair of swimming trunks and a light terry-cloth jacket, and joined her by the pool.

She poured him a glass of wine and smiled at him expectantly. "I've been officially detached to your shop for as long as I'm useful."

Lane stared at her. "Who did you see this morning?"

She studied his face, and hers fell. "Bradley Morgan. He gave me the green light." She reached out and touched his hand. "What is it, darling?"

"I'm leaving in a few days, and you're returning to London."

"I'm working for you now."

"No you're not. I'll talk to Roswell and have him arrange your transfer home."

She looked even more closely into his eyes. "Someone came here this morning while I was gone, didn't they? It wasn't Tommy, because he would have stayed. Nor was it Roswell, because there would have been a lot of fanfare, security in town, that sort of thing. I would have noticed that. So it must have been Ben Lewis. Am I right?"

Lane said nothing.

"Don't treat me this way, William. Was Ben Lewis here?"

"Yes."

"They found out something about Yernin. He's still alive, and they want you to go after him again. Is that it?" A wild look came into her eyes.

"That's part of it," he lied. "But you're no longer involved."

"The bloody hell I'm not!" she shouted. "It was me he was after, as well as you."

"I want you to go home, Frannie."

"I'm a trained intelligence officer, damnit, not some helpless female . . . if ever there was such a thing. I'm coming with you."

"No."

"Why?" she cried in anguish.

He had to look away for a minute, hardly able to face his own emotions, let alone her eyes.

"Because I couldn't stand to see you in harm's way again," he said.

"It's part of the job," she countered softly.

"Because if it came down to it, I would sacrifice the mission before I'd let anything happen to you. No matter the consequences. And this time the job is too important for that kind of a consideration."

"Then it's not just Yernin they're sending you after, is it?"

"Go home, Frannie."

"Why?" she cried again. "The truth!"

"Because I love you."

NATIONAL SECURITY AGENCY
FORT MEADE, MARYLAND

"Is he still at the British safe house in Saint-Tropez?" Bill Townsend, asked.

"Yes, but he doesn't know it belongs to the SIS," Tom Roswell replied. He was alone in his Fort Meade office, speaking to Townsend via encrypted television-telephone.

"Are the British monitoring what's going on up there?"

"They would be, except that someone disconnected the circuitry," Roswell said. He could see the concern on the national security adviser's face. If this blew up on them they'd lose a lot more than their jobs. "Ben Lewis went over and talked to him."

"He agreed to do it?"

"Yes he did."

"He knows why we want it done this way? The deniability factor?" Townsend sat forward, his face looming large in the tiny screen. "We can't have another debacle out there, Tom. You know this. OPEC is getting its act together again, and they're looking to the Far East for markets, which means we could be shit out of luck if anything goes wrong." He sat back. "Jesus Christ, even the Kuwaitis want us to get the hell out. Can you imagine that? The ungrateful bastards!"

"Nobody is in love with Hussein. Especially not now."

Townsend laughed humorlessly. "Since when has love had anything to do with anything in the Middle East? It's the leader who's feared the most who gets the most respect. And right now everybody out there is quaking in their desert sandals for fear that the crazy bastard will somehow get his hands on nuclear weapons."

"The Israelis could be convinced to take him out. We could look the other way when they did it," Roswell suggested. It was an exercise in futility and he knew it. But he played the devil's advocate because he wanted to have a leg to stand on if this operation were to blow up in their faces. His had been the only voice of reason. He glanced at the tape machine in an open desk drawer. It was working.

"They have their own problems as it is with the Palestinians. Something like this would beat them up and they know it." Townsend shook his head. "That's out."

"We could go public with it, Bill. Show and tell, starting with the raid on Bandar-é Emān, the attack on Failaka, and the Nukhayb massacre."

"That won't work either and you know it," Townsend said, disgusted. "Can we prove that Hussein was behind the raid on Iran's submarines? Can we prove it wasn't a ruse by the Iranians themselves?"

"No, but that would have to rank as one of the world's biggest coincidences."

"It's happened before," Townsend said. "But goddamnit, we've gone over this. What I want to know is, can Lane pull it off?"

"I think he has a pretty good chance of getting to Hussein and taking him out," Roswell said. "He has a habit of doing the impossible. The problem will be getting him out alive afterwards."

Townsend's eyes looked directly out of the screen, his face set in a blank expression. "That won't be *the* primary consideration."

"I understand," Roswell said after a beat.

"How are you getting him across the border?"

"Do you want to know?"

Townsend shook his head. "No, I don't believe I do."

41

KARACHI, PAKISTAN

At midnight the city was alive with the press of humanity, three and a half million people living on the disease-infested delta formed by the heavily polluted Indus River. Traffic was intense along Fatimah Jinnah and in the city center, and the smells of exhaust and decay permeated the unsettled, crime-ridden city. A man, taller than most Pakistanis but with the same dark coloration and dressed in traditional Hindi garb, stood in the shadows across the street from the Avari Towers Hotel.

Valeri Yernin waited patiently, something he had to relearn since Failaka. He'd followed his control officer for the past twelve hours wanting to make sure they were clean before he made his approach. After the disaster on the island he had become even more careful than usual.

Hussein's stupid attack on the desert village had helped focus the world's attention on Iraq. It was anybody's guess when the Western alliance would finally decide to take the man out. Though current opinion was that Reasoner did not have the guts to face up to an increasingly unified OPEC front, it could happen anytime.

Yernin had been more than happy to respond to Maslennikov's call to rendezvous tonight at eight o'clock. He was four hours late on purpose.

For five weeks he had languished on the Syrian desert with Hussein's troops, listening to the man's grandiose schemes, all the while wondering why Kiev wanted so desperately to ally itself with such a force.

He'd healed quickly under Hussein's personal physician's care, and by the second week he was exercising up to eight hours each day.

His shattered mouth had been wired and pinned back together in a series of extremely painful operations under primitive conditions. It would never heal properly. He would have a permanent scowl.

He limped a little, and his shoulder ached, but worst of all was the razor-sharp pain of the false teeth they'd made for him. Even holding his mouth stationary, he was in pain. Talking was agony, and eating was almost impossible.

But he endured, and would endure, so long as Bill Lane was alive. Hate rode with Yernin the way the fame of an Olympic gold medal stuck with an athlete; it was a part of him.

Maslennikov, dressed in dark slacks and a dark pullover, came out of the hotel and handed the parking valet something. The young man took off running down the ramp into the parking garage beneath the hotel.

Yernin stepped a little farther back into the shadows as his control officer looked across the street in his direction.

Maslennikov looked at his watch, lowered his wrist, then lifted it again to recheck the time. He took a cigarette out of a breast pocket, turned out of the wind to light it, then replaced his lighter in the pocket opposite the one he'd taken it from.

Tradecraft signs that everything was okay for the planned rendezvous. They were standard gestures. Maslennikov knew or suspected that Yernin was out there somewhere waiting for the right moment to come in.

A brown Chrysler minivan came out of the garage and pulled up in front of Maslennikov. The valet got out and Maslennikov got in behind the wheel. Seconds later nine men, dressed similarly to him, came out of the hotel and crowded into the van, and Maslennikov started down the driveway.

Yernin got on his small motorbike and maneuvered into traffic as the van headed north. He kept several cars back, continuously checking his rearview mirror to make sure that he wasn't being followed in turn.

The van continued past the Zainab Market and Saddar Bazaar and turned left to the docks on the west wharf across from the container loading complex. The port was busy around the clock. Twice they were stopped by train traffic, backing and filling, connecting with loaded flatcars, and moving empty units to sidings.

There was little in the way of security in the vast facility which was Pakistan's major port. The crush of traffic was so heavy, it would be impossible.

Maslennikov pulled up near the end of the broad pier that jutted nearly two kilometers into the harbor, where a sixty-meter luxury cruiser, *Good Hope, Plymouth, England* painted on her stern, was docked.

Yernin parked behind a stack of containers ten meters tall, and watched the men get out of the van and clamber up the yacht's ladder while Maslennikov again went through the routine of checking his watch twice and lighting a cigarette.

Yernin stepped out of the shadows and approached on foot.

Maslennikov's left eyebrow rose when he saw the disguise. "The meeting was for eight o'clock at the hotel. Why didn't you come?"

"After Failaka I wanted to make sure there would be no more mistakes."

"The mistakes were not of my making, Valeri Fedorovich," Maslennikov pointed out.

"Bill Lane—"

"You are obsessed with the man," Maslennikov interrupted sharply. "He beat you twice, there will not be a third time."

Yernin held his sudden rage in check. "You know where he disappeared to?"

"Yes, I do. But it's of no consequence at the moment. For now this mission is all that counts. You developed the plan as much as any of us. Now I'm asking, are you capable of carrying it out? Or will you take your stupid fixation with you?"

Yernin glanced up at the yacht. She looked modern and fast, exactly the kind of a vessel he'd called for. No expense had been spared. She was fitted with the latest communications and electronic intelligence-gathering equipment, as well as Magnetic Anomaly Detectors and sonars so sophisticated that the *Good Hope*'s capabilities rivaled those of any modern anti-submarine warship.

His government wanted Hussein back in Baghdad and the Middle East so destabilized that supplies of oil to the Western alliance would be permanently jeopardized.

On the face of it the plan was simple. A beholden Saddam Hussein back in power would guarantee Ukraine all the oil it needed. But there was more to it than that, Yernin suspected. Blaming the attack on Iran so that the Western allies would shift their attention away from Baghdad was only a part of it.

Maslennikov was studying him.

"My obsession, as you call it, is mine," Yernin said coldly. "But it will not interfere with this mission except to the extent that Bill Lane knows or suspects a good part of what we are up to. And it was an Iranian SAVAK officer with him in Kuwait, so the Iranians might know what we are up to now as well."

"But they cannot have guessed the how, nor the ultimate consequences."

"No," Yernin said. Nor did any of them know or suspect the consequences, because he was going to change their plans. If the madmen in Kiev thought Ukraine could profit from a destabilized world, he would give it to them.

Maslennikov glanced at the yacht. "They are a good crew. They'll do as they are told."

"How much do they know?"

"Nothing to this point, except that the mission will be as unusual as it is dangerous. But they've also been told that when it is over they will be well rewarded."

"Are you coming with us?"

Again Maslennikov studied Yernin looking for signs of weakness. "Are you capable of handling it?"

"Yes."

"Then no, I will leave it in your hands. Trust them, especially Razhin. He is a good captain. His men respect and trust him."

"Do they feel respect and trust for me?" Yernin asked.

Maslennikov laughed. "Only fear, Valeri. Only fear."

"As it should be."

42

NATIONAL SECURITY AGENCY

Thirteen hours later and ten time zones to the west a five-bell indicator chimed on one of the satellite monitors indicating that a flagged program was receiving something that the photo interpretive computer was evaluating as important.

Anthony Longo, chief photo interp officer on the graveyard shift, slid over from the console where he was playing two-handed solitaire against the computer. He knew exactly what it was the moment he looked at the monitor.

He transferred the real-time images coming from one of their KH-14 satellites in geosynchronous orbit over the Middle East onto the main viewing screen covering the back wall, enhanced the image, and started the printout sequence that would snapshot frozen time images. He selected a five-second interval.

The images were so sharp that he could recognize the uniforms and count the shoulder board pips on the two officers standing on the bridge. The angle was too high for him to read the sail number, but there was no mistaking what he was seeing.

He picked up the direct line to the situation room on the opposite side of the Fort Meade complex. His friend Ed Coney was OD this morning.

"Do you know what time it is over here, Tony?" Coney asked.

"Same time as it is here, three in the basic A.M., so quit your bellyaching," Longo, a youngish thirty-year-old with long sand blond hair, shot back. "I have an incoming hit on your GO-one-seven-one program."

"Stand by," Coney said. He was back three seconds later all business. "Okay, that's a hot one. But I'm surprised that you're coming up with anything. My screen is showing a cold front moving into the Persian Gulf. Thick overcast."

Longo looked up at the screen. The images coming down from the satellite were starting to fuzz out. "It's starting to affect us now. But I got some good shots of a Kilo-class submarine leaving the pens at Bandar-é Emān."

"How many?"

"Just one."

"Get a sail number?"

"No, the angle is too high from this bird, but if the weather gives us a break I can redirect number three."

"It won't, the front's a big one. Meteorology says it'll stick around several days."

"We got lucky this time."

"Yeah," Coney said. "Retransmit to me and to Pacific Fleet, and I'll kick the rest upstairs."

"Are the MEGAP users out of the loop on this one too?"

"So far as I know, Tony. But as soon as I see what you've got for me, I'll start waking people up."

"I just hate when that happens."

"So do they."

THE PERSIAN GULF

The Los Angeles–class attack submarine SSN 721 *Chicago* was submerged one hundred feet beneath the surface, on her assigned station in the narrow Strait of Hormuz more than five hundred nautical miles southeast of Bandar-é Emān. Her nuclear reactor was at 5 percent and her geared turbine propulsion drives were idle, allowing her to drift with the current while making almost no noise.

Her job was to monitor and identify the heavy traffic through the bottleneck. Her primary mission was to watch for Iranian submarines trying to break out of the Gulf. Once a submarine got to the open sea, she would be almost impossible to find again unless her skipper made a mistake.

Called Operation JUST WATCH, the *Chicago* was ten days into this thirty-day section of her mission. She alternated month by month with the *Honolulu,* now patrolling the open Atlantic as far south as Somalia and the Gulf of Aden at the entrance to the Red Sea. After six months, another pair of submarines from the Seventh Fleet based at Yokosuka would replace them.

Captain Glen Coburn, a slim man with thick eyebrows and a black mustache, glanced at the pair of clocks above the nav station at the rear of the control room. It was 1000 zulu, which made it 2:00 P.M. local time, 1:30 P.M. in Tehran, because the Iranians wanted to keep different time than the rest of the world. The boat's bell chimed four times.

Already in the second hour of the second day watch, sonar had tracked seven targets on the surface, designating them Sierra, for sonar contact, and a number followed by a *D* for downbound, or *U* for upbound. Of the four upbound ships, two were classified as oil tankers, one was a small freighter, and the other was a warship which they identified as an Indian gunboat sneaking into the Gulf.

In the past twenty-eight hours they had detected and identified more than three hundred boats through the strait, everything from crude oil transports to Iranian patrol ships, and a dozen unknowns classified simply as motor vessels of varying sizes from 100 feet to as large as 280 feet. Some of them were probably the private yachts of the oil sheikhs. The Persian Gulf was a very busy place.

This was Coburn's last cruise. At forty-one he was on fast track for his first star in June, and it had been loosely hinted that he'd be promoted to executive officer for submarine operations in Yokosuka. He was ready for it. These last three years of sea duty had been particularly difficult on Sandy and the kids. They might not want to be uprooted from Norfolk, where they maintained a home, but being together, even in Japan, was preferable to being a world apart.

The control room was manned by two other officers and six enlisted men. Coburn straightened up from the plotting table where he'd been studying one of the charts, eased his back, and headed to the officers' wardroom one deck down.

"I'll be in the wardroom," he told Lieutenant Brent Johansen, officer of the deck this morning.

"Aye, aye, Skipper. I have the conn," Johansen, a heavyset blond from Minnesota, said.

Coburn had to smile. The Swede was a pretty good officer and submariner, but he was a little uptight. Coburn had called him on it once, and the man was sincerely trying to change. Maybe trying too hard, the captain thought, taking the ladder down one deck.

Lieutenant Commander Mike Friend, his executive officer, was pouring a cup of coffee. "Good morning, Captain. Busy up there?"

"It hasn't let up," Coburn said, slipping in behind the table.

Friend handed him the coffee and poured a second cup for himself. He sat down and lit a cigarette. "If someone wanted to raise hell, this'd be the place for it."

"I guess so," Coburn agreed. He liked his XO, who'd graduated from Annapolis six years behind him, and was the eternal optimist.

Last year at Christmas the enlisted crew had put on a skit parodying the officers. Coburn was portrayed as a laid-back hippy from the sixties, who kept saying "No sweat" to every crisis he had to deal with. Friend called to battle stations, on the other hand, was depicted putting on a button-up sweater and tennis shoes while smiling vapidly and singing Mister Rogers's theme: "It's a beautiful day in the neighborhood."

The crew and officers were close enough that no one took offense. But there'd been a grain of truth in their portrayals, Coburn thought. Mike

Friend was a Mister Rogers right down to the smile, the sloped shoulders, and the pleasant attitude.

"So we're bean counters. I can think of worse things to do with our time," Friend offered. The captain was bored and everyone knew it.

"Skipper, conn," the wardroom loudspeaker blared.

Coburn picked up the growler phone. "This is the captain."

"Comms advises that we're receiving an ELF message."

"I'm on my way up," Coburn said. He put down the phone. "We've got some mail."

"ELF?" Friend asked.

The skipper nodded and they went up to the control room. ELF, or extremely low frequency, was a radio system by which submarines as deep as one thousand feet could be contacted. But it was slow, taking up to fifteen minutes to transmit a single three-letter code group.

"Just one group," Johansen said, handing Coburn the narrow strip of paper.

The group was TTT, which meant that the *Chicago* was supposed to come to periscope depth for an important message.

Coburn picked up the telephone. "Sonar, conn, what's it look like on the surface?"

"Conn, I show three targets, designated Sierra eighteen Uncle, eight thousand yards and opening, bearing two-six-five; Sierra nineteen Uncle, eighteen thousand yards and opening, bearing two-five-zero; and Sierra twenty Uncle, thirty thousand yards and closing, bearing one-five-five."

"Keep a sharp eye, we're heading up." Coburn put the phone down. "Diving officer, bring the boat to periscope depth."

"Aye, aye, Captain, I'm bringing the boat to periscope depth," Chief Warrant Officer Randy Doucette replied sharply. "Increase speed to five knots, turn left to two-zero-zero degrees," he told his helmsman softly. "Ten degrees up on the fairwater planes."

Coburn called the comms shack.

"This is the captain. We're on the way up, and I don't want to stay very long. As soon as you get the end-of-message indicator, acknowledge receipt and let me know so we can get out of here."

"Aye, aye, Skipper."

It took eight minutes to reach sixty feet, periscope depth, and comms reported having an uplink with a communications satellite overhead. He made a 360-degree sweep with the search periscope. Nothing was in sight. The day looked gray and lumpy.

"Stand by to dive," Coburn told Doucette.

"Standing by to dive on your order, sir."

Two seconds later the complete message was received via high-speed burst transmission.

"Conn, communications. We got it, Skipper."

"Roger," Coburn said. "Diving officer, dive the boat."

"Aye, aye, I'm diving the boat."

"Make your depth one hundred feet as before," Coburn said. "Sonar, conn. How's it look?"

"Sierra twenty Uncle is now eighteen thousand yards and closing, bearing one-eight-five."

"Any new targets?"

"Negative, Skipper."

The boat started down as Friend came back from the communications shack with the message flimsy, and handed it to Coburn without comment, though he was grinning from ear to ear.

060905 MAR 00
TOP SECRET
FM: COMSUBPAC
TO: USS CHICAGO
A.   AN IRAN NAVY KILO-CLASS SUBMARINE WAS SPOTTED LEAVING HER PENS AT BANDAR-E EMAN AT 0902Z THIS DATE.
B.   NO OTHER SUBMARINES OR IRAN NAVY OPERATIONAL VESSELS SEEN IN SUPPORT.
C.   LAST KNOWN POSITION OF SUBMARINE 29-45.00 N 49-16.50 E, COURSE 150, SPEED 8.0 K ON SURFACE.
D.   NO FURTHER SATELLITE INFORMATION AVAILABLE BECAUSE OF LOCAL WX.
E.   PROCEED COMSUBPAC POSITION 166.5E AT FASTEST POSSIBLE SPEED TO INTERCEPT AND TRACK THIS SUBMA-RINE.
F.   DO NOT ENGAGE RPT DO NOT ENGAGE.
G.   REPORT AS NECESSARY
XXX
EOM
BREAKBREAK

Friend went to one of the plotting tables where he worked out their relative positions. "Ten hours, assuming he keeps heading our way at eight knots."

Coburn smiled. Some of the others were watching him. "No sweat," he said.

43

THE NORTHERN PERSIAN GULF

The Iranian submarine *Mohammad's Star* slipped easily beneath the one-meter seas two hundred kilometers south of Bandar-é Emān a few minutes after midnight, her batteries fully charged after running on the surface for twelve hours. A thickening overcast coming in on a front from the northwest brought a chill wind that portended bad weather.

At 3,200 tons submerged, the improved Russian-designed submarine was capable of eighteen knots on the surface, and twenty-three knots submerged. With a complement of forty-seven men and officers, she was undermanned, but she wasn't going to war. This time was just practice.

Built in 1987 at the Amur Yard at Komsomolsk in the Far East, *Mohammad's Star* was sold to Iran in 1995 for $185 million in US currency (because the Russians demanded it) and oil credits. She was more expensive than the other three Kilos that Iran had purchased from the Russians because she was newer and much better equipped than the previous boats. Her electronics were more up-to-date, her electric motors quicker and more efficient, her propeller shrouded to cut down on cavitation noises, and her batteries newly designed to operate 220 percent more efficiently than the old ones.

She could sail faster, dive deeper, detect and track her enemies with more precision, and deliver more firepower at a greater distance than anyone, even the United States intelligence services, suspected.

But for all her technological marvels, her crew were still Iranian and relatively untrained compared to the submarine crews of any other nation. They had a lot to learn because they were still intimidated by the boats.

"Make your course one-six-zero," the captain, Madhlum Baram, ordered.

"Aye, one-six-zero degrees," the helmsman replied.

Unlike American submarines, the Kilo carried only one helmsman instead of two, and no diving officer. The captain and his executive officer were expected to do double and often triple duty.

Additional automatic systems had been installed by their Russian advisers because of Iran's lack of trained crew. Eventually the submarines would be efficiently operated by as few as two-thirds a normal complement. Perhaps less. But that demanded training at sea.

"Level off at eighteen meters," the captain cautioned. "Mind your bubble."

"Aye, leveling off at eighteen meters," the helmsman replied nervously after a slight hesitation. He hauled back hard on the control yoke, and the big submarine skidded to twenty-three meters before he could bring her back and level at eighteen.

Their course stabilized a few degrees past 160, but Captain Baram held his silence long enough for the helmsman to notice and then correct his error.

When the submarine was finally steady at periscope depth on a course of 160 and a speed of five knots, the captain glanced at his executive officer, Lieutenant Commander Sadegh al-Bayati, who had timed the maneuver with a stopwatch.

Bayati shook his head. "Eleven minutes, Captain," he said.

"How is the board?" Baram asked, holding his temper in check. The helmsman and most of the other crew were mere boys, but his XO was a high-ranking officer.

Bayati, realizing he'd made a serious error by not checking the boat's status board before they reached periscope depth, did so. "All green, Captain."

"Very good, Mr. Bayati. Apparently we're not sinking."

"Yes, sir," Bayati said sheepishly. Training in a classroom with Russian instructors was one thing, but at sea, submerged, was another thing completely. It was unnerving.

The captain shook his head in resignation. He raised the search periscope and made a quick 360-degree sweep. Two oil tankers were off to port, and in the distance a few degrees off their starboard bow he thought he made out a ship, hull down on the horizon. But it was so indistinct and so far away that he could not tell its type or even which direction it was sailing.

He was only one step ahead of his crew, but it was a very big step. The Russians had taken him and five other Iranian submarine commander trainees on operations in the North Atlantic aboard a Kilo boat. They'd not made many dives, but actually operating a submarine gave him and the others invaluable experience.

He lowered the scope. "Helmsman, make our depth fifty meters."

The young man looked up, surprised.

The XO stepped forward. "Captain, that is the charted depth of the water here."

"That is correct."

Bayati glanced nervously at the other crew members in the control room. "Only the Americans have accurate charts of the bottom contours here. We do not know what's down there."

"That's also correct, Mr. Bayati," Captain Baram said calmly. He wondered how far his XO was going to take this. Better to find out now when they were in no danger than later when he would have to depend upon his crew's absolute loyalty and instant acceptance of orders.

"Very well," Bayati said finally. "You heard the captain, Helmsman. Make our depth fifty meters."

"Aye sir, making my depth five-zero meters."

Bayati operated the ballast tank controls while the helmsman shoved the yoke forward and started down.

Captain Baram watched the depth indicator to make sure that the helmsman knew enough not to drive the boat bow first directly into the bottom.

"Mind your status board, Mr. Bayati," he said, as they passed thirty-five meters. The hull was groaning.

"I have all green, Captain," Bayati reported. He picked up the ship's intercom phone. "All sections, this is the executive officer. We're on our way down to fifty meters. Report any leaks, no matter how slight, immediately."

Baram smiled inwardly. The man was learning to be an executive officer and not merely an order taker.

"Watch your angle of descent," Bayati cautioned the young, nervous helmsman.

"Aye, aye, sir. I'm starting to level off now."

The depth indicator counted down to forty-eight, then forty-nine, and finally fifty meters, then stopped as they leveled off.

"Very good," Captain Baram said. "Come three degrees to starboard."

"Aye, three degrees starboard," the helmsman answered.

"Make our speed fifteen knots."

This time Bayati hesitated only a moment before he realized that the depth beneath their keel could only get greater the farther south they sailed, and he rang for the increase in speed.

Baram waited until their depth, course, and speed were all stabilized, the status board still all green, then walked around the corner to the sonar cubicle.

His chief sonar operator, Lieutenant Hamid al-Majid, headphones half on and half off, studied a waterfall display on one of the sonar screens. He looked up.

"Do you have something?"

"I have a strong target at fifteen thousand meters, bearing direct on the bow, closing with us at forty-eight knots."

It was the boat Baram had spotted hull down on the horizon. It would make a good exercise for them.

"Can you determine what kind of a boat it is?"

"The computer identifies it as a civilian vessel. Possibly a private yacht. It's not large."

"Very well, we'll pretend that it's an enemy vessel and use it for target practice."

"Yes, sir," Majid, a dark, intense young man, said, his eyes flashing with anticipation.

Baram stepped back into the control room. "Reduce speed to five knots, but maintain your present heading."

"Aye, sir." The helmsman repeated the order, and the XO rang for the slower speed.

"There is a very fast boat coming up from the south directly toward us," Baram said. "We are going to use her as target practice. So I want everyone to take special care in their duties and we shall be victorious. *In sha'Allah.*"

"Will we load actual weapons, Captain?" his weapons officer Lieutenant Uday al-Dulam asked nervously.

"No. We'll save that exercise for another time. For now we will simulate the loading and the firing."

"Aye, sir."

"Look smartly now," Baram said. "Bring us to periscope depth." He stepped around the corner. "Watch him carefully, Hamid."

"Yes, sir. I'm designating him as Sierra one."

"Very well," Baram said. He stepped back. "As soon as you have a firing solution, I want you to give it to me," he told his weapons control officer. "Then I'll want continuous updates."

"Aye, aye, Skipper," Lieutenant Dulam answered.

The submarine slowed to its new speed as it rose to a depth of eighteen meters, leveling off ten minutes after starting up.

"I have a possible firing solution on my board," Lieutenant Dulam reported excitedly.

"Roger," Captain Baram said. He reached for the periscope.

"Stand by, Captain," Majid called from the sonar cubicle.

Baram stepped around the corner. "What is it?"

"Sierra one has swung around less than one thousand meters out and has matched our course and speed." Majid looked up. "I think they are trying to communicate with us. They are using sonar, I can pick out that signal, but it also sounds as if they have lowered an underwater speaker. They're talking to us."

"What are they saying?" Baram asked, in wonder that they had closed to this distance so quickly and that his chief sonar operator hadn't seen fit to warn him.

"I can't quite make it out."

"Is it one of our patrol vessels?" Baram demanded. Some of their new gunboats were equipped with an American underwater communications system called Gertrude.

"I don't know, Captain. It might be, but the Russian computer program still identifies it as a civilian vessel."

Baram stepped back into the control room. He was alarmed; this situation made no sense.

"Load forward tubes one and two," he ordered. "This is no longer a drill."

"Aye, aye, sir," the impressed young weapons officer responded.

"Give me turns for all slow," Baram told his XO. "I want to maintain steering way, nothing more."

"Aye, Captain," Bayati said, relaying the orders.

They came to an almost complete stop, and the boat quieted down, making her nearly undetectable by anything but an active sonar or a magnetic anomaly detector.

Baram stood in front of the attack periscope. Once he raised the scope they would no longer be invisible.

"What is he doing, Hamid?" he asked. "Does he know where we are?"

"Yes, sir. He's heading directly toward us, but very slowly."

"Is he still talking?"

"Yes, sir. Stand by."

"Tubes one and two are loaded," Lieutenant Dulam reported.

"Very well," the captain said.

"Sir, it's our Special Operations people. They're sending down a man."

"How?" Baram demanded.

"To the escape trunk. Scuba gear. They say they have a man in the water now."

Baram could hardly believe his ears. He'd been told nothing about this. Nor had this sort of operation even been discussed during training. It was totally unprecedented.

"Shall we raise the mast and radio base for instructions?" Bayati asked.

Something was terribly wrong. In the first place, if a Special Operations mission had been sent out to catch up with them, it would have come from the north, not the south.

And so far as Baram knew, the Iranian navy did not own a civilian vessel.

"Can we talk to them?" he asked his chief sonar operator.

"We have the equipment, sir. But no one has been trained in its use," Majid said.

This patrol had been timed to coincide with the passage of a cold front, masking them from the American spy satellites. By surfacing now, or even by raising their communications mast, they might be detectable. Especially if attention were being drawn to this area because of the presence of the boat on the surface.

"Do they have the proper codes?"

"Yes, sir," Majid said.

Something metallic struck the deck forward of the sail. It sounded as if someone had hit the escape hatch with a ball peen hammer.

The blow was struck a second time, and then a third.

"Lieutenant Dulam, bring your sidearm and come with me," Captain Baram said.

Yes, sir," the young lieutenant said crisply.

"Let's see who is knocking at our front door, and what he wants."

Baram debated ordering the watertight doors closed and sealed, but thought better of it. Whoever had gone to this trouble to find them didn't mean to sink them.

44

Yernin struck the Kilo's forward hatch with his hammer. The water was so murky at this depth they could only see a few meters.

He held up two fingers, and Lieutenant Andrei Krasilnikov nodded his understanding. They could not afford to wait longer than two more minutes. After that the risk that the Iranian crew would become spooked and do something foolish would become too great.

In two minutes they would blow the hatch and enter the boat by force. There were materials and equipment aboard to close the opening permanently, leaving only one usable escape trunk. It was an option they were prepared to take only as a last resort because the risk of failure was too great.

Krasilnikov reached for the small shaped charge strapped to his right calf when they heard the unmistakable rush of high-pressure air as the escape trunk was cycled.

Yernin unstrapped the package he carried on his left calf instead.

A minute later the hatch popped open, a bubble of air behind it rising to the surface.

Yernin and Krasilnikov pulled themselves down into the pressure vessel, and closed and dogged the hatch above them. They hit the cycle button, and compressed air forced the water out of the chamber.

Krasilnikov's eyes met Yernin's. He nodded, pulled off his mask, spat out his mouthpiece, then undogged the lower hatch into the boat and pulled it open.

"Hello," he called down in the only word of Farsi, he knew.

Yernin pulled a short lanyard from the top of his package and dropped it hissing onto the upturned faces of the two men. Krasilnikov slammed the hatch and redogged it.

The gas was Labun-III, a variation of the old, but extremely effective, nerve agent that killed within seconds of contact. The new variation had a half-life of twenty-eight seconds, and an effective killing life of five times that long, after which it dispersed harmlessly within ninety seconds or less. A total of five minutes, including a safety margin.

The 1,200-mile sail from Karachi into the Persian Gulf through the Strait of Hormuz, where they detected the American submarine *Chicago* exactly where she was supposed to be, took forty hours. During that time Yernin got to know Maslennikov's handpicked crew.

Each of the nine men who would initially run the Iranian Kilo boat was an officer; eight of them lieutenants plus Captain First Rank Razhin.

At first they'd been wary of their new boss. He wasn't a submariner, and what little they knew about him wasn't good. He was a KGB assassin. And nobody in the old Soviet Union or in Ukraine had much love for the Komitet.

But Maslennikov, a man they loved and trusted, had given Yernin high marks, so they'd given him the benefit of the doubt. Within ten hours after leaving Karachi they had learned to respect the man because of his apparently intimate knowledge of the Kilo boat (he'd crammed during his desert sojourn), and because despite his injuries and obvious pain he bested each of them in unarmed hand-to-hand combat. He even beat Captain Razhin, who was the best infighter in the Black Sea Fleet.

Yernin had planned it this way after Maslennikov warned him that these men were prima donnas who'd follow no one they didn't trust or respect. So Yernin had shown them what respect meant.

He looked at his watch in the dim red battle light. "We'll give it one more minute before we go in."

"If they suspected that they were under attack they would have surfaced the boat," Krasilnikov suggested. He was their communications and electronic countermeasures specialist. Like many submariners, he was a slightly built man. A small size was a premium on a cramped submarine.

"At the very least flooded this compartment and locked us out," Yernin agreed.

"That's a cheery thought."

They removed their weapons from waterproof pouches and checked the loads. They carried Mac-10 compact submachine guns loaded with rubber bullets. The ammunition was powerful enough to incapacitate a man, but would not penetrate metal, such as the pressure hull or any of the hundreds of miles of vital plumbing aboard a submarine.

Yernin pulled the Mac-10's ejector slide back, thumbed off the safety catch, and motioned for Krasilnikov to open the hatch.

A very slight odor of almonds mingled with diesel oil and electronics wafted up to them when the hatch was open. The compartment below them was empty.

Yernin cautiously stuck his head through the opening. The two men who'd been waiting for them lay in a heap near a hatch a few meters aft. One of them had his hand on the dogging lever. Realizing they were in mortal danger, they'd tried to retreat and seal off this section of the boat. But they'd not had enough time.

There were no sounds in the boat except for the air-circulating fans which had helped disperse the deadly gas throughout the boat. Before the captain and his crew knew that they were in serious trouble, it was already too late.

Yernin climbed down into the boat, completely indifferent to the forty-five or fifty bodies he knew they would find aboard. But when he looked up into Krasilnikov's eyes he could see that the young man was already deeply affected by what they had done with such seeming ease.

It would put all of them on edge, which was just as well, Yernin thought. It would make them more respectful of the danger they were in.

Mohammad's Star sent one pong from its active sonar, and ten minutes later Captain Razhin and his executive officer, Lieutenant Ivan Ablakin, locked aboard and came forward to the control room.

Yernin and Krasilnikov had already begun moving bodies into the forward spaces, away from the galley and crew's quarters.

"The status board is all green," Yernin told the captain, who studied the gauges and dials at the sub's control station forward of the periscope pedestal.

"We're settling at the bow because of the redistributed weight," Razhin said.

His XO adjusted two of the ballast tanks, and the bow came up three degrees.

"*Da,*" Razhin grunted, satisfied. "The remainder of my crew will be locked aboard within ten minutes."

"How soon can we head south?" Yernin asked.

Razhin looked beyond him toward the open hatch forward of the sail. "Was anyone left alive?"

"No."

The short, wiry captain met Yernin's steady gaze. "This is a hard business."

"There was no other way," Yernin replied coolly. "You and your men volunteered."

Razhin dismissed the comment with a wave. "I agree, Comrade Yernin, with the necessity. But I do not share your disregard for life."

"Your own included?"

Lieutenant Ablakin looked up sharply.

"Anyone's life," the captain answered steadily. "How long before the bodies are out of our way?"

"Give me another man and we'll have it done in a half-hour."

"Very well," Razhin said. "In that case, providing there is nothing wrong with this boat, we'll get under way then."

"Is your brother clear on his instructions?"

"Yes. Nikolai and his crew will move the *Good Hope* to Kuwait City where they'll refuel and restock, then catch up with us," Razhin assured him.

Nikolai Razhin was captain of the *Good Hope* and a Black Sea Fleet submariner just like his brother, so he fully understood the operation. The surface ship would provide a noisy cover for *Mohammad's Star* when she passed through the narrow Strait of Hormuz. The *Chicago*'s sensors would be overloaded long enough for the Kilo boat to sneak past and get out into the open sea.

If the *Good Hope* were to be stopped and boarded, it wouldn't matter. Her paperwork was in order. Razhin and his friends were on holiday. They'd chartered the boat out of Bombay and were on their way back. An unlikely story, but there was no proof to say otherwise.

Nikolai's complete loyalty was assured by the presence of his brother aboard the Iranian submarine. If he made a mistake, his brother's life would be at risk. So he would be careful.

Maslennikov liked the idea when Yernin suggested using fathers and sons, or at least brothers, for the mission.

"We all have work to do," Yernin said. "Let's get on with it."

Captain Razhin was hunched over the plotting table checking their course when Lieutenant Ablakin brought him a glass of tea from the galley. They'd been under way for three hours, and the boat was running at twelve knots without problems.

Razhin looked up tiredly. "Thanks. Has the crew settled down?"

"Fomenko, Yezhov, and Voskoboy are getting some sleep. I've put them three hours and on and three hours off, same as us."

"Then you should be in your bunk, Ivan. Both of us should not be awake at the same time for now."

"I couldn't sleep."

Razhin glanced over at the control station on the opposite side of the conn. Yernin was taking watch-on-watch with the rest of them. Tonight he was steering the boat.

"He's a man without a soul," he said.

"In his business it would be a hindrance."

"Have you looked into his eyes?"

Ablakin shivered. "It's like looking into a graveyard. I wouldn't want him as my enemy."

"No," Razhin agreed. He held the warm glass between his hands, suddenly cold.

"What's bothering you, Captain?" Ablakin asked.

Razhin looked up. "He's hiding something."

"What do you mean?"

"We've not been told the entire story. Captain Maslennikov said that we would be told everything once we set sail. But I don't believe we have been."

"How do you know?" Ablakin asked, looking at Yernin's back.

Razhin shook his head. "I don't. It's just a feeling I have."

"Don't you trust Captain Maslennikov?"

"With my life," Razhin replied quickly. "But I don't think even he knows what's in our helmsman's twisted brain."

"I see what you mean, Captain," Ablakin said thoughtfully. "Whatever it is will involve murder."

45

THE FRENCH RIVIERA

They'd shut off the pool lights, as well as all the lights on the patio and throughout the house. The only illumination came from the stars in the perfectly clear sky.

The night breeze had died, so there were no sounds on top of the hill, not even the dry rustling of palm fronds.

Lane swam underwater toward the ghostly figure in the far corner at the bottom of the pool. He was weightless and timeless, completely out of touch with the real world above. He felt as if he could hold his breath forever, it took no effort.

At the last moment the figure unfolded itself and glided soundlessly to him. Frances, her pale skin luminous, her eyes fixed on him as if he were her savior. Captain Nemo come to the rescue 20,000 leagues under the sea.

They embraced and slowly rose to the surface, their bodies intertwined like sea creatures engaged in a mysterious mating ritual.

He swam with her to the shallow end of the pool, where wordlessly he picked her up and carried her into the bedroom. Diaphanous gauze curtains hung nearly still, moving only slightly on a chance zephyr, brushing their bodies like butterfly wings as they passed.

He laid her on the big bed beneath the skylight and went into her arms, kissing her lips, her neck, his tongue tracing patterns around the nipples of her breasts, and lower until she cried out with pleasure.

"My god . . . I love you."

"I love you too, Frannie," he said, looking into her eyes as he entered her.

Her hips rose to meet him, and although she wanted to close her eyes and hold him so tightly that he could never leave her, she kept looking at him, touching him with her fingertips, her lips brushing his chest, his neck. Her body enfolding him, a deep, sensuous joining, her knees around his hips, but not squeezing tightly. Going with their natural rhythms without forcing anything, though it took every ounce of power within her not to scream his name and clutch him madly.

For those moments neither of them wanted to be anywhere else. No fantasies, no regrets, no impatient thrustings, hurrying to get it over with. Pleasure. Slowly. Deliberately. The pleasure of making love with someone for whom it wasn't simply sex. It was something profoundly more important than that.

When they came in unison they finally held each other tightly, rolling over and over, sliding off the edge of the low bed onto the thick fur throw rugs on the floor, never wanting to let each other go. Never wanting this exact moment to end.

But gradually they parted. Tentatively at first, neither wanting to break the other's pleasure, they lay back.

"Rather," she whispered huskily.

"Every hospital should provide this exercise," Lane said languidly. "Wonderful recuperative benefits."

Frances laughed. "Is that what they meant by playing doctor when we were children?"

"Something like that."

She propped herself up on one elbow, a leg thrown over his, and traced a pattern on his chest with a fingernail.

"We could quit and go to Tahiti," she suggested playfully.

Lane smiled. "Is that why you joined the service, Frannie, to quit when things got difficult?"

"Touché," she said, lying back again. "None the less, the thought has crossed my mind."

"Then get out, there'd be no dishonor in it."

"What, and become Mrs. Somebody? Stay home and cook porridge, clean nappies, things like that?"

"Become an adviser, an analyst."

"Like you?" she shot back, and was immediately contrite. "Sorry, William."

"If you'd seen with your own eyes what he did you'd know why I took this assignment."

"Who are we talking about, Yernin or Hussein?"

Lane glanced at the clock on the nightstand. It was coming up on 4 A.M. His flight left the Nice airport at six.

He got up and padded across to the bathroom, conscious that Frances's eyes were on him. At the doorway he looked at her. She was beautiful in the soft starlight.

"Just answer me that much, would you please?" she said.

"Both," he replied, and he went into the bathroom to get ready to leave.

RIYADH, SAUDI ARABIA

The meeting was held in a rambling two-story house hidden behind a tall whitewashed wall in a back alley off Al-Jami'ah Street near the race track. Lane arrived at 1:00 P.M.

"Was Ms. Shipley understanding?" Ben Lewis asked, showing him upstairs.

"No, but she'll go along with whatever I want for the time being." Lane dumped his bag in the corridor.

"She has important friends who could screw this operation for us."

"She won't."

"If it blows up in our faces, people could get killed."

"She won't," Lane repeated harshly. "And unless you've forgotten, a lot of people have already been killed. It's why we're here."

They went upstairs to a roof garden that looked toward the city center. The skyline was dominated by the central water tower and the telephone exchange. Illegal drinks had been laid out on a low table. Several maps and a dozen or more photos were spread out on another.

"Would you like a drink, Bill? A glass of wine?"

"Where's Tom?"

"He's coming over with Walt Zimmerman, who's chief of CIA operations here. I believe you've met."

"When do I go in?"

Lewis looked at him over the rim of his glasses. In the old cold war days Lewis's Russianness was a great asset. He knew how they thought, how they would react to any given set of circumstances. He, Tom Hughes, and Lane had become an unbeatable team. They'd become so close that outsiders swore they were capable of mental telepathy. But now things were different, sometimes even strained between them. The world had changed.

"That depends on you, but the timing is getting critical. After Nukhayb it's anybody's guess what Hussein might do next. You need briefing, and you need training. Say twenty-four hours. Forty-eight at the most. If you're up to it."

"I'll manage," Lane said. "Who'll be training me?"

"The CIA. They have a station on the desert for just this sort of thing. And they'll be taking you across the border when the time comes."

"That means they know my mission."

Lewis shook his ponderous head. "Not exactly."

"But they know I'm going in to assassinate somebody."

"Yes."

"Ask us no questions and we'll tell no lies?"

"Something like that, Bill," Lewis admitted. "But we're all on the same side here. They're not the enemy."

"You'll handle briefing me?"

"Tom and I. He's up to speed now."

"What does he think about this mission?"

Lewis gave him a flat look. "I didn't ask."

Lane went to the table with the maps and photographs. They were all of the desert. The maps were topographic with latitude and longitude lines drawn at three-second intervals, which was the equivalent of a little over three hundred feet in latitude, and a little less than that in longitude.

The photos were satellite shots presumably of Saddam Hussein's desert camp. In two of the shots three shadowy figures were visible some distance from the camp. One of them was a hundred yards or more from the other two.

"We think the lead one is Hussein," Lewis said. "He likes to take walks in the cool of the evening. To clear his soul, or commune with his gods or something. The other two are his personal bodyguards."

"How recent are these?" Lane asked.

"Most of them were shot twenty-four hours ago. Before you leave you'll be given the latest information. It's about as good as it gets."

"Unless there's cloud cover."

"We're not trying to get you killed, Bill," Lewis said earnestly. "If it's cloudy, we wait. If there's some uncertainty about his exact location, we wait. Whatever it takes."

Lane put the photographs down, walked to the edge of the roof garden, and looked out over the sprawling city. Here and now he was just as vulnerable to an assassin's bullet as anyone else. Even presidents and popes with all their security were not immune. But the question came down to a philosophical issue, like all the important ones did.

If we could have killed Hitler in the thirties, before he brought the world to war, before he killed untold millions of people, should we have? Morally, ethically, should we have sent an assassin?

He had wrestled with this point of morality on two levels from the moment several weeks ago when he'd known they'd ask him to assassinate Hussein. The first was the philosophical issue for which he had no answer. But the second was the more practical issue. Morals aside, was he the man for this job? Was he capable of lying in wait in the desert, drawing a bead on the deposed Iraqi leader's head, and squeezing the trigger?

He shivered, feeling the buck of the assassin's rifle against his shoulder. Getting away would be the problem, but first he had to bring himself to pull the trigger.

Lane did not consider himself to be an intellectual. Far from it. But he was intelligent and he had a strong imagination. Qualities that were perfect for an intelligence analyst. But not so perfect for the field man because a lot of things could go wrong out there, and he could imagine every one of them and more.

"The weather over the Gulf has closed in, but central Iraq is supposed to be clear starting tomorrow night." Lewis said. "If you're ready by then, we could get the latest satellite images, pinpoint his location, and you could be in and out within a matter of hours. Certainly no more than a night and a day."

"That's a long time to hide out in the desert with a pissed-off army hunting for me."

"His position is secret, so even if they do come looking for you they won't make a big production out of it in case we take notice and call in the air force."

Hughes and Zimmerman appeared at the head of the alley and started back on foot.

Lane stepped away from the edge of the roof. "When do I leave for the training camp?"

"As soon as Tom and Zimmerman show up."

"They're here now."

Lewis's eyes were bright. "You'll do this, Bill?"

"Do I have a choice? Do any of us?"

"You have a choice."

Lane nodded. "I'll do it."

"It's a good thing—" Lewis said, but Lane stopped him.

"What about Yernin?"

Lewis was startled, but he switched gears without stumbling. "He's disappeared."

"Keep looking for him."

"We will," Lewis said.

"See that you do.

46

THE PERSIAN GULF

Technically, this was their first combat-ready patrol, Lieutenant Zaki Al-Rashid told himself. Until this moment the *PHM9 Prince Faisal* had engaged only in practice maneuvers within fifty kilometers of her home port of Al Jubayl. And this time instead of a mostly American crew, she was primarily being commanded and operated by a Saudi Arabian navy crew.

Only his XO, Lieutenant Robert Morrison, and their chief engineer, Lieutenant Kurt Moon, were American. And their orders were to defer strictly to their Saudi captain. It was a good feeling, only tainted slightly by a feeling of fear. This cruise would make or break Rashid and his crew. All of Riyadh was watching, especially the royal family, for him to maintain the proud Arabic tradition of self-sufficiency and fearlessness in the face of the enemy.

Prince Faisal was an American-built Pegasus-class hydrofoil missile patrol boat. Fantastically expensive, the Americans had only five of them in their fleet. The Saudi navy had two.

With a length overall of 45 meters, she was a technological marvel, displacing 218 metric tons, and capable, with her hydrofoils down, of speeds in excess of 50 knots.

She was armed with four Harpoon surface-to-surface missiles, four ASROC antisubmarine missiles, and a foredeck-mounted 76mm gun.

Originally designed to hunt and kill surface ships, she'd been retrofitted to do double duty since Iran had acquired submarines from the Russians. Everyone in the Gulf was highly respectful of the considerable force that the four Kilos represented, even though their crews were probably not very well trained. Yet.

The presence of American warships in the Gulf, while somewhat comforting, could not be tolerated much longer. So it was up to the Saudi navy to lead the way with the necessary countermeasures.

Lieutenant Rashid drove the *Prince Faisal* hard toward the northwest, her speed hovering slightly over fifty knots in seas that had risen above two meters over the past half-hour. The motion on the bridge was lively though not yet impossible. But as he explained to his crew, they were going sub hunting and the Iranian dogs would not wait for them.

"We have ASW ships in the vicinity," Lieutenant Morrison said. He was Rashid's opposite—tall, husky, and fair-skinned to the Saudi's diminutive, swarthy figure. They were opposites in temperament as well. Morrison was laid-back, while Rashid was excitable, sometimes too excitable.

"We appreciate your help, XO, but these are our waters," Rashid replied.

Morrison bit back the reply that if an American satellite hadn't spotted one of the Kilos leaving its pens at Bandar-é Emān, neither the Saudis nor anyone else in the Gulf would have known about it.

"Assuming they submerged, and assuming they went to top speed, I plan on taking up a position several kilometers south of their farthest possible position and wait for them," Rashid continued.

It wasn't a bad strategy, Morrison thought. Wouldn't work against a real sub driver who might not always go by the book. But the Iranians were still as afraid of their submarines as the Saudis were afraid of these boats. By tradition Arabs were desert fighters, not seamen.

"May I suggest, Captain, that we slow down to hull-borne speed every ten minutes or so, to give our sonar a chance to operate," he said. With the boat up on her hydrofoils, sonar did not work.

"That will slow us down unacceptably."

"We might miss them if they decide to take an end run. They'll hear us a lot sooner than we'll hear them."

The logic of what Morrison was suggesting began to sink in, and Rashid became uncomfortable. Morrison hated to see that happen because it had the potential of ruining a commander. But, damnit, if the Saudis wanted to operate a navy, they would have to swallow their Arab pride and get the job done right.

Rashid stared out of the windscreen for several seconds. The helmsman, navigator, and weapons officer all studiously looked away.

When he turned back there was a faint curl to his lip. "I have decided to stop and listen for one minute every fifteen kilometers. Make it so, XO."

"Yes, sir," Morrison said. They would travel fifteen kilometers in twelve and a half minutes. "Shall I inform sonar?"

"Yes, of course. And we'll come to battle stations ASROC each time. It'll give the crew practice."

Good for you, Morrison thought. You're finally acting like a captain.

Mohammad's Star continued her southerly course, her speed above twenty knots now. Even with a skeleton crew the Kilo boat was fairly easy to handle.

At these speeds the submarine made the maximum noise, but she was still quiet compared to many of her counterparts, and most nuclear submarines. It was one of the advantages diesel-electric boats had over the nukes.

Every half-hour, Captain Razhin ordered the electric motor shut down and made a sharp turn to the left in a maneuver called clearing the baffles. Submarines under way were sonar-blind aft because of the disturbed water caused by their propellers. Clearing their baffles ensured that no one was sneaking up behind them. The maneuver also allowed the sonar operator to get a much clearer picture of what was happening on the surface.

Relieved from the helm, Yernin had gotten two hour's sleep, all he normally required every twenty-four hours. When he awoke, he got a piece of lavāsh, Iranian flat bread, and a small bowl of yogurt from the galley and took the food and a glass of sweet tea forward to the sonar cubicle where he put on a pair of earphones and sat next to Lieutenant Fomenko.

Their sonar officer was a young man who looked like something out of a Nazi Youth propaganda poster. He glanced nervously a couple of times at Yernin, then went back to his job. He was very efficient, his moves precise, without wasted effort.

Twice he made grease pencil marks on one of the sonar displays, then typed something into the boat's computer memory.

"What was that last target? It looked like a big one," Yernin asked.

"It is an American Aegis cruiser, part of the *Mississippi*'s battle group."

"Are they looking for us?"

"Not very earnestly, I think," Fomenko said. "But they know we're out here."

"They think we're Iranian."

Fomenko grinned. "It's probably why they're not looking so hard. They don't think we'll go far. Least not past Hormuz where the *Chicago* is waiting to pounce."

"But they are searching?"

"Yes, comrade, they are using a standard grid search pattern of one-kilometer squares. But we are well to their south."

"Are they making any effort to search farther to the south?"

Fomenko thought about it for a moment, then shook his head. "No, sir. Their pattern is static."

"As far as they're concerned, then, we're either very close to Bandar-é Emān, or we're already south of them."

"Yes, sir."

"Not hiding on the bottom under their noses?"

"No, sir. The water is too shallow up there. Their MADs are capable of sweeping the bottom."

Captain Razhin came from the control room. "Is something bothering you, comrade?" he asked Yernin.

"The *Chicago* is no longer waiting in the strait. She's coming north to hunt for us."

Razhin looked startled. "How do you know this?"

"The American navy knows that an Iranian submarine sailed from Bandar-é Emān. The *Mississippi*'s battle group is hunting for us."

"We expected this."

"But they're not expanding their search far enough to the south. It means the *Chicago* has been told to join the hunt."

Razhin nodded. "Then I suggest that we get off this boat now and put ashore while it's still possible to escape. Because we don't have a chance against a Los Angeles–class attack submarine. Not one chance."

"I disagree, Captain," Yernin said. "We will have a chance once we provide them with a diversion."

"What kind of a diversion?" Razhin asked skeptically.

"I don't know yet, but one will come along when we need it," Yernin said indifferently. "This is a busy stretch of water. If need be, we'll sink an American oil tanker."

"They're civilians," Razhin objected.

"So what?" Yernin asked.

It was four bells of the third day watch, and suppertime aboard the *Chicago*. The officers and enlisted crew were fed the same things at meals. It was something Captain Coburn insisted on, and his men liked him for it. Tonight they were having steak, French fries, lima beans, a salad with the last of their fresh greens, and iced tea.

Coburn sat at the end of the wardroom table with his off-duty officers. They were less than five hours away from their first possible contact point with the Kilo boat and there was an increased tension aboard.

The crew went about its duties without the usual banter and with peak efficiency. In any kind of a fair fight the Kilo wouldn't stand much of a chance against a boat of the *Chicago*'s capabilities. But the Iranians were an odd, sometimes unpredictable people, and their Kilos were armed with good ordinance. The boats carried a potentially deadly sting. It made everyone keep on their toes. An attitude that Coburn heartily endorsed.

"The surface traffic hasn't thinned out much," Lieutenant Johansen said. "With all that noise it's not going to be easy picking up on that Kilo, especially if she goes deep and runs quiet until we pass."

"She doesn't know we're coming," Mike Friend pointed out.

"She'll hear us if we bull our way in up there."

"That's giving them a pretty big benefit of doubt, Brent," Friend told the weapons officer. "Everything I've read or been briefed on suggests that their sub drivers aren't so hot yet. In time maybe, but for now they probably won't try anything fancy."

"I just don't want to walk into a surprise, that's all," Johansen said.

"I agree," Coburn interjected. "We'll go into a standard run-and-drift mode three hours from now. It'll give us a couple of shots going in at picking them up."

"How about weapons readiness, Captain?" the Swede asked.

"Our orders were to find and track, Brent, not engage," Coburn replied. He grinned. "Now, who wants ice cream?"

47

Hughes stood at the window in the CIA camp's operations planning room watching the distant contrail of an airplane leaving from Riyadh's King Kahlid International Airport thirty-five miles to the south.

Lewis studied the LED computer display on his laptop computer, connected via a masked frequency through an induction interface to one of the satellite dishes outside. He was scanning the latest National Reconnaissance Office data from the Syrian desert outside Baghdad.

He looked up when Lane came in, tiredly dropped his pack on the floor, and leaned his .50-caliber sniper rifle against the wall in the corner.

"You're not going tonight. Still too much cloud cover."

"What're we getting?" Lane asked, looking over Lewis's shoulder.

The Russian director enhanced one of the photo images, and printed it out on a portable color laser printer. Some details of the desert were discernible, as were the lights of Baghdad in the distance. But finer details, such as tents or automobiles, were too indistinct to make out. The images were tantalizing, but useless.

"Can we enhance this any further?" Lane asked.

Lewis shook his head. "We're pushing it as it is." He looked up. "But meteorology says this front will be out of there by tomorrow afternoon."

"I'll go in tomorrow night," Lane said. He straightened up and massaged his back. "Unless the CIA kills me first."

"They promised me that they wouldn't go quite that far, just far enough to incapacitate you," Hughes said, straight-faced.

Lewis glanced at his computer screen as the next image came up, and Lane motioned Hughes to the door.

"I'm tired," Hughes said. "I'm going to get something to eat, and then catch a few z's."

"That's okay," Lewis said. "I want to go over this again with Bill."

"One hour," Lane said. "I'm going to take a shower and get something to eat first."

Lewis looked up at the two of them, and nodded. "I want you back here no later than that. We have a lot to go over."

Lane and Hughes left together. Outside, they headed across the compound toward the barracks and dining hall. At this moment there were only a couple dozen agents on base—many of them Saudis—in training for various CIA missions. But as Zimmerman had warned them, America's days in Saudi Arabia were numbered. Soon this camp and the three US Air Force bases in the country would be closed permanently. After that if we wanted a presence in the Middle East, it would be up to the navy to maintain one of its carrier groups in the Gulf at all times.

"How are you feeling, William?" Hughes asked, concerned. "Are you up for this mission?"

"I've felt better, Tommy, but I'm okay," Lane said. He took a cigarette and gave Hughes one.

"Lewis isn't very happy that you wanted me included. But there wasn't much he could do about it."

"I wouldn't have asked for you, except I need help," Lane said, looking at his friend. The evening had turned cool, as it usually did on the desert. But the days were still warm and dry.

"That's what I'm here for—"

"That's not what I mean, Tommy," Lane cut him off. "But a load of shit could and will probably fall out of the sky on your head if this isn't played just right."

Hughes stopped him. "How long have we been friends, William?"

Lane started to shrug, but the look on Hughes's face made him stop. "Ten years."

"Eleven and a half years," Hughes corrected. "In all that time have I let you down? Have either of us let the other down?" Hughes shook his head. "I'm sorry I asked such an insulting question." He looked away momentarily.

"I'm sorry too."

"There are damned few heroes left in the world, William. As it turns out, you're mine."

"This could get you killed."

"So could walking across the street in front of a bus," Hughes said. "Now, are you going to tell me what we're facing, or do I have to give your instructors another bribe to make your life even more miserable?"

"Yernin isn't the only one," Lane said. "There's someone else. Probably one of our own who's selling us out."

"Foolish me. Why was I hoping against hope that you weren't going to say something like that?"

"How much were you told about what happened to me at Bandar-é Emān?"

"Not much. I was taken out of the loop."

"By whom, Ben?"

Hughes nodded. "On Roswell's instruction," he said. "All I know is that they were waiting for you. Presumably you were spotted leaving Tehran, or someone saw you on the highway south."

"I wasn't followed."

"That's a short list, William. Too short for happenstance. I don't believe in coincidence in any event." Hughes again stopped Lane. "They know you're here, and why you're here. You won't have a chance out on that desert. Killed in the line of duty. No muss, no fuss, they'll even save on funeral expenses because there probably wouldn't be enough left to scrape off the sand."

"But it would tip their hand once and for all."

"Don't be stupid—"

"In order to kill me, they have to know where I'll be. If I don't show up at the staging site, but instead hide out someplace close so I can see what's happening, it might change their plans. They might make a mistake."

"They might blanket the entire region. If they can kill an entire town, one lone man would present no insurmountable challenge."

Lane smiled. "It's what I get paid for."

"This has become something personal between you and Yernin," Hughes said. "You're hoping that he'll show up out there and you can finally face him one on one."

Lane's smile widened. "Hope does spring eternal, Tommy."

Lane, dressed in clean khakis, was about to go back to the operations planning room when Ben Lewis showed up at the door. The Russian Division director looked shook up.

"It looks as if we're going to have to scrub the mission," Lewis said. "It's become impossible to contain, and the director specifically warned that we were to maintain a low profile. The lowest."

"What's happened?"

"Commander Shipley showed up."

"Here?"

"At the front gate. She says that she knows you're here, and she wants to talk to you."

"Why wasn't she sent away?"

"This camp is supposed to be secret. So the gate guards arrested her."

"Damn!" Lane said. "Where is she now?"

"I locked up our mission profiles, maps, and satellite shots, as if that makes any difference now, and put her in the operations room. One of Zimmerman's people is watching her."

"She can't know for certain that I'm here. Why not just hold her for forty-eight hours until I get back? By then whatever she thinks she knows would be a moot point."

"Can't do it, William. Her people know she came out here."

"I doubt that."

"And in the second place, if and when Hussein goes down, the shit will truly hit the fan. We're going to have to duck pretty low to keep from getting hit. She'll make that impossible."

"Don't pack your bags yet," Lane said. "I'll talk to her."

"We're going to have to let her go, of course," Lewis said dourly. "And naturally she'll report back to her people what's going on out here."

"No she won't."

Lewis stared at him. "You said that before."

"She hasn't betrayed us yet. And she won't."

Lewis started to object, but Lane held him off.

"You're going to have to trust me, Ben. It's my life on the line, you know."

"I'll reserve judgment."

Lane clapped him on the shoulder. "It's a start."

He walked over to the operations room where a CIA operative dressed in combat fatigues and armed with an M-16 stood watch by the door.

"How do you know she hasn't jumped out a window?" Lane asked.

"The windows are nailed shut, and the glass is alarmed, Mr. Lane."

"You can get out of here, I'll take over."

The CIA agent hesitated.

"She's a friend, and definitely not dangerous."

"Yes, sir," the agent said skeptically. He left.

Frances was working at the combination lock on the file cabinet when Lane came in. She looked up guiltily, but then her face lit up in a big smile.

"What are you doing here, you goddamned fool? Or did your government send you?" Lane demanded harshly.

She stopped in midstride, her face falling. "I'm here on my own. I followed you to Riyadh, and I figured you'd be training out here. It's the only logical place. So I took a chance."

"Why?"

She glanced at the door. "Is this room secure?"

"So far as I know, it's not bugged."

"You may be walking into a trap, William. I had to warn you."

"What makes you think so?"

"The house in Saint-Tropez doesn't belong to a friend of mine."

"It's a SIS safe house. I knew that from the start."

A flicker of surprise crossed her face, but she plunged ahead. "Did you also know that I disabled the bugs and recording devices?"

"You missed one. But I got it. What makes you think I'm walking into a trap?"

"Technical Services was watching the house. When you left they intercepted me on the way up to Nice and wanted to know what I was up to. I told them that I was on leave, and they warned me that a couple of French private detectives showed up the day before and were watching the house."

"Did your people talk to them?"

Frances shook her head, her gray-blue eyes penetrating. "No, but they got a solid ID on one of the detectives. His name is Jean Batérie, a former Foreign Legion intelligence officer who has freelanced for the Russians and from time to time the Ukrainian KGB."

"They weren't there to kill us."

"No, just to find out what we were doing."

Lane focused on her. "Are you sure you weren't followed here?"

"Very," she said. "No one knows I'm here."

"Except Ben Lewis, and the guards on the gate, and the one who was at the door, the chief of the CIA's Riyadh station, and whoever sponsored your stay in a hotel and car rental." Lone women travelers could not check into a hotel, rent a car, or do any number of other things in Saudi Arabia without the sponsorship of a male.

"The CIA is on our side, and I sent telegrams to the Asia Hotel and Hertz from Nice under the name of Frank Shipley, my supposed husband. I haven't checked in with my embassy so no one outside your little circle knows I'm here." She tossed her head. "I would have thought you'd give me more credit than that."

Lane looked at the file cabinet she'd tried to open. "What did you expect to find, Frannie? Something you could use to help me?"

"I just wanted to know just how far you were planning on taking this stupid stunt."

Lane went over to the file cabinet, unlocked it, and pulled out the planning maps and satellite photos. He spread them out on the table, then stabbed a finger at a spot on the Syrian Desert well west of Baghdad.

"The weather is expected to clear by tomorrow afternoon, so we can get the latest satellite updates. As soon as we pinpoint Hussein's camp I'll be helicoptered across the border, set down a few klicks from there, go in, kill the man, and then run like hell to the nearest border." He looked up.

"That's crazy," she said. "Even if you get to him you'll never make it out alive."

"It's a chance I'm willing to take."

"I'm not willing to take that risk."

"You're not coming with me."

"Nor are you going. I'll go public with it."

"I'll still try, Frannie."

"You'd get killed for sure."

"In that case, you're probably correct. If they knew I'm coming, and exactly where I was going to be set down, they'd be waiting for me."

A sudden understanding dawned in her eyes. "But you won't be there. At the last minute you'll change plans so that even if you are exposed you'll have a chance." Another understanding showed on her face. "You believe there's a mole somewhere in your service? Or perhaps in the CIA. Someone who knows your moves."

"You have two choices. You can either stay here until I get back. Say in forty-eight hours. Or you can go home."

"I can't stay that long. My people expect me to surface before then." She shook her head. "But you're not going ahead with it, are you?"

"Yes, I am."

"No."

Lane gathered up the maps and photos and put them back in the file cabinet and relocked the drawer. "You're an officer in the British Secret Intelligence Service. Go home, Frances, and do whatever it is you must do."

"Don't I mean anything to you? You said that you loved me. Was that a sham?"

"No sham, Frannie. But I have a job to do."

She squared her shoulders, and nodded. "So do I," she said resolutely. "I am a British intelligence officer."

"I understand."

"I hope you do," she replied, searching his eyes. Then she left, and for a few minutes Lane was able to do nothing except stand there.

SEVASTOPOL, UKRAINE

A bitter wind blew from Artillery Bay as Mikhail Maslennikov took the broad marble stairs two at a time into the Naval Academy's Headquarters and Operations Center. It was a few minutes past eight in the evening, and after signing in at the front desk he took the elevator up to his third-floor office. The building was quiet for the night. Except for the guards and the staff in the operations pit in the subbasement, the complex was deserted.

As he hung up his coat and hat his telephone rang. He sat down at his desk and answered it.

"*Da,*" he said, mildly annoyed. No one was supposed to know he was going to be here tonight. He wanted to get some work done undisturbed.

"It's me. Are you alone?"

The voice was intimately familiar to Maslennikov, but he got a chill up his spine. It was his private source, Red Baron. "Yes. How did you know I would be at this number?"

"Frances Shipley is in Riyadh. She's staying at the Asia Hotel."

"When she left France I thought she was either returning to Washington or going home to London. What is she doing in Saudi Arabia?"

"Presumably following Bill Lane."

"You expected it," Maslennikov grudgingly admitted. "I didn't think she would be so foolish. Will she stop him?"

"I don't know. Their relationship is close. Maybe true love will win out after all." Red Baron laughed. "If she manages to make contact with him she might have information we could use."

"Taking her would be risky."

"But not impossible. If something should go wrong she could prove to be beneficial."

"When is he scheduled to go over?"

"Tomorrow night. The front will have passed by then, giving the satellites a pass to get a current fix on the camp."

"The attempt will throw the region into a political shambles," Maslennikov said. "Just what we want. What else have you learned?"

"The president continues to try to distance himself from the assassination, but it will not work out the way he wants it to. Already there are too many people in Washington who know something is on the wind to keep a lid on it once the news hits CNN."

"There will be major political fallout."

"Yes. Worse than the Bay of Pigs or the fall of Saigon."

Maslennikov thought it over. "I'll arrange to have the woman picked up."

"Where will you take her?" Red Baron asked.

"Someplace safe," Maslennikov said. He had a few secrets of his own and he intended keeping it that way.

48

Lieutenant Ablakin had taken double duty from the captain and from their sonar operator to give both men a chance at some much needed rest. He sat in front of the display screens holding the headphones tightly to his ears as he tried to identify an unusual sound.

The waterfall display in the center screen showed a definite target on a relative bearing of 040. That was off somewhere to the southwest, toward the Saudi's southern coast. The target was at an extreme distance even for the Kilo's upgraded sonar suite. Ablakin put it somewhere outside the 50,000-meter ring. Fifty kilometers.

But what bothered him most was that neither he nor the submarine's sophisticated computer program could identify the target. The noise it made sounded to Ablakin like a thousand angry bees buzzing around inside a diving helmet. Oddly alien and dangerous because whatever it was, it was heading inbound on a course that would intercept their own.

The watch clock showed that it was a few minutes after ten in the evening, local time. The captain had been down for less than an hour, but Lieutenant Fomenko had found his way to an empty bunk around 5:30.

Yernin, who'd been wandering around the boat filling in wherever he could, appeared in the passageway with two glasses of tea. He handed one to Ablakin.

"Thank you, Colonel."

Yernin nodded to the waterfall. "What is it?"

"I don't know."

Yernin put down his tea and donned a pair of headphones. He listened intently for several seconds. "It sounds like it's moving fast."

"I'm showing fifty knots, but I don't know if this equipment is properly calibrated, or if I'm operating it correctly."

"Where is Lieutenant Fomenko?"

"Sleeping."

"Get him up here on the double. I think we've found our needed diversion."

Ablakin picked up the growler phone. "Lieutenant Fomenko to sonar on the double." He looked up. "Do you know what kind of a boat that is?"

"Of course," Yernin said. "It's a hydrofoil patrol boat that's very capable of finding and killing us if its skipper knows what he's doing."

"American?"

Yernin shook his head. "Saudi navy. But there may be some Americans aboard as trainers." Yernin smiled. "This could prove to be interesting."

Their sonar officer showed up a minute later, his eyes red from sleep, his hair standing on end. "Trouble?" he asked, taking Ablakin's seat.

The XO pointed to the waterfall display. "This showed up a few minutes ago. Colonel Yernin thinks—"

Yernin clamped a hand on Ablakin's elbow. The Black Sea Fleet officer shut up.

Fomenko donned the earphones, listened for several seconds, adjusted his equipment, listened again, then made a grease pencil mark on the display screen.

He picked up the growler phone. "Captain, sonar."

"Right here," Razhin said, coming around the corner. He too looked like he'd just awakened. He edged his executive officer out of the way. "What do you have this time, Vasha?"

"I think it's a Pegasus–class missile boat. Hydrofoil." He made another mark on the display screen. "Bearing is changing, now zero-three-eight, distance a little over forty-five thousand meters." Fomenko looked up. "He's closing with us at better than sixteen hundred meters per minute."

"I heard about that boat. Saudi navy?"

"Probably."

"Does he have us?"

"Not at that speed, Captain," the sonar officer said. "But if they were trained by an American crew, they'll slow down every ten minutes or so to make a sonar sweep. They might detect us when that happens."

"Unless we turn in the opposite direction." Razhin looked at Yernin. "Or is this the diversion you wanted?"

"Can we kill it?"

The captain shrugged. "With a few more crewmen, I wouldn't hesitate. But with so few men, it could be problematic. We'd only get one shot. Two torpedoes."

"They will be a mostly Saudi crew, and they will believe that we are Iranian. It will give us the advantage."

"Indeed it will." The captain glanced at the watch clock. "The *Good Hope* will be showing up at any time, which will provide us with the needed cover to make our escape. Important if, as you believe, the *Chicago* is heading our way."

Fomenko adjusted another display. He pulled up a file from the boat's computer memory. "During our last inboard turn there were two possible targets that could have been *Good Hope,*" he said. "Shall we stop for another look?"

Razhin stared at Yernin. "Any sign of the *Chicago?*"

"No."

Razhin picked up the boat's intercom. "This is the captain speaking. All hands to battle stations, torpedo. All hands to battle stations, torpedo." He hit the Klaxon.

"We will kill this little boat and then make good our escape," Yernin said.

"As you wish, Colonel," Razhin replied, emotionlessly.

The motion through, actually over, the seas in excess of fifty knots in the pitch dark of night was bizarre, and everybody aboard the *Prince Faisal* felt that they were tempting fate. Their radar showed them everything on the surface ahead. But they could not detect a mostly sunken log, or a barrel three-quarters filled with water that would float just at or below the surface of the water. If they hit such a half-sunken object, it might rip the hydrofoils completely off the hull, or damage them so badly that the boat could flip end over end. It wasn't a comforting thought.

Standard operating procedure was for them to go to hull speed of twelve knots during times of restricted visibility. But the last message they'd received, relayed from the *Mississippi*'s sub hunters, was that the Kilo sub was not in their neck of the woods. Nor had the boat returned to its pens at Bandar-é Emān, which could only mean that it was heading south, toward the Strait of Hormuz. And Captain Rashid meant to intercept it before it got that far.

It was general knowledge that the United States maintained a submarine presence in the Gulf. The most logical place for an attack submarine to wait for prey would be the narrow strait. But this target was an Arab target, and it would be challenged by an Arab boat manned by an Arab crew.

Lieutenant Morrison had gone below to get something to eat, and when he'd left the bridge after their last sonar sweep he asked permission to remain below for a half-hour. It meant Captain Rashid and his Saudi crew would be left to handle the next two sweeps on their own.

It was a subtle bit of encouragement that was not lost on the captain. Despite his opposite inclination he was beginning to like and respect his American XO.

The mission clock above the helmsman counted down to zero, and a red warning light flashed.

"Make your speed twelve knots," Captain Rashid told his second officer, young Ensign Ahmed Yamni. "Look smartly now."

"Aye, aye, Captain. Make my speed twelve knots."

"Sound battle stations ASROC," Rashid said. Then, realizing that his executive officer was not on the bridge to carry out his order, he hit the alarm bottom himself. "Hello all hands, hello all hands. This is the captain speaking. Come to battle stations ASROC. Come to battle stations ASROC."

The patrol boat's speed dropped rapidly, the hull settling back into the choppy sea.

Rashid picked up the phone. "Sonar, this is the bridge. Begin your sweep now—"

"Captain, there is a large mass directly in front of us!" the sonar operator shouted wildly. "One thousand meters . . . no, less!"

Rashid's heart jumped into his throat. "Is it stationary?"

"Two objects in the water, bearing direct on our . . . Captain, we have been fired on! There are two torpedoes heading directly toward us."

"Turn around and get us out of here, Ahmed!" Rashid screamed.

"Belay that order," Lieutenant Morrison shouted, coming through the door. "Bring us up on our hydrofoils and turn directly toward the torpedoes! Now!"

The helmsman, torn between his captain's orders and those of the American, hesitated.

Morrison shoved the helmsman aside and jammed the throttles forward at almost the same instant the first torpedo struck them amidships, pushing them completely out of the water.

Three-quarters of a second later the *Prince Faisal* blew up, the second torpedo charging through the debris field, exploding three seconds afterward.

Captain Razhin lowered the periscope. "The boat is dead," he said.

Yernin looked at him without expression.

"Good shooting, Georgi," Razhin told his weapons officer. He stepped around the corner into sonar. "Do we have a solid fix now on *Good Hope?*"

"Yes, Captain. She's eleven kilometers to our north and closing in at thirty knots."

"Fine. We'll intercept her and hide beneath her shadow. A lot of people are going to be taking a great interest in our handiwork, and very soon, I should think."

"Yes, Captain."

"Keep a sharp ear out for the *Chicago,* we're not out of the birches yet."

Back in the control room he called his chief engineer. "Eleven kilometers, Aleksandr. I want everything you can give me until then."

"Fuck your mother, but the batteries are running low, Captain," Lieutenant Aleksandr Pechenko replied. He was rough around the edges but he knew the Kilo boats inside and out.

"I don't care if you have to fart into the battery compartment for extra energy. I need eleven klicks at the fastest speed you can give me. Our lives depend on it now."

"Wipe your own asses up there, and stop bothering us, I have eleven kilometers to give you," the ChEng replied, then hung up.

"Conn, sonar."

"This is the captain," Coburn answered.

"Skipper, we just recorded a major event outside our one hundred thousand ring, rough bearing directly on our bow."

"What kind of an event?"

"Sounded like a torpedo hit, followed by an explosion, and what may have been second, third, and fourth torpedo hits, or subsea ordinance cooking off in a sinking boat."

"What else?"

"That's in the twilight zone, Skipper. I'm not making out any individual traffic at that range."

"Stand by," Coburn said. He walked over to the port plotting table and laid out the sonar distance and bearing. It put the event well off shore from the Saudi Arabian Navy base at Al Jubayal.

"What's up, Skipper?" Friend asked.

"Sonar picked up what might have been a torpedo attack up here," Coburn had circled the general area.

"Could be that our Kilo tangled with a Saudi patrol boat."

"It's possible," Coburn replied, but his mind was elsewhere. The Iranian sub driver had to know that the Gulf was crawling with American, Kuwaiti, and Saudi warships and patrol boats. He also had to know that an American submarine would be hanging around down south. So what was he doing terrorizing the natives unless something else was going on?

"Skipper?" Friend asked.

Coburn looked up. "Bring the boat to periscope depth, Mike. I'd like to chat with Jonesy on the *Mississippi*."

49

Lying in a shallow depression on the desert five miles outside of camp, Lane passed the time thinking about the great restaurants he'd eaten at. Tops among them had to be the Louis XV across from the casino in Monaco.

He sighted down the hill through the sniper rifle's night sights. The desert features stood out in pale, ghostly relief. The evening was cold and dark. His job was to wait with patience until Hussein and his two guards appeared below.

The restaurant's chef, Louis Ducasse, had won his third *Guide Michelin* star when he was only thirty-three, and had continued to improve with age. It was the second or third time he'd taken Frances out, and she'd been impressed. He smiled now thinking about it.

Tomorrow night the ambient light would be somewhat greater because the sky over the Syrian Desert would be clear. But there would be no moon.

He would have to be in position and well hidden before dawn, where he would remain through the day until the former Iraqi leader took his early evening walk.

"You'll freeze your ass off until sunrise, then bake it most of the day, and finish up by freezing again once the sun goes down," his instructor, Gordon O'Toole, Irish to his students, told him cheerily.

"If the spiders or scorpions or snakes don't get you, the MREs, which you'll have to eat cold, will do the trick."

The dining room looked like something out of a classic French film, with four huge chandeliers, damask linens, the best china, crystal, and silver, and tables that were not crowded together like in most restaurants. The service and the food matched the setting.

"Seriously, Mr. Lane, watch yourself out there," Irish told him gravely. "Most of the weight I'm sending with you will be water and Gatorade. I want you to keep yourself well hydrated."

"A good chardonnay would taste better."

"No way to keep it cold."

"There's always a catch," Lane said, laughing.

He'd half buried himself in the sand about twenty-five yards southwest of the position suggested for him. He turned his head left and looked toward the spot in time to catch a movement.

Moving with exaggerated care, he pointed his rifle toward the general direction and scoped the terrain. Immediately he picked out two figures dressed in desert camos crawling toward where he should have been.

He thumbed the safety catch off and fired two laser beams, simulating the silenced shots he would fire during the actual mission. The hits were picked up by the vests the two men were wearing, illuminating a Head Up Display in their helmet rims, telling them that they were dead.

"Shit," one of them said, looking around.

The other one pulled him down, and they stayed put.

Lane shifted aim back down the hill where Hussein and his two guards would be walking. A minute later they appeared, Hussein in the lead, his guards fifty yards back.

Steadying his aim, Lane took out the guards first. Both men stepped back when they knew they were hit, and looked up toward where he was supposed to be.

One of them started to gesture toward Hussein, but Lane shifted aim and fired two shots, one hitting Irish in the vest, two inches to the left of his sternum, and the second in his head, directly between his eyes.

The CIA instructor stopped in his tracks and looked directly up the hill toward where Lane should have been, then took off his helmet to signify that the exercise was over.

Lane stood up and brushed the sand from his desert camos.

"Goddamnit," one of the instructors to his left shouted, getting to his feet.

Lane waved to him.

"What in hell are you doing over there?"

"Saving his own life," Irish called up to them, "by not playing according to the rules." He laughed. "Well done, Mr. Lane. Well done."

RIYADH

Frances stood by the window in her room on the tenth floor of the Asia Hotel, looking toward the north across the city. She was filled with indecision, something new for her, and she was having trouble dealing with her emotions. Very little seemed to make much sense, except that she loved Bill Lane, and that she was desperately frightened for him.

Her London flight left at eight in the morning and she had every intention of being on it. She'd not contacted her embassy, nor had she said anything to her own service.

Which made her what? A traitor by sin of omission? England had legitimate political interest out here, and her job description included gathering information that her government could use.

Personal considerations were supposed to be set aside. For God, queen, and country. That was the drill, wasn't it?

Brad Morgan had finally given her the okay to liaise with the Americans only after she'd thrown a tantrum and threatened to quit.

"If it's a personal thing, Frances, you'd be jeopardizing your career, and everything that you've worked for," the chief of SIS Paris station told her. He was like a stern-faced uncle. He'd always been that way toward her, and they'd always gotten along well.

"I'm not happy at the UN," she'd said petulantly.

"Nor did I expect you would be when you left Paris. You could always be reassigned to me. It would be like old times."

"Do you have a crush on me, Brad? Is that it?" she shot back, and she instantly regretted it.

Morgan's face turned red, and he shook his head sadly. "What if you were to be recalled to London?"

"I'd quit."

"I see," Morgan replied heavily. "In that case it's been agreed for you to be temporarily detached to the National Security Agency. In thirty days. First we'd like you to take some more leave."

"To give me more time to think about it?"

"Something like that. Before you go over you will have to be briefed, of course."

"Of course."

She got up to leave and Morgan smiled indulgently at her. "By the way, there seems to be something the matter with the surveillance equipment at the villa. You wouldn't know anything about that, would you, love?"

"No, but I'll check on it," she'd said.

How many promises had she broken in her lifetime, she wondered. Not many. But starting now she figured they were going to begin adding up pretty fast.

Someone knocked at her door, and she hurried to the nightstand beside the bed and got her gun, a .32-caliber Browning Special automatic.

"Who is it?" she asked, standing aside, out of the line of fire if they shot through the door.

"We're from the embassy, Commander Shipley," a man said. "Mr. Morgan sent an urgent message for you. He asked that we personally saw that you received it."

The only way Brad could know that she was here was if he'd ordered her followed. But he wouldn't have done that unless he expected that there was much more to the situation than she'd told him.

"Shall we slip it under the door for you, Commander?" the man asked. His accent was British, but she couldn't place from where. North or south.

"All right," she said.

An envelope was slid under the door. Careful to remain in the line of fire only briefly, she snatched the envelope off the floor and ducked back.

"Just a moment," she said. She laid her gun on the dresser and ripped open the envelope.

The tips of her fingers suddenly went numb, and for an instant she was confused. Her heart skipped a beat, and as she dropped the envelope her legs collapsed beneath her, and the room went dark and distant.

50

THE WHITE HOUSE

Roswell's limousine was admitted through the west gate a few minutes after 4:00 P.M. The afternoon was cold and blustery, which fitted the National Security Agency director's mood as he took the elevator to the subbasement.

"Good afternoon, Mr. Roswell," one of the security guards greeted him. He handed him a security badge.

"Am I the last?"

"I believe so, sir. Traffic bad?"

"It gets worse every year."

"Yes, sir."

The president was seated at the end of the long conference table in the situation room. With him were National Security Adviser Bill Townsend, Director of Central Intelligence Roland Murphy, Chairman of the Joint Chiefs Air Force General Thomas Mooreland, J3 Admiral David Maxwell, and Secretary of State Dr. Robert P. Hatchett.

An imposing group, Roswell thought as he took his seat. He nodded his greeting at Murphy, who looked particularly sour this afternoon. They all did.

"Now that Tom is here we can get started," the president said.

"Sorry I'm late—"

"Skip it," Reasoner cut him off. "We're in a hell of a mess. What I want is information and suggestions, not apologies."

"What's happened, Mr. President?"

"The Saudis are about to declare war on Iran, and they want us to help them."

"Jesus Christ," Roswell swore softly.

"You can say that again," the president said. He turned to General Mooreland. "Bring us up to speed."

Mooreland motioned for his J3 to do the briefing, and Admiral Maxwell opened a fat file.

"At 1918 hours GMT, that was about two hours ago, the Saudi Arabian navy patrol vessel *Prince Faisal* was shot out of the water by a pair of torpedoes we believe were launched from an Iranian submarine in the central Persian Gulf." Maxwell looked up. "The *Prince Faisal* was an American-built patrol missile boat and ASW platform, crewed for the most part by Saudi naval personnel. But there were two American naval officers aboard. There were no survivors."

"Was the submarine challenged?" Roswell asked.

"Unknown, sir," Maxwell said. "But the *Prince Faisal* was sub hunting. The Kilo boat made it through the *Mississippi*'s screen so the Saudis went looking farther south."

"Did anyone see anything?" Roswell asked. "Our satellites are out of commission over there because of the weather."

"The *Chicago* reported to Bob Jones, the *Mississippi*'s commander, that their sonar detected the attack, and asked what happened. But nobody in Jones's group knew a thing. The Iranians got lucky."

"Are we currently looking for that submarine?" Reasoner asked.

"Yes, Mr. President," Maxwell said. "But it's nighttime over there, so the search is of necessity limited not only by the darkness, but by the heavy traffic. It's a busy piece of water."

"Yet nobody saw anything?"

"That's the story so far, Mr. President. If somebody did witness the attack, they're not coming forward for whatever reason."

"And now the boat has disappeared under our noses?"

"Yes, Mr. President. We have a half-dozen Orions overflying the region, but so far they've come up with nothing."

"The *Chicago* is searching for that boat as well, isn't she?"

"Yes, sir. But like I said, that's a busy piece of water. Could be that the sub is hiding in the electronic shadow beneath a surface ship. We can't stop them all. It'd be physically impossible."

"So what you're saying, Admiral, is that if that submarine commander plays his cards right, he'll be able to take his boat anywhere he wants. Through the Strait of Hormuz and out to sea, if he so desires."

Maxwell looked up, a long expression on his bulldog face. "I'm afraid so, sir. Unless we get lucky."

The president looked around the table at the others. "Up to this point they've done a good job evading the *Mississippi*, sinking a state-of-the-art sub hunter, and then eluding the best we can throw at them."

Maxwell nodded.

"That would take a pretty bright crew, wouldn't it?"

"Yes, sir."

"But it was my understanding that the Iranians were not that well trained," the president said, a harsh edge in his voice, his eyes flashing. "Someone want to explain this discrepancy to me?"

"Might not be an Iranian crew," Roswell offered.

"They're Iranians," Murphy said. "Our people on the ground in Tehran say the current Iranian Defense Ministry is thinking that the skipper has gone berserk. His name is Madhlum Baram, and he's considered to be a moderate. Which in English translates as radical."

"Is he good enough?" Roswell asked.

Murphy shrugged, and turned to Maxwell. "David?"

"I wouldn't have thought so. But they could have been sandbagging us."

"Has the Iranian government said anything officially about the incident?" the president asked his secretary of state.

Dr. Hatchett shook his leonine head and laid his pipe in the ashtray. He was the only man permitted to smoke in the president's presence. "It's too soon. But we're pressuring them."

"Do they realize what's at stake?"

"Presumably, though I don't think any one takes the Saudi threat seriously."

"I take it seriously, Bob," the president said, and his remark caused several heads to turn. The president and the secretary of state never disagreed. Never.

"Nations no longer go to war over such minor incidents," Hatchett said. "Invasions are one thing, but a skirmish between two boats in contested waters is another thing entirely."

"I'm not talking about that," Reasoner said, his eyes flashing. "I'm saying that we've been had. And I want to know why, and what else is about to fall on us."

Roswell had been having lunch in the city so he hadn't heard about the attack. But he knew exactly what the president was getting at. They were treading on very dangerous ground.

"At least they don't have nukes, Bill Lane proved that," he told the president.

"I understand that, but what I want someone to tell me is what they're up to. They had no reason to attack a Saudi Arabian patrol boat, and then disappear. Apparently they're heading south. Is that correct?"

"Yes, sir," Admiral Maxwell said.

"Are you dead certain that they have no nuclear weapons aboard that submarine?" the president asked. "They were waiting for Bill Lane. Maybe he saw what they wanted him to see."

"Valeri Yernin is a Ukrainian, not a Russian," Roswell said.

"Yes, but you showed me a photograph of Yernin's control officer meeting with high-level officers of the Russian and Ukrainian secret services in Kiev. So I think it's safe to say that the lines of loyalty are somewhat blurred. Both the Russians and the Ukrainians have their Middle East agendas that run counter to our MEGAP." The president leaned forward for emphasis. "If the goal is to destabilize the region, they're doing a damned fine job of it. Because at this point I'm inclined to go along with the Saudis. If we can prove that the attack was directed by the Iranians."

"That'll be difficult unless we can capture that submarine, Mr. President," Maxwell warned.

"There are other ways, but we still don't know what other mischief that submarine captain may be contemplating."

"I'm not sure I entirely understand, Mr. President," Roswell said. "Is it your view that the Iranians, with or without the help of either the Russians or the Ukrainians, staged the raid against their own submarine base in order to confuse us?"

"Yes, and it did," Reasoner said.

"Then their aim was to make us believe that this latest attack was carried out by someone else. Some group who somehow managed to hijack one of their subs."

"That's exactly what I'm saying," the president said. "And their admitting that the only explanation they could give was that their submarine captain was nuts strengthens the ploy."

"To what end, Mr. President?" Roswell asked.

"I don't know, and that worries me," Reasoner said. "Where is Bill Lane at this moment?"

"At our training camp outside Riyadh," Murphy said.

"When is he scheduled to go over?"

"Tomorrow."

Dr. Hatchett sat up. "Go over where?" he asked.

"I'll explain later, Bob," the president told him. "Get Lane back here. I want his input. He seems to be the only one who thinks straight. And besides, this Ukrainian spy he's been chasing somehow might provide the key we need."

"Is the mission to be canceled?" Roswell asked, exchanging glances with Murphy.

"Just delayed," the president said. "Whatever is happening in the Middle East will be stopped. Those sons of bitches aren't going to play games with my oil."

NATIONAL SECURITY AGENCY

Roswell rode back to his office, his head spinning. Wherever they looked they saw nothing but contradictions. One thing was sure, however. Whoever was responsible for the raid on Bandar-é Emān and whoever was responsible for the recent attack on the Saudi patrol boat were directed by the same hand. But for what purpose was still unknown.

His call to the CIA training camp outside Riyadh went through without delay.

"His training is finished, and he looks good, Mr. Director," Lewis said, his voice undistorted over the encrypted circuit. "But I was just about to call you. We've got a problem here."

"We're scrubbing the mission, for the moment," Roswell said. "I want all of you back here on the double. Now what problem are you talking about?"

"Frances Shipley showed up late yesterday afternoon demanding to speak with Bill."

"How did she know where he was? Did he tell her, or has the SIS gotten itself involved?"

"Apparently she followed him. But that's not the problem," Lewis said. "I had her followed back to her hotel. But now she's missing. Nobody's seen a thing. And her clothing and passport and gun are still in her room. I think she's been kidnapped."

"We've heard nothing new about Yernin's whereabouts?"

"No, sir. He just disappeared. But if it was Yernin he would have killed her and not bothered removing her body."

"Has Bill been told?"

"No. I thought it best that we hold off until he returned," Lewis said. "Why are we canceling the mission?"

"I'll tell you the details when you get here. All you have to know for now is that an Iranian submarine sank a Saudi patrol boat that was carrying a couple of American crewmen, and now it's disappeared."

"Son of a bitch."

"That's what the president said."

"What about Frances Shipley?"

"I'll ask the CIA to help us out. In the meantime don't say anything to Bill."

"Yes, sir."

"Just get back here."

CIA TRAINING CAMP
NORTH OF RIYADH

Lane was getting out of the shower when Lewis showed up at his quarters. With a towel around his middle, he let the Russian Division director in.

"The mission has been scrubbed."

"What happened?" Lane asked, studying Lewis's long face.

"Roswell just called me. He wants us back in Washington ASAP."

"Did he say why?"

"Apparently an Iranian Kilo boat got itself into some trouble," Lewis said. "Sank a Saudi gunboat, killing everyone aboard including a couple of our navy guys. The president is pissed."

"Were they provoked?"

"The Saudis or the Kilo?

"The submarine, Ben," Lane said.

"I don't know. But we're wanted in Washington, so we're going. Tom is already packing, and as soon as you get your act together the Company will chopper us down to the airport. They've loaned us one of their Gulfstreams."

Lane went back into the bathroom where he finished drying off. "The *Mississippi*'s battle group must have spotted them coming out of Bandar-é Emān. Which means if they got away with this attack they had to have successfully evaded detection. A neat trick."

"I don't have the details, Bill."

Lane came to the doorway. "I'll bet you ten bucks that no Iranian crew managed such a feat. The sub was either hijacked, or the Iranians pulled an end run on us and replaced their own crew with a ringer. The only possibilities worth mentioning are Russian or Ukrainian."

Lewis turned to go. "Shake a leg, the chopper will be ready to go in five minutes."

"Has Frances already left Riyadh?"

Lewis stopped in his tracks. "What?"

"You had her followed, Ben. I would have if I were in your shoes. She was staying at the Asia Hotel. Is she gone?"

Lewis started to say something, but then changed his mind. He shook his head. "As far as I know, she's gone. But we haven't made chasing her our number-one priority."

Something wasn't quite right about Lewis's answer, but Lane let it go for the moment. "I'll meet you guys on the pad in five."

Lewis hesitated a moment longer. "I really don't know what's going on, Bill. Except that Roswell sounded shook up. When he told me what had happened, I said 'son of a bitch.' He told me that's what the president said."

"Still no word on Yernin's whereabouts?"

"No."

"When the boss calls, we jump. Get out of here and let me get ready."

51

WASHINGTON, D.C.

Dulles was closed due to a late spring blizzard blanketing much of the eastern seaboard, so they were diverted to Andrews Air Force Base. Nothing was visible outside the windows except for the disorienting swirling snow, until less than four hundred feet from touchdown the runway lights suddenly came into view.

The Gulfstream was comfortable and their steward, a former air force steward, treated them well. Hughes and Lewis fell asleep within an hour after they'd left Saudi airspace, leaving Lane alone for most of the night with his own thoughts, which wandered back to the look in Yernin's eyes aboard the train. He had been a step behind Yernin all this time, and he chastised himself for it. Because of his clumsiness a lot of people had died. And even more would be killed unless he took off the kid gloves.

Hughes would say that his hesitance to kill was a mark of his civility. Only wild animals and sociopaths displayed the single-minded devotion to killing that Yernin showed.

Looking out the window as they touched down, Lane brought his thoughts back to the immediate problem of the Kilo boat on the loose somewhere in the Persian Gulf. He had almost none of the facts, so any guesses he might make would probably be wildly off the mark, but for the life of him he could not think why the Kilo had attacked the Saudi patrol boat unless she'd been detected and challenged. If their intent was to sneak out of the Gulf, why call attention to themselves?

"Did you get any sleep?" Hughes asked as they taxied off the main runway and followed a chase vehicle toward one of the hangers. It was 8:00 A.M. Washington time.

"A little," Lane lied. He grinned. "But you kept me awake with your snoring."

"A scandalous and scurrilous attack on my integrity."

"Moira agrees with me."

Hughes nodded. "In that case you might have a point."

Drivers were waiting for them with a pair of four-wheel-drive jeeps when they parked in the hanger and got out. Roswell climbed out of the backseat of one of the vehicles and came over. He and Lane shook hands.

"Sorry to pull you out of there like that at the last minute," Roswell said.

"What's the latest on the Kilo?"

"I'll bring you up to speed on the way over to the White House. The president asked for you personally."

"Do we get a chance to grab something to eat and clean up first?" Lewis asked.

"I want you and Hughes to get out to Fort Meade. I expect there'll be a lot of work for you when we're finished."

Hughes shot Lane a "be careful" look, and he and Lewis climbed into one of the jeeps; Lane got into the other with Roswell. They headed off base, the roads all but impassable for anything but a four-wheel-drive or a snowmobile.

"Washington has to be all but shut down," Lane observed.

"Just about," Roswell replied absently. "The president thinks that you're some kind of a superstar. The only one who seems to make any sense. And I tend to agree with him. So don't hold back. If he asks you a question, give him a straight answer."

"Ben said that an Iranian sub sank a Saudi patrol boat."

"That's right. And all hell is about to break lose over there. Did you see anything unusual at the airport in Riyadh?"

"A lot of extra security. How are the Saudis taking it?"

"They want to declare war on Iran, and the president thinks it might not be such a bad idea. A view that no one shares with him, not even Bob Hatchett."

"Did the patrol boat challenge the submarine?"

"Possibly, but not likely. One of our people aboard was executive officer. He would have known better."

"The *Mississippi* saw or heard nothing?"

"One of our satellites picked up the Kilo leaving base and the information was relayed to the *Mississippi*, of course. But then the weather deteriorated, and the last we saw of the sub, she was still on the surface heading south."

"There's a lot of traffic in the Gulf. Nobody saw anything?"

"Apparently not. One of our submarines, the *Chicago*, came up from the Strait of Hormuz. She heard the attack but it was so far away there wasn't a thing she could do. By the time they got on scene, the Kilo had disappeared."

"It's the information Yernin stole from the computer center. He knows the sailing orders for every ship and submarine in the entire Pacific Fleet."

"That's a pretty big leap, Bill. It means that Kiev and Tehran are cooperating. Goes against current thinking."

"No Iranian crew got through that blockade. And no Iranian crew attacked a Saudi patrol boat. Yernin is aboard that Kilo with a Black Sea Fleet crew. They hijacked the sub."

"The Iranians would be screaming bloody murder. They're claiming that the skipper has gone nuts."

"That's because they don't know what's going on yet."

"How could they not know?"

"Because it was done at sea, probably while the Kilo was submerged."

"Impossible."

Lane grinned tiredly at Roswell. "Not impossible, Mr. Director. Just difficult."

"How?" the president asked when they were settled in the White House situation room.

Admiral Maxwell shook his head, and the others around the big table looked just as skeptical.

"They had help," Lane said. "A well-equipped surface ship could have made contact with the Kilo, telling the skipper to come to periscope depth and to take on a passenger through one of the escape trunks."

"Wait a minute," Maxwell interjected. "You're saying that this 'well-equipped' ship of yours was able to find the sub, but that *Mississippi*'s battle group couldn't do it?"

"They had a bit of luck on their side. But Yernin has the sailing orders for every US warship and submarine in the Pacific, so he would know the search patterns we were using. He was also monitoring the *Mississippi*'s radio traffic. Our guys would have found the sub sooner or later, Yernin just beat us to the punch by looking where we weren't looking."

"What if we had beaten them to the punch?" Maxwell asked. "Assuming you're right."

"Then the mission would have ended and they would have tried again some other time."

"Okay, for the sake of argument, what comes next?"

"One of them locks through the escape trunk and kills the crew. Probably nerve gas. Acts fast through the sub's ventilation system, and dissipates just as quickly. Afterward, the rest of the crew is locked aboard, and the Kilo takes off. But now they don't need luck, because they know where our ships are."

"Then why did they attack the Saudi patrol boat?" the president asked. "Why risk exposure? At the very least they announced that they were around and willing to fight. Is it some sort of a challenge?"

Lane looked at the others around the table. "Mr. President, what's the consensus opinion at this point?"

"What do you mean?"

"Do you believe that the Iranians themselves staged the raid on Bandar-é Emān, and that it's actually their crew operating the Kilo?"

The president nodded. "I think it's a good possibility that they sandbagged us."

"Then Yernin attacked the Saudi patrol boat to reinforce that thinking. If Saudi Arabia wants to declare war on Iran, and we're thinking that it isn't such a bad idea, it'll divert our attention from Yernin's real plan."

"Which is?" the president asked.

"I don't know yet, but I'm going to ask him," Lane said.

A look of incredulity crossed the president's features. "You're going to do what?"

"Ask him what he's been ordered to do."

"How?"

"By getting aboard the submarine the same way he did."

"How are you going to find it?" Maxwell asked, his attitude even more skeptical than before.

"Because I know where he's going on the first leg of his trip and what he's going to do when he gets there."

"Would you mind explaining that to me?" the president asked.

"He's going through the Strait of Hormuz into the open sea, Mr. President, where he'll rendezvous with a cargo ship, and take on missiles. Nuclear missiles."

Everyone around the table was stunned.

"Once you're aboard, then what?" Maxwell asked.

Lane locked his ice blue eyes on the admiral's. "I'll kill him."

52

MOHAMMAD'S STAR

The biggest difficulty in piloting the submarine in *Good Hope*'s wake was keeping the warship at a steady depth in the turbulent waters. If she went too deep, her snorkel, which provided air to her diesels, which in turn charged her batteries, would submerge and drown the boat. If they rose too shallow, they could crash into the surface ship's hull.

The second problem was that only two men were capable of holding the sub that accurately. They worked two hours on and two hours off, but both of them were getting tired. And tired men made mistakes.

Lieutenant Krasilnikov looked up from the plotting table. "We have rounded the Ras Masandam," he told Lieutenant Ablakin, who had the conn. "Recommend we come right to course one-three-five."

Yernin, who was following Lieutenant Voskoboy's delicate touch on the helm, also looked up. "Have we passed the Strait of Hormuz?"

"Yes," the comms officer, who was doubling as chief navigator, said. "We'll be in the open Gulf of Oman in less than four hours, and the Arabian Sea in twenty-four."

At that point the *Good Hope* would no longer be needed, and she would turn northeast back to Karachi while they continued south to their rendezvous.

"Very well," Lieutenant Ablakin said. He picked up the handset connected to the aquaphone. "Charlie One, Charlie Two."

"Charlie Two, this is Charlie One," the officer on the bridge of the *Good Hope* replied.

"We've rounded the cape. My navigator recommends we turn to a new course of one-three-five."

"Yes, I see the lighthouse. I concur. We will start the turn on my mark."

"Helmsman, make a standard turn right to a new course one-three-five degrees on my mark," Ablakin said.

"Roger on your mark, one-three-five degrees."

"Now," the *Good Hope*'s bridge officer said.

"Now," Ablakin relayed the order, and the surface ship and the submarine made a perfectly synchronized turn to the right, at a standard rate of twelve degrees per minute.

Turbulence in the turn was ten times greater than in straight sailing, and Voskoboy had a difficult time holding the depth as well as the standard rate. Twice Yernin almost took over, but each time the younger man made the proper adjustments. His touch was as deft as it was light, and five minutes later, when they straightened, they were on course and at the proper depth.

Yernin grunted. "Well done, Lieutenant," he said. "I don't think one officer in a thousand could have done that well."

"Thank you, sir," Voskoboy acknowledged without looking up.

"One in ten thousand," Captain Razhin said at the forward hatch.

Yernin looked languidly his way. "You have a fine crew."

"Yes, Comrade Yernin. And you have balls. Sometimes that is not such a good combination."

Yernin shrugged.

"May I have a word with you in the officers' wardroom?"

"As you wish." Yernin followed the captain into the Kilo's forward wardroom, where he accepted a cigarette from the other man and sat down.

"We will be making our rendezvous within thirty-six hours," Razhin said. "About 1800 hours tomorrow."

"Providing we're in the clear."

"Yes, of course," Razhin said irritably. "It will be good to have the rest of my crew aboard, and decent food."

"*Da,*" Yernin replied noncommittally. He knew exactly where the captain was taking this, but he didn't care.

"We will be taking other cargo, I suspect. Weapons."

"A pair of SS-N-sixteen missiles."

Razhin reared back, shocked. "Black Sea Fleet Command did not order this."

Yernin reached into his jacket, pulled out a thin manila envelope, and laid it on the table in front of the captain. The seal of the Black Sea Fleet was stamped on the front, as was the warning that the envelope contained top-secret documents.

The captain looked at the envelope as if it were a deadly animal. He did not reach for it.

"Your primary orders are to put yourself under my command, hijack this submarine, and make the rendezvous."

"I expected that we would terrorize Baghdad, or perhaps even Tel Aviv if we could get that far, all under the flag of Iran. It would be good for Saddam Hussein." Razhin looked down at his hands spread out in front of him on the table. "But introducing nuclear weapons to this region is insanity. If it were to be discovered that Ukraine was behind the attacks, it would be the end of our country. No nation on earth would side with us."

"But no one will find out. It will be up to us."

"Things go wrong."

Yernin leaned forward. "Don't be naive, Captain. You've seen with your own two eyes what the Iranians have aboard this submarine. Radiation equipment, hot suits, nuclear blast radius charts."

"But no weapons."

"Yet. But that will happen very soon. And when it does, Iran will once again become the dominant power here. Iran's ally is Russia, not Ukraine. They are the enemy."

Razhin shook his head in anger and frustration. "That missile will not fire from a standard Kilo. I doubt we could even get it aboard."

"It's a Mod Three version, designed to be fired from a torpedo tube. And you also saw with your own eyes the enlargements that were made to the forward two tubes and the forward loading hatch."

"Where did these missiles come from?"

"Sevastopol."

"Those stockpiles are monitored by an international team."

"We stole them, and under cover of night loaded them aboard a ship carrying tractors bound for Bombay. When we rendezvous they will be slightly off course. But it is a big ocean."

"That makes us renegades," Razhin said, sudden understanding dawning in his eyes. "Even if we carry out our orders exactly as planned, they will deny us. We went berserk. It is too bad for us."

"Now you can see why it is up to us to make sure that the world believes this warship is being operated by Iranian fanatics," Yernin said.

Razhin tapped a blunt finger on the envelope. "What are our targets? And what will Ukraine benefit from striking them?"

"You don't need to know that yet," Yernin said calmly.

"We will refuse to follow your orders. This is insanity."

Yernin shrugged. "As you wish, Captain. When you return home, if you return home, it will not be to a hero's welcome. You will be shot as a traitor."

"It would be your word against mine," Razhin countered. "I might kill you."

"I invite you to try," Yernin replied without emotion, his eyes locked with the captain's.

After a moment, Razhin blinked. He opened the envelope and quickly scanned the two pages of orders.

He looked up when he was finished. "This says nothing about loading nuclear weapons."

"Some things are best left unwritten. Don't you agree?"

"No I don't."

"As you wish, Razhin," Yernin said. "Instruct your brother on the *Good Hope* that you will set this boat on the bottom in seventy meters of water, and we will lock up to them. They can take us back to Karachi, where with Captain Maslennikov's help I'll get a crew that is capable of following orders. I'll bring them back here, reactivate this submarine, and complete the mission."

"Goddamn your black soul," Razhin said with passion, as Yernin got up.

"I don't have a soul, Captain. Hadn't you noticed?"

"Wait!"

"Yes?"

Razhin lowered his eyes. "We will do what you wish," he said. "We will follow your orders. And God help our souls, because we have them."

CGN40 *MISSISSIPPI*

Lane was flown to Kuwait City where the same LAMPS II helicopter and crew from before were waiting to pick him up. He'd flown twice across the Atlantic and out to the Persian Gulf via Ramstein Air Force Base in the past twenty-four hours, and he was numb from jet lag.

"We're voting you passenger of the year, Mr. Lane," the copilot called back.

"Get me there in one piece, and I'll talk to someone in the Pentagon about getting you guys a raise."

"You're on, sir."

The *Mississippi* was a Virginia–class guided missile cruiser. Originally fitted with a helicopter deck on the fantail, the landing area had been converted to a Tomahawk missile firing platform eight years ago. But with changing missions in the Middle East, the *Mississippi* and one of the other cruisers in her class had been converted back to a helicopter platform. It made the ships more versatile.

The weather over the central Gulf and south was still overcast and lumpy, although a high-pressure system was beginning to make its way down from Iran and Iraq, bringing with it cooler temperatures and clearing skies.

Good weather for assassinations, or finding submarines, Lane thought, as the helicopter came in over the cruiser's fantail and set down hard.

They were surrounded by ground crew, and the fantail elevator lowered them to the hanger deck. It was 0900, a long Friday yet to come.

A young ensign greeted Lane when he climbed down from the helicopter. "Mr. Lane, the captain sends his compliments, sir. He'll see you in the officers' wardroom now."

Lane nodded. He turned back to the helicopter's crew. "Keep this bird warmed up. We're going out again shortly."

"Nobody said anything to us, Mr. Lane," the pilot called down.

"They will," Lane assured him.

He followed the ensign forward to the officers' wardroom where the ship's skipper, Commander Jones, and his executive officer, Lieutenant Commander Martin Prescott, waited. Jones was a large, swarthy man with a delicate nose and cheekbones, and piano player's hands. He was a study in contrasts. His XO, on the other hand, looked like he'd just stepped out of a magazine ad for Armani suits: tall, well built, handsome.

"Welcome aboard," Commander Jones said. They all shook hands.

"I won't take much of your time, Commander. I need to get out to the *Chicago* as soon as possible."

"I see," Jones said, exchanging glances with his XO. "Is there time for a cup of coffee first?"

"Barely," Lane replied. "So I'll make this short and to the point. The Iranian submarine is no longer in the Persian Gulf. By now she's made her way through the Strait of Hormuz and is probably well out into the Gulf of Oman."

Prescott shook his head. "We have assets in the strait that could have picked them up."

"She's hiding beneath a surface ship."

"Neat trick," Jones admitted. "If that's in fact what they're doing, we'll never catch up with her. Do you realize how many ships pass through the strait in a twenty-four-hour period?"

"They came in with the same ship," Lane continued. "Look for a private ship, maybe a big yacht or a research vessel of some sort, that came into the Gulf about the same time the Kilo sailed from Bandar-é Emān, then, a half-day later, turned around and left."

"That we can do," Jones said. He motioned for his XO to get on it.

"Look for a ship that came in fast, but suddenly slowed down on the way out."

Prescott nodded and left the wardroom for the CIC behind the bridge.

"Getting you out to the *Chicago* won't be easy, if it can be done at all," the captain said.

"I know, I saw the Clancy movie, *The Hunt for Red October*," Lane said.

"Well, you're going to have to convince me, so that I can convince Glen Coburn, who probably didn't see the movie."

"The Iranian navy is no longer in command of that Kilo. She was hijacked by a Black Sea Fleet crew. Probably a very good crew."

Jones looked at Lane with a new interest. "It would explain a few things."

"The attack on the Saudi patrol boat was a diversion to keep your attention on this end of the Gulf while they headed south."

"Assuming that you're right, and they do get into the open ocean, what then?"

"Sometime in the past two or three weeks, a pair of SS-N-sixteen Mod

Three nuclear missiles disappeared from the Black Sea Fleet depot at Sevastopol. At least one of the Iranian's Kilo subs has been modified to load and fire that missile."

"Jesus H. Christ," Jones said. "All right, Lane, you've got my attention. Where are you taking this?"

"I think the Kilo is heading toward a rendezvous somewhere in the Arabian Sea with a Ukrainian civilian ship that's carrying those missiles."

"What targets are they looking at? Riyadh, Kuwait City, hell, Tel Aviv? The sixteen has a range of ten thousand miles. That's a damned big circle."

"I don't know," Lane said absently. He looked up. "That's why I have to get to the *Chicago*. Have I convinced you?"

"I'll order an Orion down there and put a comms buoy in the water. We'll see what Coburn has to say."

"We don't have a lot of time, Captain."

"I understand." Jones telephoned the communications shack and sent the message to the Orions searching the Gulf.

Prescott came back twenty minutes later and spread a chart on the table. "The *Good Hope*, home port of Plymouth, England, recently sailed on charter from Karachi. She came into the Gulf the day before yesterday making over thirty knots through the strait, showed up in Kuwait City for provisions and headed back the way she came. She passed through the strait nine hours ago. Only now she's making less than eighteen knots."

"Is she big enough for a Kilo to hide beneath her?" Lane asked.

"Possibly. But I suspect she's making so much noise it wouldn't matter."

"Do we have anything in the Arabian Sea that could intercept that boat?"

"Nothing near enough with any teeth," Prescott said. "I checked. Looks like the *Chicago* is your best bet after all. But until this front passes, the satellites are going to be worthless."

"Do we have a course and speed?"

"Nothing past the strait," Prescott said.

"We'll find the *Chicago*, and I'll bring Glen up to speed," Jones said. "In the meantime we'll get you started in that direction, unless there's something else."

"What's your relationship with the Saudi navy?"

Jones gave him a hard look. "They're here and so are we. We lost two men aboard the *Prince Faisal*. I'd just as soon lose no more. The Saudis declaring war on Iran—even if you're wrong and it is an Iranian crew aboard that Kilo—is plain nuts."

"I agree, Commander. So let's not give them any more ammunition by telling them what we know."

"It wouldn't help," Jones said. "It's a big mess out here."

We started it, Lane wanted to say, but he held his peace.

"Good hunting," Jones said.

53

Yernin had set the off-duty crew the task of moving more bodies of the Iranian crew out of the way.

Nobody liked the job or understood why he'd ordered it, but they couldn't complain because the captain went along with him, and because Yernin did not shirk his share of the dirty work. In fact, they had a grudging respect for the man. Whatever could be said about him, he would have made a fine submariner.

He came forward to the control center, a tired but otherwise neutral look on his face. "We're finished," he said.

"A necessary job well done," Razhin replied. He thought he understood what Yernin was up to.

The assassin didn't acknowledge the compliment, "What's our present position?"

"We've passed Muscat on the Oman mainland, and we're coming up on Ras al Hadd. It is the final headland before we reach the open sea."

Yernin glanced up at the navigator's master clocks. It was 1500 GMT, which made it 7:00 P.M. local. By now it was dark on the surface.

He picked up the aquaphone handset. "Charlie One, this is Charlie Two."

"Roger Charlie Two," the officer on *Good Hope*'s bridge responded. It sounded like Razhin's brother.

"What does your radar show?"

"We have multiple targets. There's a lot of traffic up here. Mostly oil tankers."

"Any military vessels?"

"None that we can see."

"What about airborne?"

"An airliner twenty-eight kilometers to the southeast, heading away from us, probably to Bombay. Nothing else."

Yernin thought about it for a moment. "Is any of the surface traffic within visual range?"

"I can see the lights of a supertanker about five miles behind us heading up into the Gulf. If they're looking for us, they'll see our lights. But there's nothing else, although we're showing up on a lot of radars."

"Is this Captain Razhin?" Yernin asked.

"Yes, it is."

"Then thank you, Captain. This is Colonel Yernin. You and your crew have done an excellent job. You may return to Karachi. Your part in this mission has been completed."

"May I speak with my brother?"

A momentary flash of irritation crossed Yernin's face. "Very well." He held the phone out to Razhin. "Your brother wishes to speak with you. When you are finished, submerge the boat to three hundred meters, and increase speed to twenty-four knots on our present course. I'm going to get some sleep."

CHICAGO

Lane's transfer to the submarine went without a hitch. The deck was well lit from portable spotlights on the sail bridge, and by a spotlight on the hovering helicopter. The air crew and the deck crew were experts at this sort of thing, and the weather hadn't turned choppy enough for the submarine to wallow too badly.

He was glad to get safely below, however, because lowering a man from a helicopter to a submarine at night was never routine.

It had taken a team of four Orions most of the day to find the *Chicago* even though they knew her general position, and only then because Coburn allowed himself to be found. Had he wished to evade, he could have easily done so. But he wasn't happy about having a civilian passenger and it showed on his face when Lane was brought up to the red-lit control room.

The boat was already being dived, so Lane was motioned to keep out of the way. He went over to one of the plotting tables and, bracing himself against the forward slope of the deck, studied the chart under the clear plotting sheet. It was a large-scale chart of the central Persian Gulf.

Lane opened a drawer and rifled through several charts until he found one showing the entire Gulf and a big section of the Arabian Sea, the Indian subcontinent to the east, Africa to the southwest.

He took it to the other plotting table, overlaid it with a clear plotting sheet, and, using the plotting arms, marked their present position from the other table.

Several of the crewmen watched him nervously until Lieutenant Commander Friend came over.

"Can I help you with something, Mr. Lane?"

"Is this our present position?" Lane asked, pointing to the small cross he'd marked on the plotting sheet.

Friend glanced at it. "Close enough."

"We're level at two hundred feet," the diving officer reported.

"Very well," Coburn said. "Come right ten degrees, to a new course of zero-three-zero, make your speed ten knots."

"Aye, aye, coming right to course zero-three-zero, speed ten knots."

Lane marked the new speed and course on the plotting sheet with the depth notation in a small square box to the right.

Coburn came over, glanced at Lane's handiwork, then looked up. "All right, you're here and no one got hurt. Now how much of what Jonesy told me is fact, and how much is speculation? A lot of lives could depend on this."

"That's what I want to find out, Captain, but I'm going to need your help to do it."

"I'm listening," Coburn said impassively.

Lane turned back to the chart and drew a series of lines from the *Chicago*'s present position in the central Persian Gulf, south through the Strait of Hormuz, through the Gulf of Oman, and into the Arabian Sea. Next he drew a line between Karachi and the Oman headland at Ras al Hadd. He drew a circle around the spot where the two lines intersected.

"I need to be there as soon as possible."

"You can be out there in a couple of hours by air."

"We're going submarine hunting," Lane said. "If it comes down to it you might have to shoot a couple of torpedoes."

"At this Iranian submarine?"

Lane nodded. "Possibly at a civilian freighter as well."

"Under what flag?"

"Ukraine."

Coburn exchanged glances with his XO. "Let's continue this in the wardroom."

Lane stood rooted to this spot. "We need to start now at the very best speed you can give me."

"I'll decide when and where this boat will go," Coburn said.

"I'll explain on the run—" Lane started, but Coburn stepped close and cut him off.

"You'll do as I say, right now, mister."

"Captain—"

Coburn stepped back. "Ask the quartermaster to come up here on the double, with his sidearm."

"Put up a comms buoy, and send a message to the White House Situation Room. I'll give your comms people the proper codes. Tell the president that I'm unable to carry out his orders at this time. In fact, I'm under arrest."

Coburn's eyes locked with Lane's for several long seconds. Finally he turned to his XO. "Raise a comms buoy and go ahead and send that message."

Friend stepped over to the control station and used one of the growler phones.

The quartermaster came into the control room, his sidearm drawn. "Captain?" he said.

"Stand by, Stu," Coburn said. "Diving officer."

"Aye, Skipper."

Coburn studied the plot Lane had laid out. "Make our course one-six-five degrees."

"Aye, aye. Changing course to one-six-five degrees."

"Ring for maximum turns." Coburn looked into Lane's eyes.

"Aye, ringing for maximum turns."

"Very well," Coburn said, leaning back against the plotting table.

Three minutes later Lieutenant Commander Friend had the uplink with one of their communications satellites, and Lane gave him the special number that would connect with the president at any time of day or night, wherever in the world the president might be. Friend put it on the overhead speaker.

"You have reached the White House Situation Room, special circuit Delta-Delta-Bravo. Please give your authenticator now."

"Alpha-Seven-Bravo, Lane" Lane said.

Friend relayed the code.

"Stand by."

A half-minute later the distinctive voice of President Reasoner came over the speaker. "Lane, is that you?"

"No, sir. This is Lieutenant Commander Friend. I'm the executive office aboard the *Chicago*."

"Is he aboard?"

"Ah, yes, sir," Friend said. "We're just confirming who he is."

"Give him what he needs, Commander," Reasoner said. "He's the only one at the moment who knows what the hell is going on. Do you understand?"

"Yes, sir."

The connection was broken, and Friend hung up the phone. He ordered the comms buoy reeled back in on its long wire.

"My apologies, Mr. Lane," Coburn said. He stuck out his hand. "Welcome aboard."

Lane grinned. "I would have done the same, Captain. Now I'd like to talk with your communications and ELINT officers, as well as the SEALs you have aboard."

54

MOHAMMAD'S STAR

It was after midnight when they turned at right angles to their course and slowed to all stop so that they were drifting dead in the water. It gave sonar a chance to make sure no one was behind them.

A sweep to the Kilo's maximum passive range showed no targets of interest within twenty kilometers. It was a precaution, Yernin explained, because the critical part of their mission would develop very soon.

The engineering and control room staffs had been raided, leaving only Captain Razhin on the conn and sonar, and his chief engineer, Lieutenant Pechenko, in the engine spaces.

The first of the bodies had been brought back into the forward torpedo storage and launch area and placed at their normal duty stations. If and when this submarine was finally boarded, everything would look normal.

Yernin stood at the hatch open to the cramped torpedo room. Ablakin came back to him.

"Are you almost finished?" Yernin asked. He hadn't been able to get much sleep. His mouth ached horribly.

There was the ghastly smell of flesh beginning to rot in the confined spaces. They wanted this job to be finished so that they could get on with their mission, and abandon the boat.

"Da," Ablakin said in a subdued voice.

They stepped aside as two men wrestled a body through the hatch, and hoisted it up into one of the bunks.

"This is a bad business," the young executive officer said. He was pale.

"It's better than going to the bottom with them," Yernin shot back harshly. He was tired.

Ablakin looked at him sharply. "What do you mean, going to the bottom?"

Yernin realized that he had made a mistake. But it didn't matter. "A slip of the tongue," he replied indifferently.

Ablakin snapped. "What are you talking about, you crazy bastard? What insane plans are we expected to carry out for you?" He gestured at the bodies stacked like cordwood. "Those were all decent men, some of them with families. Men of the sea, no matter what flag they sailed under. Now they are dead because of you. How many more are we supposed to kill in the name of . . . what?"

Everyone else in the compartment was busy hoisting bodies into bunks, so they did not hear Ablakin's outburst. Yernin wanted to kill him, but for the moment such an act wasn't practical. Captain Razhin and the others on the crew would certainly rebel, and he needed them for just a little while longer.

"I'm sorry," Yernin apologized, a contrite expression on his face. He looked at the bodies and shook his head sadly. "These aren't my orders, Ivan Petrovich. Like you, I just do what I'm told. And it's getting to me." He looked Ablakin in the eye. "Fuck your mother, can you understand this? Half the time I'm so tired I don't know what I'm doing, let alone what I'm saying. But I'm in charge of this mission so I cannot show any weakness. I must be strong even if it seems like I'm an insensitive bastard."

Ablakin's expression immediately softened. "I know what you mean, comrade. But when you said 'go to the bottom,' I suddenly saw stars."

Yernin clapped the executive officer on the back, and smiled ruefully. "We'll be at our rendezvous soon. When the cargo is loaded, we'll be on the last leg of the mission. After that it won't be long. I promise you. Not long at all."

"Good."

When the job was finished no one had any appetite, nor was anyone interested in sleep, so everyone went back to their duty stations. No one said much. The enormity of handling so many corpses had affected them all, even Captain Razhin on the conn and the ChEng in the engine room, because some of the bodies had been brought to where they were stationed.

Yernin went to his quarters, and when he returned to the control room he brought two bottles of vodka. He handed one to Lieutenant Kedrov. "Bring this back to engineering. Tell them thank you for me."

"Yes, sir," the younger man said, pleased. He headed aft.

Yernin opened the second bottle, took a deep drink, and handed it to Razhin. "I will tell Captain Maslennikov what a fine crew this is."

Razhin nodded. "They are." He took a drink and passed the bottle to Ablakin.

"*Buzhmo*," Cheers, the executive officer gave the Ukrainian toast. He took a big drink, which brought a little color back to his still pale cheeks, then handed the bottle to Krasilnikov.

The comms officer took a drink and brought the bottle around the corner to Lieutenant Fomenko in sonar.

"That was good of you, comrade," Razhin said. "The men appreciate it."

Yernin shrugged. "The least I could do after such hard duty. But I have my orders."

"Yes," Razhin said and he glanced over at Ablakin. "Which I am sure you will share with us when the time comes."

"*Da,* when the time comes." Yernin looked at the master clocks. It was past 2100 GMT, which put it after 1:00 A.M. local.

"We have crossed the line," Razhin said, pointing at the mark on the chart. A line had been drawn between Karachi and Ras al Hadd, which intersected with their course.

"It is time then to come to periscope depth and send our message," Yernin said.

Razhin stepped around the corner to sonar. "What is on the surface?"

"I have six targets, designated Sierra nine through fourteen, all at my extreme range. And then Sierra fifteen."

Razhin studied the waterfall. Sierra fifteen was much stronger than the others.

"Range nineteen thousand meters and closing. Relative bearing zero-four-five," Fomenko said. "Her speed is steady at seventeen knots."

"Is there a positive identification in our computer?"

"*Da.*"

"Anything under the water?" Razhin asked.

"Not since we cleared our baffles fifteen minutes ago," Fomenko said looking up.

"We will do it once again, and then send our message." Razhin squeezed his sonarman's shoulder. "Keep a sharp watch, Vasha."

CHICAGO

It had been over thirty hours since Lane had come aboard, and the crew was tense. Operating at extreme speeds in confined waters was tough. Everyone was glad when they'd broken out into the Gulf of Oman, and even happier as they approached the Arabian Sea.

"Conn, sonar."

Coburn glanced at Lane and Friend standing by at the plotting table. He picked up the growler. "This is the captain."

"I have a definite subsea target now, designated Sierra forty-seven Baker. Range thirty-one-thousand yards, bearing zero-nine-zero. Skipper, she's a Kilo boat."

Everyone in the control room glanced at Lane with amazement. The Kilo was right where he said it would be.

"What are they doing?" Coburn asked.

"Sounds like they're clearing their baffles."

"Can they hear us?"

"Negative," the sonar operator said. "Stand by, Skipper. They're on the way up. I'm picking up venting noises now, and hull popping."

"Very well. What about Sierra forty-six Alpha?"

"Same course and speed as before. Range now fourteen thousand yards, bearing two-one-seven."

Sonar had identified the ship as a civilian vessel, probably a freighter, coming up from the southwest making seventeen knots. It was happening just as Lane said it would.

"ESMs, conn." ESMs were electronic support measures, which, among the section's duties, included electronic intelligence gathering, or ELINT.

"Conn, ESMs."

"Roger."

"Send up the intercept buoy now," Coburn ordered.

"Aye, Skipper."

With the noise the Kilo was making, the *Chicago*'s intercept buoy would not be detected. Once on the surface the buoy would raise an extremely low profile omnidirectional antenna which was capable of picking up radio emissions in a wide variety of bands over a considerable distance.

The intercept buoy was up in two minutes, and the Kilo leveled off at periscope depth nine minutes later.

"Stand by," Coburn told the ESMs officer Lieutenant (j.g.) Charles Meierhoff.

"Roger."

"Skipper, the Kilo is sending out an extremely low power signal on the VHF band. Probably not more than a few milliwatts. It's in code."

"Ask him if it's in Farsi or Russian," Lane said.

"Charlie, is that Kilo transmitting in Farsi?" Coburn asked.

"Negative, Skipper. Russian," Meierhoff reported, and he sounded impressed. "Okay, the transmission has stopped."

Lane tensed.

"They're getting a reply from that freighter to the southwest. Also in Russian and in code."

Lane smiled. "Bingo," he said softly.

"Sonar, conn. What's the Kilo doing?"

"She's starting to move, range thirty-one thousand five hundred yards and increasing, changing bearing zero-eight-zero and narrowing. Skipper, she'll cross our bow, heading southwest."

"Toward Sierra forty-six Alpha."

"Aye, aye, sir. Sierra forty-six Alpha is changing course too, bearing now two-two-five, and she's slowing down. They're definitely on an intercept course."

"Very well, keep a sharp watch."

55

The submarine lay in the lee of the cargo vessel which had sailed from Odessa twelve days ago. Because of the running seas, it was tricky maneuvering the Kilo next to the much longer motor vessel. But once they were in the wind and wave shadow created by the bigger boat, fendering off and tying fast was possible, if dangerous.

Lighting would be kept to a minimum during the four-hour loading operation. The skies were still overcast, so they were safe from satellite observation. But they did not want to attract the attention of a passing ship. *Mohammad's Star,* riding low in the water, and dark, would be difficult to spot. But a well-lit cargo ship with her raised house and masts would be visible for many kilometers.

When the boats were made fast, Yernin scrambled up the rope netting over the side, and went immediately to the bridge where Captain Arseni Orlov was waiting for him.

"Keep your eyes open," Orlov told the man at the big radar set. "If anything looks like it might come this way, sound the alert."

"Yes, sir."

Yernin followed the captain back to his cabin, but not before he looked down the deck and saw that the *Gorki*'s forward hatch was already open and the first missile was being loaded into its slings. Razhin's people had opened the submarine's forward loading hatch, ready to receive the weapons.

"Did you run into any trouble since Odessa?" Yernin asked.

"No, our voyage so far has been uneventful. But all hell is breaking loose behind you, Comrade Colonel," Orlov said through fat, moist lips and teeth black from chewing tobacco.

"Because of the Saudi Arabian patrol boat?"

"Yes. The Saudis are on the verge of declaring war on Iran."

Yernin laughed humorlessly. "It is the effect we wanted to produce. What is Tehran saying?"

"That their submarine captain has gone crazy. They are throwing up their hands in despair."

"And Moscow?"

Orlov grunted, flecks of tobacco tumbling down on the front of his jacket. "They are calling for calm." He slapped his leg. "Fuck your mother, but they are shitting cherry pits, their assholes are so tight." He looked shrewdly at Yernin. "But they are making noise, Comrade Colonel. Nothing more. It strikes me as strange, doesn't it you?"

"No one can predict how a government will react under every circumstance," Yernin replied indifferently.

"If they knew about the missiles, I could guess what they would do."

"Indeed," Yernin agreed.

"What are the targets?" Orlov asked, his pig eyes glittering.

"You have done a fine job to this point, Captain, do not spoil your record by becoming overly curious at the wrong moment."

Orlov shrugged. "Tel Aviv, maybe. It would teach those bastards a lesson. More than twenty percent of their population are Russian or Ukrainian. They gave up their country. Let them roast in it."

"In fact you're correct."

Orlov licked his lips. "What about the second? Kuwait City? It would teach the Western alliance a lesson about sticking their noses where they didn't belong. It would make Iraq's oil all the more valuable."

For the moment it amused Yernin to play with the gross man. Being aboard the submarine with the smells of the dead bodies and the smells of the unwashed crewmen had begun to get to him. Orlov wasn't any better, but there was fresh air up here.

"The second missile will be aimed at Baghdad."

Orlov's eyes narrowed. "Hussein would have nothing to return to."

"Remember the Iranians are inept. The second missile will miss its mark and explode harmlessly in the desert. There will be little doubt in the West who ordered the attacks."

"What about afterward?" Orlov asked. "Where will you go?"

"We'll sink the submarine, and a boat will pick us up and take us to Karachi where we will disperse." Yernin's lips curled in a faint smirk. "Now that you have this dangerous knowledge, Captain, what do you intend to do with it?"

"My job, Comrade Colonel. Just as you are doing yours so capably. And when we are finished there will be a new government not only in Baghdad, but in Kiev as well."

"I would take very great care whom you tell that to."

"Don't worry about me," Orlov assured him. "When will you launch your little birds of prey?"

Yernin forced a lighthearted laugh. "You can't know everything, Captain. Now, I need to use your quarters for the next hour."

Orlov nodded. "As you wish."

"Send Captain Zamyatin up to me."

"If he and the other crewmen haven't already gone aboard your little boat."

"He hasn't," Yernin said.

CHICAGO

At ten thousand yards, passive sonar had lost engine noises from the submarine as well as from the freighter. But enough machine noise and metal-against-metal noises were being picked up that they had no problem accurately pinpointing the bearing and range to the merged targets.

Over the course of a half-hour the *Chicago* worked its way slowly to periscope depth.

Coburn and Lane were in the sonar room looking over the chief operator's shoulder. What he was listening to was piped to a loudspeaker.

"The grinding noise is a power winch. A big one," Ensign Smith said. He made a grease pencil mark on the display screen, then punched a series of keys. The noise was partially filtered out so that they could hear the other sounds more clearly.

"Big enough to handle four or five tons?" Lane asked.

"Yes, sir," Smith said. "Sounds to me like the sub has tied up alongside the freighter, and something big is being loaded aboard."

"Like a missile," Coburn said.

"It's possible, Skipper."

"We're at periscope depth," Friend called from the control center.

They were at battle stations torpedo and rigged for silent running. Nobody aboard spoke much above a whisper, and all work in the galley was forbidden.

"Keep me informed," Coburn told his sonar crew, and he went back around the corner into the control room.

The Mark 18 search periscope was raised so that only a few feet of the masthead stuck up out of the water. The mast was coated with the same radar absorbing material (RAM) that stealth airplanes used, but Coburn wanted to take as few chances as possible, so he kept it raised to a minimum height.

"I have them," the captain said. He made an adjustment. "Range ten thousand two hundred yards, bearing zero-zero-five degrees."

The data was automatically transferred to the submarine's combat system, called BSY-1, or Busy-One, and what Coburn saw through the periscope was evaluated as a possible target for any weapons system he might choose.

He switched the image to the overhead television monitors, which showed an indistinct black lump on a slightly less black background until he switched on the low-light operating mode. The silhouette of the freighter suddenly showed clearly enough that they could make out the eight-story superstructure aft, and the booms for loading.

Lane pointed up at the image. "There," he said. "It's a missile."

Coburn raised the magnification. The image blurred and darkened somewhat but it jumped in size. They were definitely seeing a missile being loaded over the opposite side of the ship.

"The sub must be in the freighter's lee," Lane said.

"Makes sense," Coburn agreed. "In these seas it's a dicey operation even at that. Somebody could get hurt."

"The sub is tied to the freighter."

"It'd have to be," Coburn said.

"No other way of transferring the missiles?"

"What do you mean?"

"Say, submarine-to-submarine," Lane suggested.

Coburn glanced at his XO, who shook his head. "I don't think it's possible. I can't imagine the engineering."

Lane went to the plotting table and studied the small-scale chart which showed the entire Arabian Sea from the tip of India in the southeast to Somalia's coast in the southwest.

Coburn came over. "What are you getting at, Bill?"

"There's no port along here where they could have loaded missiles aboard the submarine in secret. The only way they could have done it, in fact, is exactly how they're doing it now."

"That's right."

"If it is Yernin aboard the Kilo, he would not be as willing to martyr himself for the cause as would an Iranian crew. Yet he wants the world to think that the Iranians are running the show."

"I don't understand," Coburn said.

Lane looked up from the chart. "When those missiles are launched they'll start showing up on radars all over the place, right?"

Coburn nodded.

"It'll be no problem to extrapolate backwards along their trajectories to see where they came from. Which means once the missiles are fired, the Kilo is as good as dead." Lane studied the chart again. "Unless the submarine gives up, it'd be fired on and sunk. Afterwards we'd send equipment down to verify the kill. And to verify, if possible, that it was Iranians and not someone else aboard."

Coburn nodded. "Under the circumstances we'd have to do something like that. We'd have to verify who made the attack."

Lane grinned. "I see," he said.

"You see what?" Coburn asked, confused.

Lane focused on the captain. "Can you get us to the other side of the freighter, and maybe in closer? Say, to within a couple thousand yards without being detected?"

Coburn shrugged. "With all the noise they're making it's doubtful they'd hear us." His expression hardened. "But I've seen all I need to see. I'm going to challenge them to stand down. If they resist I'll shoot them out of the water."

"Not yet," Lane said. "We're still not sure it isn't the Iranians after all. We can't make a positive identification on those missiles from this distance. And we still don't know their intended targets."

"I'll go along with you on the first two," Coburn said. "But the targets are my least important consideration right now. Because if those are nukes, there is no acceptable target."

"You're wrong, Captain. It's the most important piece of information. More important than you can imagine."

"They won't fire them. Nobody would be that crazy."

"Don't count on it," Lane said, the image of Yernin's eyes clear in his mind.

"I disagree with you," Coburn said. "The oil fields aren't worth it."

"What's the range of an SS-N-sixteen Mod Three?"

"Ten thousand miles. Maybe more."

Lane's ice blue eyes locked with the captain's. "How far is it by great circle route from here to Washington, D.C.?"

A startled expression crossed Coburn's face, and he paled. "I see what you mean."

56

Both missiles were safely transferred to the submarine within the four-hour limit Yernin had imposed on the crew, and he ordered them to be made ready for loading into the two innermost torpedo tubes.

The seas were starting to get up, but the missiles could be tube-launched from practically any depth, even with the submarine riding on the surface, still attached to the freighter. However, they were beginning to wallow, and because their underwater configurations were completely different, their rocking motions were different. If it got much worse the ships could crash against each other, doing damage to the submarine that *could* make it impossible to launch the missiles. But no one cared because they all thought they'd be away and submerged within the hour.

Razhin took the crew up to the *Gorki* for a hot Ukrainian meal, and to get away from the stench of dead bodies. The submarine was very quiet. Only the whir of the air recirculating fans, and the groan of the ropes and fenders holding them to the freighter, broke the deathly silence. The submarine was a tomb.

Yernin stood braced against one of the missiles in the torpedo room, an ear cocked, listening to the sounds of the boat. He looked at one of the dead Iranian crewmen crumpled in a heap beneath tube six. The man's head lolled back, his mouth open as if he were gasping for air (which he had been) or screaming.

The sight was disquieting.

Two bodies, lying in their bunks, were also screaming silently, their lips pulled back in a grimace. One of them had dried blood beneath its nostrils.

Yernin felt a wave of nausea come over him. It was the stench, the closeness of the cramped torpedo room, the rolling motion caused by the seas.

He looked over his shoulder through the hatch leading aft. He could make out the form of another dead Iranian sailor in the dim red light.

The submarine came up short against the heavy lines holding it to the *Gorki,* nearly tossing Yernin to the deck. Several of the torpedoes shifted noisily in their racks, and he looked at them with indifference.

He believed in fate beyond his own abilities. If he did all that he could, nothing else mattered. Not objects, not money, not people. He would either win or lose. It was fate.

Bracing himself against the rolling, heavy deck, he checked the serial number of the missile poised in front of tube three. It matched the one that was set to explode in the desert fifty miles north of Baghdad at the edge of the Zagros Mountains. The SS-N-16 was a multiple independently targetable reentry vehicle, or MIRV, with three 40-kiloton warheads. The other missile was set to detonate at three thousand feet above Tel Aviv, Haifa, and Jerusalem.

The effect would be even more devastating than Captain Orlov could imagine. Israel would cease to exist as a nation state. Ninety percent of its population would be dead or severely injured. The entire country would become a nuclear wasteland.

The targets had been selected by Ukraine's defense minister, Andrei Grechkov, a crazy man, but one easily manipulated. Soon he would become president and then the country would go back to the old ways. The better ways. In effect, the KGB would once again be in control.

The targets had been selected to place the blame squarely on Iran, allowing a beholden Saddam Hussein to return to power in Baghdad. But Grechkov and his advisers had underestimated the American government's resolve in this region.

Yernin pulled a small screwdriver from his pocket and began removing the eighteen screws from a small plate one-third of the way back from the nose, just behind the MIRV payload on the Baghdad missile.

The American government needed a diversion. Something to keep it occupied while Hussein's Ukrainian-backed government marched into Baghdad to consolidate power and then attack Iran.

The first twelve hours would be decisive, Yernin thought, laying the screws in a tray beneath the missile. Given the proper distraction, it would take the American military at least that long to react.

He pulled the eighteen-centimeter square plate loose, set it in the tray, and removed a smaller clear plastic cover from the electronic guidance system director and set it aside.

Working from memory, Yernin set the fourteen rotary switches, each with twenty-four possibilities, to the code he'd worked out himself from the missile's technical manuals.

Now the SS-N-16 was no longer pointed at the desert north of Baghdad. Now it was pointed to the west on the great circle route over the African continent, across the North Atlantic Ocean and finally to separation over the American eastern seaboard.

The growler phone above the torpedo tube control board rang, and Yernin looked up from what he was doing.

After two more rings the phone fell silent, and he went back to his work.

The three targets did not matter, though nominally the missile would cross the American coast in the vicinity of Washington. Long before the impact, however, the missile would be detected and shot down. The American antimissile systems were very efficient.

But the political damage would be done. And it would be severe. An Iranian submarine that had slipped by the *Chicago* had launched an attack not only on Israel but on the United States. The Middle East would never be the same.

The entire world wouldn't be the same, Yernin thought. And Grechkov and the KGB would get what they desired, control of the region, only in a different, more interesting fashion than they thought possible.

"What are you doing?" Lieutenant Ablakin demanded from the hatch.

Yernin looked up. "Checking the targeting codes," he said. He replaced the clear plastic cover, then started on the outer plate's eighteen screws.

"The missiles were preset," Ablakin said. His eyes were wild. They darted from Yernin to the bodies lying in the bunks and crumpled on the deck.

"Return to the control room. We're leaving soon."

"*Nyet,*" Ablakin shouted. "Get away from there!" He clawed for something beneath his tunic.

Yernin calmly withdrew his Heckler & Koch and fired a single shot, hitting the young lieutenant in the heart. No rubber bullets this time, he thought, as Ablakin fell back dead, halfway through the hatch.

He listened for several seconds to make sure no one had heard the silenced shot and was coming to investigate, then pocketed his gun and turned back to the missile.

When the outer plate was securely fastened, he opened tube three and, using the electric chain fall, lowered the missile onto its loading tray and powered it into the tube.

The operation took less than ten minutes. Once he had the inner door secured, he loaded the Israel-bound missile into tube four and closed and latched the inner door.

Next he flooded both tubes, and opened the outer doors. Now the missiles were ready to fire from the weapons control panel in the control room. It would take only one man to do that job.

He stared at Ablakin's body. On the way back to Karachi, with the Middle East on the brink of all-out war, and with Israel nothing but smoking cinders, he would allow himself the pleasure of planning Bill Lane's death. It would be the crowning glory of his career. Afterward he would retire. Somewhere very far away from here and from Ukraine, because in the end what really happened would come out.

Hussein would do something crazy. Grechkov would make a mistake. Another smart one like Bill Lane would come along and the deception would finally unravel. When it did, Yernin wanted to be long gone.

He found a set of Iranian navy coveralls that would fit Ablakin's medium frame, put them on the boy's body, and hefted him up onto one of the bunks.

He wiped the blood from the deck with the boy's shirt, then bundled it with Ablakin's trousers and took them up to the galley. He stuffed them in a plastic garbage bag and took the bag up to the control room.

Razhin came around the corner from the sonar compartment.

"Is the sonar usable with all this noise?" Yernin asked, keeping the consternation from his face. The bastard was supposed to be on the *Gorki* with the others.

"No. Where is Lieutenant Ablakin?" Razhin asked.

"I don't know. Isn't he supposed to be with you?"

Razhin nodded. "What do you have in the bag?"

Yernin held it up, and shrugged. "Garbage. I'm going to toss it over the side."

"Let me see."

"It is nothing, Captain," Yernin said.

Razhin unhurriedly stepped back into the sonar compartment. When he came back he had a gun. He pointed it at Yernin. The action was unexpected.

Yernin grinned. "Well, if you want to see the garbage that badly, I'll show it to you." He opened the bag, and with one hand tipped the bloody contents onto the deck.

Razhin was distracted for a moment. "You bastard—"

Yernin took out his pistol and shot the captain in the chest, just missing his heart, but shoving him backward against the bulkhead. Razhin grunted, his eyes glassy.

"You'll kill us all," Razhin whispered. He tried to raise his gun, but couldn't. His knees slowly buckled and he sat down on the deck.

Yernin walked over to him. He felt no remorse, but Razhin's death was something of a waste. The man had been good at what he did. "I programmed one of the missiles to fly across the Atlantic to Washington, D.C. Would you have tried to stop me had you known?"

Razhin looked up at Yernin, the effort costing him nearly everything he had left. He nodded. "Yes," he croaked.

Yernin watched the captain's eyes as he died. The light faded and went out. Nothing else. And Razhin slumped over, his head clunking on the deck.

A waste, but necessary, Yernin thought. He went to the captain's cabin and dug out a pair of Iranian navy trousers and a shirt with officer's pips on the shoulder boards.

He stripped Razhin's body, dressed him in the Iranian uniform, and stuffed his body in a corner of the sonar room.

Next he wiped the blood off the control room deck with Razhin's shirt, and put those clothes and Ablakin's into the garbage bag.

He pocketed Razhin's American Colt .45. The safety catch was still on. Even at the last the captain had not believed he would have to shoot a fellow Ukrainian officer. Too bad for him to have learned such a tough lesson so late, Yernin thought.

It took another ten minutes to remove the front panel from the weapons control console, figure out the wiring, and clip an electronic counter he'd brought with him from Karachi to the circuits that controlled torpedo tubes three and four.

Setting the countdown clock for six minutes, Yernin replaced the front panel, then uncaged the firing switches for three and four.

When those buttons were pushed, a six-minute countdown would begin, after which time both missiles would launch.

He stepped back and looked at his handiwork. His mission was nearly finished. Then there would only be Bill Lane.

MV *GORKI*

Yernin dumped the bag of clothes into a trash barrel below decks, and went up to the bridge where Captain Orlov and KGB Captain Boris Zamyatin were studying the radar display.

"Is someone approaching?" he asked.

They looked up. "I thought so, but it's just an oil tanker coming out of the Gulf," Captain Orlov said. "She'll pass well west of us."

Zamyatin motioned toward the door. "Are you finished down there?"

Yernin nodded. "Where are the rest of your people?"

"In the crew's mess with Razhin's people."

"He and his first officer surprised me aboard the submarine," Yernin said.

Zamyatin shrugged. "It caused you no difficulty?"

"No, but it could have."

Zamyatin said nothing.

Yernin turned to the captain. "How soon can we get under way?"

"Cut the lines and we can leave now," Orlov said, his eyes darting from Yernin to Zamyatin.

"We'll leave in thirty minutes," Yernin told him. He turned back to Zamyatin, whose eyes were nearly as lifeless as his. "Kill them."

A flicker of a smile crossed Zamyatin's lips. "As you wish," he said.

57

CHICAGO
They were running out of options. Coburn had moved his submarine to within two thousand yards of the lee side of the Ukrainian freighter. The images appearing on the periscope low-light monitors showed the picture clearly. The loading operation was finished, which meant both missiles were aboard the Iranian submarine.

"They won't remain tied together like that much longer unless they want to hurt that submarine," Coburn said.

The seas continued to rise, and it looked as if the Kilo boat was starting to take a pounding.

No one was on the deck of either the freighter or the sub, nor did either show any lights. The operation was professional, there was little doubt of it in anyone's mind. Nor was there much doubt in Lane's mind that whatever was about to happen would happen very soon.

"I'm going over there," Lane said. He'd agreed on a plan of action with Lieutenant Charlie Gilbert, the leader of the eight-man SEALs team.

"I can't let you take the risk," the captain said.

"It's a Ukrainian ship and an Iranian submarine, that's all we know for certain," Lane said. "And to this point they've done nothing wrong, by American law."

"They attacked and sank a Saudi patrol, with two of our people aboard," Coburn pointed out, a pinched expression coming over his face.

"But we don't know if the Saudis challenged them first," Lane argued. "We don't have all the facts."

"Which you're going to get by boarding the ship and asking them."

"That's right. Along with the targeting data programmed into the missiles."

Coburn looked up at the periscope screen. The others in the control room were watching the interplay between Lane and the captain with interest. They were all tired, and jumpy. And they were siding with their captain because among other considerations they wanted to get this operation over with so that they could go back to a normal watch schedule. Since they'd detected the Kilo, the galley had been closed for everything except sandwiches and bug juice.

"You figure that this Ukrainian spy you've been chasing after is aboard that sub," Coburn said. "Is that right? You figure he's running this show?"

"I think it's a very real possibility, Captain," Lane said. He knew what was coming. One of the communications crew had let it slip that the captain had raised the comms buoy and got a message to COMCINCPAC about him.

"You're saying that if I challenge him directly, he's going to do something drastic."

"He's planned for the contingencies," Lane said.

Coburn looked at him coldly. "You want to swim over there and spit in his eye. Put a bullet in his brain for what he did to you. You fucked up against him in Richmond, and nearly got yourself killed. And you fucked up against him in Kuwait, and nearly bought the farm."

"That's right," Lane said. He wondered how CINCPAC in Honolulu got the information.

"There've been a lot of casualties that could have been avoided if you'd played it a little differently."

"Like backing off and giving him some breathing room?" Lane shot back.

"You could have at least waited until the bystanders were cleared away," Coburn retorted. "Then you could have blown him away. No questions asked, just pulled the trigger."

"Like right now?"

"Like right now," Coburn agreed. "You want me to send my SEALs over there in harm's way, so that if something starts to develop I'll be faced with the choice of doing nothing or firing on my own people. Something you seem to be an expert at."

"Leaves you two choices, Captain," Lane said. "Either send over a couple of torpedoes right now, or challenge them."

"I won't shoot first."

"What are you going to do when they tell you to go to hell? They're in international waters carrying out the legitimate business of two legitimate governments. Are you going to put a shot over their bows?"

"If need be."

"What if they cut the lines, and the Kilo submerges and turns tail for home?"

"I won't let that boat loose with nuclear weapons aboard."

"Assuming what they loaded aboard were in fact the two SS-N-sixteens missing from Sevastopol, what gives you the right to use deadly force? Because that's what it will take. Did CINCPAC give you launch discretion in situations other than a direct threat on American lives or property?"

Coburn was fuming. "That warship is responsible for the deaths of two US naval officers."

"Yernin is aboard that boat," Lane said, looking up at the monitor. "And you're right, I do want to go over there a put a bullet in his brain. But I also want to avoid a bloodbath. The moment you challenge him, he'll launch the missiles. It'd be risky, but it could be done while they were still tied up to the freighter."

"You said he wasn't willing to become a martyr."

"Nor is he willing to be captured."

Coburn shook his head, his face a study of indecision. "He's gotten this far, which means he's not an amateur, nor is he insane. He won't launch."

Lane snatched the growler phone from the overhead and held it out to Coburn. "Ask your sonar people to replay the tapes for the past hour. Tell them to filter out everything except the noises of flooding tubes and opening doors. Two of them."

Coburn took the phone. A note of uncertainty crossed his face. "Sonar, conn, this is the captain," he said, putting it on the speaker.

"Sonar, aye."

"I want you to search the tapes on that Kilo for tube-flooding noises. It would have happened within the past hour."

"That might not be possible with a hundred percent certainty because of the other racket they were making, Skipper."

"Just do it."

"Sir, we already recorded what could have been flooding noises. But the computer gave it a probability of less than twenty percent, so we just logged it as an unknown event."

"Was it just the once?"

"No, sir. Twice, one right after the other."

"Damn," Coburn swore softly. He lowered his head for a moment. "Is there any sign that they've detected us?"

"Not by sonar, Skipper."

"Keep your ears open," Coburn said. He reached up and punched a different button. "ESMs, this is the captain."

"Aye, Skipper."

"What's the radar picture look like?"

"We're detecting at least five lower-band units to the horizon. Low-power civilian signals."

"Is Sierra forty-seven Baker emitting?"

"No, sir. The Kilo is quiet. But Sierra forty-six Alpha is searching."

"Do they have us?"

"It's not likely, Skipper."

"Okay, keep a sharp eye."

"Yes, sir."

"Jesus Christ," Mike Friend said, staring at the periscope monitor.

Everyone looked up. Several men were at the freighter's rail. They were lowering something onto the deck of the submarine where several black-suited figures waited.

"Bodies," Friend said.

"What the hell?" Coburn said softly.

"The Ukrainian submarine crew, unless I miss my guess." Lane said. "They'll dress them in Iranian uniforms. Which means Yernin plans to fire the missiles, sink the boat, and get away aboard that freighter."

"But why kill his crew?" Coburn asked in disbelief.

"That's the way he does things."

Coburn focused on Lane, a note of foreboding in his eyes. "I'll send my SEALs over now."

"I'm going with them."

"This is a military operation, and you're a civilian."

"Your people don't know what they're up against, Captain," Lane said coolly. "But I do. As you said, I went up against him twice and fucked up both times. I know whereof I speak."

"You shouldn't even be aboard this submarine, mister."

"But I am. Under presidential order," Lane responded. He hated like hell to pull rank. But Coburn was being stubborn, and they were running out of time.

"It's like that, is it?" the captain asked frostily.

"If need be," Lane matched the captain's tone. "But this is why I was sent out here. To stop that maniac."

Coburn glanced up at the monitor again. A total of seven bodies had been lowered to the pitching deck of the submarine, and now they were being hustled below.

"As you wish," he finally said, his eyes locked into Lane's. "But I will not let that boat submerge. If it tries to get away, I'll kill it."

"I'll keep that in mind," Lane said.

"*We'll* keep in it mind. Mr. Lane," Friend interjected. "I'm coming with you."

"What are you talking about?" Coburn demanded.

"Bill doesn't know the Kilo boats, and neither do our SEALs. But I do."

"I need you here, goddamnit," Coburn argued. "You didn't sign on to do the job of a UDT rating."

"It's the same uniform, Glen," Friend replied. "My master's thesis was on Soviet bloc submarines. There's no one else to do the job."

"He's right," Lane said.

Coburn looked at the screen. "This changes nothing, Mike. If that boat submerges I'll kill it."

"I wouldn't expect you to do anything different, Captain," Friend said. "Good luck."

"Aye, aye, Skipper," Friend said, and he and Lane hurried aft to the lockout chamber where Lieutenant Gilbert and his people were standing by.

"Don't get yourself killed," Lane said.

"I won't," Friend assured him.

"Good. Because I don't think the captain would forgive me if I didn't bring you back in one piece."

58

"I want no external evidence of why this submarine sank," Yernin told the two KGB officers crouched in the bilges beneath the engine room.

Azarov, a former Kilo–class submariner under Maslennikov, looked up through the opening in the floor grating. His eyes squinted against the harsh glare of the work light. "If you wish to take my place in this stinking hole, you are welcome to it, Comrade Colonel."

"I don't want any mistakes made," Yernin said. He was starting to get jumpy, but he didn't know why. Unless it was because they were so close to completing their mission.

"If they raised this submarine, and took her apart at a yard, they would find that the main and backup high-pressure air directors both failed at the same time," Azarov explained. "Bad luck, but the ballast tanks flooded, the boat went down, and there was no way for her valiant crew to bring her back up."

The submarine lurched against her lines, sending Yernin sprawling against a maze of pipes and cable runs. He cracked his head against the bulkhead, making him see stars for a moment.

Azarov laughed. "You see, Comrade Colonel, a submarine is a dangerous place after all."

"How much longer before you're finished down there?"

Vitali Lomakin, the other officer, looked up impatiently. He was a hawk-faced demolitions expert originally from Armenia. Maslennikov warned that he was a prima donna. But his work was so good it was worth indulging him.

"We may never get out of here if you keep bothering us, Comrade Assassin."

Yernin swallowed a sharp retort. He wanted to pull out his pistol and shoot the greasy bastard in the face. Instead he nodded. "I'm launching the missiles and sending this ship to the bottom in twenty minutes. Will you be ready by then?"

Azarov looked serious. He glanced over to where three Iranian crewmen lay in a heap. They were engineers like him. "You'll send our boys down with them?"

"They were criminals," Yernin lied. "But their families will be provided for because now they are heroes."

Azarov gave Yernin a harsh look. "We learned a lot from Moscow. Maybe too much."

"Do you wish to renew the old alliance?"

Azarov shook his thick, peasant head after a moment. "Leave us now, Comrade Colonel. We'll be ready by your deadline."

"I'll be in the control room. When you're finished let me know, and then you can go back up to the *Gorki* and stand by to cast off our lines."

"Don't make a mistake."

"I won't," Yernin replied coldly. "See that you don't." He turned on his heel and left the engine room, the big diesel engines and the electric motor silent now and forever.

The rolling motion was becoming increasingly violent as Yernin made his way forward and up two decks. He had to work his way hand over hand down cramped passages and up slippery ladders. In some parts of the submarine the stench of rotting bodies was so overpowering it was all he could do to keep from vomiting. This boat had become hell on earth.

One of the other former Kilo officers who'd worked for Maslennikov, Leonid Yaskov, was the only one in the control room. He was an older man, in his early fifties, with a heavily pockmarked face, a sallow complexion, and a cigarette at the corner of his mouth. He had the front panel off the weapons control console.

"What are you doing?" Yernin asked, reaching inside his pocket for his gun.

"Your rewiring job is a cock-up," Yaskov said unconcernedly. "Before you fire a missile you do a diagnostic on your computer. This one was all off, so I figured you must have screwed up something. I was right."

"Get away from there."

Yaskov unclipped the timer from the torpedo circuitry and tossed it across to Yernin. "In the unlikely event that this boat is ever raised, they would find this little toy of yours, Comrade Colonel. It is evidence linking the missile firings back to Kiev. I am covering our asses."

"Are you volunteering to wait until we are gone and then fire the missiles yourself?"

Yaskov looked at him with disdain. "You may be good at what you do,

Yernin, but so am I. Unless you mean to kill the rest of us, which would leave you no crew to bring the *Gorki* into port, you'll have to trust me."

Yernin said nothing, but he was fuming inside. His normally indifferent composure was beginning to slip away. Something was eating at him, nagging at the back of his head. Something was wrong, but he couldn't put a finger on it.

"These systems have delay circuits already built into them. You didn't read far enough into the manuals." Yaskov replaced the front panel and refastened the screws. "Six minutes is cutting it close. Are you sure that's all the delay you want?"

"Who authorized you to do this?" Yernin asked.

"Captain Zamyatin, of course."

"Where is he now?"

"He said he was going to the captain's cabin to open the safe." Yaskov said. He entered a series of figures into the sub's targeting computer.

"I know of no such delay system," Yernin said. "Show me."

"There isn't an actual timer," Yaskov said. "So we're going to fool the computer into believing that there's a real target out there. When the bogey comes to a specific range and bearing, the computer has been instructed to shoot torpedo tubes three and four."

Yernin watched over his shoulder as Yaskov entered the data into the targeting computer.

"Push the Engage button, and the bogus target I've programmed into the system will come in range in six minutes and the missiles will fire."

"Ingenious."

Yaskov grinned wolfishly. *"Da."* He flipped another series of switches. "Now it is set," he said. "You only need to enter the proper five-digit safeguard code."

"Which only you know," Yernin said.

Yaskov nodded. "I will call it down to you when I am once again safely aboard the *Gorki*."

"What will stop me from killing you later?"

Yaskov shrugged. "There will be no need for it, Comrade Colonel."

Yernin held his eye for a long moment. "You are probably correct, Lieutenant. Return to the *Gorki* now. I would like you to stand by on the bridge. I'll be needing that code within the half-hour."

Yaskov nodded.

"If you do not have the code when I need it, you will most certainly be incorrect about my not killing you."

"Da," Yaskov grunted, and he left the control room.

Yernin studied the panel for a long moment. There was no real way of knowing if Yaskov was lying. But these men were the best of the best, according to Maslennikov. Captain Razhin and his crew were expendable, these men were not. But trust was something alien to Yernin's way of thinking.

He took the screwdriver from his pocket and, bracing himself against the weapons console, quickly removed the front panel and wired his six-minute timer back into the torpedo circuitry.

The water was very deep here. The chances that the submarine's hull would remain intact all the way to the bottom, and then remain in one piece should the Americans try to raise her, was remote.

It was a chance he was willing to take in exchange for the certainty that when he pushed the button, the missiles would fire in six minutes.

Suddenly conscious that he was no longer alone, Yernin straightened up and turned around. Captain Zamyatin stood in the hatchway leading aft, a manila envelope in his hand, and a grin on his face.

"I see you do not trust us yet," Zamyatin said.

"I trust no one," Yernin replied emotionlessly. His right hand was in his pocket, his fingers curled around the grip of his Heckler & Koch.

Zamyatin pointed to Yernin's gun hand. "If you kill us you will not make it back to Karachi."

"I have no intention of killing you or your people, as long as you do as you're told."

Zamyatin nodded. "Captain Maslennikov told me that you would say that."

"What was his advice?"

"Do as I was told and I would probably survive."

"Only probably?"

Zamyatin shrugged. "This is a hard business."

"Yes it is," Yernin said. "What did you find in the captain's safe?"

"I'm surprised you didn't open it yourself," the KGB captain said. "The Iranian bastards were practicing a nuclear patrol."

"What were their targets?"

Zamyatin laughed. "It is rich. But their targets were the same as ours. Baghdad and Tel Aviv."

Yernin's left eyebrow rose.

"Don't you see, Comrade Colonel. If these orders were to be leaked to the West it would prove beyond any doubt who was behind this attack."

"Return the orders to the safe."

"It would be a wasted opportunity."

"None the less, put the orders back in the safe, and get up to the *Gorki*. We're leaving."

Zamyatin wanted to press the argument, but he backed down. "You're in charge of this operation."

The growler phone rang, it was Azarov from the engine room. "We're set down here, Comrade Colonel. When do you want to do it?"

"Set the timer for fifteen minutes, then get aboard the *Gorki*."

"Very well."

Yernin hung up. Zamyatin was still standing in the hatchway, an odd expression in his eyes.

"You've changed the targets," he said in wonderment. "Fuck your mother, but you've done something that will get their attention for sure."

"In fifteen minutes this boat will sink," Yernin said. "I suggest you not delay any longer. When you get topside, stand by to cut the lines."

"When will you set the missiles to fire?"

"One minute after this boat begins to sink. By then I would like to be several hundred meters away."

"So would I," Zamyatin said, and without further encouragement left.

Yernin waited a moment, then glanced at his watch and turned back to the weapons control panel. He uncaged the firing buttons for tubes three and four, then braced himself against the motion of the submarine. At T minus five minutes he would hit the launch switches and get off the boat.

IN THE SEA

They locked out of the *Chicago,* took five undersea sleds, each capable of pulling two divers, from the locker at the base of the sail, and headed the two thousand yards across to the freighter and submarine. They wore oxygen rebreathers strapped to their chests.

One hundred yards from their target, Lieutenant Gilbert motioned for them to head up, and they surfaced in the six-foot ragged seas.

The submarine rode low in the black water. It was dwarfed by the freighter. They had come up off the bows of both ships, and for the first seconds they had trouble picking out what was happening. Except that there was movement at the rail and up the side of the freighter.

Two figures dressed in black clambered up a landing net draped over the side of the freighter and scrambled over the rail. Several other figures seemed to be standing by topsides where the lines holding the submarine passed through the limber holes and hawseholes. Both vessels slowly drifted downwind.

Their headsets clicked. "Copy?"

"Roger," Gilbert radioed to the *Chicago.*

"Sitrep." Coburn wanted a situation report.

"Stand by."

A third figure came out of the submarine's sail hatch and scrambled up the landing net. Halfway up he stopped and looked back, as if he expected that someone would be coming, then climbed back down and reentered the submarine.

Lane swam over to Gilbert. "Take your people to the weather side of the freighter and get aboard. Secure the ship by whatever means you deem necessary. Lieutenant Commander Friend and I are going aboard the submarine."

Gilbert gave Lane a hard look through his face mask. "If they drop those lines before we get to them, and the Kilo starts to move, get out of there, sir. The skipper is a man of his word."

"I expect he is," Lane said. "I've got no desire to go down with the ship."

"Watch yourself, sir," the young man said. Like the rest of his SEALs, he was in his twenties, and at the peak of his physical prowess. Lane hated to think what it would be like going up against him and his team. It wouldn't be pleasant.

"We're going aboard Baker," Gilbert radioed his terse message to the *Chicago.*

"Copy."

59

MOHAMMAD'S STAR

The sail hatch was closed, Yernin had heard it with his own two ears. But now it was open again. He could smell the sea, and hear the disturbed water between the submarine and the *Gorki* slamming against the hulls.

He pulled out his gun and stepped around the corner into the sonar room, where he switched off the dim red lights, and lowered the intensity on the display screens, putting himself in relative darkness. He listened for someone to come.

Zamyatin was the last man off the submarine. But he was the only man alive who knew, or at least suspected, that the missiles' targeting computers had been tampered with.

He looked at the battle clock above the sonar displays. In a little more than ten minutes the high-pressure air directors would fail, the submarine's ballast tanks would begin to fill, and she would go down. In a little more than five minutes he had to start the missile launch timer.

Maslennikov had been a very good agent runner. His work was precise and to the point, without the knee-jerk political histrionics of so many people in his position. And he'd been careful, something Yernin had always been appreciative of.

"I'll never leave you hanging, nor will I lead the FBI to your door because of my mistakes, Valeri," Maslennikov had promised in the beginning. Yernin had cause to remember the exact words. "I expect good things from you. With imagination. Do not let me down."

But he *had* let his control officer down. In Richmond, and again in Kuwait. This time would be different.

"Boris Nikoleiavich, is that you?" he called from the darkness.

The submarine lurched and something or someone fell against the bulkhead.

Yernin fired one shot toward the open hatch forward of the control room. The bullet ricocheted off the walls, and high-pressure water suddenly sprayed from a pipe somewhere down the corridor.

Nothing moved. He waited ten seconds, then slipped around the corner into the control room. Everything was in readiness. He could not fail this time because he'd thought of every contingency. Even the *Gorki* and her crew. With his left hand he reached into his pocket and fingered the detonator. If need be he would send the *Gorki* to the bottom and take his chances out here in one of the lifeboats. The coasts of Africa and India weren't that far away. He'd been in worse spots before and had come through.

He approached the forward hatch, flattened himself against the bulkhead, and listened. The only sound was water spraying from a burst pipe.

"Captain Zamyatin, you came for something. What do you want?"

There was no answer.

He darted across the open hatch, hoping to draw the KGB captain's fire, but there was nothing. Was the man a coward, had he changed his mind?

Someone fired from behind him. The bullet smacked into the bulkhead, centimeters from his head. He fell back, while bringing his gun around, in time to see Zamyatin's figure outlined in the hatchway. The bastard had climbed down one deck, passed beneath the control room, and come up from behind.

Yernin fired, catching Zamyatin high in the chest, knocking him off his feet. He struggled to get up as Yernin hurried across the control room to him.

"You bastard," Zamyatin said, the front of his black coveralls wet with blood. "You'll destroy us all."

"You'll never know," Yernin said indifferently, and he shot the man in the face just above the bridge of his nose.

The master clock in the control room showed that he had a few minutes to spare before he had to start the launch timer. He started aft to one of the officer's cabins to find an Iranian uniform for Zamyatin when he heard the distinct sounds of gunfire from outside.

He was stopped in his tracks. Was it a mutiny lead by Zamyatin's people? That was simply inconceivable. Zamyatin was nothing but an aberration, a mistake. Maslennikov picked his people better than that.

Yernin braced himself against the bulkhead as he tried to sort out what he was hearing. There was a lot of gunfire, but from two different kinds of weapons. Were they under attack?

He pulled himself aft, beneath the stream of ice-cold sea water, and then up one level to the sail hatch open to the deck.

The firing came from the *Gorki,* but it was becoming sporadic now. Nothing was visible from where he stood in the hatchway except the occasional muzzle flash. It sounded to him like whoever had attacked had come over the rail from the weather side, and had pinned down his people crouched in front of the lee rail.

He weighed his options. The radar lookout had not sounded a warning, which meant the attackers could have come from a submarine. It was even possible that the *Chicago* had detected their presence after all and had followed them out here to this rendezvous.

But they might not have been in time to see the missiles being loaded. If they had, they would have fired on them by now.

The mission was of the utmost importance. There was still time. He would take his chances with the sea.

Yernin pulled a fire ax from its bracket just within the hatchway and, keeping low, darted out on deck and raced to the bow, the footing on the sharply heaving deck treacherous.

He cut the two hawsers, and the bow immediately swung away from the freighter, the rolling motion already easier now that the two ships weren't bound along their entire lengths.

A fresh burst of gunfire from above made him stop. He crouched in the darkness about a third of the way between the bow and the forward edge of the sail, and listened. No one cried out, no one shouted orders or demands. Two well-disciplined forces were facing each other, and from where he crouched there was no telling what the outcome would be.

He jumped up, sprinted around the lee side of the sail, and made it to the stern, where he cut the two lines up to the *Gorki*. He tossed the ax overboard and raced back to the open hatch, clawed open one of the life raft lockers, and pulled a canister out. He shoved it overboard on the weather side of the boat; it popped open and began to inflate automatically. The action of the wind and waves would keep the life raft against the hull of the Kilo until he needed it.

Before he went back aboard the submarine he took the detonator out of his pocket, and without hesitation hit the proper buttons. A muffled explosion deep in the bowels of the *Gorki* rippled the water. A second later a much larger explosion lit up the night sky, fire and debris blowing two hundred feet into the air from amidships, shattering every window in the ship's superstructure.

MV *GORKI*

Adams and Karsten were both gone, and now the freighter was definitely down at the bow. Lieutenant Gilbert sat wedged behind a winch trying to make some sense of what happened. His head was spinning and his ears ringing from the explosion.

Three of the bad guys were down, and there was returning fire from only four others. Gilbert had sent Patterson and Lear aft and Mason and Cunningham forward to flank them. It left Adams, Karsten, and Biermeier with Gilbert. Biermeier took a hit in the throat coming over the rail, and had fallen back into the sea. He was dead before he hit the water, there wasn't much doubt about that.

Then the explosion.

His people were all dead, and he knew it. Something was wrong when only the squad leader survived.

Something crashed below as the stern continued to rise up into the air.

His headset clicked. "Copy?"

"Roger," Gilbert radioed, surprised he could even talk. He'd been hit in the shoulder, just above his vest, and the bullet had spiraled down into his chest. Every time he breathed it felt as if a pair of scissors were working on his lungs.

"This is the captain, what's your situation?" Coburn radioed. He sounded strung out.

"The bad guys are down, Skipper. So are my men. I'm the only one left."

"Are you still aboard that ship?"

"Yes, sir."

"Get off now. Do you hear me?"

"Aye, aye, Skipper. But no can do. I'm hit and we're going down."

"Get out of there, Lieutenant!" Coburn shouted, but the radio signal fell on dead ears as Gilbert slumped over on the canted deck.

MOHAMMAD'S STAR

They were all dead aboard the *Gorki*. No one could have survived. Yernin hung by the hatchway, fascinated despite himself as the freighter's stern rose into the night sky. The flames cast blood red reflections across the water, and on the submarine's superstructure.

Time now to do what he had come for.

He turned and started below when something fell on the deck forward of the sail, near the bow. He stepped back out on deck and looked forward. In spite of the flames from the *Gorki,* now several hundred meters away, the night was dark and the submarine's black hull and deck nearly feature-less, except for the open loading hatch. He could see nothing.

But he'd heard something.

A black figure rose up over the leeward edge of the deck, like some apparition rising from the sea, pulling itself up by a rope. It straightened up, and turned toward Yernin. It had been a grappling hook he'd heard.

He stepped back involuntarily.

The figure pulled something off its chest, tossed it aside, then pulled off its face mask and head covering.

Yernin was staggered to the bottom of his soul. It was Bill Lane, come like the bogeyman in the night for him. He had the flash of an image that nearly caused him to cry out. He was a small child locked in a tiny black box. He screamed to be let out, the darkness was suffocating. He was going mad.

"Vasha, you bastard," Lane called out in Russian. "I've come for you!"

Lane fired as Yernin suddenly came alive and grappled for his pistol. The shot hit him in the side, above his left hip, slamming him through the hatchway and up against the dogging wheel.

The sharp pain instantly cleared his head. He pulled out his pistol, extended his arm out the hatchway, and fired three shots toward the bow of the submarine.

When there was no answering fire, he took a quick peek forward. Nothing.

For an instant he thought he might have hit Lane, but then he realized that the loading hatch was closed.

The son of a bitch was aboard the submarine.

Mindless of his wound, Yernin turned and rushed back down to the control room.

He held up in the shadows to listen for a few seconds. But except for the water still streaming from an overhead pipe, the submarine was deathly still. The stench of dead bodies was even more ghastly than before.

Yernin hobbled across to the weapons control panel and looked up at the master clock. Only three minutes left and the submarine would begin to sink.

He hit both launch buttons, and his timer circuitry began to count down.

The submarine would be on the way to the bottom when the missiles launched. He didn't know if there was a depth that would be too deep for a successful launch, but he didn't think the sub would submerge that far in only three minutes.

He looked forward toward the dark bowels of the ship. Lane was somewhere up there, and when the boat went down he would be trapped.

Yernin would have given anything to have it out with the American here and now. But it would have to be enough knowing that Lane would go down with the submarine.

He turned and started toward the hatch; the light for torpedo tube three suddenly changed from green to red indicating that the tube was no longer ready to fire.

Lane! The bastard was in the torpedo room, and was trying to stop the launch.

For a split second Yernin weighed his chances of escape, but he had no choice. He started forward, pulling out his stiletto, because a stray bullet in the torpedo room might damage something vital.

Lane fought his way from the stream of water blasting through open torpedo tube three, and braced himself in front of tube four. The compartment was filled with bodies, but he was mindless of the stench as he worked the manual controls for the other loaded tube.

The lights over the firing panel showed that the missiles were in the countdown mode. With both the outer and inner doors open, the submarine would eventually sink, but the missiles would not be launchable. The tubes had to be pressurized first.

A thump below somewhere aft shook the submarine. It sounded like a small explosion, or as if they'd hit something. Perhaps a piece of debris from the *Gorki.*

Lane looked up. Besides the water streaming past the missile in the open torpedo tube, he heard another, deeper, more ominous sound, and the submarine started to go down by the bow.

The crazy bastard was submerging the boat! The ballast tanks were filling, and Coburn would think that the mission had failed and would order the Kilo to be killed.

He redoubled his efforts, acutely conscious that he was running out of time.

No one could have survived the explosion aboard the *Gorki,* and unless Mike Friend, who'd been hit in the head by a piece of debris from the explosion, got some help soon, he would die too.

The dead look in Yernin's eyes came back to him. The man was beyond evil. He was an emotionless killing machine. Life meant nothing to him. His or anyone else's.

Lane spun the locking wheel the last two turns and started to ease back the bolts when something sharp raked his left arm and shoulder.

He fell to the side as Yernin slashed the air with his stiletto, missing Lane's face by a scant half-inch. Before he could recover, Lane grabbed the knife hand and shoved Yernin up against the bulkhead.

"What are the targets?" Lane shouted over the noise of the rushing water.

Yernin tried to shove him away, but Lane kneed him in the groin, and slowly bent the Ukrainian assassin's knife hand forward.

"Where?" Lane shouted.

Yernin gave a mighty heave, shoving Lane backward, off balance, but dropping his stiletto in the rapidly rising water, which was already over their ankles.

Before Lane could recover, Yernin pulled out his pistol. "Time now for you to die," he said matter-of-factly. There was no triumph in his eyes, just a flat, dead calmness.

Lane scrambled to the right on his hands and knees as Yernin fired, the bullet splatting in the water.

Shifting his aim, Yernin stepped into the stream of water blasting through the open torpedo door and was spun to the left.

Lane jumped up and slammed Yernin back against the forward bulkhead, the Ukrainian's head cracking against one of the torpedo tube doors.

The light faded from the man's eyes and he dropped his gun. His knees buckled beneath him.

Lane shoved him aside, and pulled himself back to torpedo tube four, but now the locking mechanism seemed to be jammed.

The water was up to his knees and still rising as he put his back into it. The locking bolts eased back a quarter of an inch, stopped, and then suddenly slid the rest of the way clear.

Lane was pushed backward as the torpedo door burst open on a jet of water, the green light on the console above switching from green to red. Neither missile would fire.

He turned in time to see Yernin clamber up the ladder into the forward escape trunk.

"No!" he shouted, pulling himself up and splashing through the deepening water to the ladder. The locking wheel spun home, and the ready light winked red. Until Yernin locked himself out of the escape trunk and closed and secured the outer hatch, something he wouldn't do, Lane was stuck here.

The bastard had won again! The missiles wouldn't launch, but within minutes the *Chicago* would fire.

Lane turned and faced aft. Yernin would try again, and keep trying until he was successful. The body count would continue to rise.

He could not allow that to happen. He was the only one who knew the true measure of the man. The only one who knew to what lengths the assassin would go.

He shoved away from the escape trunk ladder and pulled himself hand over hand up the sloping corridor. He put everything out of his mind except escape, except surviving so that he could face Yernin. That thought alone drove him beyond his normal level of endurance, turning him into a machine, not for death like Yernin, but for life.

The water was halfway up his chest when he made it aft and scrambled up the ladder into the escape trunk. It seemed to take forever to close the hatch and start the cycle.

He filled one of the Steinke survival hoods, pulled it over his head, and, when the water had completely filled the trunk, cycled open the outer hatch and started up, inflating his life jacket as he rose.

The water was pitch black, and for an eternity he had no sense of up or down, but finally he broke the surface and seconds later the water all around him erupted in a massive geyser from somewhere far below.

His last conscious thought as his body was tumbled end over end was that the *Chicago* had fired a torpedo on the submerging Kilo and scored a direct hit.

PART
FOUR

60

THE WHITE HOUSE

National Security Agency Director Tom Roswell was in good spirits as he rode in the back of his chauffeured limousine to the White House. He'd explained the high points to Bill Townsend, who'd told him that despite the fact it was a Saturday the president wanted to see him immediately.

His limo pulled up at the west portico where he was met by a staffer who escorted him back to the Oval Office in the executive wing.

The president was speaking with his speechwriter, appointments secretary, media adviser, and national security adviser when Roswell came in. Reasoner gave him a knowing smile.

"All right people, I need a half-hour, no interruptions. Slide everything back," Reasoner said.

Everyone left except Townsend. The president's mood was up, if guarded. "Bill's told me that you have some good news."

"We just got word from the *Chicago* that the submarine was stopped in the Arabian Sea as it was about to launch two missiles. Once again it was Bill Lane who figured it out and pointed our guns in the right direction."

The president exchanged glances with Townsend. "Thank God," he said. "Were they the missing nuclear missiles from Sevastopol?"

"It's possible, Mr. President, but there was no way of confirming it. The navy can send down one of its Deep-Submergence Rescue Vehicles, but the submarine is probably scattered over a wide area. The *Chicago* reported they hit it hard."

"Any chance of a radiation leak?"

"I'm told there might be some, but we'll just have to wait and see."

"In that case we'd put pressure on Kiev to do the cleanup," the president said, grim-faced. "The Russians are complying with SALT, but they're the only ones."

"They have the most to lose," Townsend suggested cynically.

"Maybe it's time we started spreading the responsibilities around. Did we take any casualties?"

"Eight SEALs from the *Chicago*. They boarded the Ukrainian freighter that delivered the missiles to the submarine, and apparently had the situation in hand, or nearly so, when the ship blew up."

"Was there another submarine out there? Black Sea Fleet?" Reasoner asked.

"No, sir. The ship was probably sabotaged."

The president's jaw tightened. "Was it Yernin?"

Roswell nodded tiredly. "Yes, sir. That's his style."

"Did we nail the bastard?"

"It's not that simple," Roswell replied hesitantly. "We haven't seen Lane's full report yet, but what he did tell us was gruesome. Yernin was the only one left alive aboard the submarine. Everyone else, the Iranian crew, were all dead. And had been dead for a while, because the stench aboard was bad."

The president had a hard time accepting it. "Lane actually got aboard the submarine?"

"Yes, sir. Two missiles were loaded into a pair of torpedo tubes and were in the countdown mode. He opened the inner doors so that they couldn't be launched."

"That would sink the boat."

"Yes, sir," Roswell agreed. "It was either that or allow them to be launched. Yernin tried to stop him at the last moment. They fought, and it's possible that Yernin got away through one of the escape hatches just before the *Chicago* fired its torpedoes."

"Has his body been found?" Townsend asked.

"No," Roswell admitted. "The *Chicago* searched for twelve hours with no luck."

"Were any bodies recovered?" the president demanded.

"Two of our boys. Everyone else went down with the freighter."

"Six of our people are missing?"

"Yes, Mr. President, six of our people."

"Any chance some of them were still alive?" Townsend asked.

Roswell shook his head, but said nothing. They were all moved by the enormity of what had happened, and what had almost happened. In the space of seventy-two hours they'd lost ten American servicemen in addition to those killed in Kuwait and Norfolk, as well as the civilians.

"Was Lane hurt?" The president sounded tired.

"He was stabbed in the arm and the back, and was shook up pretty badly when the submarine was sunk. Apparently he was in the water less than fifty yards from the epicenter of both torpedo hits."

The president's left eyebrow rose. "He's one tough bastard, I'll give him that."

"Yes, sir."

"Where is he now?"

"En route to the *Mississippi*," Roswell said. He'd been able to read the last president, but not this one. "After that it's up to you, sir, whether we bring him home, or send him back to Riyadh."

Reasoner gave the NSA director a hard stare. "There's no proof that the missiles were nuclear, or that Iraq was part of this scheme."

"The proof is on the bottom of the Arabian Sea, but recovering anything from the submarine would be difficult if not impossible."

"What are the Ukrainians saying about it?"

"We've heard nothing," Roswell admitted. "Of course if it was a legitimate freighter on a legitimate cruise, it might not be overdue yet. In any event I would expect them to handle it as an accident at sea. Apparently the explosion was so severe that none of the automatic signaling devices designed to activate when a ship goes down did so. The *Chicago* reported that there were no electronic emissions from the ship before she went under."

"Or from the submarine?"

"That's correct, Mr. President."

"Iran is asking for help finding their missing submarine," Townsend put in. "What do we tell them?"

"We're going to stonewall it for now," Reasoner said thoughtfully. "Because there's still no proof who was behind this other than this Ukrainian spy who could have arranged everything without the legitimate government in Kiev knowing a thing about it."

"Lane mentioned Defense Minister Grechkov," Roswell said. Townsend tried to dismiss the suggestion, but the president held the national security adviser off.

"If that's the case, he might have cut his own deal with Hussein. I wouldn't put it past him."

"There's another consideration," Townsend said ominously. "I just got off the phone with Murphy. It's about Commander Shipley."

A cold fist clutched at Roswell's heart.

"She's the Brit on the UN team who first blew the whistle about the strike on Bandar-é Emān, isn't she?" the president asked.

"Yes, sir. And it turns out that she and Bill Lane are involved with each other. It was her place on the Riviera where Lane chose to recuperate after Failaka. And she followed him to the camp in Riyadh."

"Last I heard she'd returned to England," Roswell said.

Townsend eyed him coolly. "The chief of CIA operations in Riyadh thinks that she was kidnapped. A chambermaid at the hotel admitted she'd been paid to look the other way the night Commander Shipley left."

"By whom?" Roswell asked.

"The maid wasn't sure, but they were Arab," Townsend said. "The point is, she never showed up in London or New York. She's no longer in

Riyadh, so far as Murphy's people out there can determine. And that night a small cargo airplane with a flight plan for Baghdad was reported missing and possibly down in the desert north of the city."

"Hussein's people have her?"

"It's possible, Mr. President."

"Are they trying to send us a message? Are they that stupid? Gadhafi tried to thumb his nose at us, and we bloodied it for him. Didn't Hussein get the message that if he pushes us we'll take it directly back to him in a very personal way?"

"Evidently not, Mr. President, because it's possible that's exactly what he's trying to do," Townsend said.

Roswell listened to the exchange with a growing sense of disbelief. "You're not suggesting that we send Bill in there after all?"

The president looked at him with a blank expression. "They might not expect him to show up."

"It'd be a trap. He wouldn't have a chance," Roswell blurted.

"Bill Lane seems to be like a cat who always lands on his feet. Maybe he has nine lives as well. But we'll give him help if he needs it. And we won't force him into it."

"I'll order him not to go."

Reasoner turned on his National Security Agency director. "You'll do no such thing, goddamnit!" he shouted. "We've lost too many people for me to back off. Who in Christ's name does Hussein think he's dealing with?"

"We can take him out with a stealth fighter. A surgical strike."

The president shook his head. "We had only a partial success with Gadhafi, and this time I don't want to risk hurting Commander Shipley or anyone else out there except for Hussein himself and his personal bodyguards if need be." He eyed Roswell coldly. "Put it to Lane, and I expect he'll take the assignment."

"It's a trap," Roswell repeated weakly.

"Then prepare him for it," the president ordered. "Turn a disadvantage into an advantage. Because I'm telling you, we stopped his fanatical plans this time. But unless we kill him, he'll keep trying until he's successful."

61

The guided missile cruiser lay about one hundred miles south-southeast of
Kuwait City, approximately the same place she'd been stationed when one
of her helicopters had plucked Bill Lane from Bandar-é Emān. The sky
had finally cleared, and under the influence of a high-pressure system the
Persian Gulf was like a duck pond in August.

"This is becoming a habit," Lane tiredly told the LAMPS-II pilot when
they touched down.

"Yes, sir," the young chopper pilot said. "Something to tell my
grandkids."

"You know these guys?" Mike Friend asked from his stretcher. His
head was swathed in bandages, and he complained of constant blinding,
debilitating headaches.

"Sure do. Didn't you know us NSA types have our own ships and
chopper pilots?"

Friend laughed and then winced, tears coming to his eyes. It was a
wonder he'd survived. After their torpedo attack, the *Chicago* had surfaced
and sent out a search party. They'd found Lane almost immediately, but
it had taken another hour and a half before they'd picked up Friend and
then the bodies of the two SEALs. And they might not have found them
at all, except that Lane had threatened to shoot the captain unless they
continued to search.

"You might as well," he said. "You have your own submarine."

"I'm angling for a flattop, something with a little more elbow room."

"In that case, I'm putting in for a transfer," the chopper pilot said. "To
destroyers."

"Turncoats," Lane told them. He felt as if he'd been run over by a Mack truck. The medic aboard the *Chicago* had patched up his stab wound, but he felt like hell, mentally as well as physically.

It was Yernin's eyes. The bastard wasn't human.

After they'd found Friend, and got him aboard to sick bay, the *Chicago*'s search teams had scoured the vicinity without luck for another twelve hours for any signs of the Ukrainian assassin. There was a lot of debris in the water, bits and pieces of wood, and plastic and clothing, as well as an oil slick. But Yernin was gone. Drowned or escaped, he was gone.

When the helicopter was secured, the ground crew helped Lane get out, and Friend was hustled below.

The *Mississippi*'s executive officer, Lieutenant Commander Prescott, came up and shook Lane's Hand. "Hell of a call, Bill."

"We got chewed up pretty badly. The *Chicago* lost eight SEALs."

"We heard," Prescott said heavily. "But it could have been a lot worse."

"Yes, it could have been," Lane agreed. Yernin had lost this round, but everything within Lane told him that the Ukrainian was not dead, and that there'd be more to come. Next time it might be worse.

He looked out across the fantail toward the north. Someone was waiting for him, he could feel the pull. In the early days he used to think his gift was ESP, but later he'd come to learn that his gut feelings were generated by a subconscious analysis of a developing situation. His imagination played a constant game of what-ifs, juggling the almost infinitely possible variations in any given situation. It was an analyst's way of looking at the world.

"The captain would like to have a word with you, unless you want something to eat first."

"A cold beer would be nice, but I'll settle for a cup of coffee."

"Even the British navy has cut out its ration of rum," Prescott said wryly. "A sober navy is an effective navy."

"Bullshit," Lane replied good-naturedly.

"I agree wholeheartedly."

Commander Jones was waiting for them in his cabin aft of the bridge. He got up and shook Lane's hand. "Glen Coburn said that you did a hell of a job for them out there."

"He's a good man."

Jones looked at him in appraisal. "He says the same thing about you, Lane." He cocked his head. "Actually he said he'd never seen anyone with a bigger pair."

Prescott poured Lane a cup of coffee and perched against the bulkhead. "Able chopper is being refueled, should have it ready to roll in twenty minutes," he told the captain.

"Good," Jones replied. "How's Mike Friend?"

"He's in one piece. Doc says he'll let us know ASAP if he can leave with Lane."

"Okay," Jones said and he turned to Lane. "I'd like to offer you a hot meal and a soft bunk, but I have an urgent message from your boss that I'm to get you to Kuwait City. They have a jet standing by for you."

"Who sent it?"

"Ben Lewis. You're going to Riyadh. He said you'd know where to go when you got there. The jet will take Mike Friend to Ramstein, unless you need it."

"If I did I could make other arrangements," Lane said absently. "Mike needs to be in a proper hospital right now."

He missed the look of satisfaction that passed between Jones and his XO because he was lost in thought, his steel blue eyes focused elsewhere. There was only one reason for recalling him to the CIA's training camp outside Riyadh. It meant that they wanted to go ahead with their plans to assassinate Hussein. At first it had been little more than a desperate gamble to stop whatever insane plan the deposed Iraqi leader had cooked up. But that had been stopped on the Arabian Sea. So unless something else had come up, something just as desperately urgent as the submarine and missiles, he wouldn't go along with them.

He was an analyst, not an assassin. And floating in the water after the *Chicago*'s torpedo attack, he had come to answer his own question. Knowing what we know now, should we have assassinated Hitler in 1930 before he become chancellor? The answer was no. Because by carrying out an assassination we would have become no different than the people we were trying to stop. And no one could foresee the future with 100 percent accuracy.

"Mr. Lane?" Jones prompted.

Lane looked up. "Right."

"Glen Coburn said that you were aboard the Kilo when it submerged. What about the crew?"

"They were dead."

"Iranians?"

"It looked like it," Lane said.

"Where were the Ukrainian crewmen?" Prescott asked.

Lane shook his head. "I don't know. Probably aboard the freighter, which had been sabotaged to blow. Coburn's SEALs didn't have much of a chance."

"Thing is you made the right call, because if you'd been wrong there would have been a carnage."

The phone buzzed, and Jones answered it. "This is the captain." He looked at Lane, then nodded. "Very well." He hung up. "Mike Friend will be ready to go in five minutes."

"I'll take Bill back to the chopper deck," Prescott said.

Lane got to his feet and shook hands again with the captain.

"What about the missiles? Glen said you told him that they were loaded and ready to launch. How'd you stop them from firing? He said you told him, but that I should ask you because I'd never believe him."

"I opened the inner doors."

"But the outer doors must have been opened, and the tubes flooded," Jones said.

"That's right."

Jones smiled and shook his head. "Glen was right, I wouldn't have believed him."

"What else could I have done?"

"Close the outer doors," Prescott said. "That would have disabled the firing circuitry, least that's what they taught me at Annapolis."

Lane considered it for a moment, then shook his head. "Nope. It wouldn't have been nearly as exciting that way."

THE SYRIAN DESERT
SOUTHWEST OF BAGHDAD

Frances Shipley stood in the darkness of her quarters peering through the small hole in the heavy fabric of the tent as the guard disappeared around the corner twenty feet away. It was evening and she figured that she was in Saddam Hussein's camp on the desert somewhere in Iraq because of the uniforms the guards wore.

At this evening's meal, which she was served here alone, she managed to break her tea glass and hide one of the shards. When the uniformed guard returned to collect her dishes and utensils he asked politely if she had cut herself.

"No, I didn't," she said. "But sorry about the glass, it was rather stupid of me."

The guard shrugged indifferently, and he counted the utensils. But he didn't piece the glass together to make sure none of the shards were missing.

After he was gone, Frances used the piece of glass to slice a two-inch hole in the tent wall at about eye level, giving her a narrow view of the area behind her.

About thirty yards to the left, several satellite dishes were protected by camouflage netting. Thick cables snaked a few yards to a low, expansive bedouin tent. In the past hour she'd seen a half-dozen people come and go from the tent, all of them seemingly intent on what they were doing.

The same distance to the right, a dozen camels stood or lay around a watering trough. At first they'd looked quite natural. But after a few minutes when they hadn't moved, Frances realized that they were fakes.

She could make out several other tents to the right, at the edge of her peripheral vision, but except for the lone guard patrolling the rear of her tent, and the activity in what she took to be the camp's communication center, there was nothing preventing her from escaping out into the desert.

Five minutes later the guard passed from her left to right and disappeared in opposite direction.

As soon as he was gone, Frances wrapped her jacket sleeve around the glass shard and started back to work on the slit, extending it toward the floor until it was big enough for her to crawl through. The material was tough, and the job took longer than she'd expected.

Since she'd stupidly allowed herself to be kidnapped from the hotel in Riyadh four days ago, she'd not been mistreated. When she'd recovered from the effects of the chemical-laced notepaper, she found herself in an old red Mercedes racing across the desert. Her hands and feet were bound, but she was not blindfolded or gagged. In any event there'd been nothing much to see, other than the featureless countryside, but she had a very good idea where she was being taken, and why.

Her captors were indifferent to her, refusing to answer any of her questions. At one point, however, they asked if she had need to relieve herself. They stopped the car, allowed her to walk a dozen paces from the road, then politely turned their backs to her.

She'd contemplated running then, but decided to wait until her chances were better.

For the last three nights after her evening meals, she'd been left alone until morning. If the passing guard did not notice the slit in the tent wall she would have eight or ten hours to put distance between herself and the camp. It was a thin margin, but better than nothing.

Checking to make certain that the guard was not coming, and that no one was approaching the communications tent, she slipped through the hole and crouched for a moment in the darkness.

Off to the right she could hear men talking and laughing. A generator on the opposite side of the communications tent was running, and she could hear music coming from somewhere.

She pulled the tent material together to make the hole less conspicuous, then turned and straightened up just as the guard, his Kalashnikov rifle slung over his shoulder, came around the corner.

He pulled up short, hesitated for an instant, and then reached for his gun.

The delay was long enough for Frances to rush him. Before he could cry out she smashed the side of her left hand against his Adam's apple, damaging his larynx and crushing his windpipe.

He staggered back, disbelief and shock coming into his eyes.

Frances kneed him viciously in the groin, yanked the rifle away from him, and, as he started to collapse, smashed the butt of the heavy gun against his skull, cracking it like an eggshell in a spray of blood.

"Bloody hell," she said to herself.

Apparently no one had heard the brief struggle because there were no alarms. The desert was ten yards away, and fifty yards beyond that it was a no-man's land where a body could remain hidden for a very long time.

If she moved now!

Frances pulled the Iraqi soldier's body to a sitting position, then, squatting down in front of it, heaved the corpse up over her shoulders. The man was lightly built, but she was barely able to straighten up under his weight, and that of the nine-pound Russian assault rifle.

She stood, wavering for several seconds, her legs threatening to buckle, then she staggered off toward the open desert, praying for just five more minutes of luck.

She'd gone fifteen paces when a pinpoint of red light hit her chest. An instant later a half-dozen more pinpricks of light came out of nowhere, and she stopped.

Laser sights, she thought bitterly.

She let the body fall to the ground, then dropped the rifle and held her hands over her head. She never saw the club that hit her in the back of the head.

62

The billion stars flung across the desert sky were made more than brilliant because the Saudi Arabian capital city was dark. Even the international airport was under blackout except when an airliner came in for a landing or departed on a highly curtailed schedule. The entire nation was on a war footing because of the *Prince Faisal* incident.

Friend had been given a sedative aboard the *Mississippi,* and Lane was able to catch a little sleep on the short flight down from Kuwait City. But when he left the plane he felt as if he'd been drugged; his mouth was pasty, his eyes burned, and something gnawed at his gut.

He'd done a lot of thinking about what Tom Hughes had told him, that things were getting strange at the Agency. Someone very well placed was reading Roswell's mail and blowing the whistle. At first Lane had thought it might be another Ukrainian spy. Someone within the NSA or possibly the CIA. Someone independent of Maslennikov, who had apparently left Washington for good. It would make sense to have a backup team or agent in place against the time that Maslennikov and Yernin outlived their usefulness.

But Lane had begun to wonder if the answer was that simple; although the leaks had consistently concerned him, the pattern was erratic.

First the Ukrainians knew what his moves were, and therefore so did Hussein's loyalists. But it had been the Russian First Directorate chief meeting with Maslennikov in Kiev. And it had been the Iranians who'd known he was coming to Bandar-é Emān.

It made no sense. It was as if whoever was passing information was doing so for a political purpose that was not clear. Unless the aim was simply to destabilize the entire Middle East, in which case the mole was very successful.

Lane traveled on a diplomatic passport, which eliminated a lot of hassles, and which allowed him to carry a weapon in his luggage, because it was never searched.

The airport was a bedlam. Thousands of people jammed the terminal trying to get seats on the few airplanes leaving the country. Serious-looking armed guards were everywhere. And a steady stream of announcements in Arabic and then English warned that anyone not holding tickets or advanced reservations was to leave. There were no unbooked seats on any airplane departing within the next twenty-four hours.

Incoming customs, which was blocked from the main terminal by a tall iron barrier, was empty except for two officials, and three armed guards who nervously watched Lane come across the hall.

He handed his passport to the agent, who opened it, studied the information, and compared the photograph to Lane's battered appearance.

"What is the purpose of your visit to Saudi Arabia, Mr. Lane?"

"I'm on a diplomatic mission. My government ordered me here."

The agent stamped his passport without a word, and Lane walked over to the customs counter and was waved through without a question.

It was possible that Lewis had sent a car and driver for him to avoid the confusion of trying to rent something tonight. Lane was headed toward the mobbed information kiosk at the center of the main concourse to see if any messages had been left when someone came up behind him and touched his arm. He turned and looked into the face of Amin Zahedi, who was dressed in traditional Saudi head covering and long, loose robe.

"We must leave the airport immediately," Zahedi said. "It is very dangerous for me."

"How did you know I'd be here tonight?"

"I'll tell you on the way, but you won't like it."

"On the way where?"

The Iranian's expression softened. "To the CIA training camp north of the city."

"I see," Lane said. Zahedi was right, already he wasn't liking it.

He followed Zahedi outside to a battered dark blue Taurus parked in the short-term lot and tossed his bag in the backseat, after first retrieving his 9mm Beretta.

"I didn't sneak into Saudi Arabia to do you harm," Zahedi said, eyeing the gun.

"Does your service know that you're here?"

Zahedi had a resigned look. "No. Only my partner knows what I'm doing and why. He'll cover for me as long as he can."

They headed away from the airport, the outgoing highway clear but the incoming lanes jammed with traffic for miles. Some people had even abandoned their vehicles at the side of the road and were making their way on foot toward the terminal. What they didn't know was that the road was blocked by armed soldiers who were letting almost no one through.

"How did you get across the border?" Lane asked.

"That doesn't matter," Zahedi replied, concentrating on the road. "When will Washington go public with what you found aboard our submarine? It would relieve the pressure here."

Lane was stunned, but he kept the extent of his shock from his expression. "What are you talking about?"

"Don't be coy with me. It's already too late for that. I'm trying to save your life because of what you did for us. For our dead boys at the bottom of the Arabian Sea."

"Where are you getting your information, Colonel?"

"I cannot tell you how I come to know what I know, except that someone very high in your government is selling you out. What we cannot fathom is why he is doing this. We don't know what he has to gain."

"Who is it?" Lane asked, careful to keep his emotions in check. A great many people were dead because of the traitor.

"I can't give you a name, because I don't know it," Zahedi said tiredly. "I swear by Allah."

"A God your country has made bloody by state-sponsored terrorism," Lane said harshly. "If you don't have a name, where are you getting your information?"

Zahedi said nothing.

"Who are you protecting?"

Zahedi shook his head, his jaw tight.

"Do you want me to tell you about all those dead boys aboard your submarine?" Lane asked. "Do you want me to tell you why no one in Washington will go public with the truth, because nobody gives a damn about Iran? You can kill each other off for all we care. If it comes to that, we'll climb over your dead bodies to pump your oil. And whoever is feeding your government information is planning your destruction."

"General Sultaneh," Zahedi said softly.

"What about him?"

"The calls come to him on his personal line. He's the only one who receives the information."

"Go on," Lane prompted.

"Sometimes he shares with us, but most of the time he simply . . . knows things."

"How did you find out?"

Zahedi was acutely uncomfortable. "I've suspected something for months. There were certain things that he told me that I couldn't verify anywhere in SAVAK. Only the general had the right answers, and no one knew how he got them."

"How did you find out about the submarine? Did you put a tap on his line?"

The Iranian nodded. "The call came this morning from Washington. It was a man who identified himself as Red Baron."

"Did you recognize his voice?"

Zahedi shook his head. "No. He told the general about what you did aboard our submarine, and about *Chicago* firing two torpedoes, one sinking our submarine and the other sinking the Russian freighter."

It was as if one of the tumblers in a complicated lock fell into place. Zahedi said *Russian* freighter, not *Ukrainian*. "What else?" Lane asked.

"He told the general that you would complete your training here, and that you would cross into Iraq to kill Saddam Hussein." Again Zahedi glanced at Lane. "But he said Hussein's Mukabarat knows that you are coming and are waiting for you. They have a surprise. And that when you are captured the truth about the submarine will be made public."

"That doesn't make sense. What could Red Baron have to gain by helping Iran? And what would my capture by Hussein have to do with anything? It would serve both our country's interests to see Hussein eliminated."

"I don't know," Zahedi said. "But it sounded as if the general knew. Apparently it has something to do with President Reasoner's policies. Red Baron said he was naive, and the general agreed with him."

A second tumbler fell into place with a sickening click.

"What's the surprise they have for me?" he asked absently.

Zahedi didn't answer immediately, and Lane looked up out of his thoughts.

"You said they had a surprise."

"Commander Shipley," the Iranian intelligence officer said softly. "She was kidnapped from her hotel here in Riyadh. Saddam Hussein has her in his desert camp."

63

Zahedi dropped him off at the gate, and Lane signed in with the guard, then walked over to the operations center. The camp, like the rest of Saudi Arabia, was blacked out.

The guard telephoned Lewis, and the Russian Division director was waiting for Lane. "We were about to send out the militia. Where the hell did you disappear to?"

"Did you have a car waiting?" Lane asked tiredly, dropping his bag in a corner.

"We left a message for you, but when you didn't show up, Walt Zimmerman sent his people looking."

"You'd better call him off. I caught my own ride."

"With who?"

Lane looked at his boss. His short list of possible traitors was very short and Lewis was on it. But if the man was hiding anything, he was a very good actor. All Lane could see were signs of frustration and deep concern.

"Colonel Zahedi."

Lewis whistled. "He's taking a hell of a big risk being here. What'd he want?"

"Where's Tommy?"

"In town with Zimmerman looking for you," Lewis said. "What'd Zahedi want?"

"He knew what happened aboard the Kilo, and he wanted to know when we were going public with it so that the Saudis would stand down."

Lewis worked it out in his head, and his face lit. "I knew it," he said. "The dirty sons of bitches, it was their operation after all. They're working with the goddamned Ukrainians."

"No, Ben. He knew *everything* that happened down there, including the fact the Iranian crew was dead, and that the *Chicago* ended up sinking their boat."

Lewis's face fell, and he shook his head. "That's impossible, Bill. No one knew the details until you sent the message from the *Chicago*. If Zahedi found out, it means the bastards have the capability of reading our encrypted traffic, something I think is entirely too far-fetched to even consider."

"You're right."

"It doesn't leave a lot of options," Lewis said.

"Who'd Tommy pass off my message to besides you?" Lane asked. He'd sent the encrypted message eyes-only directly to Hughes.

"As far as I know I'm the only one. I hand-carried it to Roswell, who took it over to the White House."

"What about the CIA?"

Lewis shrugged. "Roswell would have passed a copy directly to Murphy, who I think would have held it close to the vest. At least initially. But Zahedi must have gotten the information almost as fast as we did in order to have made it this far." Lewis's eyes narrowed. "What's his source?"

"He wouldn't say."

"Well, goddamnit, everybody knows what's going on, but nobody wants to admit anything," the Russian Division director exploded. "Why'd he come over here to tell you that? What's his point?"

Lane watched Lewis's eyes. "He told me that Hussein's people knew I would be coming, and that they were waiting for me . . . with Frances."

Lewis paled.

"He said she was kidnapped and taken to Hussein's desert camp."

"Oh, Jesus Christ," Lewis said. He looked away for a moment. "I was going to tell you, Bill, I swear it."

"How did you find out?"

"The CIA found out about it after you had left here. There was no way of reaching you. And frankly it wouldn't have mattered. Not then."

"Someone knew that I'd turn down the assassination assignment at the last minute. But for some reason they want me to go through with it. Instead of putting a bullet in my brain in some dark Washington alley, they want me killed by Hussein's people so that my body can be put on display. Frances is the bait to make sure I go along."

Lewis shook his head. "There are other ways."

"Like what?" Lane asked coldly.

"Commander Shipley is British. If we simply step away from the plate, her government will negotiate her release. Iraq's beef is with us, not the Brits."

"I can't do that."

"Don't be a fool!" Lewis spat. "You said it yourself: You're being set up. They're waiting for you to make the assassination attempt."

"That's right," Lane agreed. "And they even know how I'm going to do it."

"So don't go."

"I won't."

Lewis wanted to be relieved, it was plain in his expression, but he wouldn't let himself be. "What have you got in mind?" he asked warily.

"Call Roswell and tell him I turned the assignment down. I'm not up to it physically. The aftermath of stopping Yernin makes it impossible for me. Zimmerman can file the same report with Langley."

"Just like that?"

Lane nodded.

"Roswell won't buy it. He knows you too well."

"Then convince him," Lane shot back. "Because I am going after the bastard, and I'm bringing Frances out with me. But not the way we planned it."

"They'll want to talk to you, find out what's going on."

"You'll have to hold them off," Lane said grimly. "Because if there's another leak, it will have to have come from here."

"From me."

"Or Zimmerman," Lane said to ease the pressure slightly. "I'll come back and kill him, *whoever* it is."

"What about Tom? He's on the list, right? Are we going to tell him?"

A sudden flood of despair washed over Lane, threatening to drown him. But he shrugged it off. Fate and his own abilities, there was nothing more than that.

"We'll tell Tommy so that he can be eliminated too."

"How are you going to do it?" Lewis asked, his eyes bright.

"I'll save the explanations until Tommy and Zimmerman return," Lane said. Hold on, Frannie, he said to himself. Just a little longer.

"Do you want something to eat?"

"Yeah. In the meantime, is there a documents man in this camp?"

"I think so."

"Get him over here on the double. He's got just a few hours to make me a convincing set of papers that will hold up in Iraq."

"Under what name?" Lane asked.

Lane smiled grimly. "Colonel Valeri Yernin, Ben, who else?"

Lewis was startled. "Is he dead?"

"I hope so."

64

SADDAM HUSSEIN'S CAMP

The desert night wind sent a chill up Saddam Hussein's spine. He stood with his Mukabarat chief Rashid Emir and his personal guards looking at the hole the infidel bitch had cut in the tent.

His brain was alive with a dozen conflicting thoughts and emotions that buzzed like angry sandflies, chief among them Valeri Yernin's apparent failure aboard the Kilo submarine. They would have heard by now if the launching had been successful. Saudi Arabia was on the verge of war with Iran. All it would take was one more push to topple the entire region into an all-out war that Iraq could win.

Without that vital nudge, however, he was in limbo out here. Alone, away from the reins of power. Cut off from decision making important to the survival of his beloved people.

In weakness lay disaster. *In sha'Allah*. But in strength the path toward victory and glory was open to him. He'd made that abundantly clear to his nation, and to the world, by eliminating the traitors at Nukhayb.

One man had almost single-handedly bested them all. He had ruined nearly everything, setting their plans back as if he were swatting an irritating insect. And he'd been promised that man would come here for the woman's sake.

Without the rocket attack, without Yernin, and without the Ukrainian help, they would have lost. Bill Lane would become meaningless.

Except, Hussein thought, looking up at the stars, as a means to vent his rage.

"Pardon me, Dear One, but the next infidel satellite will come within range in less than ten minutes," Emir said obsequiously. "We must get under cover until it passes."

Hussein turned his dark eyes to the portly man. "What about the young soldier the woman attacked?"

"He is dead."

Hussein's powerful hands balled into fists, and the veins stood out on his neck. He would attend her dying and it would not be very pleasant for her.

"His family is to be generously compensated," he said.

Emir looked suddenly uncomfortable. "Dear One, his family was from Nukhayb. But he was still loyal to you."

Hussein smiled. "Then he has already been compensated. He must be very happy now, being with his loved ones in Allah's paradise."

"Yes, Dear One," Emir agreed. Lately their leader had not been himself. He was forgetful, and at times he lapsed into worrisome silences. But worst of all were his terrible mood swings when he became a madman. Irrational, and very dangerous. The massacre at Nukhayb had been the result of one of those black rages.

A dark figure came out of the communications tent and hurried over. Hussein stepped back, then realized that it was one of his Ukrainian-trained communications specialists.

"Mr. President, you have a telephone call," the young technician said respectfully.

"Is it from Kiev?" Emir demanded.

"No, sir. From Washington."

Hussein's gut tightened. "Who is it?"

"Mr. President, he said that you would know him. It concerns Colonel Yernin and William Lane."

Hussein knew who it was. He'd spoken only twice to the man, but he knew who it was and why he was calling. It was as if he had received an electric charge directly to his brain.

"Gather my staff in the receiving chamber, Rashid. I will join you soon."

"Yes, Dear One. But what about the woman?"

"Do whatever you want with her, but do not kill her, she is still needed."

"As you wish," Emir replied.

Hussein and his guards followed the technician to the communications tent, where he ordered all of them to wait outside under the netting. He cleared the other technicians from the tent, then sat down at one of the equipment-laden tables and picked up the telephone.

"Yes," he said.

"Do you recognize my voice?" the man asked. The circuit was crystal clear, as if the man whose code name was Red Baron was seated in the same room.

"Yes, I do. It is good to hear from you again. Do you have some information for me?"

"Valeri Yernin has failed. The American submarine *Chicago* sank the Kilo and the freighter, destroying the missiles as well as the crew. There were no survivors other than Bill Lane."

Hussein's grip tightened on the instrument. "He was there?"

"Yes. He was instrumental in the disruption of your plans."

A red haze seemed to fill his eyes, and it was with the utmost control that he held himself from flinging the telephone across the room. His English wasn't very good, but he didn't misunderstand the message.

"Why are you telling me this?" he asked, when he'd recovered his composure.

"Because at this point in history your aims are similar to ours."

"Does your president agree?"

Red Baron laughed. "He is a fool who does not understand the wider implications of Middle Eastern politics. He will not be reelected."

"What about me?"

"You must have patience now, Mr. President. Very soon the situation will turn to your benefit if you are willing to strike when it's time."

"I'm listening."

"No announcement will be made about the Kilo except that it was sunk by the *Chicago* with a loss of all hands. All *Iranian* hands. The Saudis will subsequently attack Iran from the south through Kuwait. When that occurs you must make your attack directly against Tehran. It will be unexpected, and your chances for success will be very great."

"That will leave my southern flank exposed, and my army's position will no longer be secret."

Again Red Baron laughed, his tone nonchalant. It infuriated Hussein.

"Your position has always been known, Mr. President."

Was there a sneer in the infidel's voice? Hussein suspected there was. Control was difficult. "You will give me a signal when it is time?"

"Yes."

"What about William Lane?"

"In this too you must have patience," Red Baron said "He is in Riyadh now, recovering from his wounds. It will take some persuasion, but he will finally come to you, if for no other reason than to save his whore. When the time comes you will be told of his exact plans."

Was it enough? Hussein asked himself.

"For the moment your fight is not with the British. So the woman must not be damaged. When the time comes, she will be returned to her people, and Bill Lane will be put on display for the world to see."

"She killed one of my young soldiers," Hussein said.

"I don't care if she kills a hundred of your cousins, do not harm her. If you do I will immediately withdraw my support. The only way you will get to Baghdad is in a body bag."

"If I told the world your identity you would be jailed as a traitor."

"No one would believe you."

"I am tape-recording your conversation, as I did the others."

"Have you tried to listen to those tapes, Mr. President?" Red Baron asked. "Because if you haven't, I suggest you do at your earliest convenience. You will find that they are filled with noise that blankets everything we've said. It's a marvelous technology that was designed by our scientists at the National Security Agency."

Hussein said nothing.

"Patience, Mr. President, and you shall receive everything that you so richly deserve."

The connection was broken, and after a long pause Hussein hung up.

"Rashid," he shouted, jumping up.

Moments later his secret service chief rushed in. "What is it, Dear One? Has something happened?"

"Call your men off. The woman is not to be molested after all."

"Mr. President?"

"Do as I order!" Hussein exploded. "Immediately!"

65

AR'AR, SAUDI ARABIA

Lane stood at the edge of the tarmac studying the Syrian Desert wasteland through a pair of powerful Steiner binoculars the Cobra pilot had loaned him. The western horizon was tinged red with the sunset, and in a few minutes it would be time to go.

The border with Iraq was twenty-five miles to the north, and because of the trouble brewing in the southeast, this area was all but unguarded. They would have to avoid a radar site to the northeast, but the CIA pilot was confident it would give them no trouble.

Although the government in power now in Baghdad was friendly to the Western alliance, it still looked with nervousness toward the south because of the Saudis' war preparations. But this was Saddam Hussein's stronghold, so Baghdad kept its wary distance.

Lane had tried to avoid thinking very much about Frances, because each time he did, his analyst's mind imagined all sorts of terrible things. She was a trained intelligence officer, so she'd either been taken by surprise or by an overwhelming force. Zimmerman's people hadn't seen a thing until after the fact, even though the operation had apparently been carried out under their noses.

But he didn't think Hussein would have harmed her yet. He wanted her for bait. If Lane were to be killed or captured, however, she would become useless, and they would probably kill her.

"Something to think about, William," a worried Hughes had told him last night at the CIA camp outside Riyadh.

"I won't leave her, Tommy."

Hughes had shrugged, and managed to smile. "When we get back home, Moira and the girls will insist, and I do mean *insist*, that you bring her over for dinner."

Lane had laughed tiredly. "It's a date."

"Get some sleep then, while the rest of us toil the night through preparing for your latest mad stunt."

This afternoon the CIA had flown them aboard a Gulfstream jet the six hundred miles up here to the northern border where they maintained an airstrip and a small camp which they used to insert agents into Iraq.

Lane lowered the binoculars and turned as Hughes came over from the camp's operations hut past the helicopter, which had been trundled out from under its camouflage netting. "Is it time to go?"

"Just about. Bob Davis will be out in a minute." Hughes said. Davis was the CIA pilot who would take Lane across in the modified Cobra attack helicopter. Fast and low to avoid detection, but with enough firepower to fight their way out if it became necessary.

"Roswell sounded relieved when he found out that you refused the mission," Hughes said. "They all did over there." He grinned. "Still not too late to back away from this one, William."

"Bad feelings?"

Hughes nodded. "From the day I saw Maslennikov's picture." Hughes stepped closer and lowered his voice. "Use your head. They're gunning for you over there. We'd be better off taking this investigation back to Washington where the real trouble lies. That fight's not going away."

"I agree."

Hughes's eyes were bright. "Do you know who it is?" he asked.

"Ask me when I get back."

"It could be one of us, you know."

Lane nodded.

"If it is, you'll be walking into a hornet's nest."

"That's right, Tommy, but at least I'd know," Lane said. "Keep your eyes open over here for me."

"Will do," Hughes replied. "Just make sure that you're at the rendezvous point on time, and in one piece."

"Count on it," Lane said.

They walked back to the Cobra as Davis and Ben Lewis came out of the operations hut. The ground crew had already prepped the chopper, and it was ready to fly.

"You'll have to do the last five miles on foot, because going in the front door will be trickier than the back," Lewis said. "But your papers should hold up when you're stopped."

"Sounds good."

Lewis shook his head. "Beyond that you're on your own."

"Just give me twenty-four hours, Ben."

"I can't promise to hold them off any longer than that," Lewis warned. "So, good luck."

EN ROUTE OVER IRAQ

They flew about fifteen feet off the ground at two hundred knots, the desert rushing past them in a nearly featureless blur. From time to time Davis pulled back on the stick to climb over a hill, then immediately dropped back to the deck with a sickening plunge on the other side. His flying was precise even though his manner was nonchalant. Lane had taken to him the first time they met.

The plan was to drop Lane near the highway that ran between Baghdad in the east and the border with Syria in the west. All of this area was Hussein's stronghold, and sooner or later Lane, carrying the identification of Valeri Yernin, would be picked up and brought into the camp.

"That'll get you killed as soon as someone who knows Yernin sees you," Lewis said, and Lane secretly agreed with him.

"Hussein will want to talk to me first," Lane said. "And when he does I'll tell him why letting me and Frances go is in his interest."

Lewis looked at him in amazement. "Just like that?"

"You'll have to trust me on this one, Ben."

"This is crazy," Lewis said. He turned to Hughes. "Talk him out of this insanity."

Hughes shook his head. "When's the last time either of us ever talked him out of something he wanted to do?"

Lane sat above and behind the pilot. He unplugged his headset, loosened his restraints so that he could lean forward, and tapped Davis on the shoulder.

Davis cocked his head, but didn't look away from the Head Up Display on the windshield.

"Unplug your headset," Lane shouted.

Davis hesitated but then did as he was told. "The cockpit recorder is off."

"That's okay, but I'm changing plans and I'm going to trust you to keep your mouth shut about it when you get back."

Davis chuckled. "Zimmerman warned us that you were a maverick. But he said that you were the best. What do you have in mind?"

Another tumbler fell into place with a satisfying click. The list was getting even shorter.

"Were you in on the original mission planning?"

"From the git-go."

"Then that's the spot where I want you to put me down. How soon can you get me there?"

Davis did something with his flight computer. "About fifteen minutes."

Lane checked his watch. It gave him a thirty-minute leeway from the time he touched down until Hussein took his evening walk. *If* he was on time tonight.

"Can you tell me what's going on?" Davis asked.

"You don't want to know, Bob. But I want you to refuel and stand by to take off again."

"Without looking like I'm standing by."

"You catch on quick," Lane said. "I'll radio your comms center, wait a half-hour, and then send you a signal you can home in on."

"What about your Ukrainian ID?"

"It's buried behind the barracks."

"Is the sniper rifle aboard?"

"I put it aboard a half-hour before we took off."

Davis chuckled again. "You sure got balls, Mr. Lane."

"I've heard that before," Lane said. "I just hope they don't get shot off tonight."

ON THE DESERT

The Cobra gunship set down in the middle of a swale, low sand hills hiding it to the north and east. Lane tossed out his equipment bag and the canvas satchel containing the partially disassembled .50-caliber sniper rifle, then clapped Davis on the shoulder.

"Get out of here," he said.

"Yes, sir. Good luck."

Lane climbed down from the chopper, closed the door, and before he got ten feet saw Davis haul the Cobra up and back toward the south. Within thirty seconds it was gone, the desert utterly still.

For a full minute Lane crouched low, listening for sounds that someone was coming to investigate the helicopter's landing and takeoff. But the desert remained silent.

He reassembled the sniper rifle, then took off his jacket and trousers, revealing the Iraqi army desert camos he wore beneath them. The clothes went into the rifle bag, which he buried.

He checked his position on a plasticized map with his handheld GPS navigator, slung the equipment bag with his radio, medical kit, water, and provisions over his shoulder, and headed northwest in a dogtrot with twenty-eight minutes to spare.

If Saddam Hussein showed up with his two guards as usual it would mean that no one in Riyadh had betrayed him. It would mean that he wasn't expected to come across, here or at the site he'd worked out with Lewis, Hughes, and Zimmerman's people.

The going was rough. At times the sand was very soft, making it difficult to make good speed; at other times the ground was hardpan and rocky, some of it lava outcroppings, dangerous if he took a fall.

The sky was clear, perfect viewing for the KH series satellites that the National Reconnaissance Office maintained. If one of them was in position, the observers in Washington would know by now that a helicopter had landed here, and then took off back to the south. But it would take time for the downloaded images to be analyzed, and for the information to be sent to the NSA. And even more time before the images were sent to the CIA, the Pentagon, and the White House.

Longer than twenty-eight minutes. He was counting on it.

He had a fair idea who the traitor was, and why. But he didn't want any surprises, because a surprise could kill you.

It came down to his short list. Every name on the list was devastating to him personally as well as to the nation. Under any other circumstances he would not have believed such a list possible. But he'd been in the business long enough to realize that the CIA's old acronym for why spies spy— MICE:-Money, Ideology, Compromise, and Ego—was still just as valid as it was during the height of the cold war when it was penned.

In this case if he was right about the traitor, it wasn't money, ideology, or compromise. It was ego. One man thinking he was better than the rest, and willing to sacrifice lives to prove that he was right.

66

THE WHITE HOUSE

President Reasoner was at lunch with his budget director, Stanton Cross, and the House and Senate leadership in the White House dining room wrangling over the new budget bill, when his chief of staff, Warren Zeuch, came in.

"Sorry to break in like this, Mr. President, but it's your daughter at school. There seems to be a little problem," Zeuch said apologetically. He was a short, stocky bulldog of a man who'd been with the president for a lot of years.

"Nothing serious, I hope," the Senate majority leader, Martin Wood, said.

"No, sir. She scraped her knee or something, and they need parental consent to get her stitched up."

The president was suddenly cold. There was nothing wrong with his daughter. It was a code. "Parental consent" meant something had come up that required the president's immediate attention. And "stitched up" meant it was serious.

He pushed back from the table, got up, and put his linen napkin down. "Continue your lunch, Stanton can hold the fort for me until I get back." He laid a hand on Cross's shoulder. "Don't give away the farm while I'm gone."

"No, sir."

The president went down the walkway back to the Oval Office with Zeuch. "What's up?"

"Roland Murphy is on the way over from Langley. He suggests that you gather your staff in the situation room. There's apparently been a coup in Tehran, and Saudi troops are starting to mass at the Kuwait corridor."

Reasoner had been expecting something like this, or some variation of it, for a number of months, ever since the second Gulf War. Kicking Hussein out of power and installing a puppet government in Baghdad had not stabilized the situation out there as he'd hoped it would. It seemed like every time they took a step in the right direction something happened that would push them back two.

It was as if a shadow of rotten luck was riding over his shoulder—over all of their shoulders. Now this.

If war broke out between Saudi Arabia and Iran the entire oil-producing region could be embroiled in ugly fighting for a very long time. It wouldn't be anything quite so tame as the two near destructions of Kuwait and the terrible damage done to her people and oil fields. This time the carnage would be a hundred times greater. A thousand times more terrible.

"Where's Bill Townsend?"

"He was speaking at the National Press Club," Zeuch said. "I got word to him, and he's on his way. But I held off on the others. I figured you would want to talk to Murphy first."

The president nodded. "Anything on CNN?"

"It was just starting to break when I came for you, so I didn't get a chance to see how much they knew."

"How long before Roland gets here?"

"He called from his car, so he should be showing up any minute."

Reasoner's secretary had a cup of tea for him when he arrived, and she and his appointments secretary followed him into his office. It was snowing again outside the bowed windows, but the president's attention went immediately to the television set. CNN was reporting live from Tehran.

"Earlier this evening while he was leaving his office, the director of Iran's secret service, General Mohammed es Sultaneh, was shot to death by three so far unknown assailants who apparently escaped by car," Sam Bradley, CNN's chief Middle East correspondent said.

"Get Hatchett and Powers over here on the double," the president ordered, and Zeuch picked up one of the phones to call the secretaries of state and defense.

"It's still unclear whether this was an isolated incident or part of a much larger operation to weaken the stranglehold that the religious right is said to have on the more moderate secular arm of the government," Bradley reported. "Tanks surround every major government building in the city, as well as the telephone exchange and radio and television stations.

"But no one is saying if the tanks are part of a coup to overthrow the government, or are there by order of the government to protect itself."

Reasoner's press secretary, Toby King, and his chief speechwriter, Lawrence Prest, came over from their offices, worried but excited expressions on their faces. This president had always shined in crisis situations, and they'd been with him all the way. Like the willowy King told her staff, "This is what we get paid for, so let's make the boss look good."

"The cat's out of the bag already, so we'll have to give them something, Mr. President," King suggested.

"Schedule a news conference for four o'clock," Reasoner instructed.

"They'll want a briefing before then."

"No," Reasoner said.

King wanted to argue, but she backed off. Now wasn't the time, she could see it in his set expression.

Townsend and Murphy came in together.

"I see you've already got some of it," the CIA director said, nodding at the television set.

"How close to the mark are they?" Reasoner asked.

"They have most of the high points, but what they're missing is who did the killing and why," Murphy said.

"That's still only speculation, Roland," Townsend countered angrily.

"We have the radio and telephone intercepts to prove it," Murphy said heavily. "Roswell is on his way with the actual transcripts and some of the tapes."

"Could have been staged for our benefit. No one but the religious right had any political reasons to kill Sultaneh," Townsend argued. "He brokered Bill Lane's release from Bandar-é Emān, and the mullahs couldn't forgive and forget."

"You're saying let the situation develop on its own out there?" Murphy asked the president's national security adviser.

"I'm telling you that we've done enough. Sultaneh's death may be a blessing in disguise. In the confusion the Saudis could waltz right into Tehran and take over with relatively little bloodshed. And if Bill Lane can be convinced to take out Hussein, the region would be a clean, manageable slate for the first time in seventy-five years."

"No," Reasoner said.

Townsend shot the president a glance of hate that changed to one of confusion so quickly that his first reaction was impossible to read. "We have a once-in-a-lifetime opportunity to finally bring peace to a region that has been at war for centuries, and that is so vital to our national interests we just can't step away. Respectfully, Mr. President, you must do something."

"I won't further our aims by encouraging people to kill each other," Reasoner said.

"Forgive me, sir, but that's just plain naive," Townsend argued. "Vietnam, Grenada, Panama, and two Gulf wars. The precedent *has* been set."

Reasoner looked at his NSA with a little sadness. "Yes, I'll forgive you for the remark, but now the precedent stops. Bill Lane won't be ordered into Iraq after all. He was right all along and we were wrong."

"It might be a little late, Mr. President," Murphy said. "I got part of an NRO alert on the way over that one or more helicopters have made an incursion into Iraq and may be headed in the direction of Saddam Hussein's command camp. We're not sure about it yet, the first reports were sketchy, but it means something."

Townsend's face went white.

"Do you think it was Lane?"

"I'm trying to get an answer, but if I had to guess, I'd say it was possible."

"That's just great," the president said, his gut hollow. "I want him out of there as soon as possible. Do whatever it takes."

"Yes, Mr. President," Murphy said.

The president eyed him. "Who killed General Sultaneh?"

"His own people, Mr. President," Murphy said. "Because they think he's been committing treason against Iran by working with someone here, in the United States. Someone high up in the government or military. Somebody in a position to know about our policies."

"Who is it?" Townsend demanded.

Murphy looked at him. "I don't know, Bill. But it scares the hell out of me thinking of who it might be."

67

SADDAM HUSSEIN'S CAMP

The camp was in darkness as it was every evening that there was no cloud cover. A television set tuned to CNN, however, provided a ghostly illumination in the big room of the main tent. Saddam Hussein stood just within the doorway watching the pictures and listening to the rapid-fire Arabic commentator, his stomach still heavy from the evening meal of cous-cous and lamb.

It was happening, not exactly as Red Baron had promised, but very closely. Because of the Tehran coup the Saudis were poised to strike and the American government was doing nothing to prevent it.

"It's fantastic, but King Fahd and that half-brother of his, Prince Abdullah, will do our work for us," Ali Sidqi blurted excitedly.

Hussein gazed at his minister of foreign affairs through lidded eyes. "We have enough enemies, take care we make no more."

"Of course, you are right, Dear One," Sidqi agreed automatically, while thinking that once Baghdad was theirs again, it would be time to change leadership for a man more moderate. For a man who knew how to deal with foreign governments.

"When peace comes we must embrace it. We must become its champion. *In sha'Allah.*"

"Of course."

"By the time the Saudi army pushes its way across the high plains it will be greatly weakened. Then our moment will come."

All eyes in the room were locked on him now. Whatever mistakes he'd made in the past, whatever excesses he'd gone to, whatever weakness and mental lapses he showed recently, he was still a Tikriti. A man of strength and charisma from a powerful, proud family. He was their leader, there was no doubt in any of their minds, not even Sidqi's.

He turned his gaze to his secret service director, Rashid Emir. "Are your agents fully in place in Baghdad?"

"*Balé*, yes," Rashid said.

"Alert them that their time is coming very soon. Possibly within the next twenty-four to forty-eight hours, depending upon how organized Iran's army remains in the aftermath of the coup."

"Yes, Dear One."

Hussein turned to his defense minister. "Place all my troops on full alert. But they must be very careful of satellites."

"Yes, they understand this, Dear One," General Nuri replied. "They are fully ready and dedicated."

Hussein stared at his cousin for a long moment. "Would that they had that dedication six months ago."

No one said everything. It seemed as if Hussein was working himself into another of his dark moods. When that happened, people died.

But he glanced at the television set and smiled sadly. "A waste of young lives that will not be so quickly replaced. *In sha'Allah.*" Better to lose Saudi and Iranian lives than Iraqi, he told himself. They were brothers, but better them than us.

"I will take my walk now," Hussein said.

"Is that wise, Dear One," Emir asked nervously, "considering everything that is happening?"

Hussein ignored the warning. "Where are our Ukrainian advisers?"

"In their quarters," General Nuri replied.

"Gather them and my staff in one hour. I have something to say to them and you."

"Yes, Dear One."

Hussein cracked a smile. "We will discuss our plans for the return to Baghdad, and for the invasion of Iran to help our Saudi brothers."

The others laughed carefully.

"Our triumph is at hand. *In sha'Allah.*"

IN THE DESERT

It took Lane the full twenty-eight minutes to get into position above the dirt track down which Hussein was expected to take his nightly walk.

He took a drink of Gatorade, pocketed the radio, GPS, and plastic map, then flattened himself into the sand behind a small rise and aimed the silenced sniper rifle down the low draw.

The desert night was very dark despite the stars, making it impossible to pick out the line of the horizon. He shivered. Out here he was as completely alone as if he had been adrift at sea.

He brought the night-spotting scope up to his eyes and swept the track left to right. Pale green images stood out in sharp contrast to the blackness of the night. If Hussein came down this road Lane would not miss him.

In small measure he almost wished there'd be a shoot-out here because somebody back in Riyadh had betrayed him. In a way it would make everything simpler. Not easier, just simpler, because it would mean that the leak was at a lower level and therefore less serious than he feared. But it would mean that the traitor was one of his friends, and he didn't know how he would be able to take that. Especially if it turned out to be Tom Hughes.

The thought was impossible to bear, and he turned away from it, as he had tried to avoid thinking in too much detail about Frances and what was happening to her. Except that in both Gulf wars the Iraqis had clearly shown how they treated female prisoners. Rape, to them, was a legitimate tool of war. Just as it had been in Nazi Germany, and then a half-century later in Bosnia.

Laying the rifle down, Lane took his pistol from its holster strapped to his chest beneath his camos and checked the action. He carried two spare magazines of 9mm ammunition, and the silencer, which he took out of his pocket and screwed on the end of the barrel.

He reholstered the pistol as he detected a movement below on the track. He lifted the sniper rifle and searched the road, finding, then passing, and finally returning to a lone figure walking from his right to his left.

It was Saddam Hussein. Lane could tell from the way the man moved, from his size and shape, from his profile, and from his uniform. But it was confirmed when Hussein turned his head and Lane got a full view of his face.

The crosshairs of the night-spotting scope centered on the middle of Hussein's face. Lane slipped the safety catch off and moved his forefinger to the trigger.

A few ounces of pressure and the deposed Iraqi leader would be dead.

Sweat popped out on Lane's forehead. His insides seethed with hate and rage as he thought about the dozens of innocent people who'd lost their lives because of Yernin's insane scheme to help Hussein. And about the thousands of people killed in the two Gulf wars because of one man's aggrandizing plans.

The massacre of women and children at the desert town of Nukhayb had outraged the world. But no one had done a thing about it. Not the ineffectual government in Baghdad, not the United States, not even the Western alliance, which administered the MEGAP peace treaty.

Hussein came to a position about thirty yards down the long defile, and Lane started to pull the trigger. At the last moment he switched aim, sweeping the night-spotting scope to the right.

Two Iraqi guards, Kalashnikov assault rifles slung over their shoulders, walked side by side about forty yards behind Hussein.

Lane fired two shots, the first catching one of the bodyguards in the head, knocking him down, and the other kicking up a puff of sand across the track.

The shots were all but soundless, the direction all but impossible to determine. The bodyguard was very good, however. Figuring that the assassin could only be hiding above them in the sand dunes, he spun left and raced for the protection of an outcropping of rock, raising a walkie-talkie to his lips.

Hussein stopped and turned back, realizing that something was wrong. His hand went to the gun at his hip as Lane fired three shots in rapid succession, hitting the bodyguard in the side of his torso, in his leg, and finally in the side of his head, flinging his body to the ground as if it were a rag doll.

Lane switched aim back to the former Iraqi leader, who'd pulled out his pistol, dropped to a crouch, and studied the sand dunes a few yards to Lane's left.

"Drop your weapon or I will kill you," Lane shouted.

Hussein's head snapped to the direction of Lane's voice, but he didn't raise his pistol. In the darkness he could not pick out a target, but in the space of a couple of seconds two of his best personal bodyguards had been killed by an unknown assailant.

"Put it down and step away," Lane called just loudly enough for the man to hear him.

Hussein hesitated for several seconds, weighing his chances, but then tossed his pistol down, straightened up, and stepped a few paces down the track.

Keeping the rifle aimed at the center of Hussein's chest, Lane got to his feet and made his way down the hill. The Iraqi rebel leader watched his every move.

"I believe you've been expecting me," Lane said when he reached the man.

Sudden understanding dawned in Hussein's eyes. "William Lane," he said, and a momentary look of fear crossed his features. "Your woman has not been harmed."

"For your sake, I hope she hasn't, because I'm taking her out of here with me in exchange for your life."

68

SADDAM HUSSEIN'S CAMP

Lane took a Kalashnikov rifle and extra magazine of ammunition from one of the dead bodyguards, leaving the heavy sniper rifle behind. Dressed in Iraqi camos and carrying the Russian assault rifle he figured he could pull off his deception long enough to penetrate the camp's outer perimeter without raising the alarm.

After that his next moves would be determined by what he found, and by how cooperative Hussein was.

"You are a dangerous man," Hussein said over his shoulder as they walked down the wadi toward the camp. His English was fair, but heavily accented. "Everyone has a great respect for you. And fear, I think, rightly so."

"You knew that I was coming, but not when?" Lane prompted.

"I was told that you had changed plans, but that you could be convinced to come here if I had patience. It was the first time Red Baron was wrong."

All but the last few tumblers fell into place for Lane. "Who is Red Baron?"

Hussein laughed delightedly. "Do you believe that you will escape and return to Washington to confront him?"

"Either that or I'll kill you."

Hussein stopped and faced Lane. "Why didn't you kill me back there when you had the chance? Is this British secret service agent so precious to you?" Hussein studied Lane's face. "She tried to escape, and killed one of my brave young soldiers. Red Baron says she is not to be harmed, but I don't think that you and she will leave Iraq alive."

Lane raised the rifle, but Hussein waved him off.

"I might be willing to consider a trade. Her life for yours. I have no trouble with Great Britain. My struggle is with your country. Give me your word that you will cooperate with me, and I will arrange to have Commander Shipley flown to the main highway outside of Baghdad where she will be safe."

"Why should I accept the word of scum like you?" Lane shot back.

Hussein's expression hardened. "You didn't come here this time to kill me or you would already have pulled the trigger. Nor am I going to bargain with you like a commoner." He fought to control his rage. "Commander Shipley has not been harmed."

"Take me to her."

"Then what?"

"The three of us will walk out into the desert, and when I think it's safe I'll let you return to your camp."

"Why should I accept your word, assassin?"

Lane flicked the safety catch off. "Because you have no choice."

"I'm not afraid of martyrdom . . . ," Hussein said, and Lane laughed out loud.

"Save that lie for your loyal troops who've been brainwashed and don't know any better."

"The desert is very big, and my army is positioned in a dozen different places. Give up now and at least the woman will live."

"Fuck you," Lane said.

Hussein's face turned dark. "You motherless bastard, I'll see you roasted over a very slow fire and listen to your screams while I violate your woman in ways you cannot imagine."

"I doubt if you could get it up," Lane said. He motioned down the path with the rifle. "Shall we go, or do you want a bullet through your brain now?"

Hussein stood a moment in stunned disbelief that he had not been able to intimidate this man. It was the first time it had ever happened to him.

Lane motioned again with the rifle, and Hussein had turned and started down the dirt track when a series of loud explosions came from the direction of the camp.

Moments later all hell broke loose, gunfire erupting in the near distance, tracers lighting up the night sky, and what sounded to Lane like a dozen or more big helicopters coming in low and fast from the east.

The camp was under attack by some unknown force, and all Lane could think of was Frances down there unable to defend herself.

Hussein took off in a dead run toward the camp as more explosions flashed like strobe lights, the booms rolling around them like thunder, echoing off the sand dunes.

Lane sprinted after him, catching him and spinning him around. "Take me to Frances, and then you can help defend your camp!"

Hussein snarled at him like a cornered animal, but immediately regained control. "She's being held behind the communications tent."

"Show me!"

The gunfire intensified as Hussein's troops started to get themselves organized and began to fight back.

Hussein hesitated again, weighing his chances of somehow overpowering his captor and making his escape.

"I swear to Christ, if she's been hurt in all this I'll kill you without blinking an eye," Lane shouted over the increasing noise of the battle.

"This way," Hussein said.

They raced up the last hill and over the crest into the camp, parts of which had already been destroyed and were on fire.

Half-track mounted antiaircraft guns fired from beneath camouflaged positions ringing the camp. A dozen rocket launchers were raising their missiles.

One, less than a hundred yards away, took a direct hit from a helicopter-launched rocket, but in the confusion and darkness Lane could not tell if the chopper was American or Russian.

A captain and four elite guards rushed up to them. They nervously eyed Lane, not sure who or what he was.

"Mr. President, your convoy is ready to take you out of here! But we must leave now!" the captain shouted over the din.

Hussein moved left, away from Lane, and raised an accusing finger. "He's an American assassin! Kill him!"

Lane expected something like that, and before the captain and his men could react, he switched the Kalashnikov to full automatic and emptied the clip into the officer and four soldiers, blowing them off their feet.

Hussein squealed like a pig as he backed away.

Lane popped the empty magazine out of the receiver, rammed a fresh one home, cycled the ejector lever, and pointed the gun at the terrified man.

The fighting around the camp was so intense that no one noticed that their leader was in trouble. But it wouldn't last much longer.

"Take me to her, you bastard!" Lane shouted.

A helicopter came in very fast from the northeast, its guns firing, tracing a path directly toward them, when it suddenly exploded in midair on the tail of a truck-launched rocket. Debris and burning fuel fell all around them, and ammunition started to cook off in the flaming wreckage.

Lane took a hit in his left side, his flak vest saving him; he was knocked back, nearly off his feet, when something smashed into the side of his head. A wave of dizziness sent him to his knees and caused his vision to double momentarily.

He dropped the rifle in the sand and rolled away from a large chunk of flaming metal that landed within inches of his legs.

Hussein screamed in triumph as he snatched the Kalashnikov and swung it back to bear on Lane. "Die, infidel!" the Iraqi leader snarled.

Lane yanked his Beretta out of his chest holster and, before Hussein could fire, shot the man three times in the chest, driving him backward off his feet.

The camp's defenses were concentrated on the north and east perimeters. Incredibly, no one saw their leader fall as the fierce fight continued to rage. From Lane's perspective, however, it was clear that it would only be a matter of minutes before the camp was overrun.

He struggled to his feet, stood swaying as a wave of dizziness passed over him, then got his bearings and headed toward what he took to be the communications facility. The big bedouin tent was burning furiously, and the satellite dishes beneath camouflage netting were mostly destroyed, but there was enough of the installation left for Lane to recognize it for what it was.

Behind it, the generator and fuel tank exploded, flames shooting fifty feet into the air.

Beyond that, a small bedouin tent had just caught fire. Two guards crouched in front of the tent fired their rifles at the helicopters angrily buzzing in from the east.

Lane ran at them, firing as fast as he could pull the Beretta's trigger as he zigzagged around the comms facility.

At first the two men had no idea they were being attacked from behind. At the last minute, however, they started to bring their weapons to bear on the figure dressed in camos outlined by the fires. But it was too late. The first guard took a direct hit in his forehead, the bullet destroying his brain, and the second took hits in his side and in his throat, and he fell to the ground, drowning in his own blood.

Lane ejected the Beretta's spent magazine, fumbled one of the spares out of his pocket, and rammed it into the butt of his gun as he jumped over the fallen guards and burst into the tent.

He was in a large, smoke-filled room, empty except for a low table surrounded by cushions.

"Frances!" he shouted.

He thought he heard a noise in another room at the rear of the tent.

"Frances!" he shouted again, racing across the main room.

He yanked the flap aside. Frances, her blouse ripped open, pulled a long, curved knife from the throat of a dying guard lying half on top of her, and raised it threateningly. The wall behind her was on fire, and in the flickering light her face was mottled red. She looked like a feral animal, cornered, ready to kill anything or anyone who approached her. There was an insanity in her eyes.

"We have to get out of here, Frannie," he shouted, trying to keep his tone gentle.

She shook her head fiercely.

A big explosion rocked the earth. The front part of the tent collapsed in a storm of sparks and fire.

Frances's face suddenly brightened in recognition. "Bill?" she cried.

He went across to her, rolled the dead guard away, and pulled her to her feet.

"The camp's under attack. We've got to get out of here now!"

"Who is it?" she demanded, her voice still wild.

"I don't know," Lane said. "Are you okay, can you walk?"

"I can bloody well do better than that," she shouted. She sliced a big hole in the back wall of the tent with the knife, and Lane followed her outside.

The fighting, although still mostly concentrated to the north and east sectors of the sprawling camp, was moving toward them.

They headed southwest into the desert, directly away from the attacking forces, moving as quickly as they could through the darkness.

A couple hundred yards out, they angled to the south on a path that Lane figured would intercept the dirt track where he'd ambushed Hussein and the two guards. He'd left his pack with the provisions where he'd hidden in wait. And he wanted to retrieve the Kalashnikov and ammunition from the other bodyguard he'd killed. There was no telling who'd be coming after them.

Frances kept up with him even though she was battered and obviously in pain. When he tried to slow down she made him pick up the pace.

He'd underestimated her on more than one occasion, he thought wryly. And he figured a lot of other people had probably made the same mistake.

Ten minutes later, the sounds of the battle still intense, but well behind them, they scrambled down a shallow series of sand dunes to the floor of the dirt track Hussein had taken. The downed guards were a half-mile farther to the west.

They'd gone ten yards when a Soviet-built helicopter swooped in low overhead from the east. It carried no markings.

Lane's first thought was that Hussein's people were making a breakout, and he shoved Frances into the scant protection of a small pile of rocks.

The chopper made a tight 180-degree turn and pulled up short in a hover less than fifty yards from where they were crouched.

A second Hind pounded in from the east and took up a position behind them, while a third and a fourth unmarked helicopter touched down on the dirt track in front of them.

"I'm not going back," Frances said. She was shivering. "They'll have to kill me first."

"Us," Lane replied, taking aim with his Beretta on the rotors of the nearest helicopter hovering above them. "And the next time, follow instructions, will you please?"

69

ON THE DESERT

"BILL LANE, LOWER YOUR GUN, WE MEAN YOU NO HARM," an amplified voice came from one of the helicopters on the ground, before he could shoot.

The English was accented, but the voice was recognizable. Lane lowered his gun and uncocked the hammer.

"Is it a trick?" Frances asked.

"If it is, it's a damned good one," Lane replied. He took Frances's arm and they got to their feet.

Amin Zahedi, dressed in Iranian desert battle gear, stepped down from the helicopter and, keeping low, hurried up the dirt track to them. The other helicopter on the ground lifted off in a blizzard of sand, and it and the two hovering machines peeled off back to the diminishing fight for Hussein's camp.

"You're a tough man to keep up with," Zahedi said, his rugged face all planes and angles in the darkness.

"Considering the trouble brewing along your southern border, you're something of a surprise yourself, Colonel," Lane replied. "What are you doing here?"

"We came to kill Hussein. But someone beat us to it."

Lane said nothing.

"Was it you?"

"I shot at a lot of people," Lane replied. "How did you know I would be here?"

"Red Baron told General Sultaneh that you'd decided not to come after all, but that you could be convinced," Zahedi said. "When I spotted you and Commander Shipley running away, I could hardly believe my eyes."

"Red Baron was passing information to Hussein as well."

Zahedi nodded. "I thought it was possible. But now both fools are dead."

Lane's surprise showed on his face.

"General Sultaneh is dead. I killed him. And now I want to avert a war with Saudi Arabia, and I need your help."

"The Saudis are our allies. Iran is our enemy."

"Peace is everyone's ally," Zahedi countered. "Maybe it's time for the moderates in my government to gain power."

"The mullahs will fight you."

A flicker of a smile played at the corners of Zahedi's mouth. "One in particular." He shook his head. "First we need to convince King Fahd that our submarine was hijacked."

"Who is Red Baron?"

"I don't know, except that he is someone very high in your government. Someone in a position of power, and knowledge. Someone who would stand to gain by keeping all of us in the Gulf at war with each other." Zahedi studied Lane's eyes. "But you know, or suspect who it is."

"I have an idea."

Zahedi turned to Frances. "Are you all right, Commander?"

"Just peachy," she said coldly.

Zahedi bit off a sharp reply, then turned back to Lane. "You got this far, how did you plan on getting back to your base across the Saudi border? Needless to say we cannot take you back. But time *is* of the essence, as they say in America."

"How close would you care to take us?"

Zahedi considered it for a moment. "There's radar at Ar'ar. But our pilot is good. If we keep low, maybe fifty kilometers from there. Will this help?"

Lane nodded. "As you said, time *is* of the essence."

Frances looked back toward Hussein's desert camp, the battle all but over. Then she looked up at Lane. "Just that easy?"

"You and I are having dinner with an old friend in Washington tomorrow night, if you're up to it."

"Rather," she said, smiling.

AR'AR, SAUDI ARABIA

The Cobra could carry only one passenger besides the pilot, so Davis came out for them in one of the old Bell Rangers.

He had a lot of questions to ask, but he held his silence during the short flight back across the border. When they set down, he helped them out of the helicopter.

"I sure am glad to see you, Mr. Lane," he said.

Lane shook his hand. "Honest, I'll never bad-mouth the Company again."

"I'll hold you to that, sir."

Hughes came out of the operations hut in a dead run, the fastest Lane had ever seen his old friend move. By the time he reached them he was winded and even more red in the face than normal.

He stared first at Lane and then at Frances. Finally he took her in his arms and gave her a gentle bear hug, his eyes glistening.

"Oh goodness, am I ever glad to see you, my dear," he said. "And if I may say so, I've never seen a woman look more radiant."

"Slow down," Lane said. "I want to get all this on paper. Moira will want a blow-by-blow description for her divorce lawyer."

The CIA's Gulfstream was warming up on the tarmac. Frances glanced over at it. "Before I get on that thing, I need the loo."

"The building next to Ops," Hughes said. "We have a few things laid out for you. But they're not very pretty, I'm afraid."

"Pretty I can do without," Frances replied. "Clean is what I lust after." She gave Lane a searching, vulnerable look, then headed away.

"Ben has been on the scrambler with Roswell since we heard you were coming out," Hughes said. "We think Iran attacked the base."

"That's right," Lane said. "Hussein is dead."

"They kill him?"

Lane looked into his friend's eyes. "No."

Hughes nodded after a beat. "Ben called Roswell as soon as he realized that you'd switched plans. And Zimmerman called Murphy. But they're not part of this. They made the calls openly."

"Did Davis tell them what I did when he came back?"

"He didn't have to. We watched you all the way in on radar. The Company hid a couple of low-profile self-contained radar units out on the desert that Zimmerman forgot to mention."

"We all have our little secrets," Lane murmured, his gaze going to the Gulfstream. "Are we flying to Riyadh first?"

"No, Washington direct. We'll refuel in Málaga," Hughes said. "Do you know who it is?"

Lane turned back. "I think so, Tommy. The list is down to three names now."

"Who are they?"

"If I'm wrong this time, I want to be wrong on my own."

Hughes started to object, but Lane held him off.

"Is that invitation to dinner still open?"

"What do you think?"

"Better call Moira from the plane, see if tomorrow night's okay."

WASHINGTON

The city was like a dream. It had snowed for the past two days, and when the storm passed, the sky cleared and the capital lay under a magnificent blanket of white; a fairyland, but with dark undertones. One job was left to be done.

Hughes went with Lane and Frances directly over to Bethesda Naval Hospital, where over her objections she was given a sedative and put to bed.

"It's obvious she's had quite a trauma," the doctor warned. "She needs the rest."

"She's a British citizen," Lane said.

"I called the embassy," Hughes told him. "They're sending someone over to check on her."

"We might have to wait a day or two for dinner, Tommy," Lane said tiredly. The CIA medic aboard the Gulfstream had patched him up and he'd managed to get a few hours' sleep on the way over. But he was suffering from serious jet lag and the accumulated effects of his wounds. His body felt like a gigantic bruise.

"You could use a few days' rest yourself," the doctor told him.

"Soon," Lane said, but riding over to his apartment with Hughes he wondered if this business would ever truly be over, because it would live with him and Frances for the rest of their lives. Lewis had assured them that they had done what had to be done. But somehow Lane wasn't quite sure.

He took a shower, shaved, and put on a pair of slacks, a cashmere turtle neck, and a hand-tailored blazer. When he came out Hughes poured him a small cognac neat.

"Did you make the two calls?"

"Roswell and Murphy will meet you at the White House," Hughes said.

"Did they ask why?"

Hughes shook his head. "And neither will I. I'm not even going to ask if you're sure, because it would be redundant." Hughes studied his friend's haggard expression. "What about afterward?"

"I'll be with Frances at the hospital," Lane said.

THE WHITE HOUSE

Hughes dropped Lane off at the west gate and he walked up to the White House where he was taken to the Oval Office. The president was waiting for him with Townsend, Rosewell, and Murphy.

"Welcome home, Bill," the president said. "You've done a hell of a job for us. Once again your country owes you its gratitude."

"Saddam Hussein is dead, Mr. President," Lane said curtly, in no mood for platitudes. He felt betrayed. The entire nation had been deceived by one man who thought he knew better than everyone else what was right. Because of him a lot of people were dead for no reason at all, other than ego.

Townsend walked over to the door and closed it.

"Did you kill him?" President Reasoner asked, a strained look of awe on his face.

"Yes, sir."

"We're not a nation of assassins." Townsend spat the words in disgust.

"I didn't assassinate him," Lane said. "At that point the camp was under attack, and Hussein was pointing a rifle at me. I just shot first, that's all."

"You were there with him, in his camp?" Roswell asked. "You actually got that far?"

"Yes, sir. I waited in the desert for him to take his walk. And when he came by I killed his two bodyguards and took him captive. I was there to trade his life for Frances Shipley's, not assassinate him."

"We'll never know, will we," Townsend said, his face a mask of loathing. "There are no witnesses. No one who knows."

"There's one man who knows, sir," Lane said. "Hussein called him Red Baron."

"What's this all about—" Townsend blurted, but the president waved him off.

"What are you talking about?" Reasoner demanded.

None of them was seated. There didn't seem to be the time for it.

"Hussein said that a man code-named Red Baron, who was highly placed in our government, had fed him intelligence information. It was one of the reasons his army managed to elude direct confrontation with the forces out of Baghdad for so long."

"Preposterous," Townsend said.

"Do you think it's one of us?" Murphy asked.

"Walt Zimmerman told you about my last-minute change of plans. Did you report that to anyone here?" Lane asked.

"There wasn't enough time," Murphy answered darkly.

"Ben Lewis called me," Roswell said. "But we were already tracking the Iranian sweep across the border. We had our hands full."

"The Iranians rescued me and Commander Shipley. Their commander admitted he was involved with General Sultaneh's assassination because it was time for the moderates to take over and Sultaneh was anything but moderate. They want to avoid war with Saudi Arabia."

"They're a nation of terrorists," Townsend all but screamed. "Rabid dogs . . ."

"General Sultaneh was also receiving intelligence information from Red Baron," Lane said.

Townsend stepped back, his face screwed up in a grimace of fear. He raised a hand in appeal to the president.

"Why?" Reasoner asked, and the question hung in the air because no one was sure who it was directed to.

"Because he didn't agree with your policies, Mr. President," Lane said. "With the entire Middle East in turmoil, and with the Ukrainian government implicated in a terrible scheme to help Hussein, the United States would have been forced into picking up the pieces and managing the entire region over the foreseeable future."

"Over the dead bodies of how many?" Reasoner asked, again directing his question to no one in particular.

"Terrorists," Townsend repeated himself. His face was beginning to fall apart.

The president looked at him. "You?" he asked.

Townsend turned to Lane, a last spark of hate curling his lips, narrowing his eyes. "How could you have been so sure? I made no mistakes."

Lane managed a weary grin. "Sorry, Mr. Townsend. But to tell the truth, I wasn't sure, until this moment."

70

Moira Hughes always came as a surprise to anyone who'd met her husband first. Half expected her to be a diffident, mousy woman with averted eyes, overawed by her husband's superior intelligence. The other half, learning that the Hugheses had six children, expected a short, matronly, gray-haired woman dressed in a soiled apron over a flower print housedress.

The woman who opened the door of the huge three-story brick house that had once been a Civil War–era tobacco farmer's mansion for Lane and Frances was anything but. She was nearly as tall as her husband, with medium-length auburn hair, a statuesque physique, a milky complexion, a lovely face filled with good humor, and deep green, sparkling eyes that lit up like Fourth of July fireworks and then almost immediately glistened with tears.

"Oh, William," she said softly, her voice gentle and mellifluous. "We were so relieved when Thomas said you'd come safely home."

Mindful of his wounds, she took him in her arms and held him tenderly for several moments.

"I missed you," Lane said.

"She's going to make the perfect wife for you," Moira whispered in his ear.

He stepped back as if he'd been slapped. "That, you wicked woman, was a dirty, deceitful trick to pull on a battle-scarred man."

She laughed brightly. "Piffle," she said, and she took Frances by the arm and led her inside to the vast stair hall. "You're even more lovely than Thomas told us."

"You're exactly as I pictured you'd be," Frances replied, her eyes filling.

The two woman embraced warmly, leaving Lane standing alone on the threshold.

A second later utter bedlam engulfed the entire house as girls came running from seemingly all directions, shouting and screaming: "Uncle Bill! It's Uncle Bill!"

A large black Lab careened around the corner from the back hall, barking and baying wildly, as two huge cats streaked down the stairs, hissing as if they were jungle animals on the attack.

The dog stopped long enough to sniff cautiously at Frances, then, with the cats and the girls, raced around the stair hall completely out of control.

Frances laughed so hard her knees became weak, and Lane was dragged the rest of the way into the house and completely mobbed.

"Ladies, mind your decorum, if you please," Tom Hughes called mildly as he came nonchalantly down the stairs in his slippers and smoking jacket.

The noise stopped instantly. The girls lined up by ages, the dog and cats came to heel beside the oldest, and Moira looked up warmly at her husband, who came to her side and pecked her on the cheek.

"We have company, darling, you should have worn your blue smoking jacket."

"I'll get it," three of the six girls shouted in unison.

Hughes glanced their way, and they stopped. He smiled. "It's not back from the cleaners."

"He beats them with a willow stick every night before bed," Lane told Frances.

"Piffle," she said, kissing Hughes on the check. "Thank you both for inviting me to your home."

"Something like this will be yours once you and William are married."

"Thomas," Moira said, shooting her husband a warning glance.

Hughes grinned innocently. "You've met Moira; let me introduce my daughters." He turned to his girls. "Susan is seventeen, our oldest."

The young woman was tall, with a perfectly oval face and her mother's eyes and good looks. She curtsied the old-fashioned way.

"Deborah is sixteen, and her twin sister, Kathleen, is thirty-eight seconds younger."

"Oh, Father," the younger twin said.

"Winifred, named after one of my aunts, is fourteen. Beth Ann, named after Moira's cousin, is nine. And Proxaida, little Proxie, named after my grandmother, will be three next week."

The little one had been shivering with anticipation, and she couldn't hold it any longer. "Uncle Bill!" she cried, and she raced past her father and mother. Lane scooped her up.

Hughes shook his head. "That one hasn't quite got the idea yet, but we're working on it," he said, smiling broadly. "The three incorrigibles on the end are Bo Jo, a miserable excuse for a dog, and the two real rulers of this madhouse, Scott and Zelda the cats."

Again pandemonium broke out, the younger girls mobbing Lane and the three older ones speculatively eyeing Frances, who was loving every minute of it.

"William is godfather to the girls," Moira told Frances as they went into the living room. "I don't think this family would be the same without him."

"A lot of us wouldn't be," Frances said.

A fire burned on the hearth, and something classical played on a stereo. The large room was pleasantly furnished and was crammed with books. There wasn't a television in sight.

The girls served Frances a glass of white wine, Lane a cognac, and then brought wine for their parents. When they were settled, Susan looked sweetly at Frances.

"Tell us all about it, would you please, Ms. Shipley?" Susan said, smiling.

Frances was nonplussed for a moment, and she glanced at Lane. "I don't know if I can. I suspect much of it is classified."

The girls tittered.

"I'm sorry, I didn't mean that dreadful operation with the Kilo submarine, and the SS-N-sixteen nuclear missiles, or Saddam Hussein and the war that almost happened between Saudi Arabia and Iran. I meant about how you and Uncle Bill first met."

Frances opened her mouth but nothing came out.

"I hoped you warned the poor girl about the grilling she would be subjected to," Hughes said to Lane.

"Nope. I figured I'd let her learn the hard way. Same way I did," Lane said. "At least Bo Jo didn't bite her like he did me the first time I came over."

"He didn't bite you," Moira corrected. "I remember the incident clearly. He piddled on your leg."

The girls howled in delight, and Frances basked in a warmer family glow than she'd ever know in her upper-class reserved English household.

"It was three years ago, when your Uncle Bill was stationed in London," Frances said.

"I told you," Kathleen whispered, poking her twin in the ribs.

"He was on temporary assignment, and the first time I laid eyes on him I thought he was the most gorgeous man I'd ever seen in my life."

Susan smiled. "I'm jealous, of course. I wanted him to wait until I got a little older and then I was going to run away with him to some deserted island."

"You're talking about your uncle," Hughes cautioned his daughter.

"Piffle," she said seriously, and they all broke up laughing again.

KIEV

It was 3:00 A.M. when Maslennikov's bedside telephone rang. He'd not been sleeping well lately because of the aftermath of the failed operation. Despite Grechkov's assurances that nothing had changed in their struggle for political power, he had his doubts. He expected to be arrested at any moment, and he had salted away enough money in two Channel Island accounts to ease his way into a new life in the West should his escape become necessary.

He turned on a light and picked up the phone on the second ring. *"Da?"*

"It's me," the caller said.

The connection was poor, and in the background Maslennikov could hear traffic noises, but he recognized the voice. Was it possible?

"Where are you?" he asked.

"That doesn't matter," Valeri Yernin said. "By now you know that I failed, and you know why I failed."

"I can help. It's not over yet."

"Fuck your mother, you're right, it's not over. It won't be over until I kill him."

"Don't be a fool," Maslennikov shouted. "There are other considerations now. Other projects. We need you."

"I'm going to kill him," Yernin said. "When I've done that, I'll return. But not until then."

"You stupid fool!"

"This time I won't fail, because I know his Achilles' heel!" Yernin said. "Do you hear me? I know his Achilles' heel."

NATIONAL SECURITY AGENCY
INTERCEPT CENTER

"That's it," communications specialist Art Shannon said, thickly padded earphones on his head, his fingers playing rapidly over a keyboard.

His supervisor, Dale Delmonico, came over from his console. "Is that Bill Lane's voice search and recognition program?"

Shannon nodded, hit the Play button, and looked up. "The voice print is a ninety-eight percent match. The call originated in Karachi."

Valeri Yernin's voice came up on the loudspeaker.

"This time I won't fail, because I know his Achilles' heel! Do you hear me? I know his Achilles' heel."

TO BE CONTINUED . . .

F
FLANNERY   FLANNERY, SEAN

KILO OPTION